VICTORY

RESISTANCE
BOOK 3

First Second

New York & London

Text Copyright © 2012 by Carla Jablonski
Illustrations Copyright © 2012 by Leland Purvis

Published by First Second
First Second is an imprint of Roaring Brook Press, a division of Holtzbrinck Publishing Holdings
Limited Partnership, 175 Fifth Avenue, New York, NY 10010

Distributed in the United Kingdom by Macmillan Children's Books, a division of Pan Macmillan.

Design by Colleen AF Venable
Colored by Hilary Sycamore and Sky Blue Ink. Lead colorist: Alex Campbell

Library of Congress Cataloging-in-Publication Data

Jablonski, Carla.
  Victory / written by Carla Jablonski ; art by Leland Purvis.
    p. cm. — (Resistance ; bk. 3)
  Summary: In 1944, as Allied forces move to retake France from its Nazi invaders, the Tessier siblings
risk their lives once more and journey to Paris, where they are to deliver top-secret intelligence to
Resistance workers.
  ISBN 978-1-59643-293-2
  1. World War, 1939–1945—France—Juvenile fiction. 2. France—History—German occupation,
1940–1945—Juvenile fiction. 3. Graphic novels. [1. Graphic novels. 2. World War, 1939–1945—
France—Fiction. 3. World War, 1939–1945—Underground movements—France—Fiction. 4. France—
History—German occupation, 1940–1945—Fiction.] I. Purvis, Leland, ill. II. Title.
  PZ7.7.J32Vi 2012
  741.5'973—dc23

                                                                                    2011030504

First Second books are available for special promotions and premiums.
For details, contact: Director of Special Markets, Holtzbrinck Publishers.

First Edition 2012
Printed in China

10 9 8 7 6 5 4 3 2 1

VICTORY

RESISTANCE BOOK 3

Written by
Carla Jablonski

Art by
Leland Purvis

Color by
Hilary Sycamore

First Second
New York & London

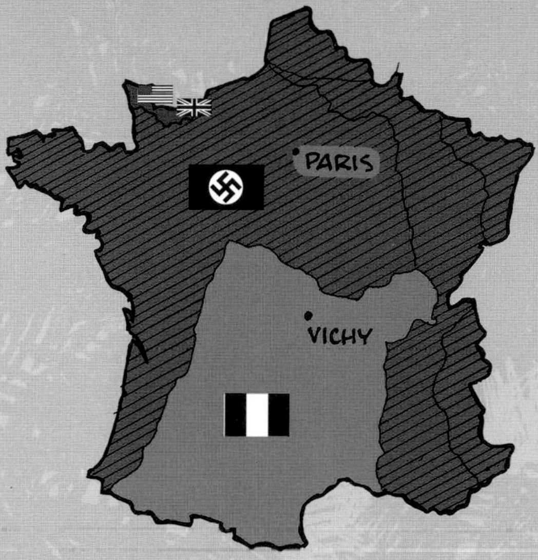
PARIS
VICHY

On June 22, 1940, the French and the Germans signed an armistice agreement. Not even a year had passed since the British and French declared war on the Nazis. But the German forces were too powerful, the attacks too effective, and the French knew they could never win a war against them. So the Vichy government was established in France to support the German war effort.

Now, four years into the occupation, the tide is turning. There has been a plot to assassinate Hitler perpetrated by his own generals; even more important, the Americans have finally entered the war. There is hope now that the Allied forces will come to France's aid.

But even as victory seems possible, things in France are getting worse. Dwindling food and other resources, fewer men, longer separations. Nazi reprisals are becoming more vicious and less predictable. And the renewed hope of the French people is mixed with anxiety and dread — for the Allied bombs pounding France don't only kill Germans, and they decimate cities and farmlands.

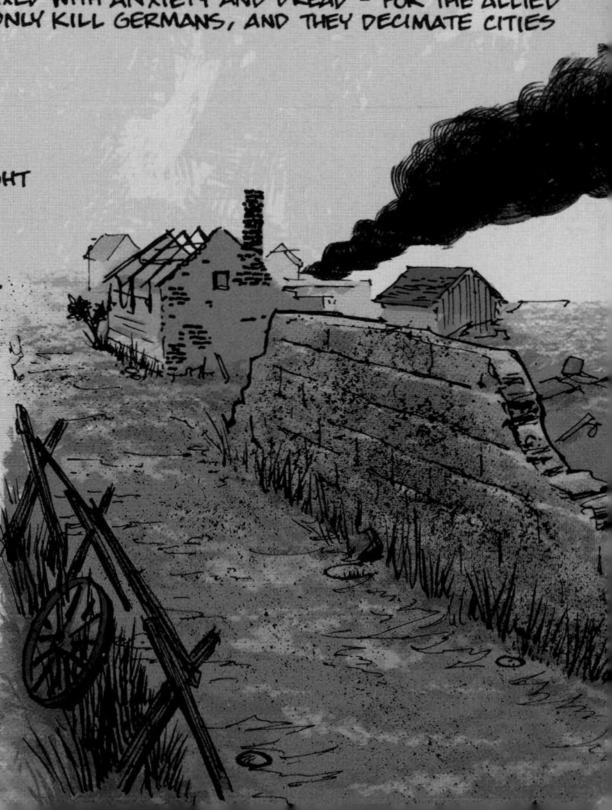

The French who worked to fight against Germany both within France and abroad are having other troubles. Potentially most damaging is the fighting among the resistance groups — as well as between the Allies and Charles de Gaulle (head of the Free French, but in exile in London). Even those who could agree had different ideas of how best to liberate France.

Tensions run very high — and every choice anyone makes could have life-changing consequences.

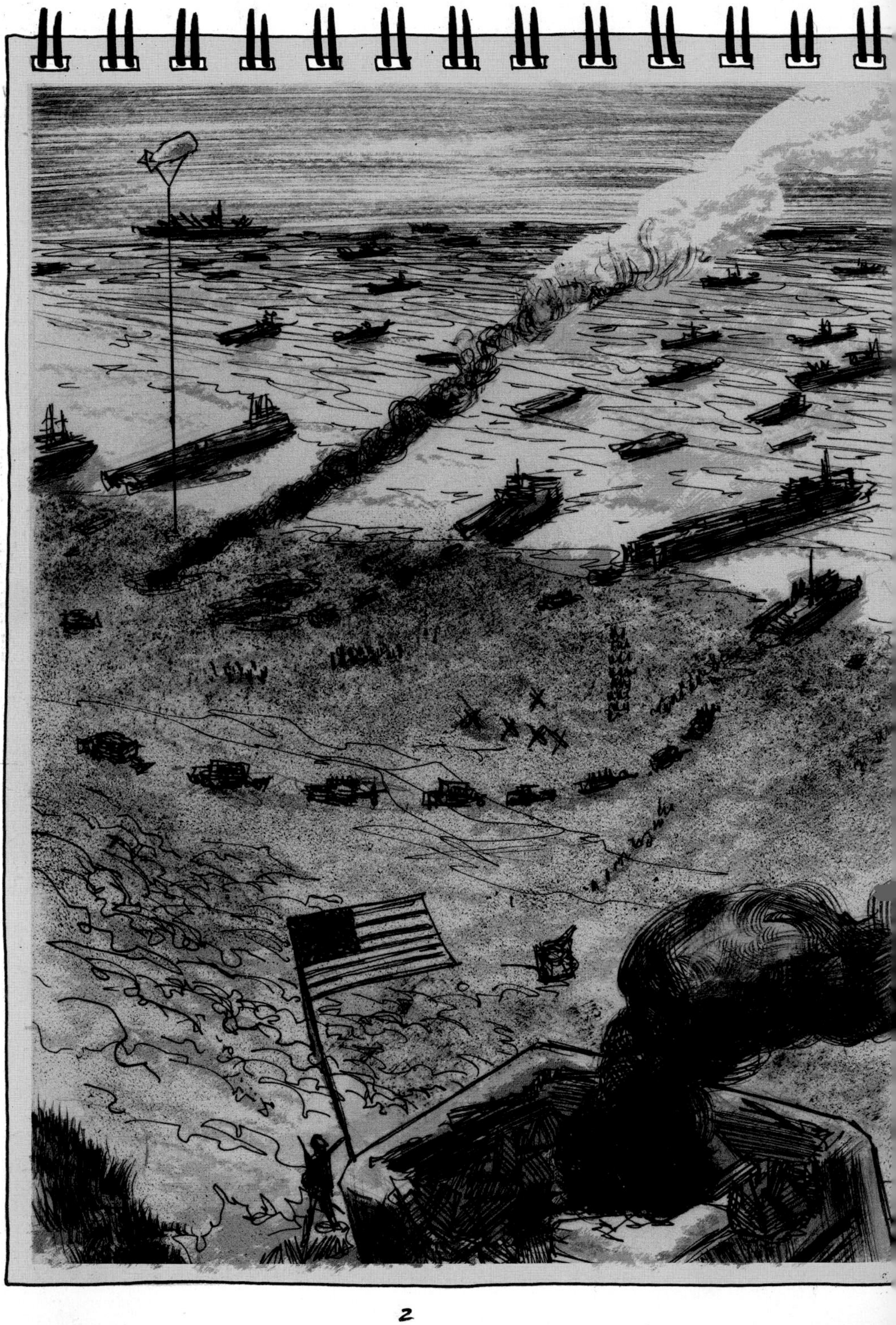

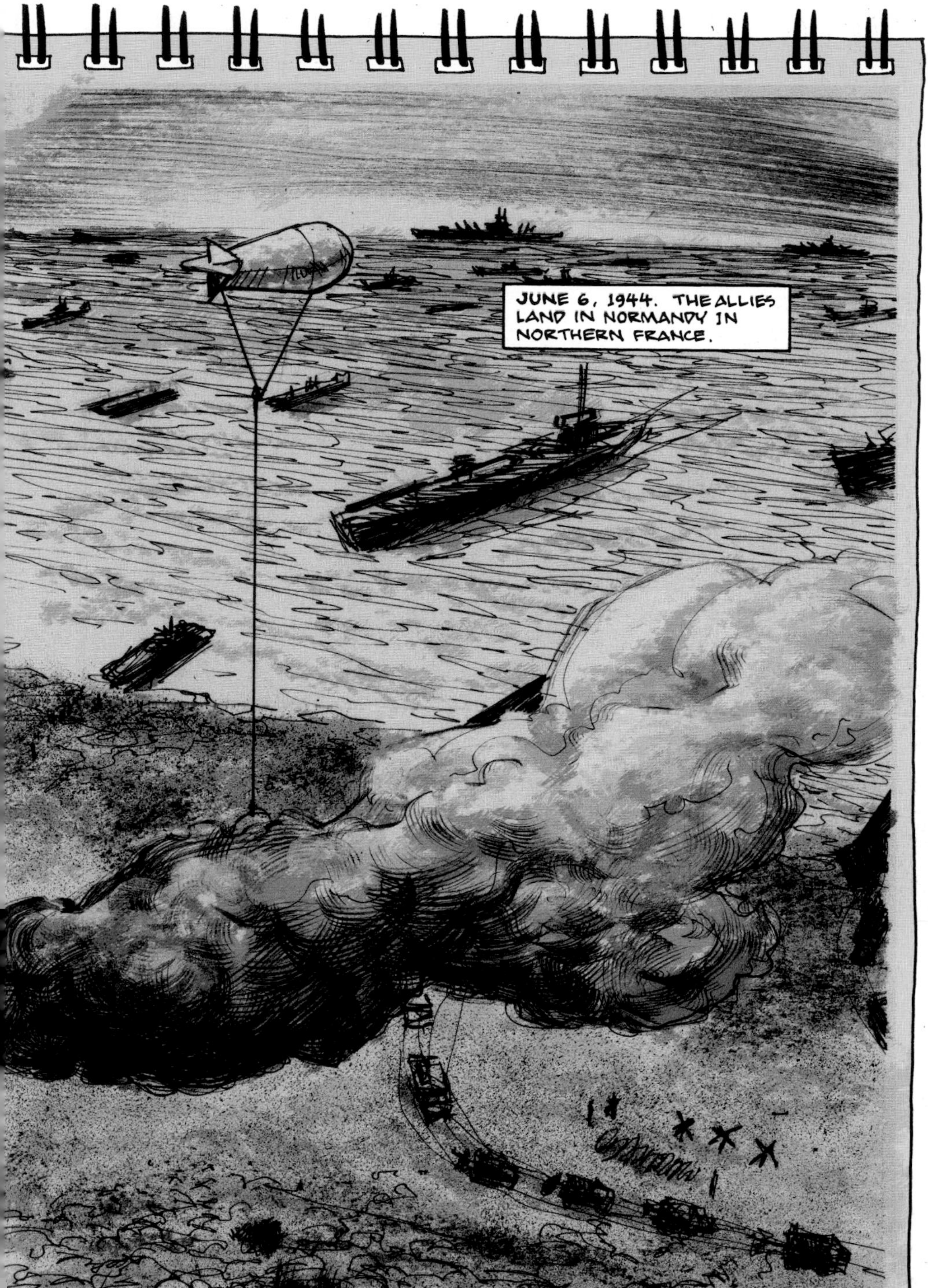
JUNE 6, 1944. THE ALLIES LAND IN NORMANDY IN NORTHERN FRANCE.

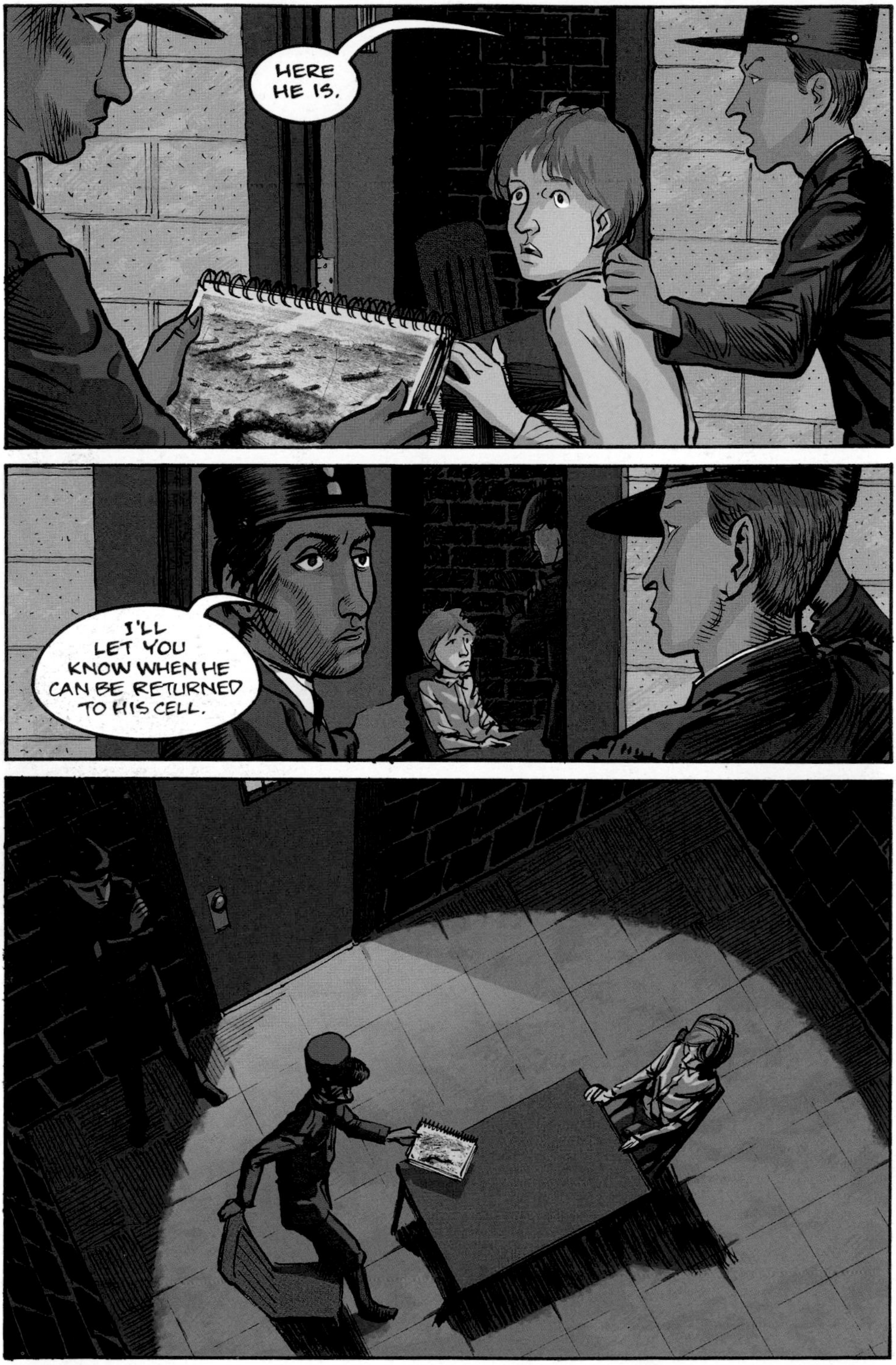
HERE HE IS.
I'LL LET YOU KNOW WHEN HE CAN BE RETURNED TO HIS CELL.

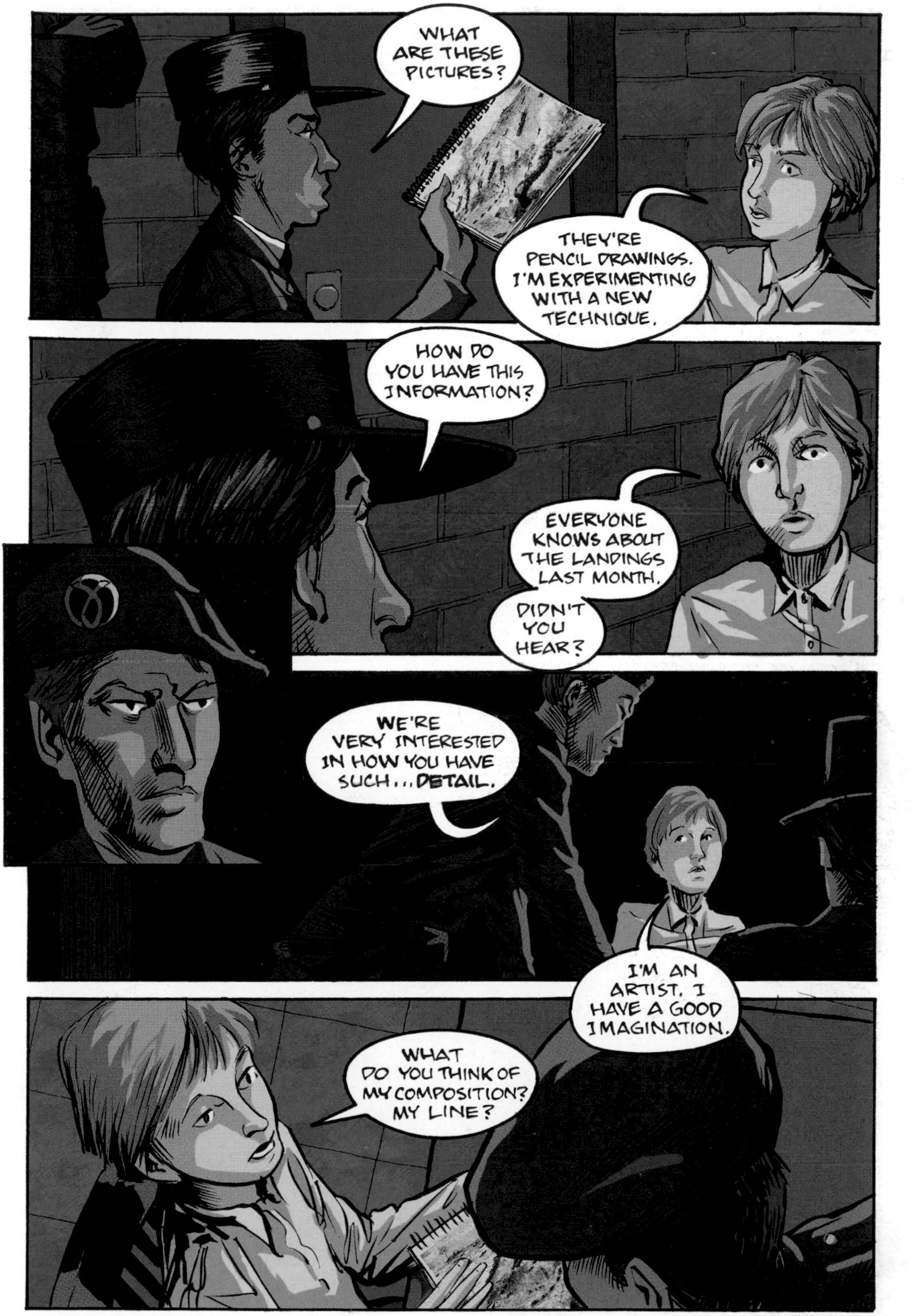
WHAT ARE THESE PICTURES?
THEY'RE PENCIL DRAWINGS. I'M EXPERIMENTING WITH A NEW TECHNIQUE.
HOW DO YOU HAVE THIS INFORMATION?
EVERYONE KNOWS ABOUT THE LANDINGS LAST MONTH.
DIDN'T YOU HEAR?
WE'RE VERY INTERESTED IN HOW YOU HAVE SUCH... DETAIL.
I'M AN ARTIST. I HAVE A GOOD IMAGINATION.
WHAT DO YOU THINK OF MY COMPOSITION? MY LINE?

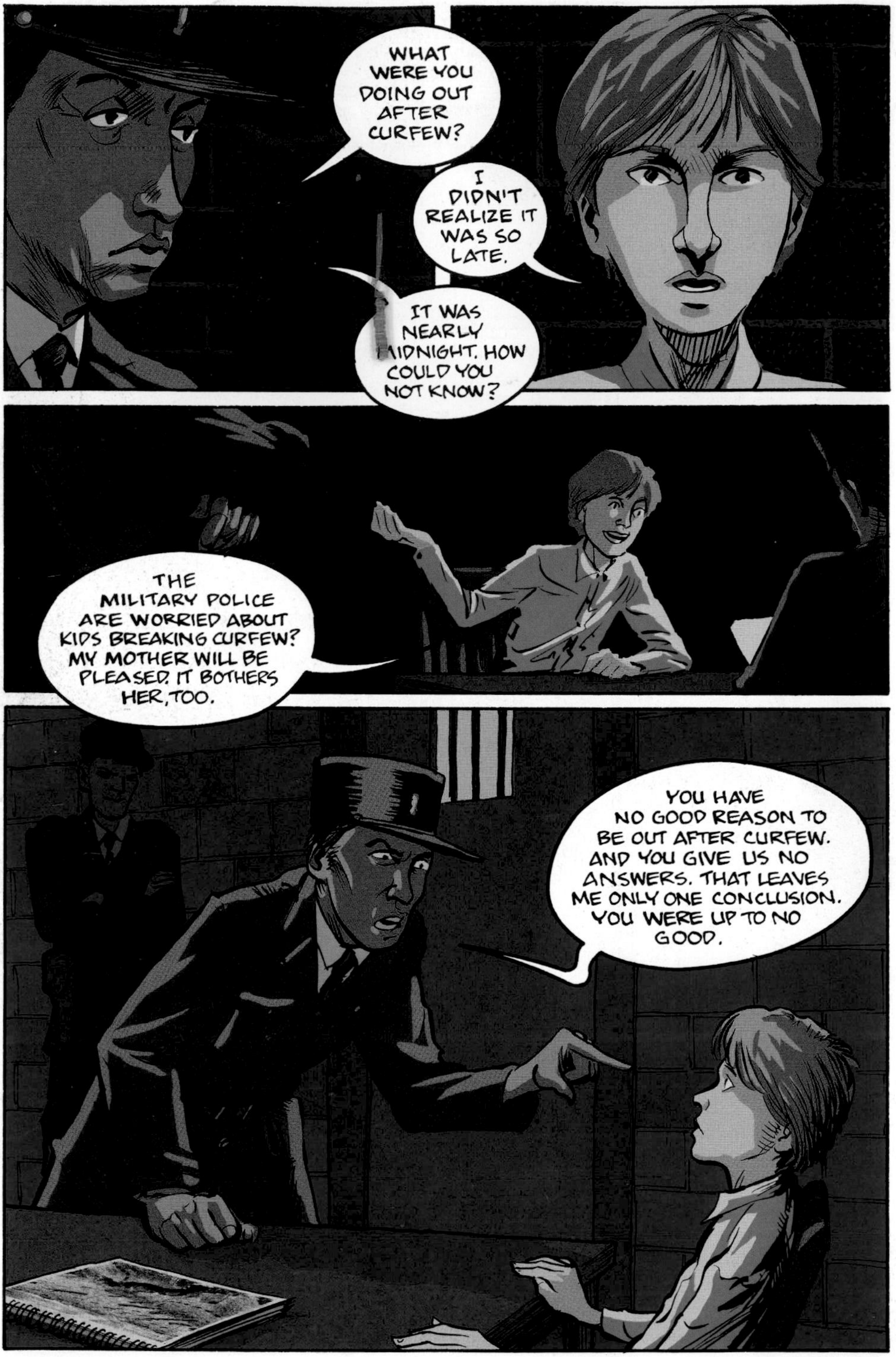
WHAT WERE YOU DOING OUT AFTER CURFEW?
I DIDN'T REALIZE IT WAS SO LATE.
IT WAS NEARLY MIDNIGHT. HOW COULD YOU NOT KNOW?
THE MILITARY POLICE ARE WORRIED ABOUT KIDS BREAKING CURFEW? MY MOTHER WILL BE PLEASED. IT BOTHERS HER, TOO.
YOU HAVE NO GOOD REASON TO BE OUT AFTER CURFEW. AND YOU GIVE US NO ANSWERS. THAT LEAVES ME ONLY ONE CONCLUSION. YOU WERE UP TO NO GOOD.

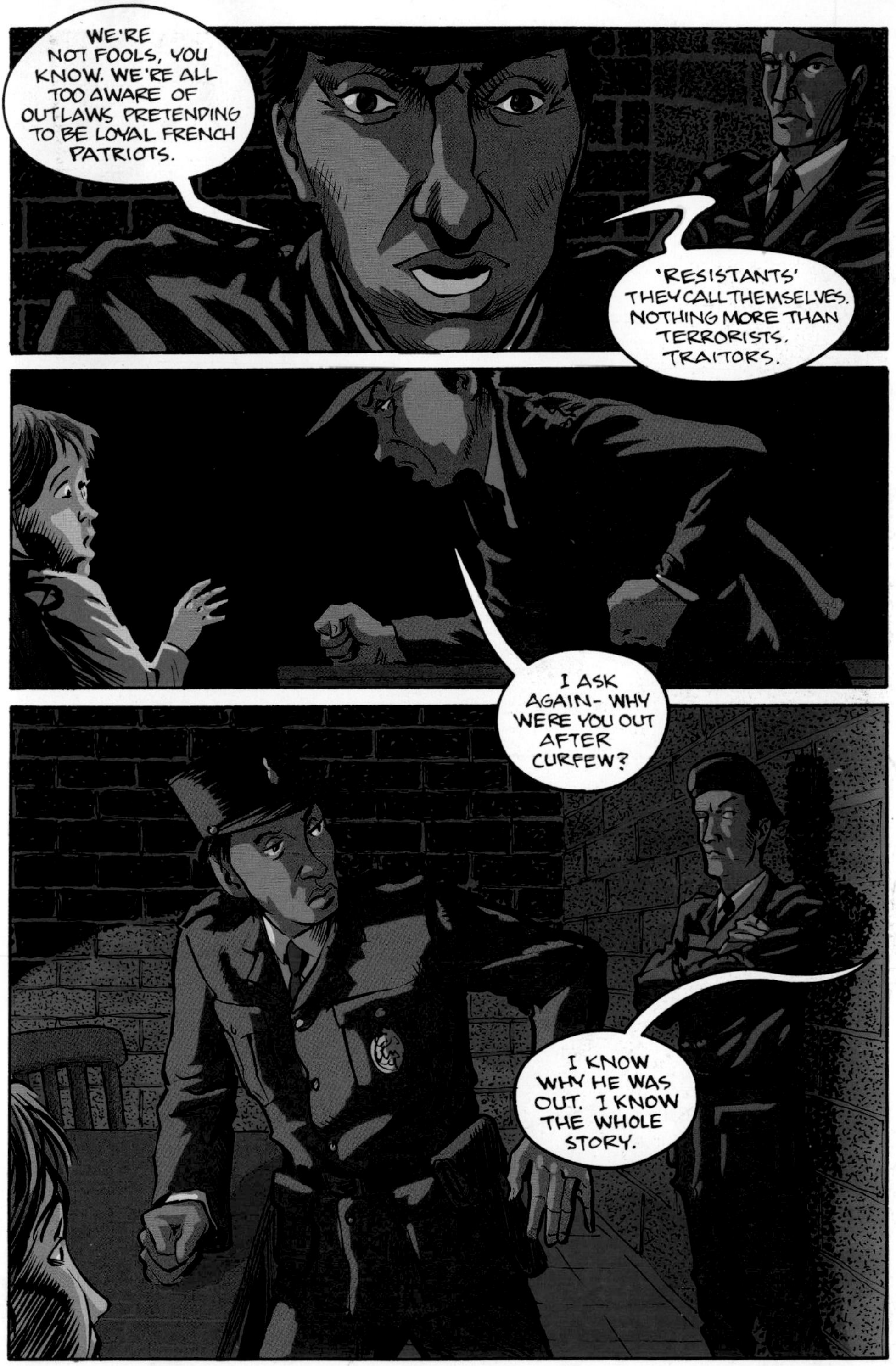
WE'RE NOT FOOLS, YOU KNOW. WE'RE ALL TOO AWARE OF OUTLAWS PRETENDING TO BE LOYAL FRENCH PATRIOTS.
'RESISTANTS' THEY CALL THEMSELVES. NOTHING MORE THAN TERRORISTS. TRAITORS.
I ASK AGAIN- WHY WERE YOU OUT AFTER CURFEW?
I KNOW WHY HE WAS OUT. I KNOW THE WHOLE STORY.

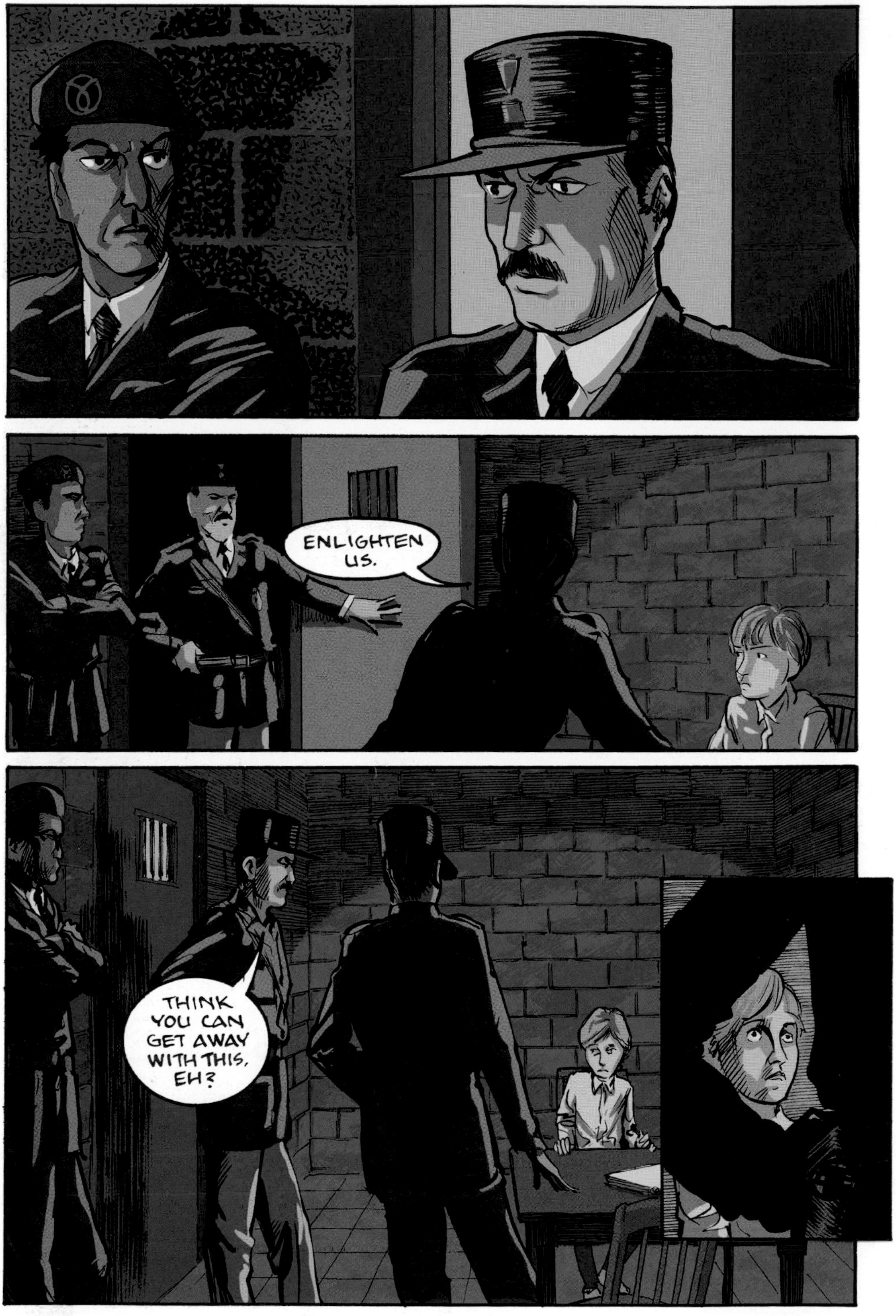
ENLIGHTEN US.
THINK YOU CAN GET AWAY WITH THIS, EH?

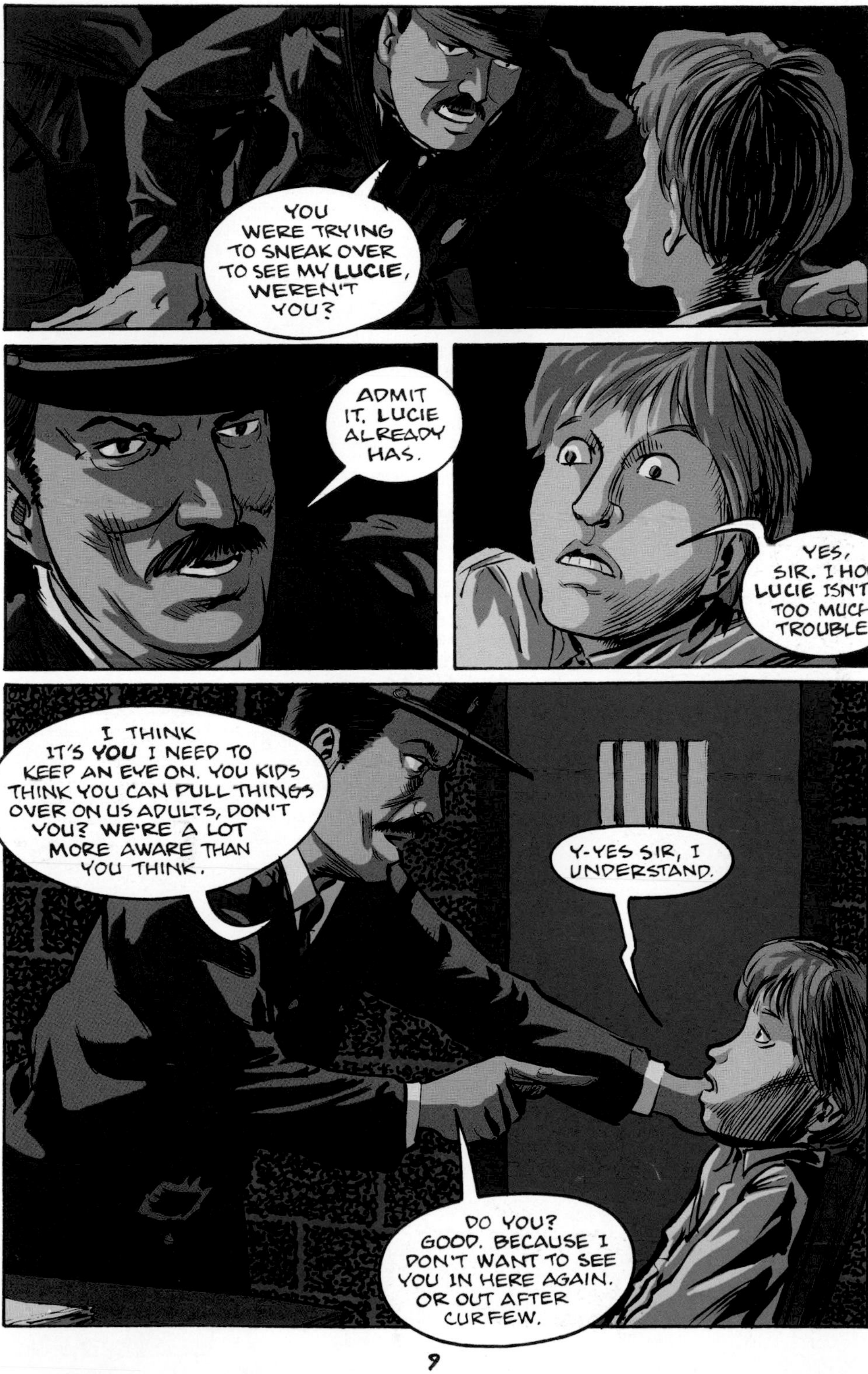
YOU WERE TRYING TO SNEAK OVER TO SEE MY LUCIE, WEREN'T YOU?
ADMIT IT, LUCIE ALREADY HAS.
YES, SIR. I HOPE LUCIE ISN'T IN TOO MUCH TROUBLE.
I THINK IT'S YOU I NEED TO KEEP AN EYE ON. YOU KIDS THINK YOU CAN PULL THINGS OVER ON US ADULTS, DON'T YOU? WE'RE A LOT MORE AWARE THAN YOU THINK.
Y-YES SIR, I UNDERSTAND.
DO YOU? GOOD. BECAUSE I DON'T WANT TO SEE YOU IN HERE AGAIN. OR OUT AFTER CURFEW.

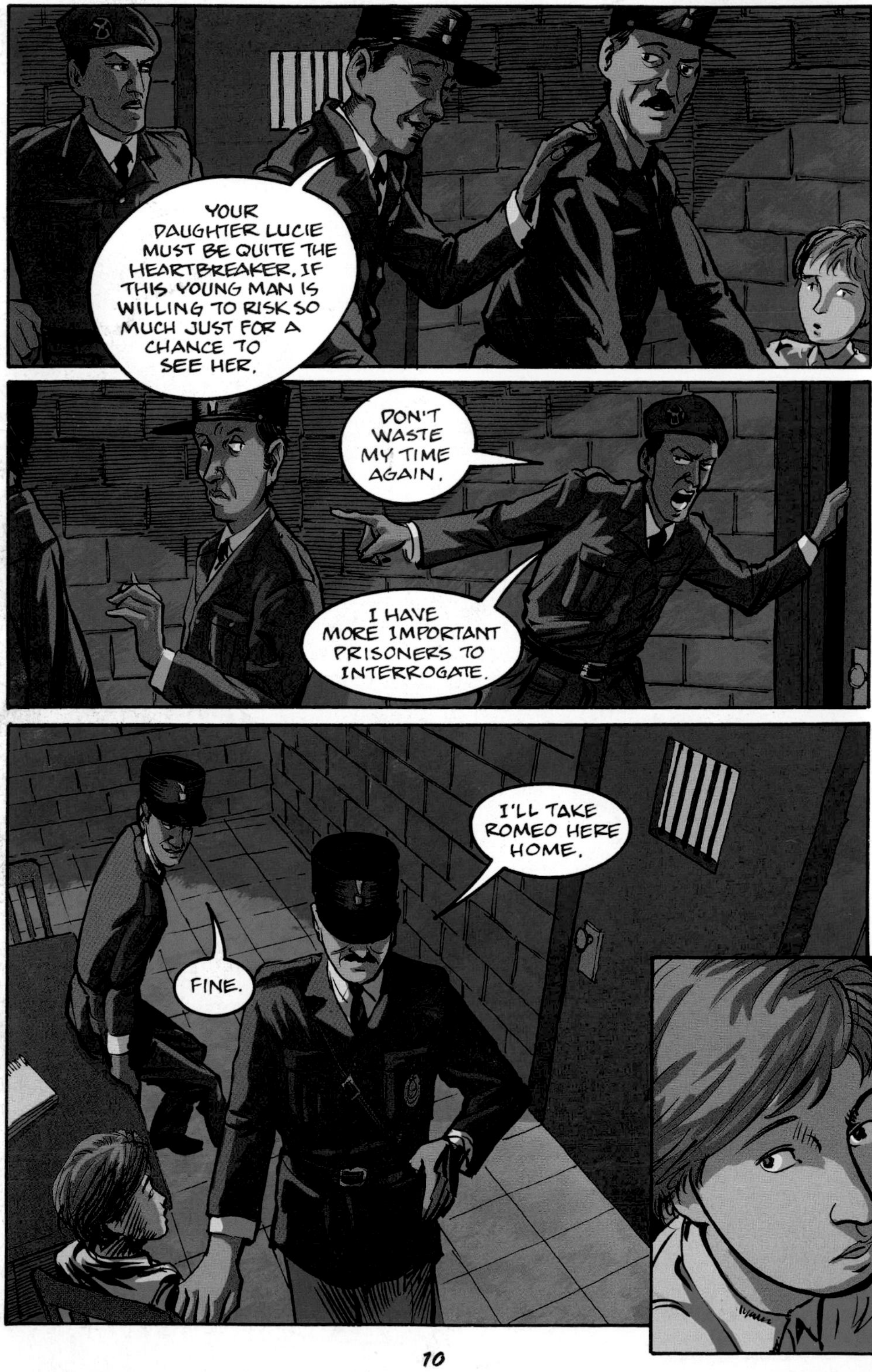
YOUR DAUGHTER LUCIE MUST BE QUITE THE HEARTBREAKER, IF THIS YOUNG MAN IS WILLING TO RISK SO MUCH JUST FOR A CHANCE TO SEE HER.
DON'T WASTE MY TIME AGAIN.
I HAVE MORE IMPORTANT PRISONERS TO INTERROGATE.
I'LL TAKE ROMEO HERE HOME.
FINE.

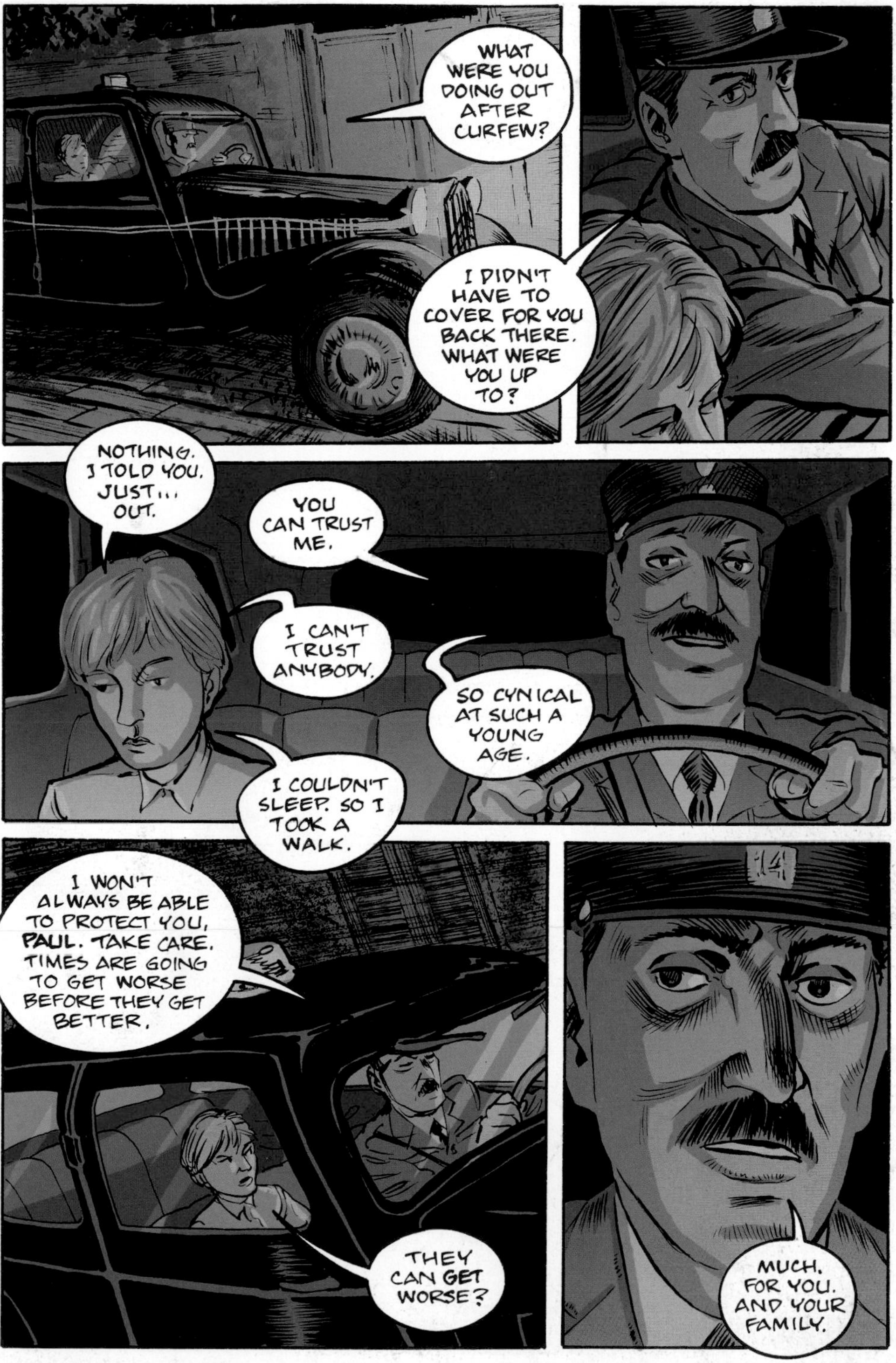
WHAT WERE YOU DOING OUT AFTER CURFEW?
I DIDN'T HAVE TO COVER FOR YOU BACK THERE. WHAT WERE YOU UP TO?
NOTHING. I TOLD YOU. JUST... OUT.
YOU CAN TRUST ME.
I CAN'T TRUST ANYBODY.
SO CYNICAL AT SUCH A YOUNG AGE.
I COULDN'T SLEEP. SO I TOOK A WALK.
I WON'T ALWAYS BE ABLE TO PROTECT YOU, PAUL. TAKE CARE. TIMES ARE GOING TO GET WORSE BEFORE THEY GET BETTER.
THEY CAN GET WORSE?
14
MUCH. FOR YOU. AND YOUR FAMILY.

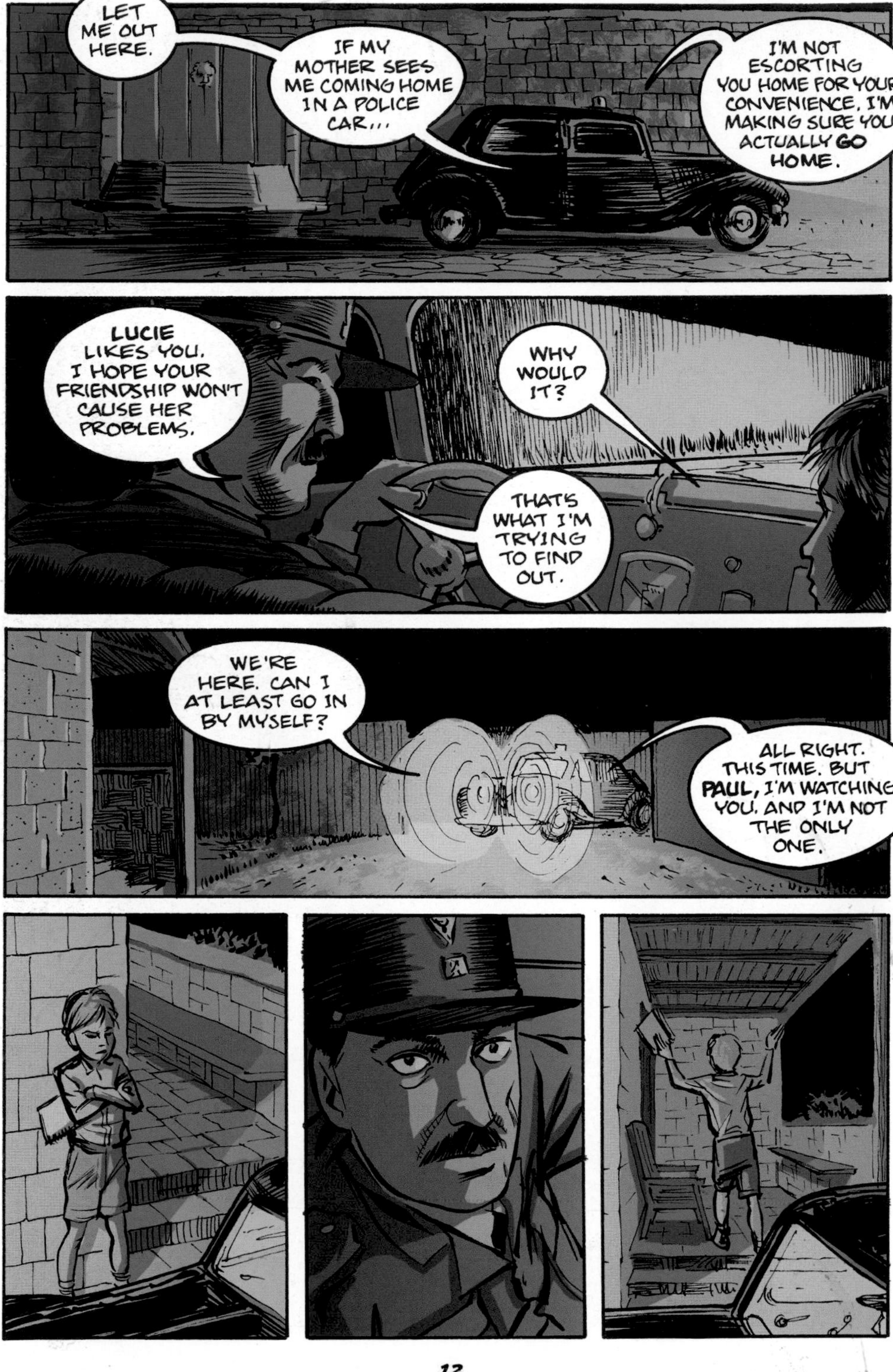
LET ME OUT HERE.
IF MY MOTHER SEES ME COMING HOME IN A POLICE CAR...
I'M NOT ESCORTING YOU HOME FOR YOUR CONVENIENCE. I'M MAKING SURE YOU ACTUALLY **GO HOME**.
LUCIE LIKES YOU. I HOPE YOUR FRIENDSHIP WON'T CAUSE HER PROBLEMS.
WHY WOULD IT?
THAT'S WHAT I'M TRYING TO FIND OUT.
WE'RE HERE. CAN I AT LEAST GO IN BY MYSELF?
ALL RIGHT. THIS TIME. BUT **PAUL**, I'M WATCHING YOU. AND I'M NOT THE ONLY ONE.

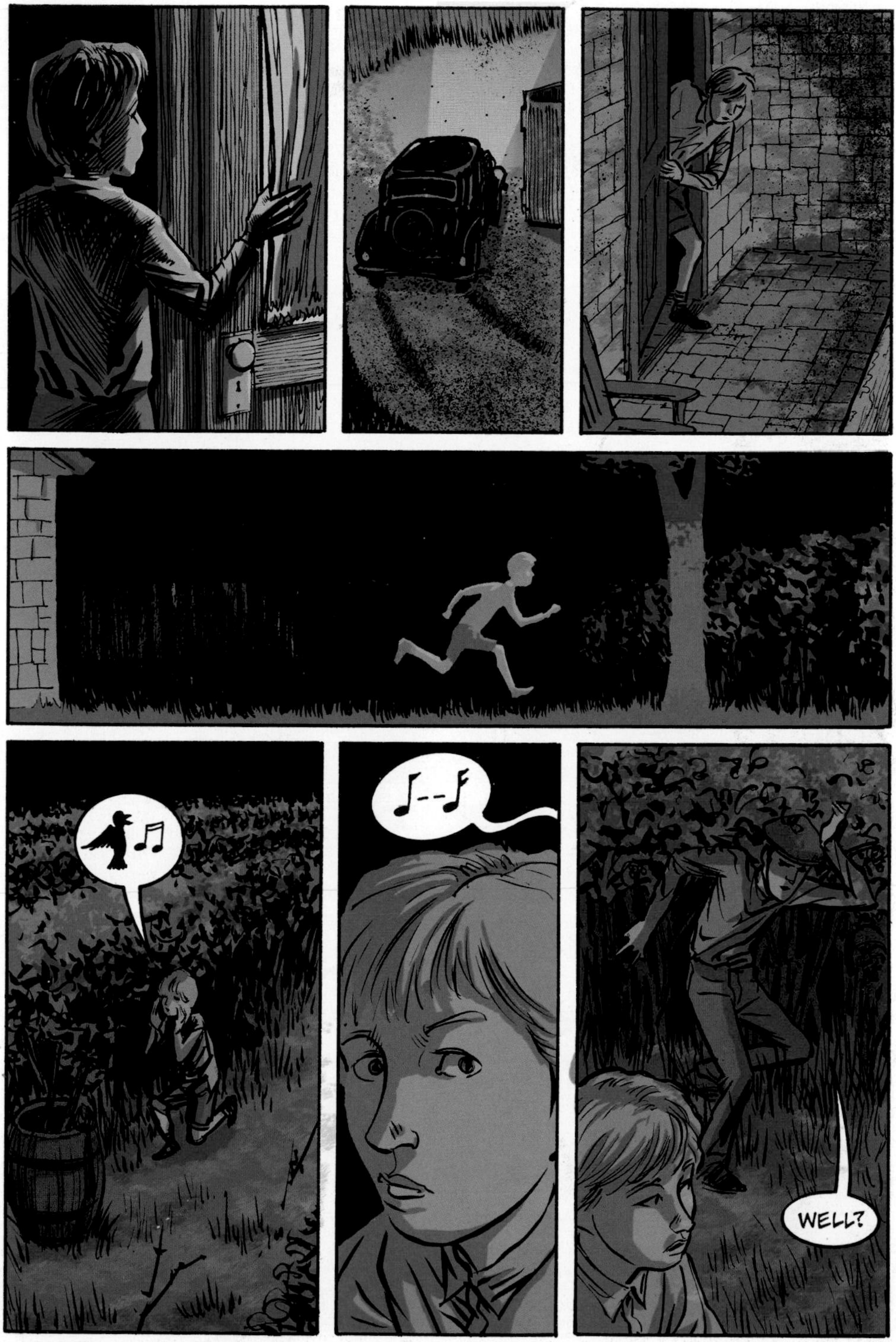
WELL?

OKAY, **JACQUES** YOUR MAN IS IN THE THIRD CELL FROM THE FRONT DOOR. THE **MILICE** ARE THERE. THEY'RE GOING TO MOVE HIM TOMORROW.
THEN WE GET HIM OUT TONIGHT.
HOW WILL YOU-?
YOU KNOW BETTER THAN TO ASK. GOOD WORK.
GETTING HAULED INTO THE JAIL WAS EASY.
GETTING OUT IS HARDER.

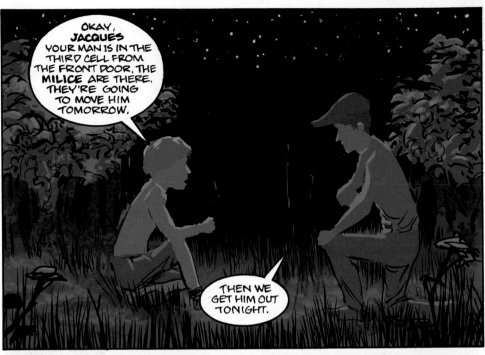

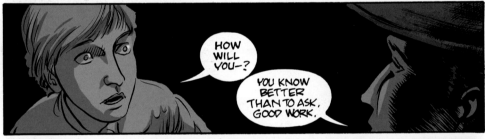

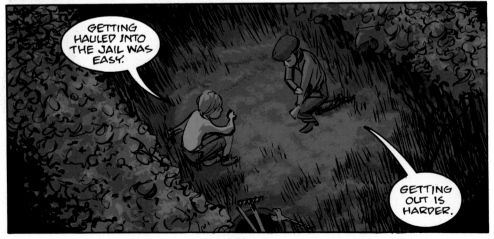

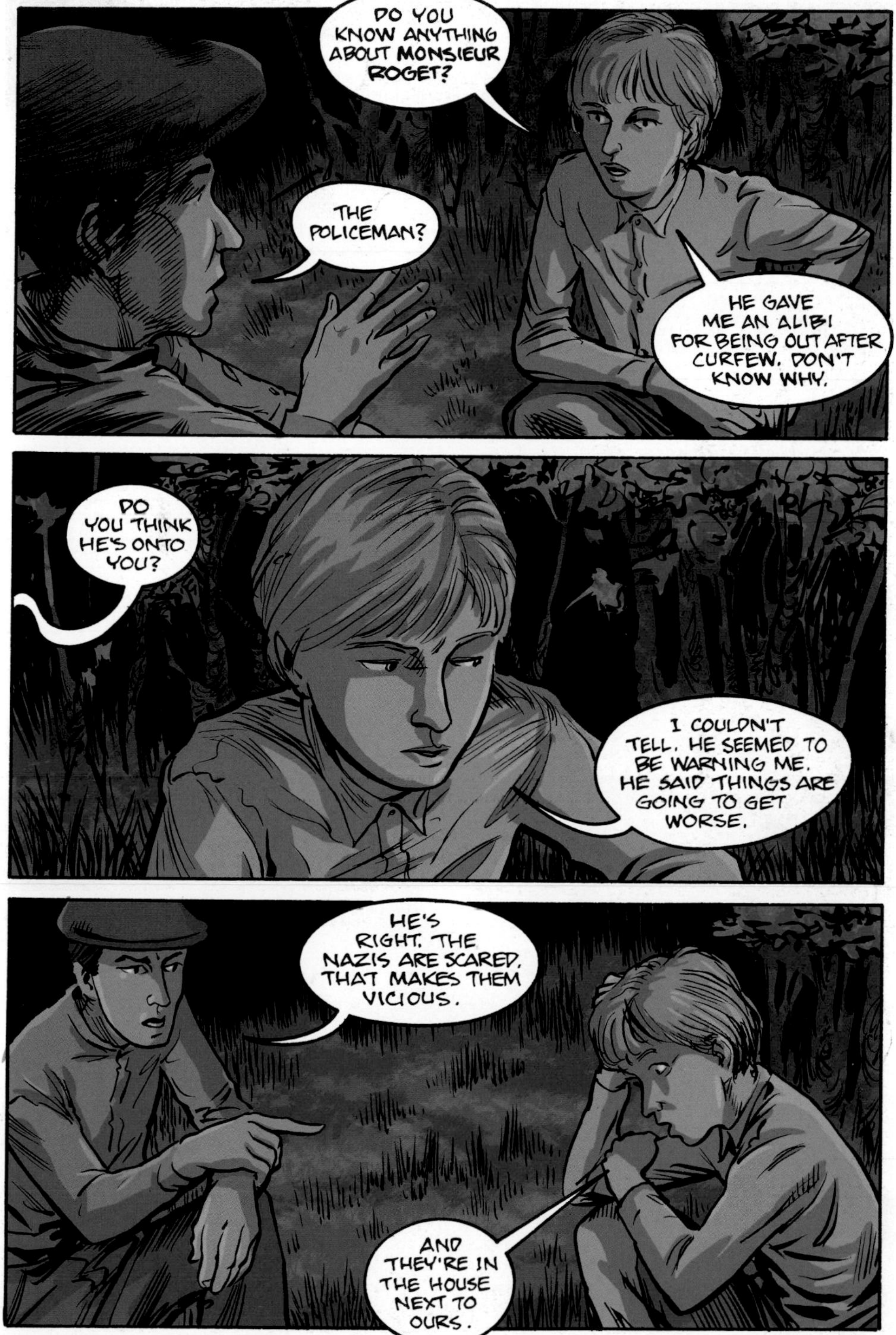
DO YOU KNOW ANYTHING ABOUT MONSIEUR ROGET?
THE POLICEMAN?
HE GAVE ME AN ALIBI FOR BEING OUT AFTER CURFEW. DON'T KNOW WHY.
DO YOU THINK HE'S ONTO YOU?
I COULDN'T TELL. HE SEEMED TO BE WARNING ME. HE SAID THINGS ARE GOING TO GET WORSE.
HE'S RIGHT. THE NAZIS ARE SCARED. THAT MAKES THEM VICIOUS.
AND THEY'RE IN THE HOUSE NEXT TO OURS.

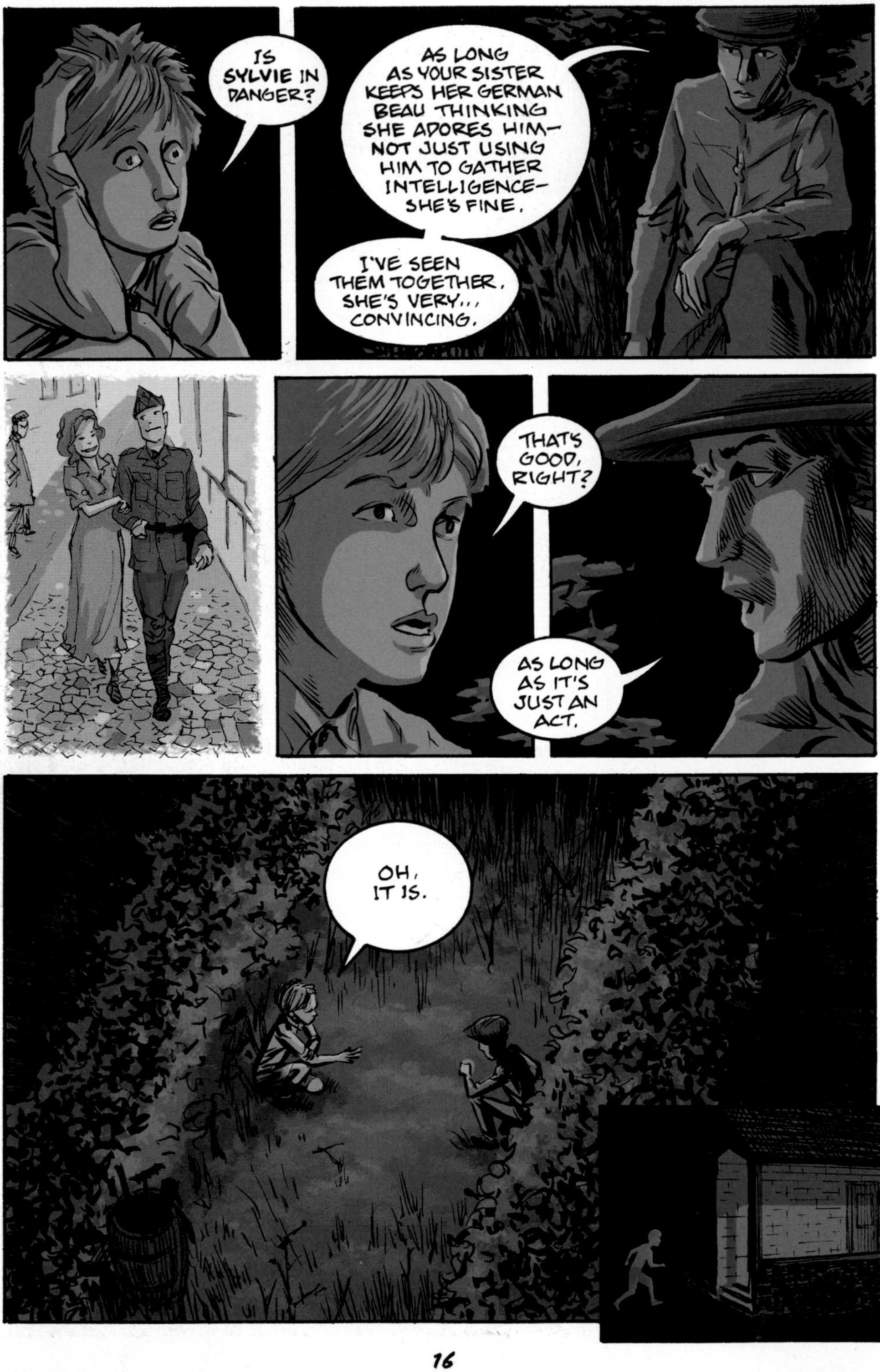
IS SYLVIE IN DANGER?
AS LONG AS YOUR SISTER KEEPS HER GERMAN BEAU THINKING SHE ADORES HIM– NOT JUST USING HIM TO GATHER INTELLIGENCE– SHE'S FINE.
I'VE SEEN THEM TOGETHER. SHE'S VERY... CONVINCING.
THAT'S GOOD, RIGHT?
AS LONG AS IT'S JUST AN ACT.
OH, IT IS.

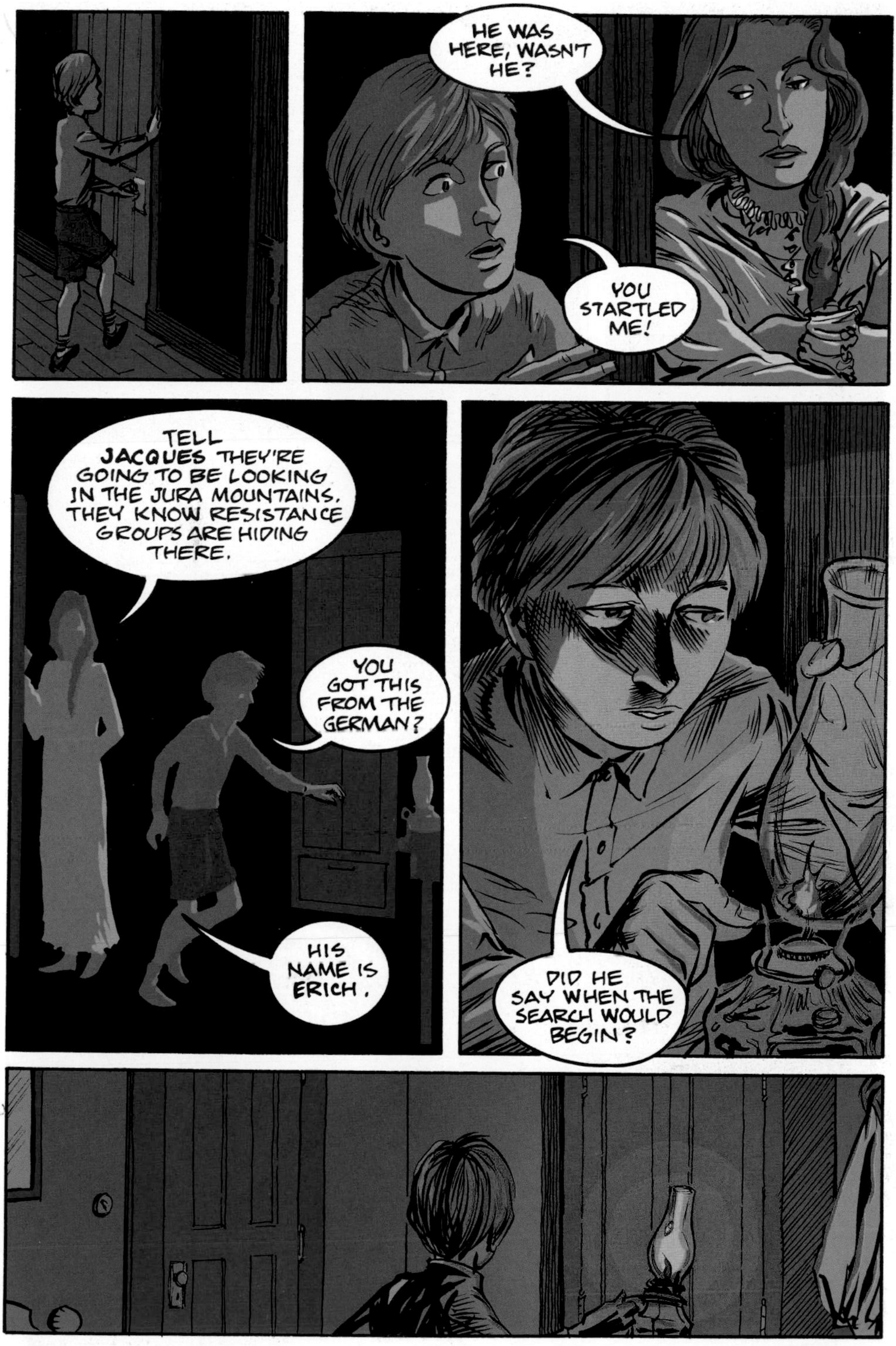
HE WAS HERE, WASN'T HE?
YOU STARTLED ME!
TELL JACQUES THEY'RE GOING TO BE LOOKING IN THE JURA MOUNTAINS. THEY KNOW RESISTANCE GROUPS ARE HIDING THERE.
YOU GOT THIS FROM THE GERMAN?
HIS NAME IS ERICH.
DID HE SAY WHEN THE SEARCH WOULD BEGIN?

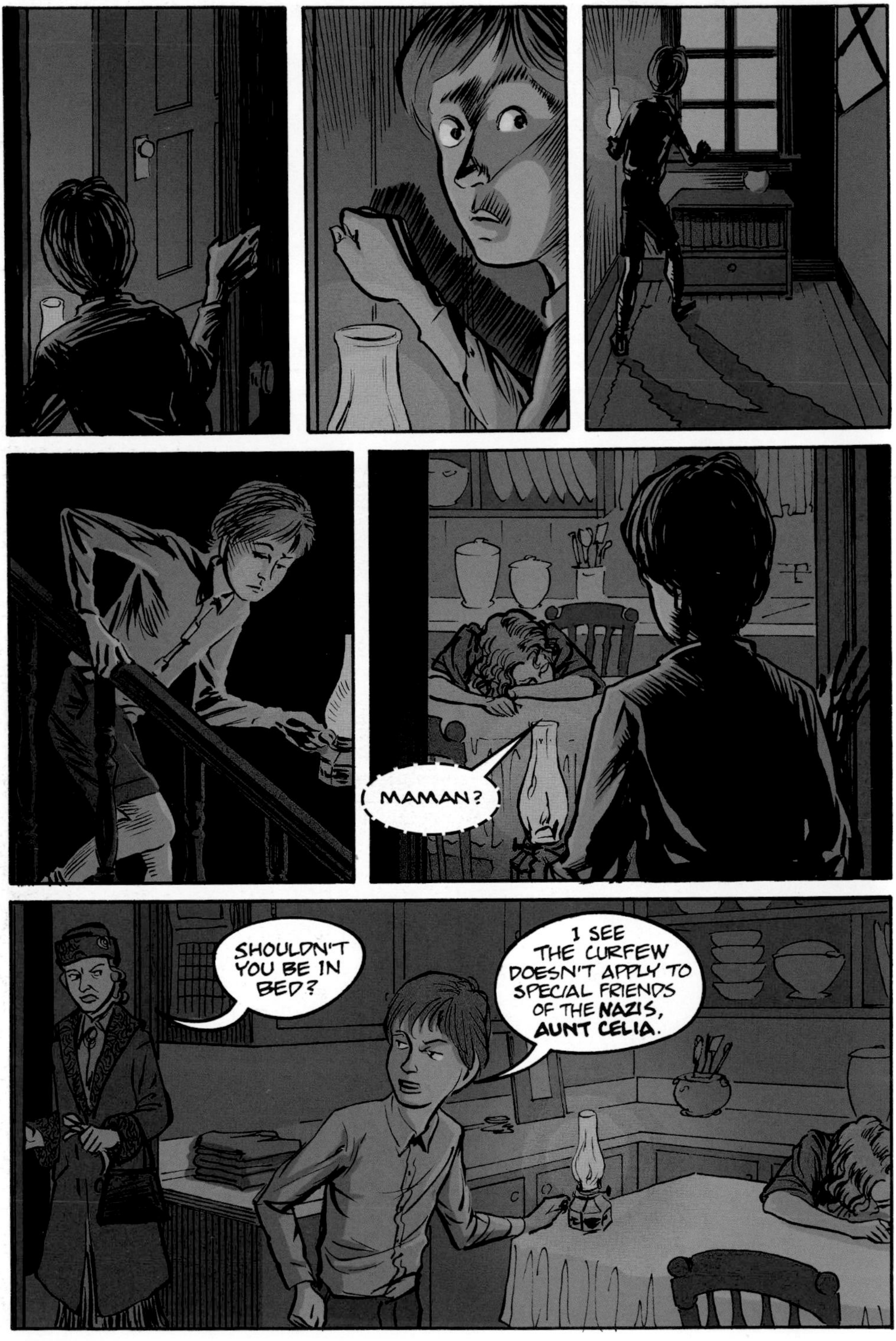
MAMAN?
SHOULDN'T YOU BE IN BED?
I SEE THE CURFEW DOESN'T APPLY TO SPECIAL FRIENDS OF THE **NAZIS**, **AUNT CELIA**.

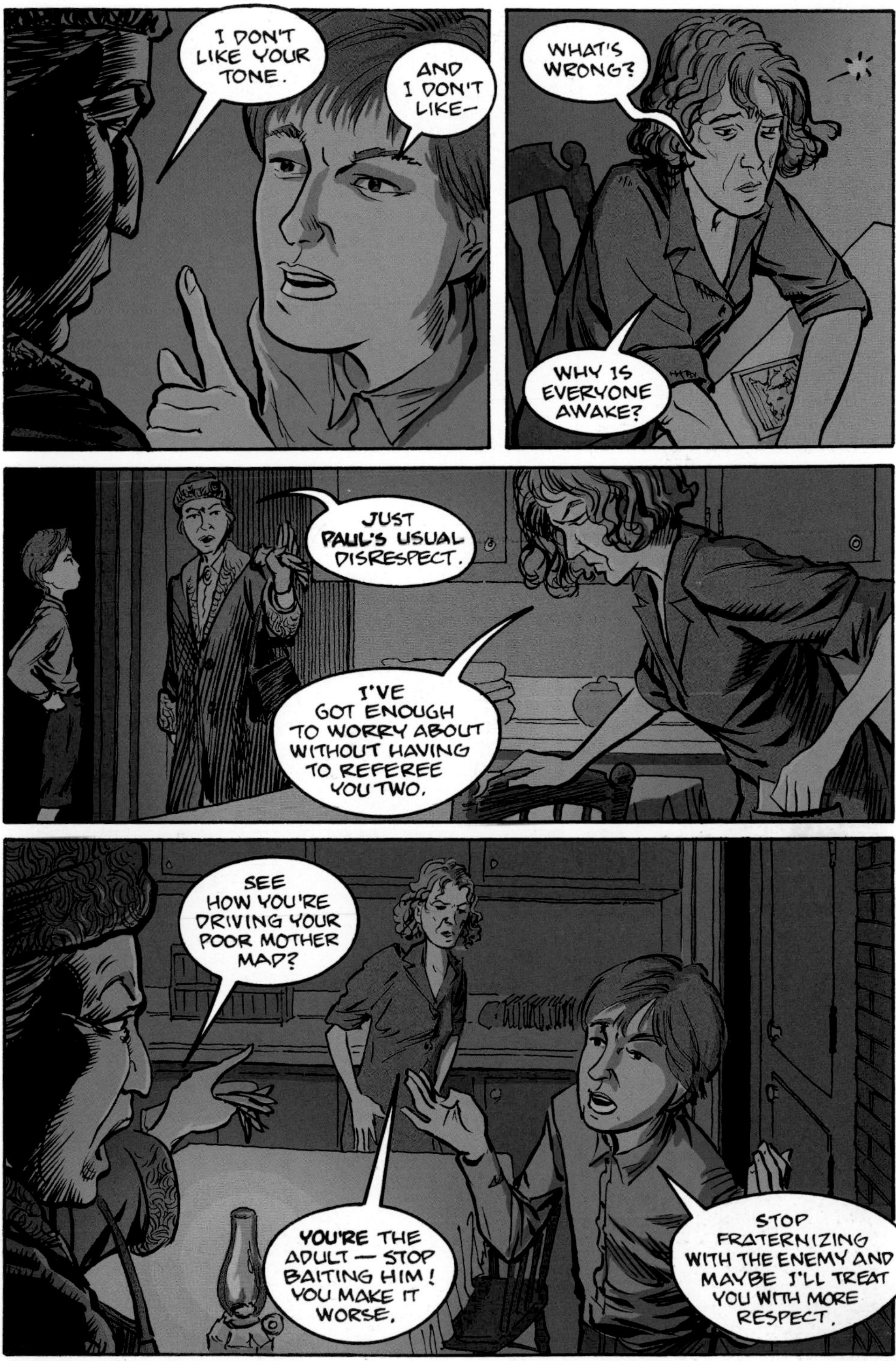

I DON'T LIKE YOUR TONE.
AND I DON'T LIKE–
WHAT'S WRONG?
WHY IS EVERYONE AWAKE?
JUST PAUL'S USUAL DISRESPECT.
I'VE GOT ENOUGH TO WORRY ABOUT WITHOUT HAVING TO REFEREE YOU TWO.
SEE HOW YOU'RE DRIVING YOUR POOR MOTHER MAD?
YOU'RE THE ADULT — STOP BAITING HIM! YOU MAKE IT WORSE.
STOP FRATERNIZING WITH THE ENEMY AND MAYBE I'LL TREAT YOU WITH MORE RESPECT.

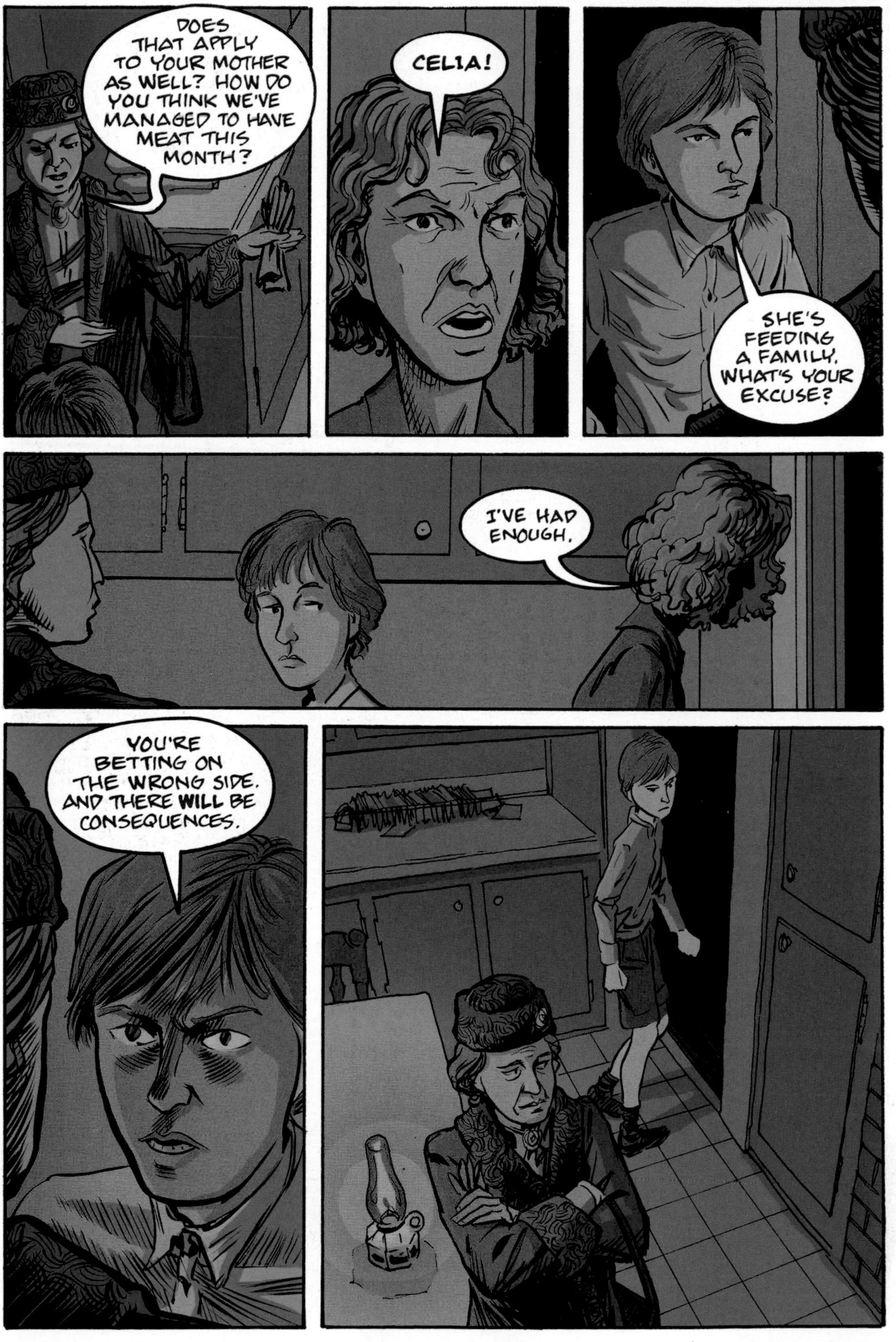
DOES THAT APPLY TO YOUR MOTHER AS WELL? HOW DO YOU THINK WE'VE MANAGED TO HAVE MEAT THIS MONTH?
CELIA!
SHE'S FEEDING A FAMILY. WHAT'S YOUR EXCUSE?
I'VE HAD ENOUGH.
YOU'RE BETTING ON THE WRONG SIDE. AND THERE **WILL** BE CONSEQUENCES.

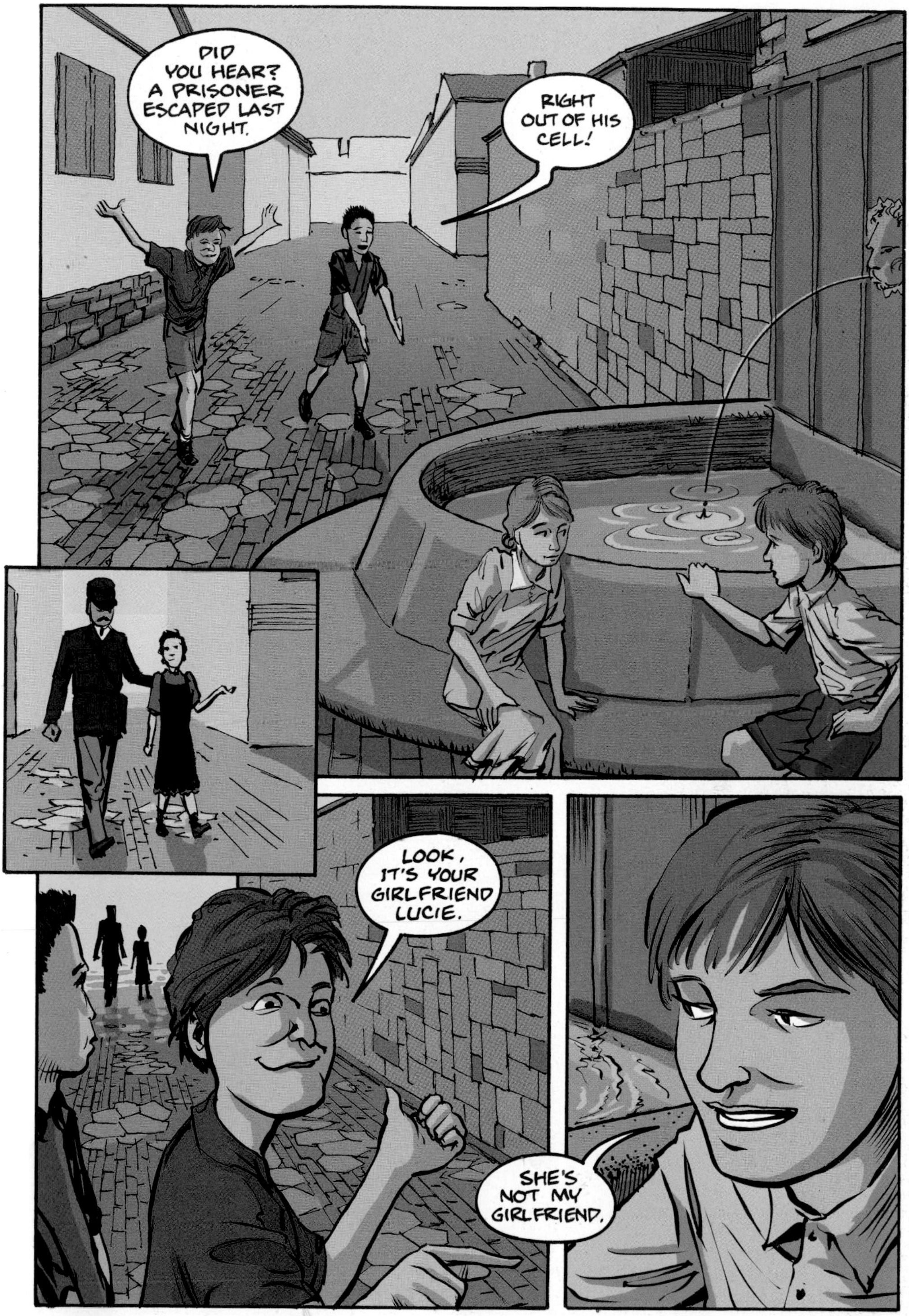
DID YOU HEAR? A PRISONER ESCAPED LAST NIGHT.
RIGHT OUT OF HIS CELL!
LOOK, IT'S YOUR GIRLFRIEND LUCIE.
SHE'S NOT MY GIRLFRIEND.

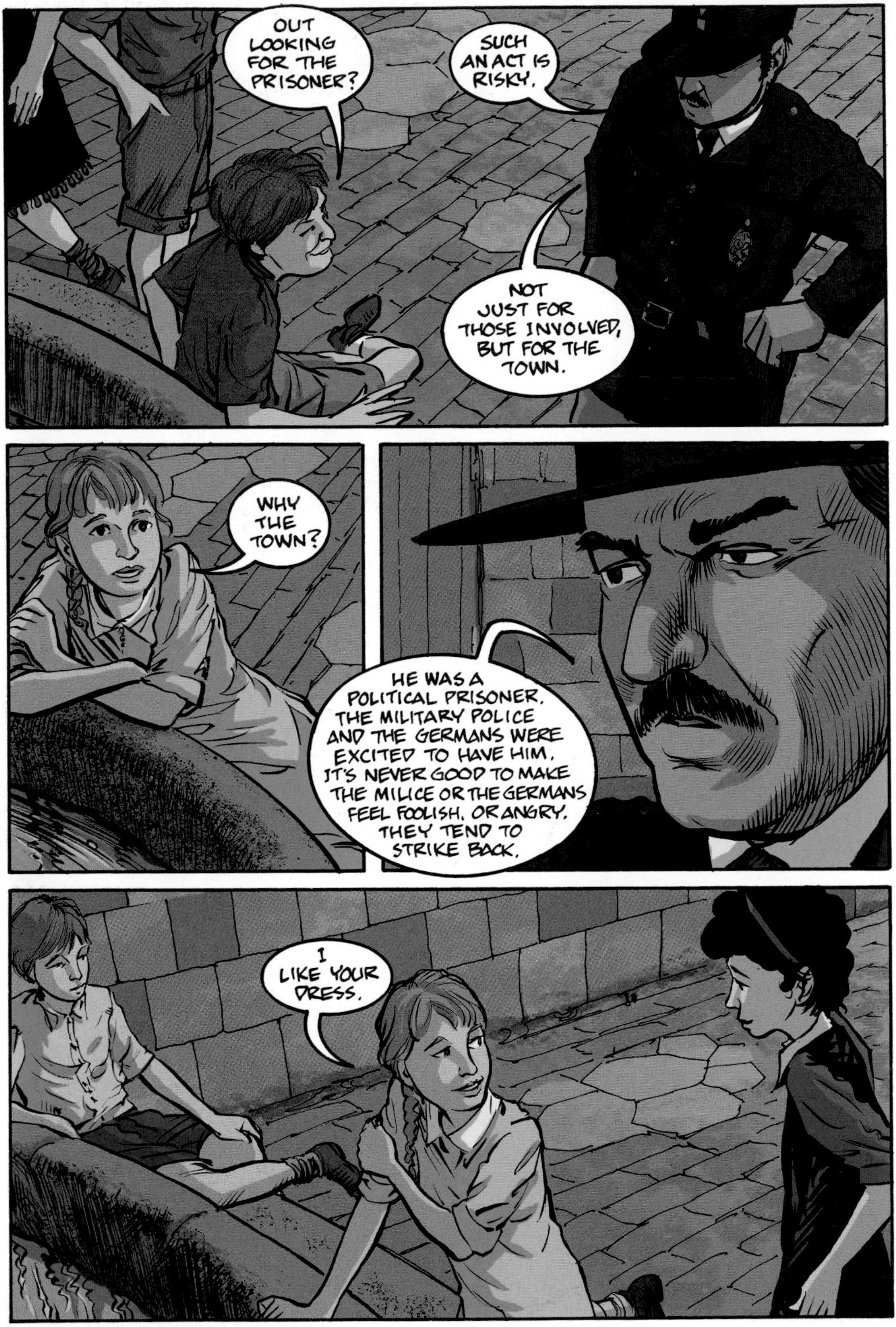
OUT LOOKING FOR THE PRISONER?
SUCH AN ACT IS RISKY.
NOT JUST FOR THOSE INVOLVED, BUT FOR THE TOWN.
WHY THE TOWN?
HE WAS A POLITICAL PRISONER. THE MILITARY POLICE AND THE GERMANS WERE EXCITED TO HAVE HIM. IT'S NEVER GOOD TO MAKE THE MILICE OR THE GERMANS FEEL FOOLISH, OR ANGRY. THEY TEND TO STRIKE BACK.
I LIKE YOUR DRESS.

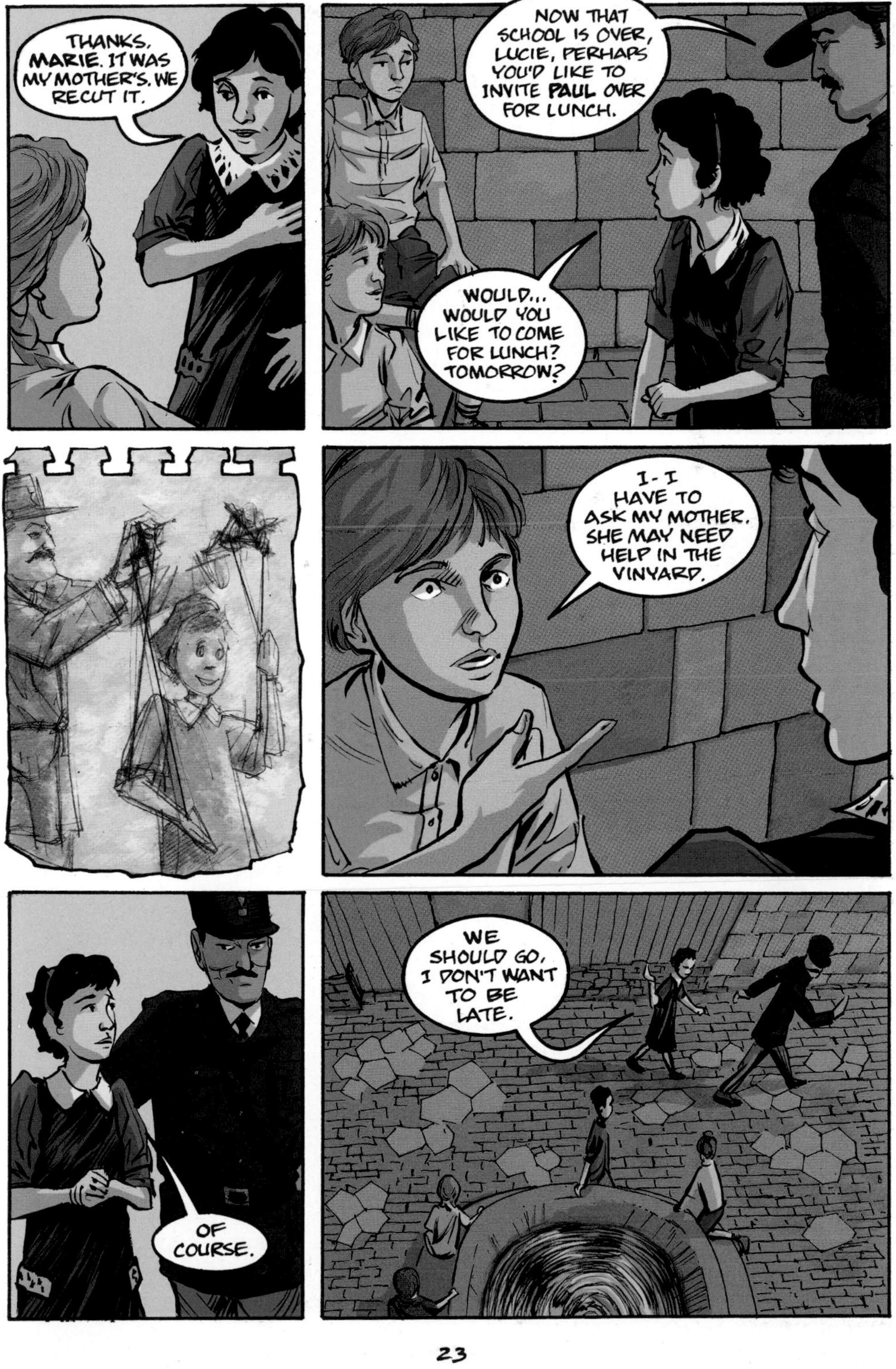
THANKS, MARIE. IT WAS MY MOTHER'S. WE RECUT IT.
NOW THAT SCHOOL IS OVER, LUCIE, PERHAPS YOU'D LIKE TO INVITE PAUL OVER FOR LUNCH.
WOULD... WOULD YOU LIKE TO COME FOR LUNCH? TOMORROW?
I- I HAVE TO ASK MY MOTHER. SHE MAY NEED HELP IN THE VINYARD.
OF COURSE.
WE SHOULD GO, I DON'T WANT TO BE LATE.

WATCH OUT, PAUL. YOU'RE GOING TO WAKE UP MARRIED TO LUCIE ONE DAY.
YOU REFUSE AND HER FATHER WILL ARREST YOU!
I WOULDN'T WANT MY GIRLFRIEND TO BE THE DAUGHTER OF A POLICEMAN.
YOU'LL BE LUCKY TO EVER GET A GIRLFRIEND.
IF I COULD GET A GIRLFRIEND LIKE SYLVIE...
SHE'S OUT OF YOUR LEAGUE. YOU'LL HAVE TO MAKE DO WITH SOMEONE LIKE... MARIE.
NO WAY! I WANT MY GIRL TO LOOK LIKE A GIRL! LIKE SYLVIE.
SYLVIE WOULD NEVER EVEN LOOK AT YOU! YOU DON'T EXIST TO HER!
WHAT DO YOU SAY, MARIE? TAKE PITY ON POOR GEORGES HERE.
YOU KIDDING? I'D BE TAKING PITY ON HER.
SHUT UP!

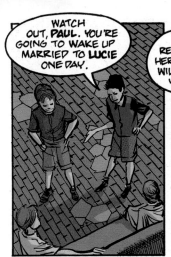

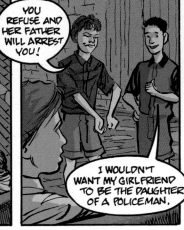

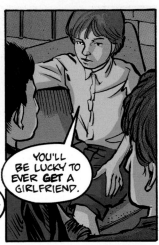

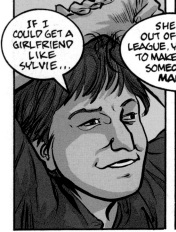

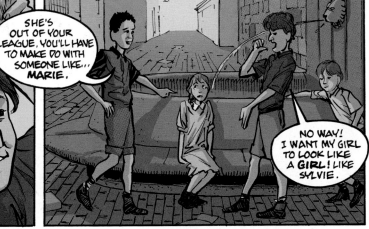

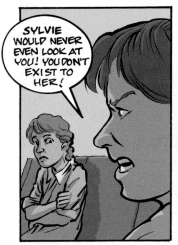

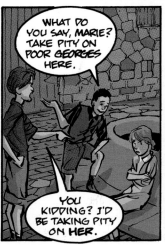

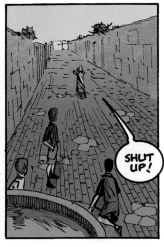

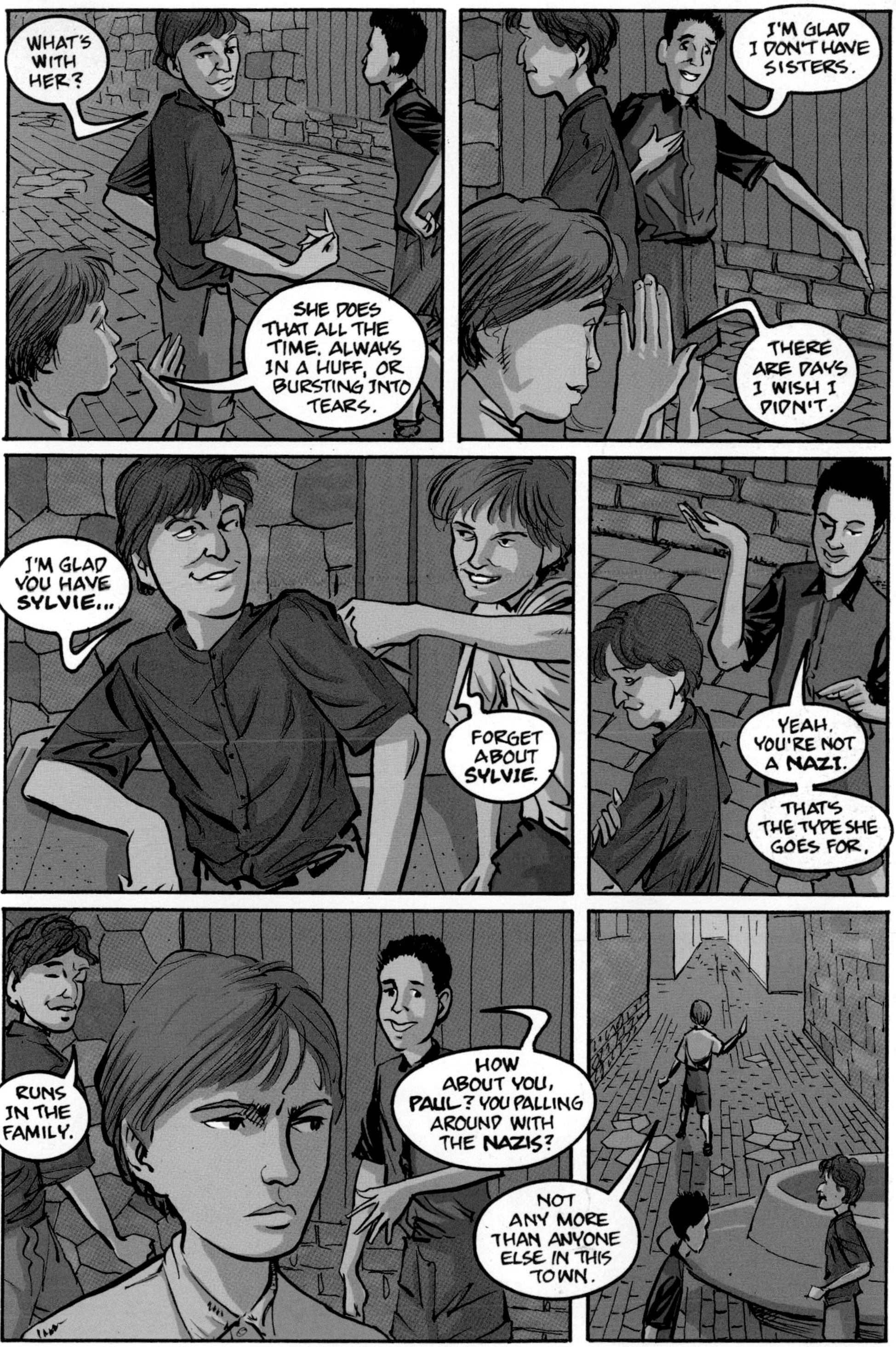

WHAT'S WITH HER?
SHE DOES THAT ALL THE TIME. ALWAYS IN A HUFF, OR BURSTING INTO TEARS.
I'M GLAD I DON'T HAVE SISTERS.
THERE ARE DAYS I WISH I DIDN'T.
I'M GLAD YOU HAVE SYLVIE...
FORGET ABOUT SYLVIE.
YEAH. YOU'RE NOT A NAZI.
THAT'S THE TYPE SHE GOES FOR.
RUNS IN THE FAMILY.
HOW ABOUT YOU, PAUL? YOU PALLING AROUND WITH THE NAZIS?
NOT ANY MORE THAN ANYONE ELSE IN THIS TOWN.

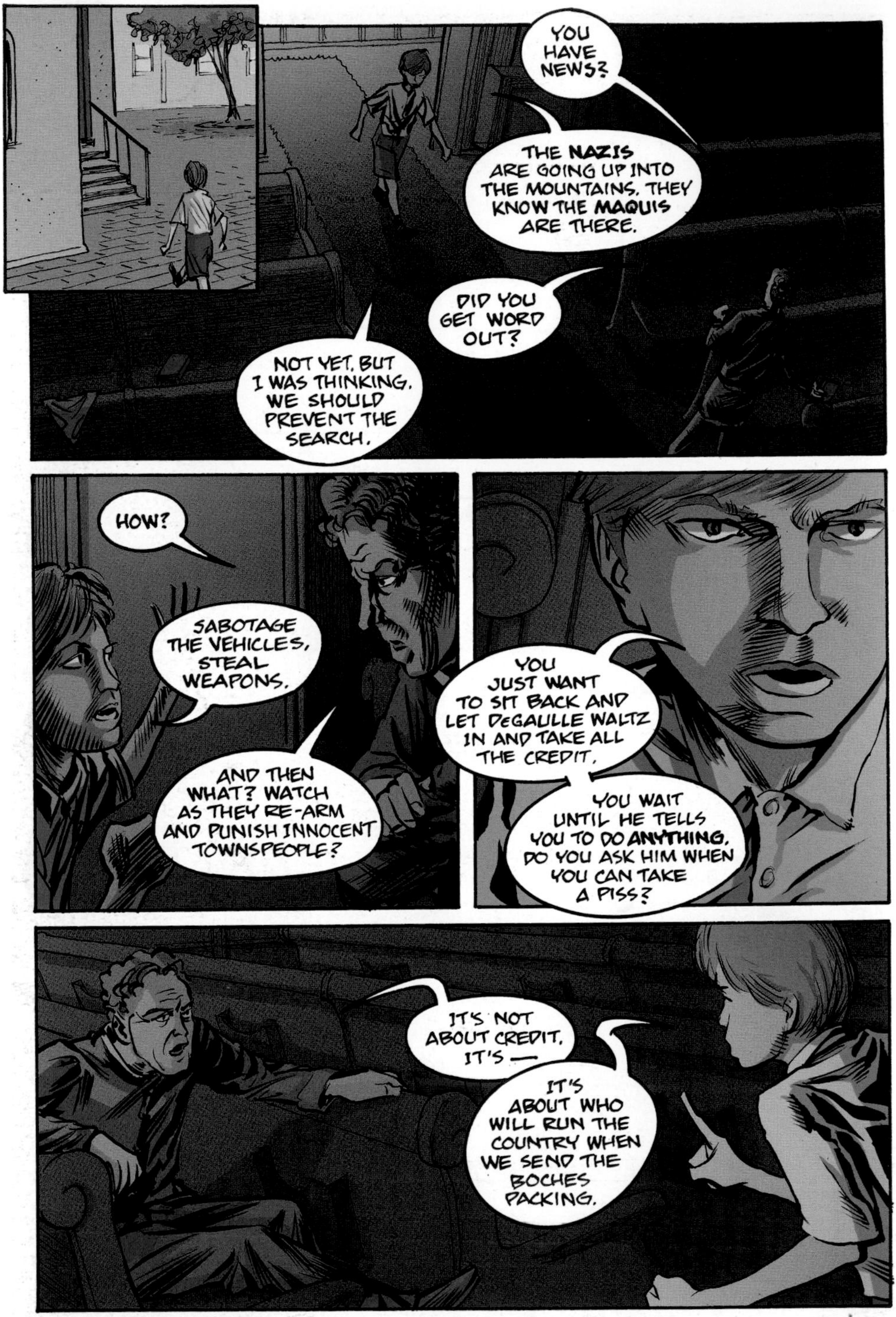
YOU HAVE NEWS?
THE NAZIS ARE GOING UP INTO THE MOUNTAINS. THEY KNOW THE MAQUIS ARE THERE.
DID YOU GET WORD OUT?
NOT YET, BUT I WAS THINKING. WE SHOULD PREVENT THE SEARCH.
HOW?
SABOTAGE THE VEHICLES, STEAL WEAPONS.
AND THEN WHAT? WATCH AS THEY RE-ARM AND PUNISH INNOCENT TOWNSPEOPLE?
YOU JUST WANT TO SIT BACK AND LET DEGAULLE WALTZ IN AND TAKE ALL THE CREDIT.
YOU WAIT UNTIL HE TELLS YOU TO DO ANYTHING. DO YOU ASK HIM WHEN YOU CAN TAKE A PISS?
IT'S NOT ABOUT CREDIT, IT'S —
IT'S ABOUT WHO WILL RUN THE COUNTRY WHEN WE SEND THE BOCHES PACKING.

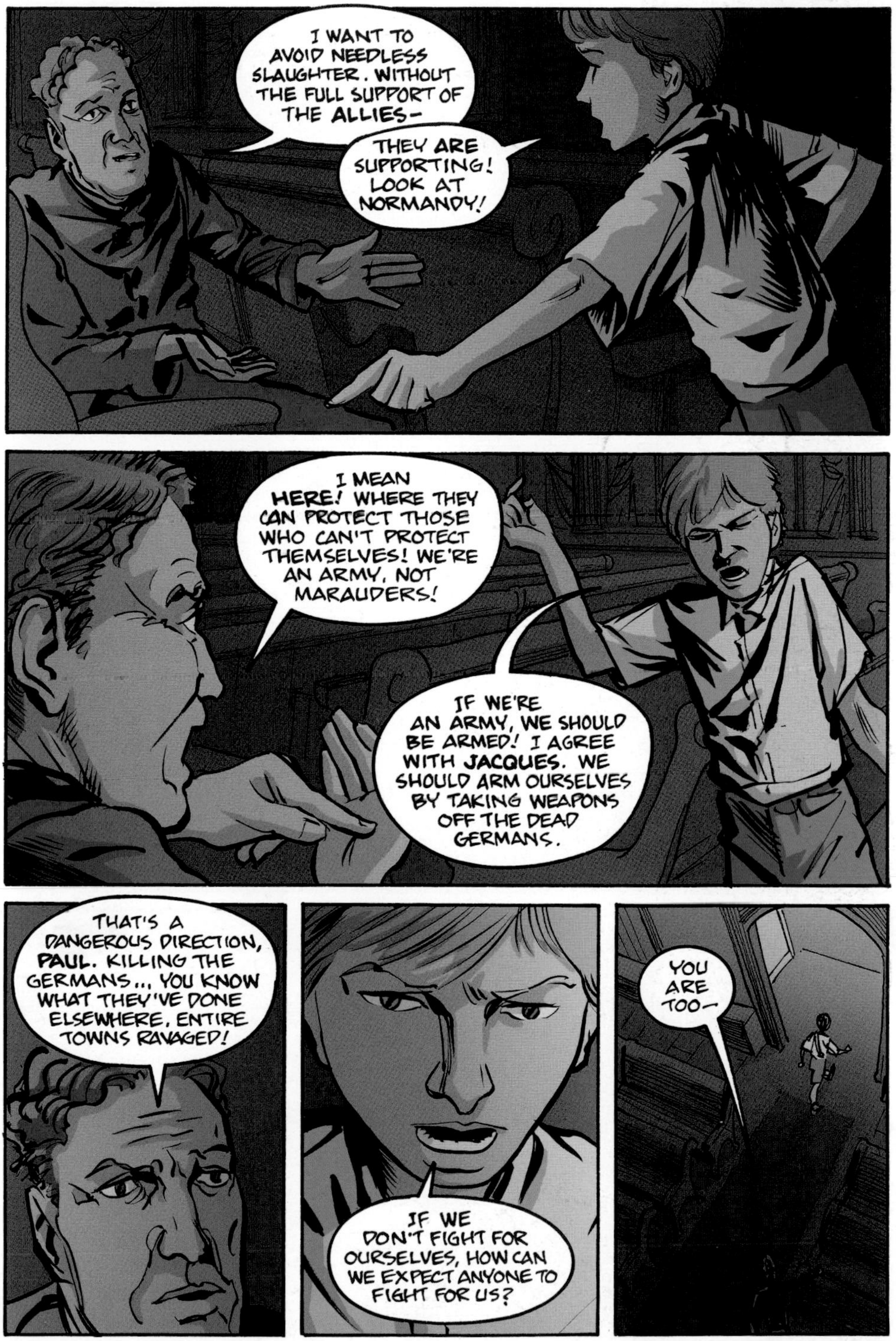
I WANT TO AVOID NEEDLESS SLAUGHTER. WITHOUT THE FULL SUPPORT OF THE ALLIES–
THEY ARE SUPPORTING! LOOK AT NORMANDY!
I MEAN HERE! WHERE THEY CAN PROTECT THOSE WHO CAN'T PROTECT THEMSELVES! WE'RE AN ARMY, NOT MARAUDERS!
IF WE'RE AN ARMY, WE SHOULD BE ARMED! I AGREE WITH JACQUES. WE SHOULD ARM OURSELVES BY TAKING WEAPONS OFF THE DEAD GERMANS.
THAT'S A DANGEROUS DIRECTION, PAUL. KILLING THE GERMANS... YOU KNOW WHAT THEY'VE DONE ELSEWHERE. ENTIRE TOWNS RAVAGED!
IF WE DON'T FIGHT FOR OURSELVES, HOW CAN WE EXPECT ANYONE TO FIGHT FOR US?
YOU ARE TOO–

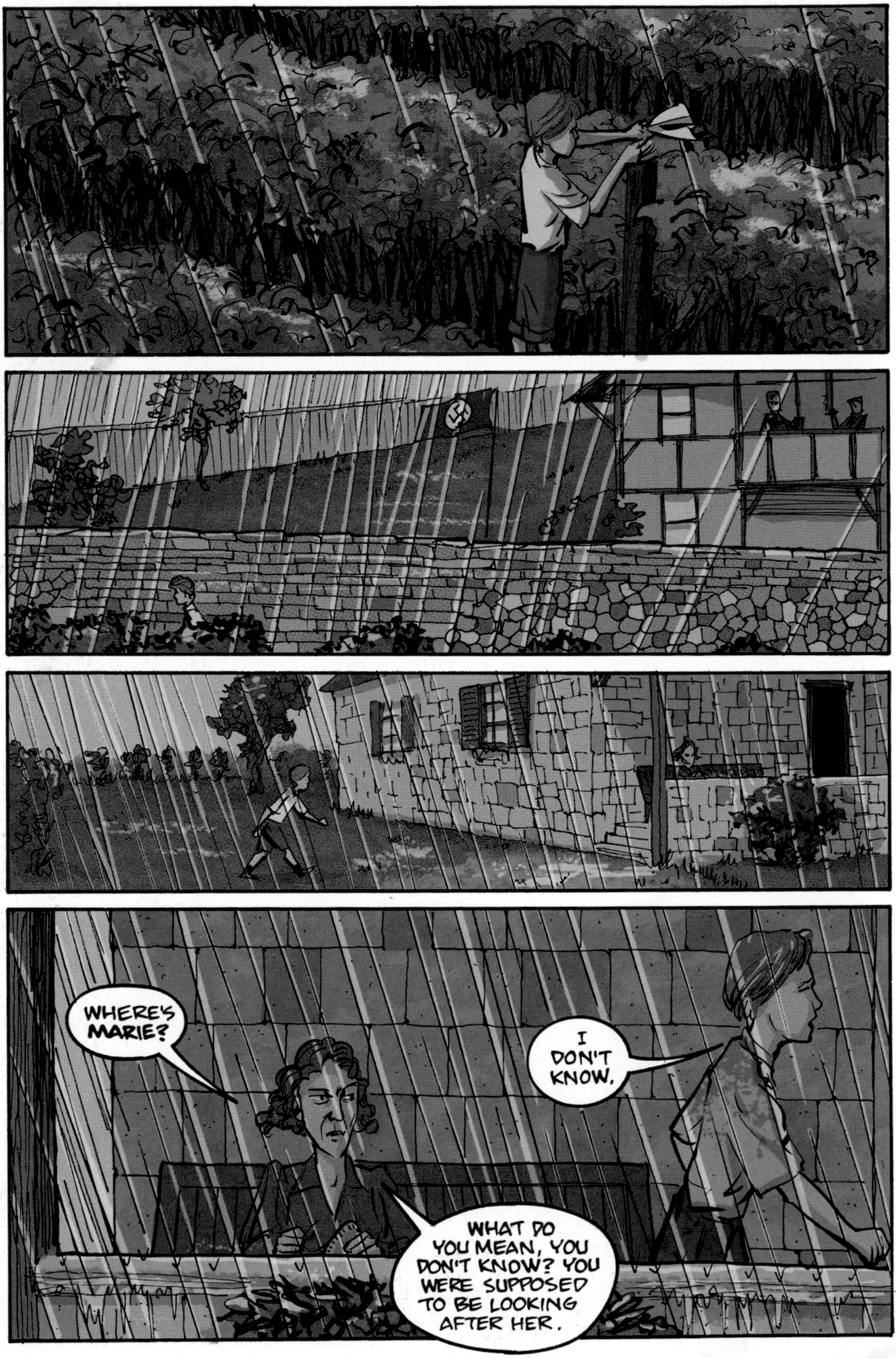
WHERE'S MARIE?
I DON'T KNOW.
WHAT DO YOU MEAN, YOU DON'T KNOW? YOU WERE SUPPOSED TO BE LOOKING AFTER HER.

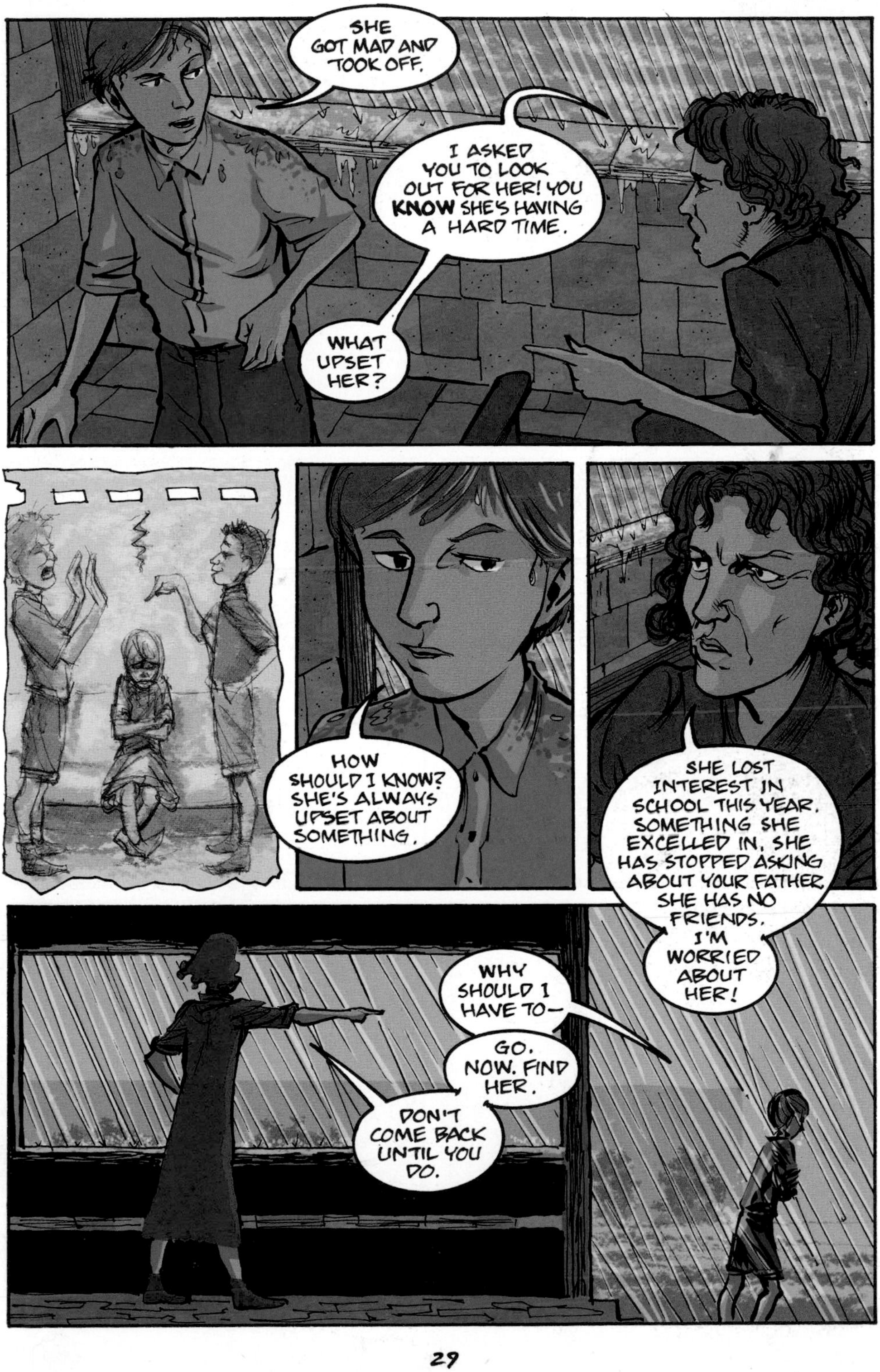
SHE GOT MAD AND TOOK OFF.
I ASKED YOU TO LOOK OUT FOR HER! YOU KNOW SHE'S HAVING A HARD TIME.
WHAT UPSET HER?
HOW SHOULD I KNOW? SHE'S ALWAYS UPSET ABOUT SOMETHING.
SHE LOST INTEREST IN SCHOOL THIS YEAR. SOMETHING SHE EXCELLED IN. SHE HAS STOPPED ASKING ABOUT YOUR FATHER. SHE HAS NO FRIENDS.
I'M WORRIED ABOUT HER!
WHY SHOULD I HAVE TO—
GO. NOW. FIND HER.
DON'T COME BACK UNTIL YOU DO.

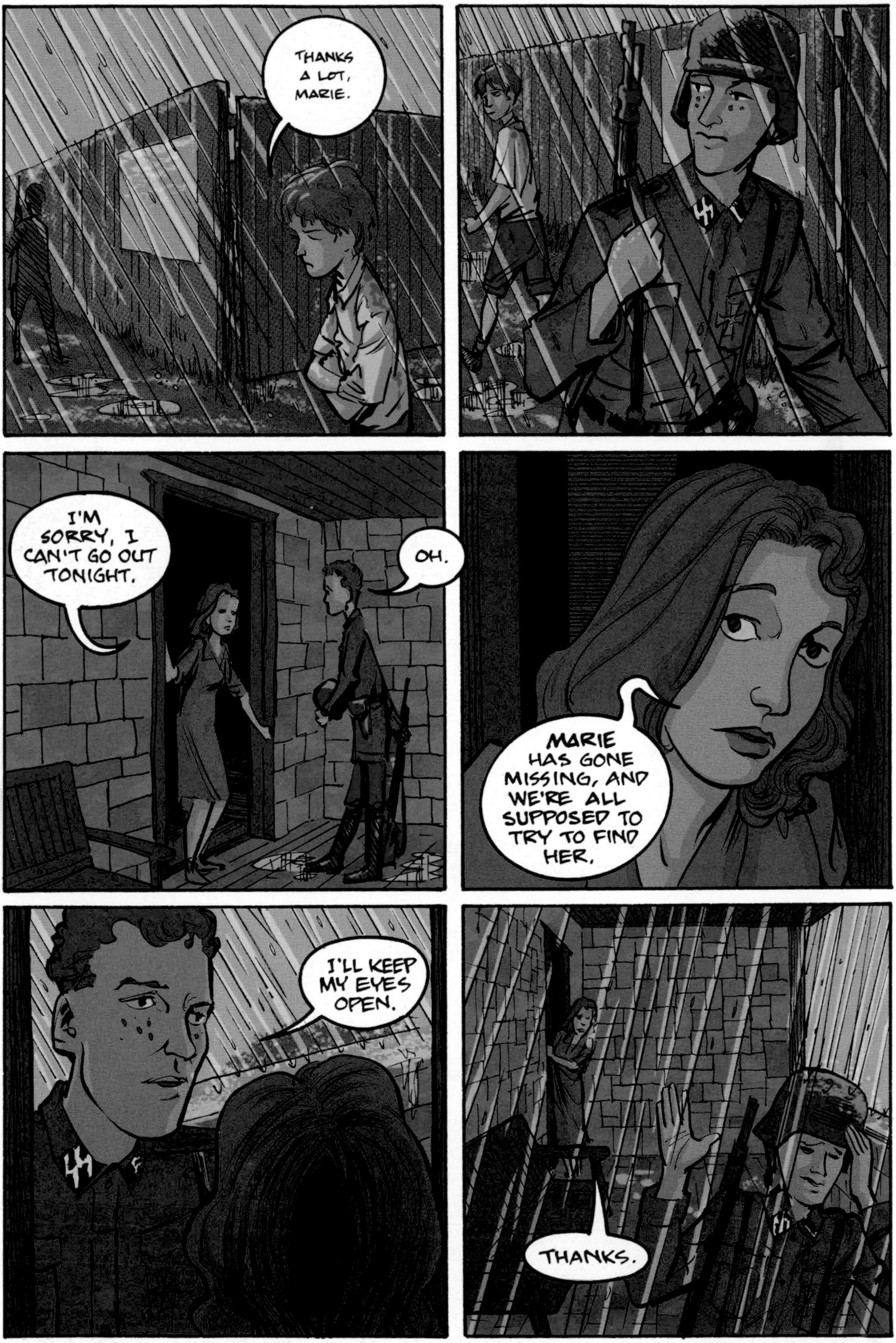
THANKS A LOT, MARIE.
I'M SORRY, I CAN'T GO OUT TONIGHT.
OH.
MARIE HAS GONE MISSING, AND WE'RE ALL SUPPOSED TO TRY TO FIND HER.
I'LL KEEP MY EYES OPEN.
THANKS.

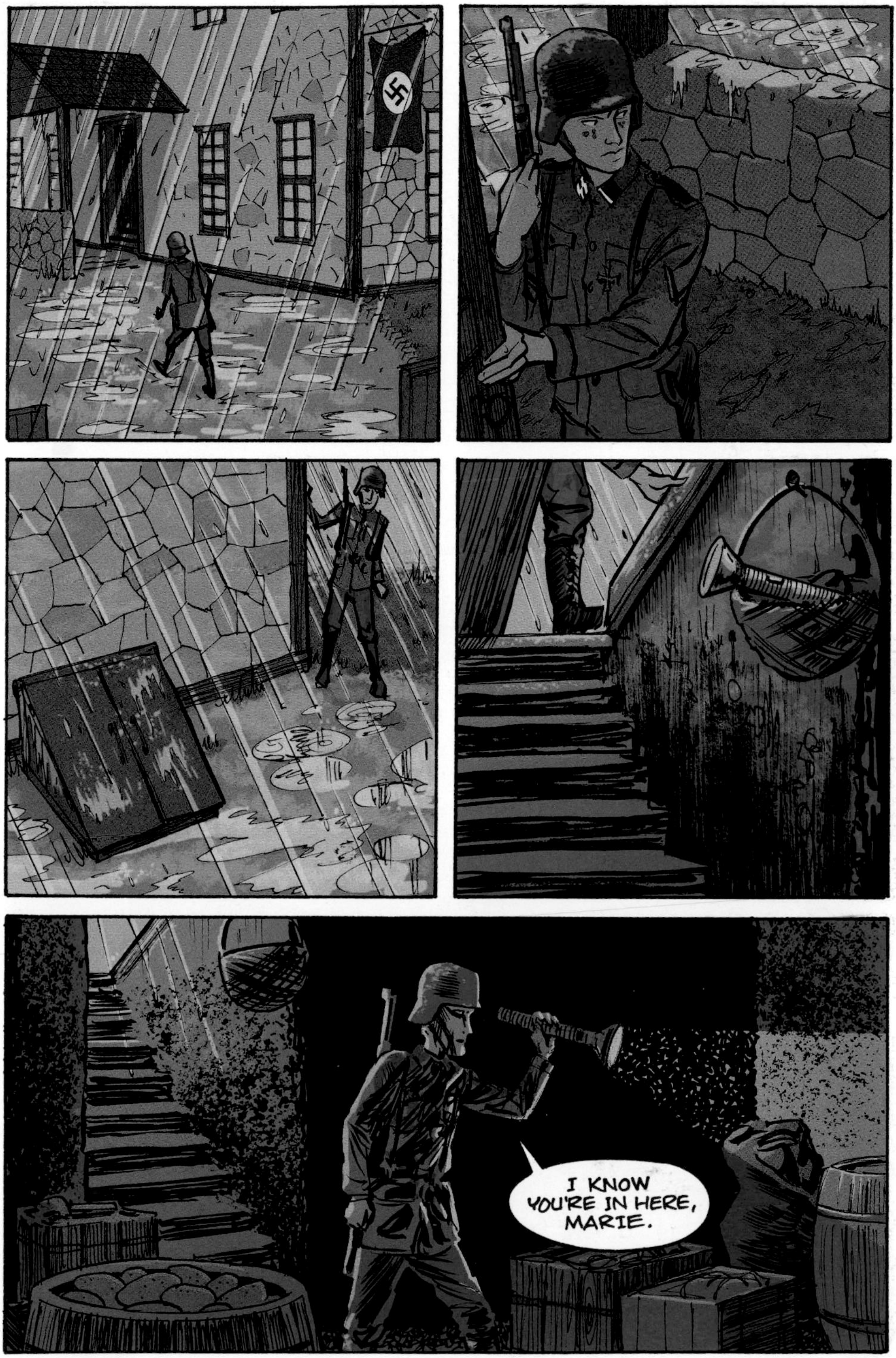
I KNOW YOU'RE IN HERE, MARIE.

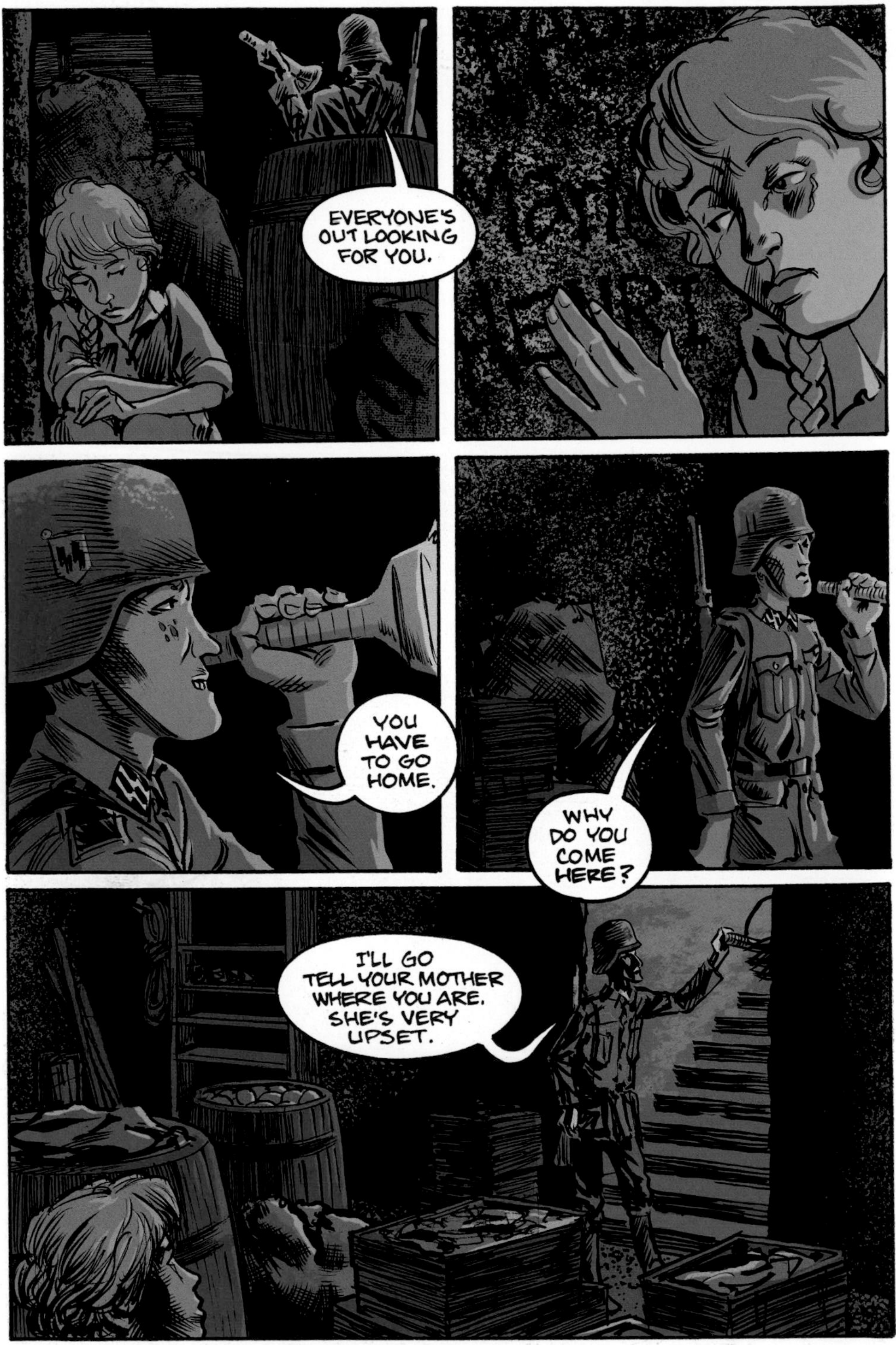
EVERYONE'S OUT LOOKING FOR YOU.
YOU HAVE TO GO HOME.
WHY DO YOU COME HERE?
I'LL GO TELL YOUR MOTHER WHERE YOU ARE. SHE'S VERY UPSET.

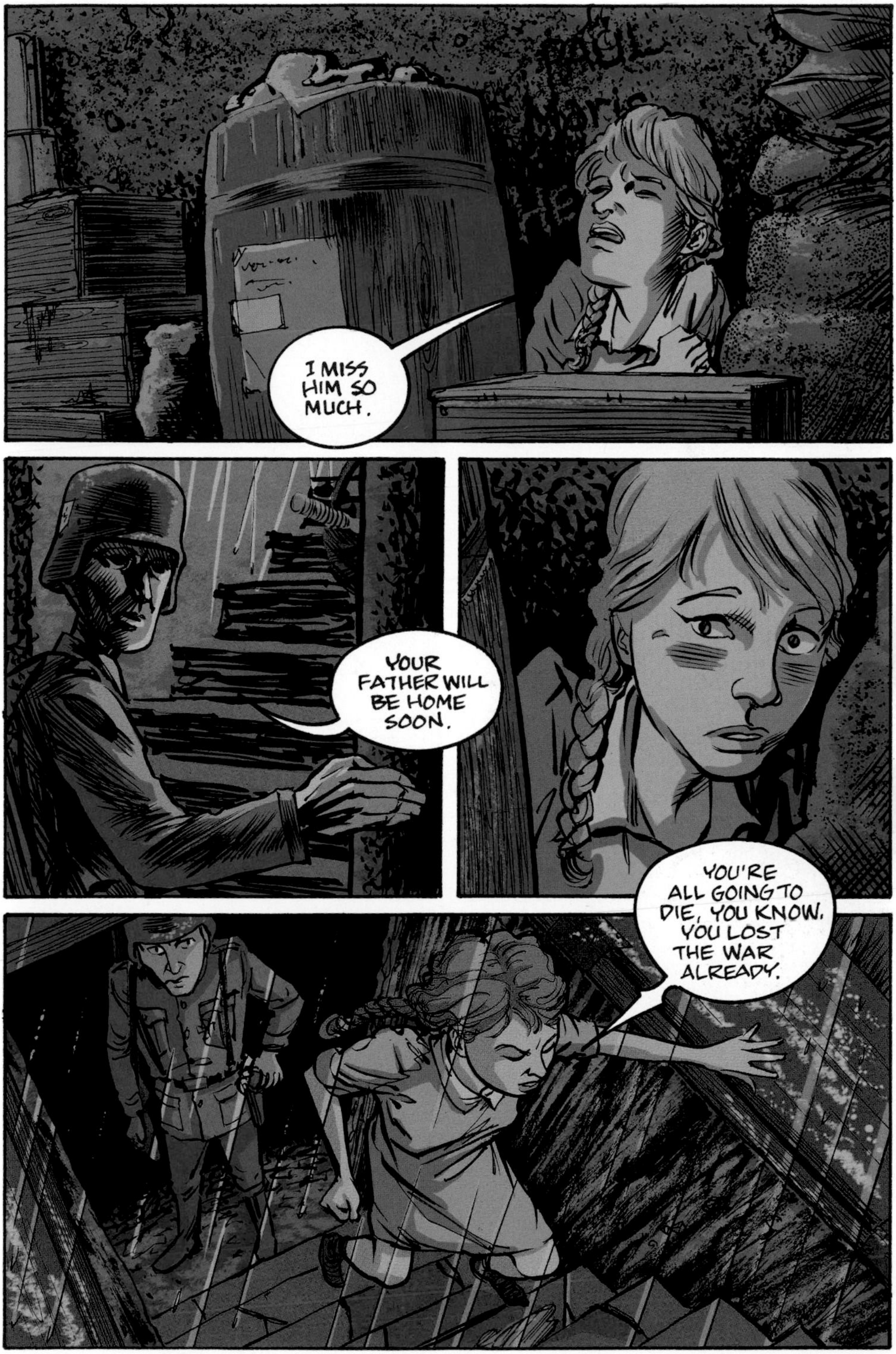
I MISS HIM SO MUCH.
YOUR FATHER WILL BE HOME SOON.
YOU'RE ALL GOING TO DIE, YOU KNOW. YOU LOST THE WAR ALREADY.

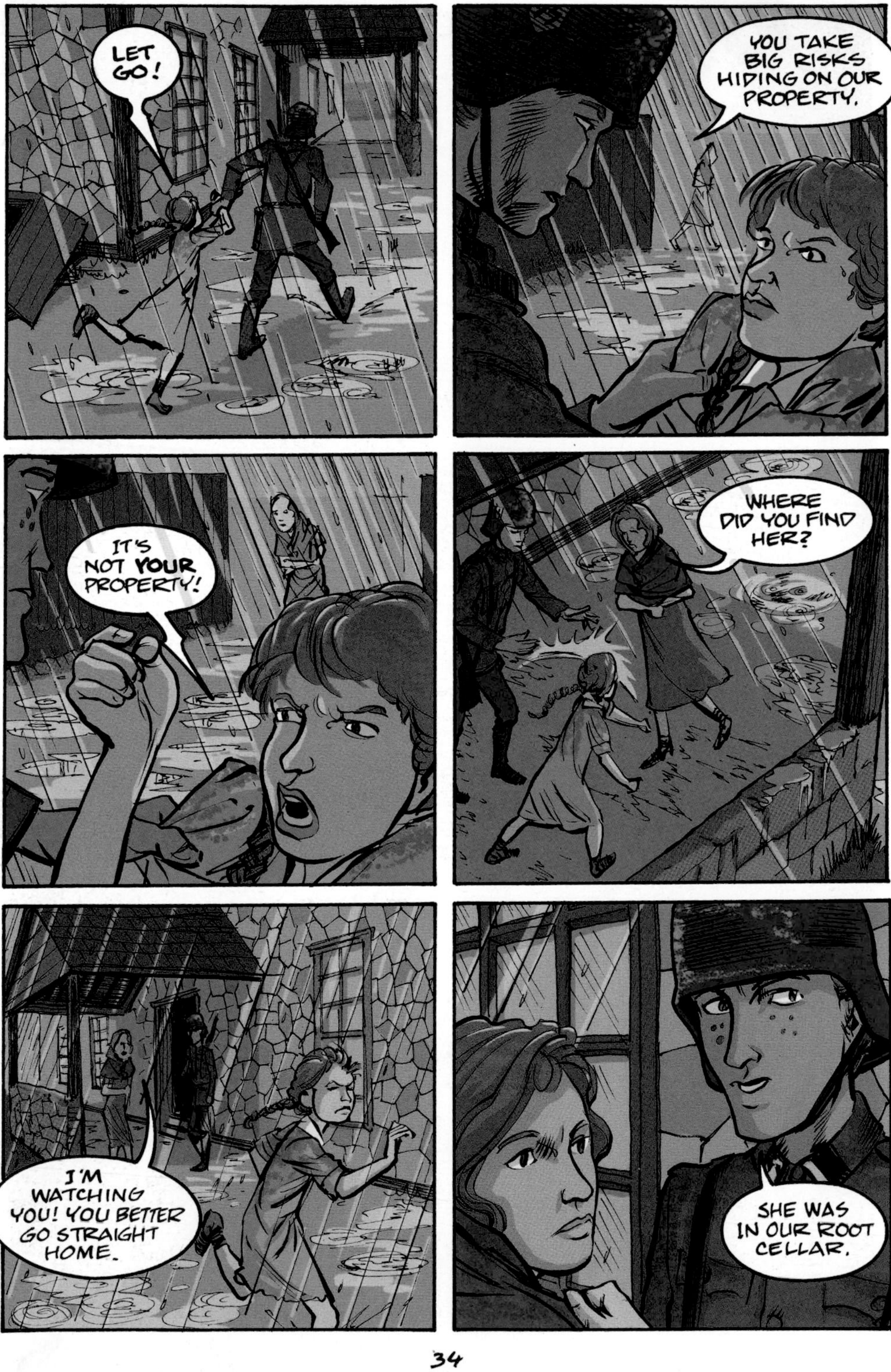
LET GO!
YOU TAKE BIG RISKS HIDING ON OUR PROPERTY.
IT'S NOT **YOUR** PROPERTY!
WHERE DID YOU FIND HER?
I'M WATCHING YOU! YOU BETTER GO STRAIGHT HOME.
SHE WAS IN OUR ROOT CELLAR.

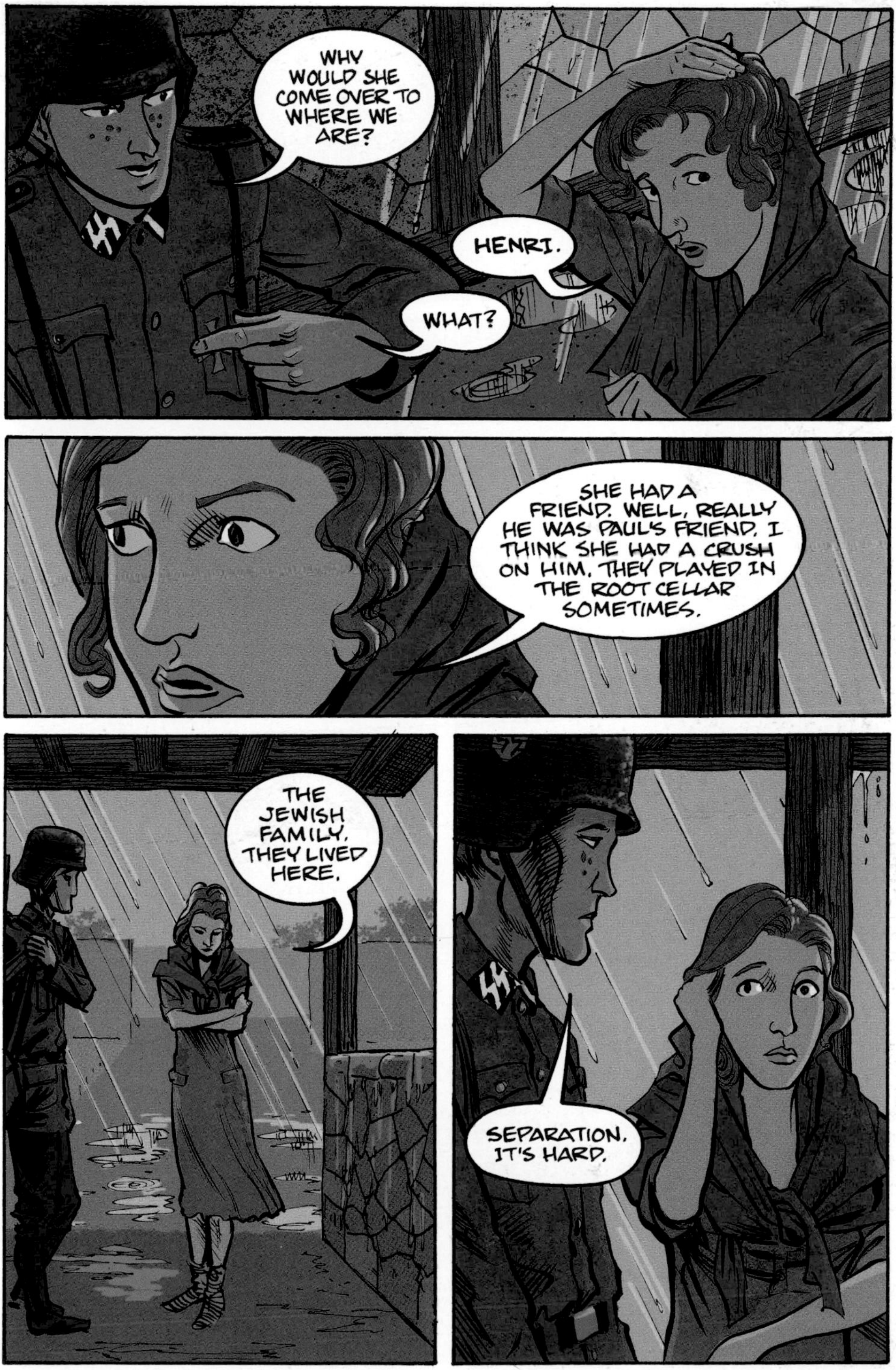
WHY WOULD SHE COME OVER TO WHERE WE ARE?
HENRI.
WHAT?
SHE HAD A FRIEND. WELL, REALLY HE WAS PAUL'S FRIEND. I THINK SHE HAD A CRUSH ON HIM. THEY PLAYED IN THE ROOT CELLAR SOMETIMES.
THE JEWISH FAMILY. THEY LIVED HERE.
SEPARATION. IT'S HARD.

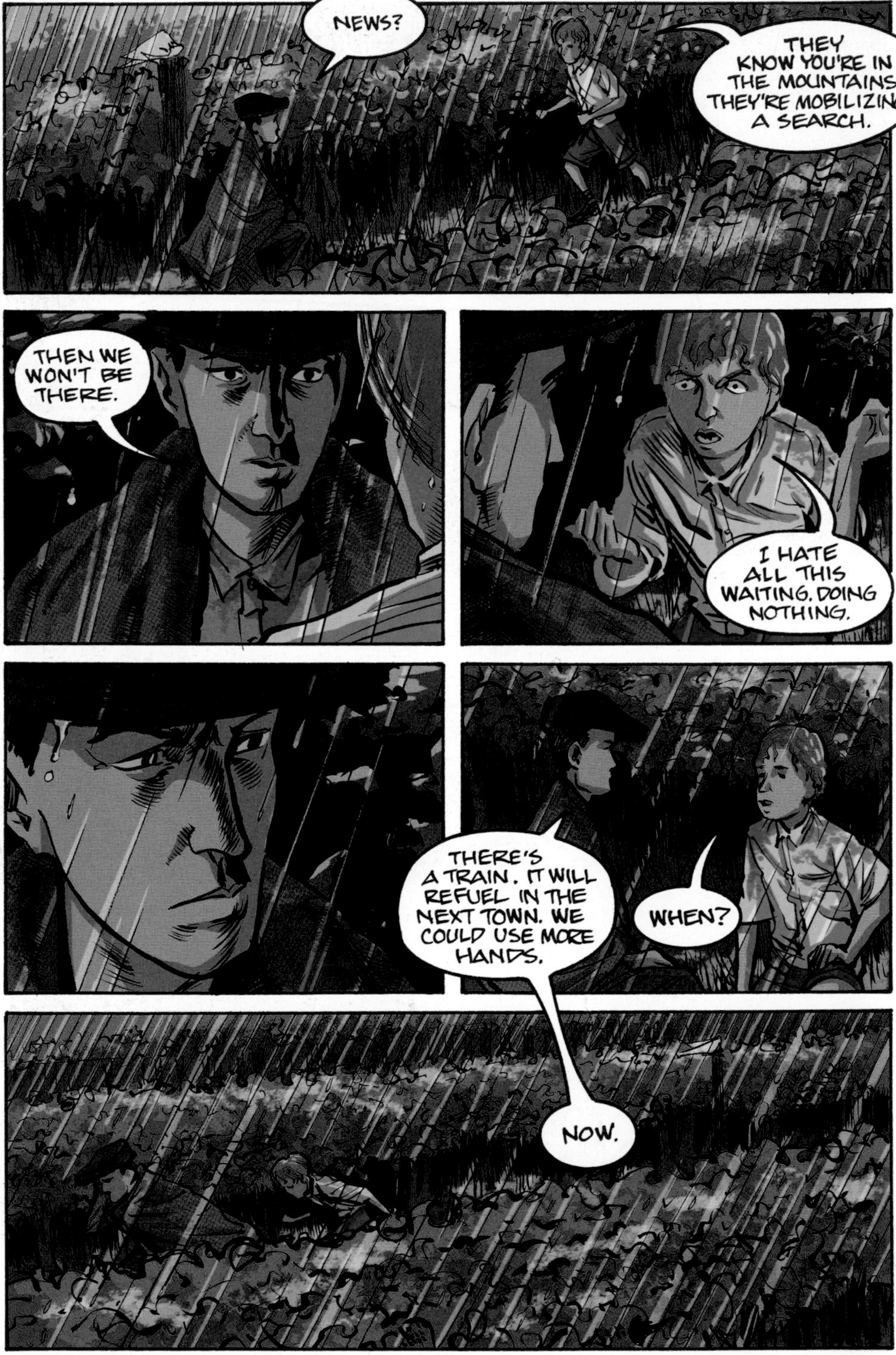
NEWS?
THEY KNOW YOU'RE IN THE MOUNTAINS. THEY'RE MOBILIZING A SEARCH.
THEN WE WON'T BE THERE.
I HATE ALL THIS WAITING. DOING NOTHING.
THERE'S A TRAIN. IT WILL REFUEL IN THE NEXT TOWN. WE COULD USE MORE HANDS.
WHEN?
NOW.

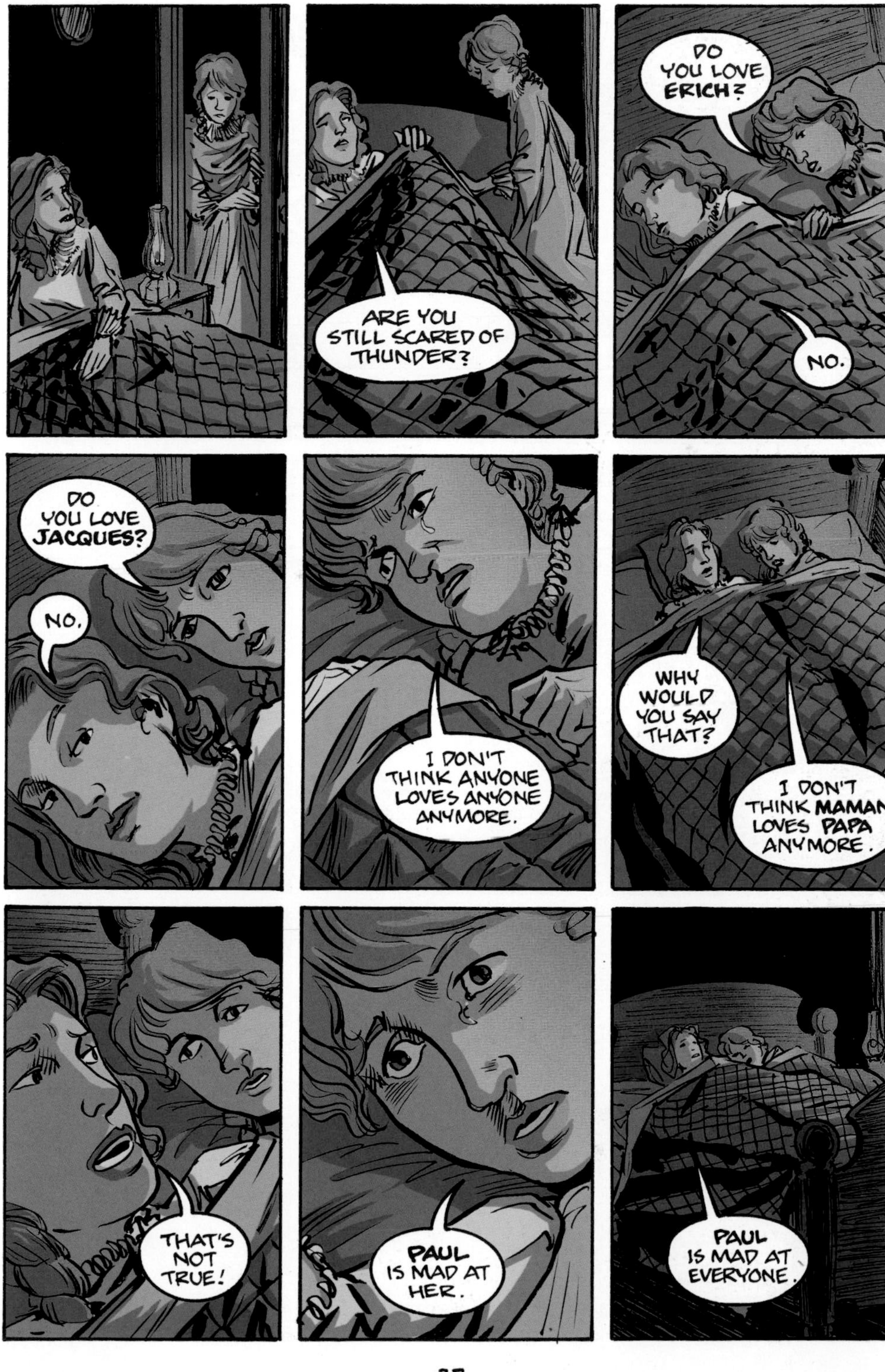
ARE YOU STILL SCARED OF THUNDER?
DO YOU LOVE ERICH?
NO.
DO YOU LOVE JACQUES?
NO.
I DON'T THINK ANYONE LOVES ANYONE ANYMORE.
WHY WOULD YOU SAY THAT?
I DON'T THINK MAMAN LOVES PAPA ANYMORE.
THAT'S NOT TRUE!
PAUL IS MAD AT HER.
PAUL IS MAD AT EVERYONE.

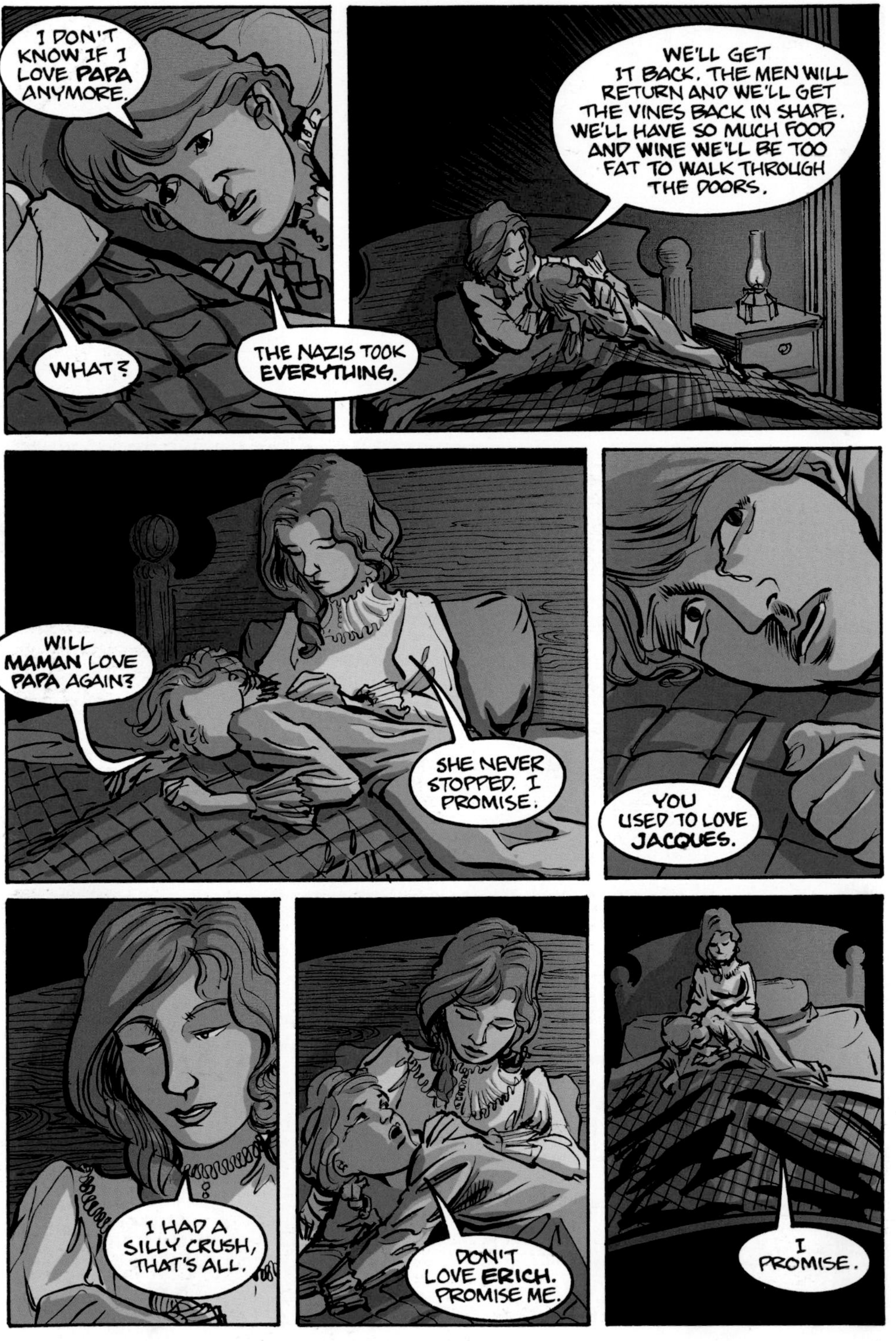

I DON'T KNOW IF I LOVE PAPA ANYMORE.
WHAT?
THE NAZIS TOOK EVERYTHING.
WE'LL GET IT BACK. THE MEN WILL RETURN AND WE'LL GET THE VINES BACK IN SHAPE. WE'LL HAVE SO MUCH FOOD AND WINE WE'LL BE TOO FAT TO WALK THROUGH THE DOORS.
WILL MAMAN LOVE PAPA AGAIN?
SHE NEVER STOPPED. I PROMISE.
YOU USED TO LOVE JACQUES.
I HAD A SILLY CRUSH, THAT'S ALL.
DON'T LOVE ERICH. PROMISE ME.
I PROMISE.

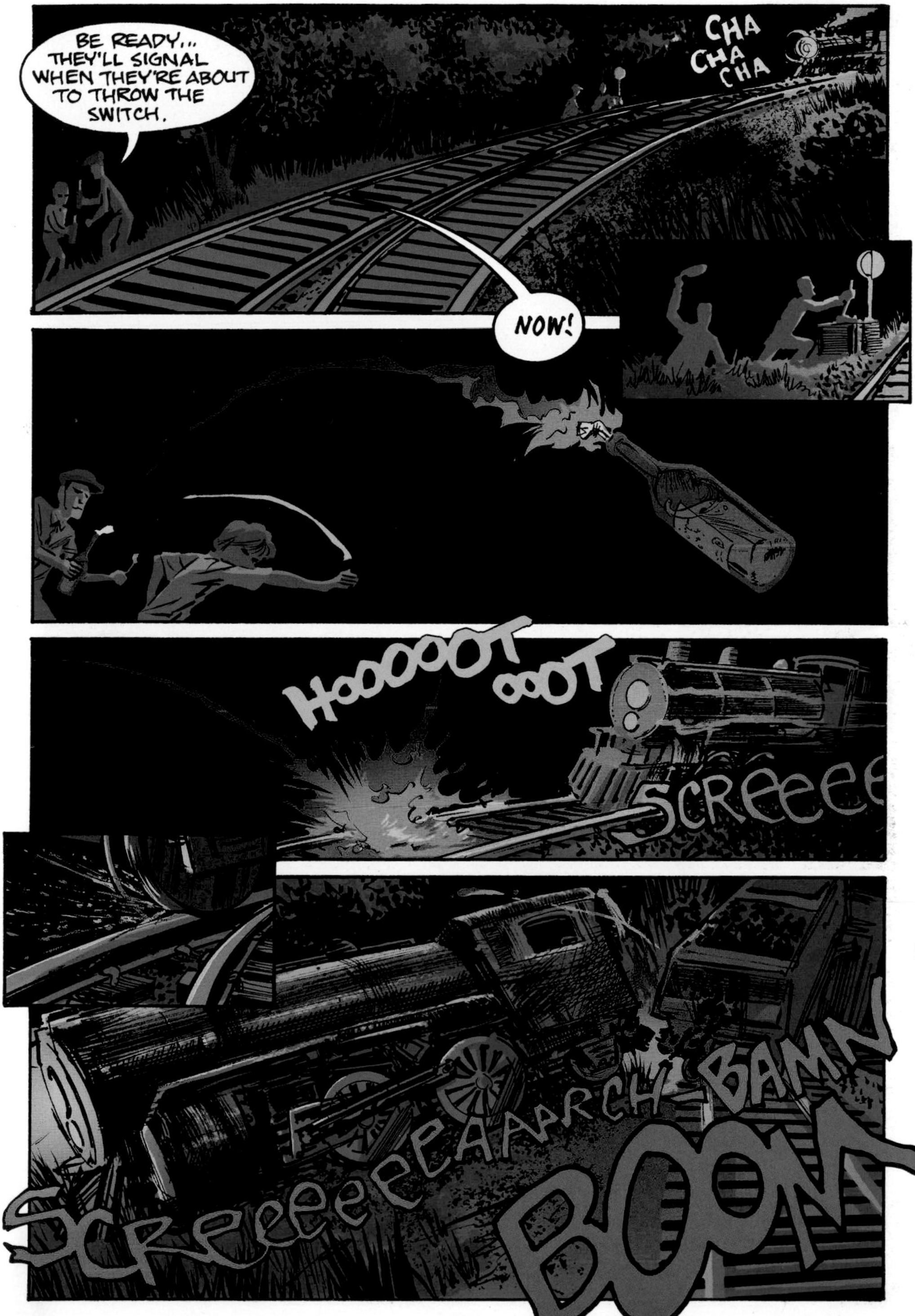
BE READY... THEY'LL SIGNAL WHEN THEY'RE ABOUT TO THROW THE SWITCH.
CHA CHA CHA
NOW!
HOOOOOT OOOT
SCREEEE
SCREEEEEEAAARCH
BAMN
BOOM

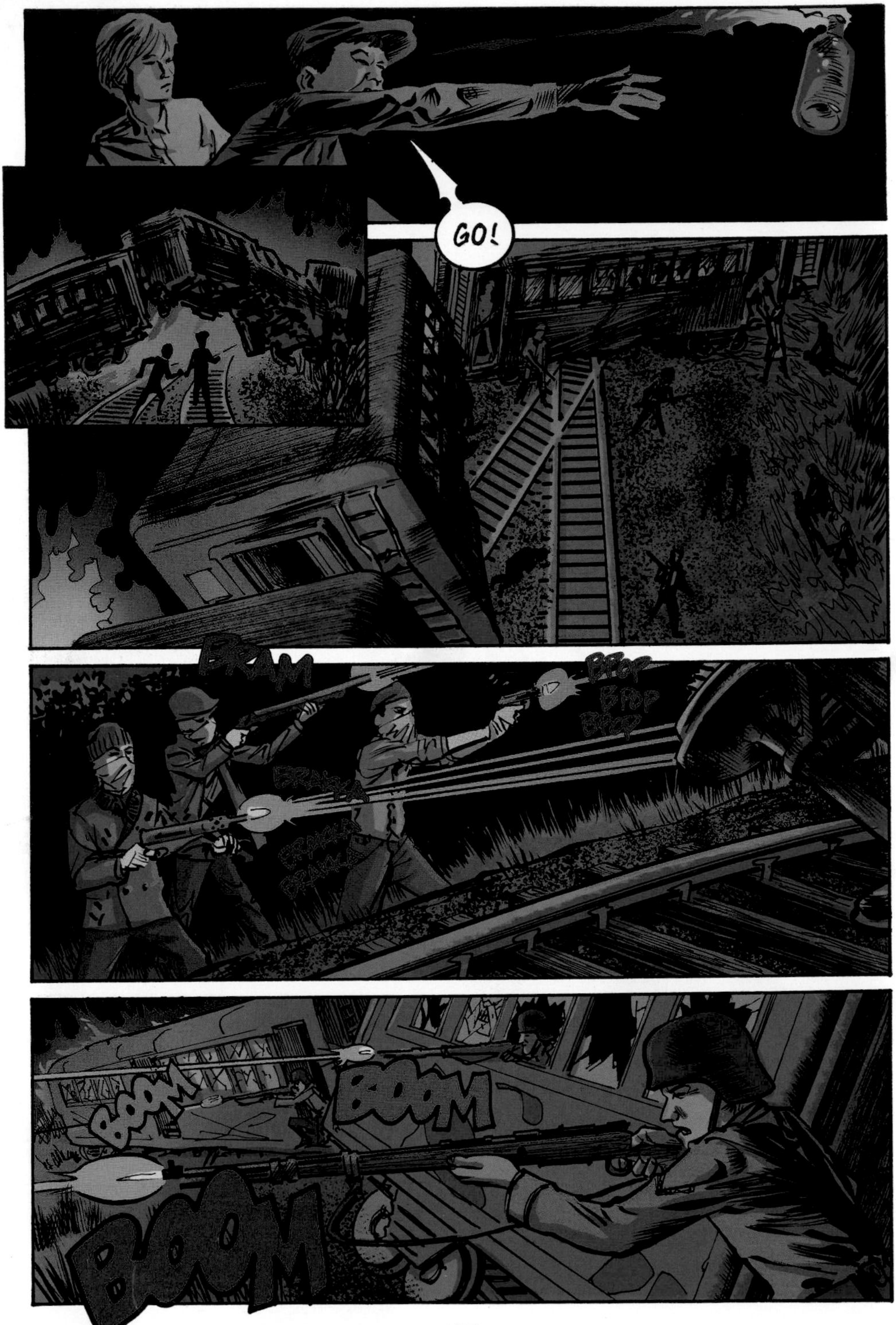
GO!
BRAM
BPOP
BPOP
BPOP
BRAKKA
BRAKKA
BRAKKA
BOOM
BOOM
BOOM

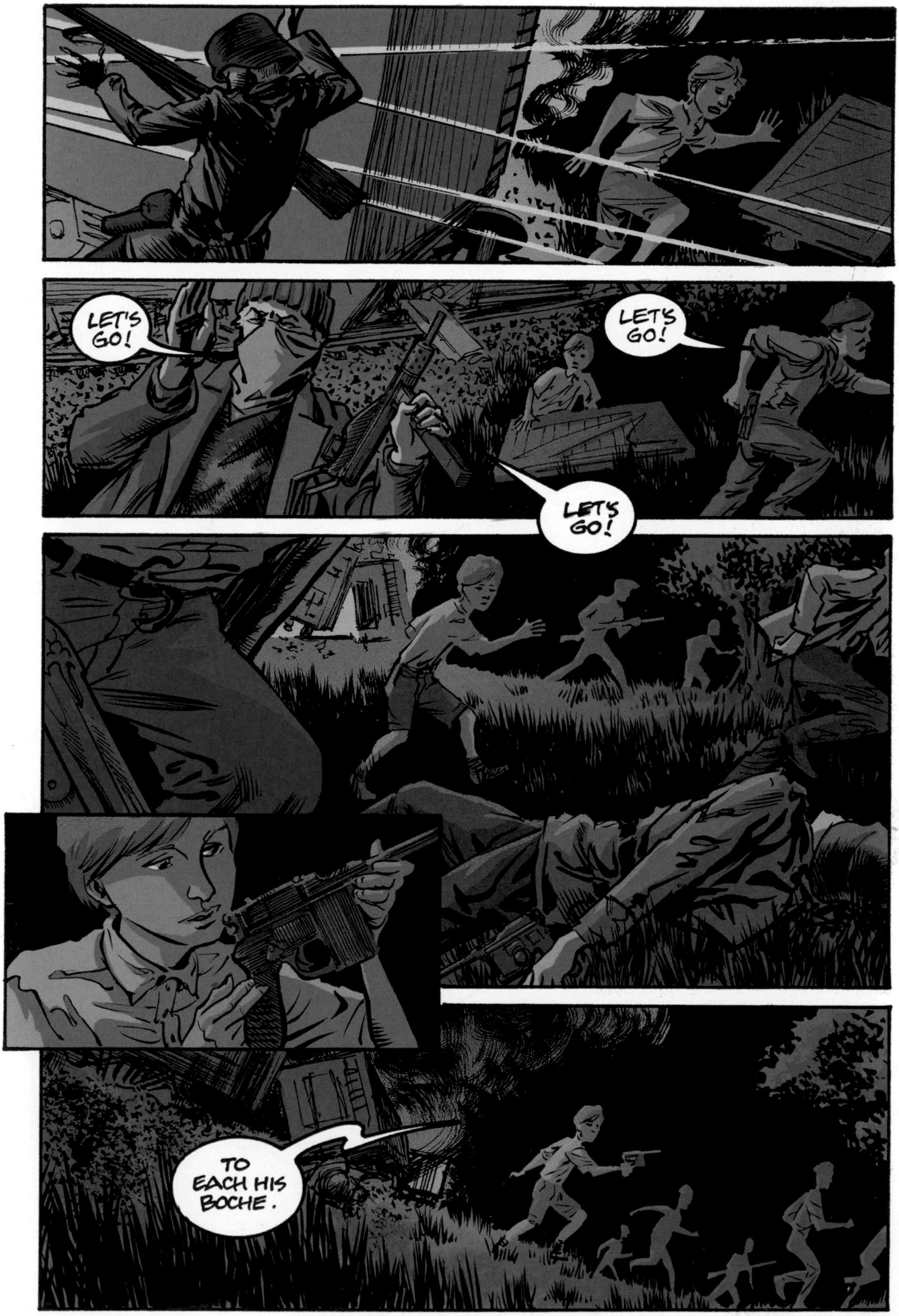
LET'S GO!
LET'S GO!
LET'S GO!
TO EACH HIS BOCHE.

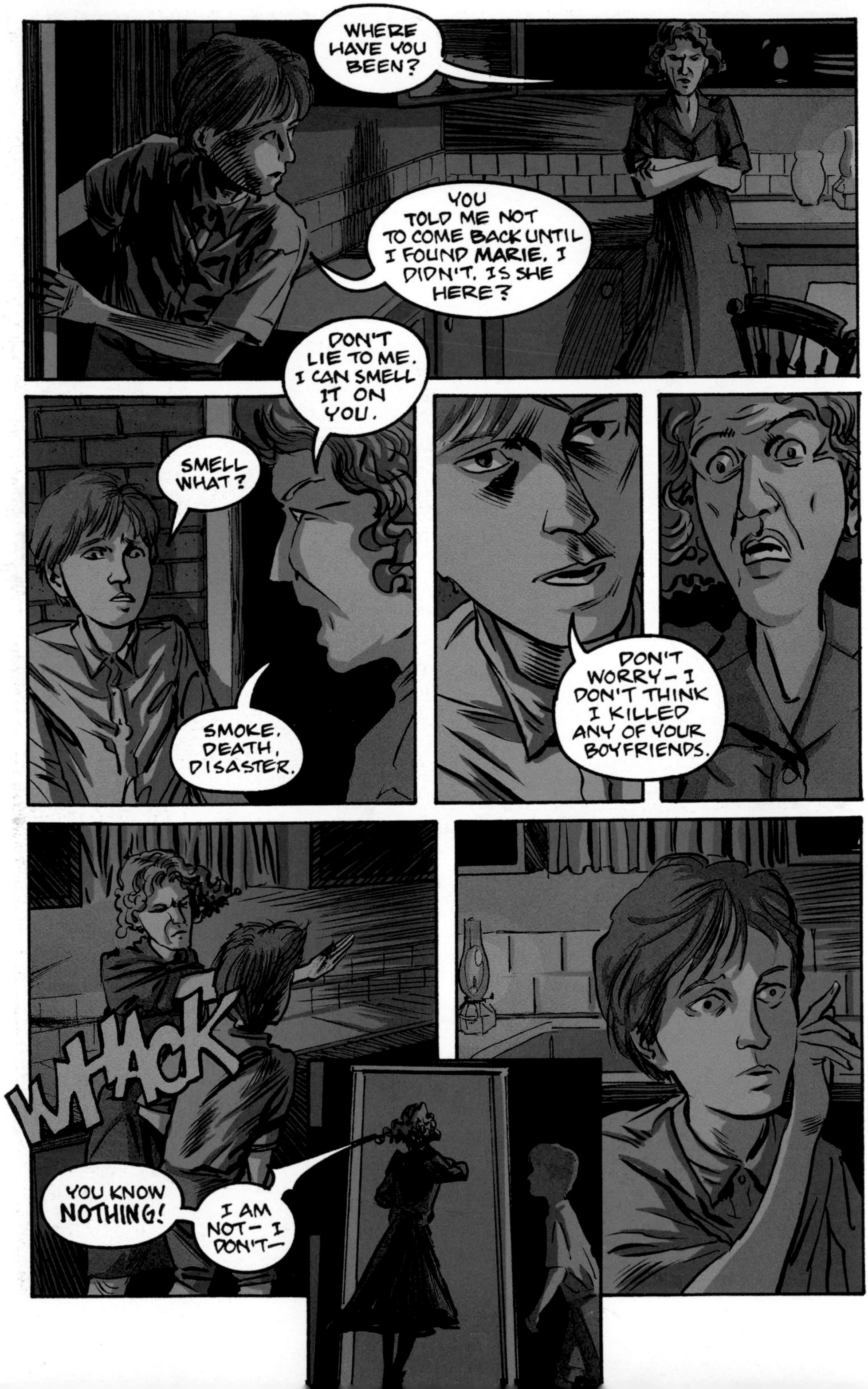

WHERE HAVE YOU BEEN?
YOU TOLD ME NOT TO COME BACK UNTIL I FOUND MARIE. I DIDN'T. IS SHE HERE?
DON'T LIE TO ME. I CAN SMELL IT ON YOU.
SMELL WHAT?
SMOKE. DEATH. DISASTER.
DON'T WORRY– I DON'T THINK I KILLED ANY OF YOUR BOYFRIENDS.
WHACK
YOU KNOW NOTHING!
I AM NOT– I DON'T–

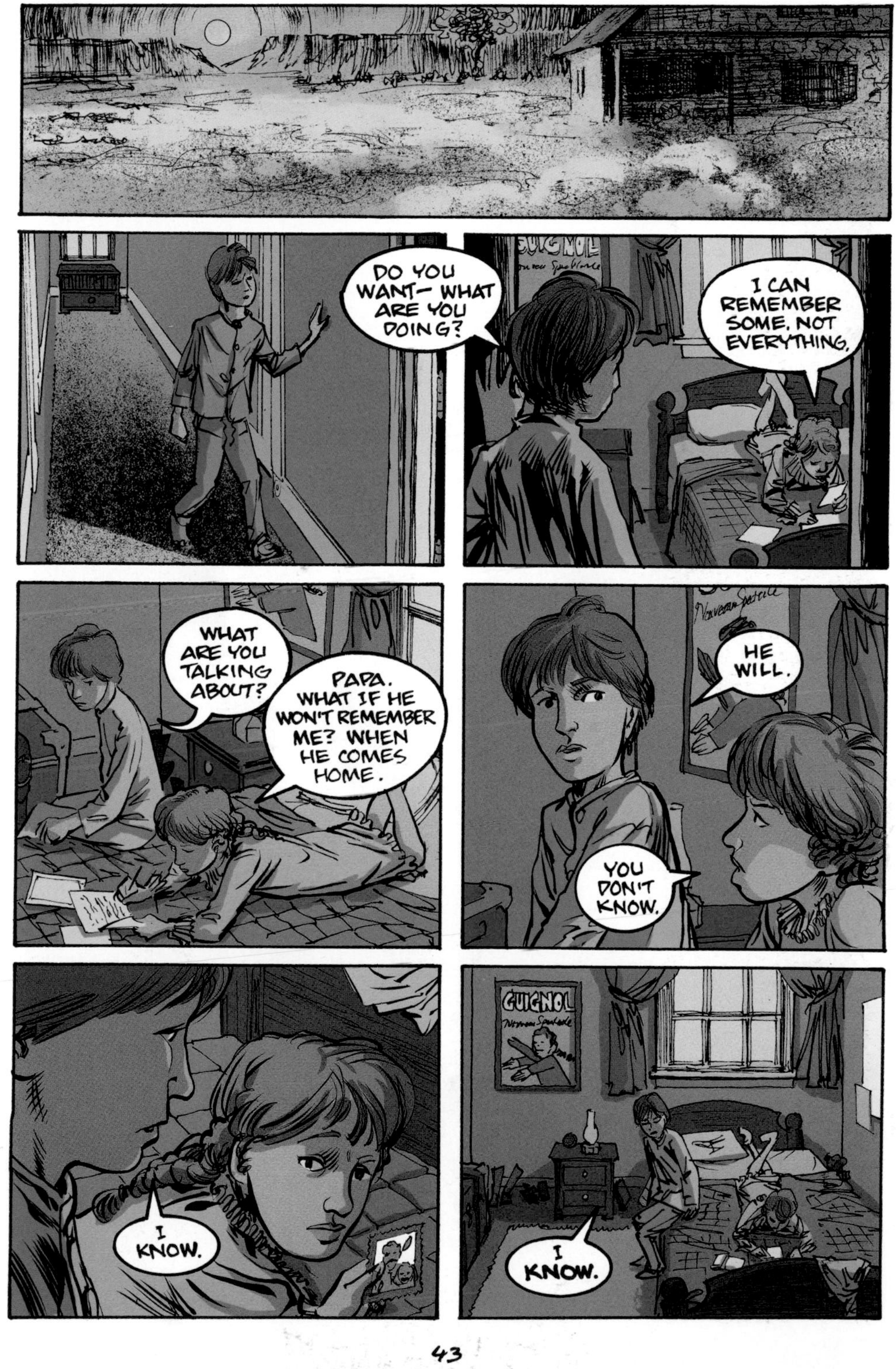
DO YOU WANT— WHAT ARE YOU DOING?
I CAN REMEMBER SOME, NOT EVERYTHING.
WHAT ARE YOU TALKING ABOUT?
PAPA. WHAT IF HE WON'T REMEMBER ME? WHEN HE COMES HOME.
HE WILL.
YOU DON'T KNOW.
I KNOW.
GUIGNOL
I KNOW.

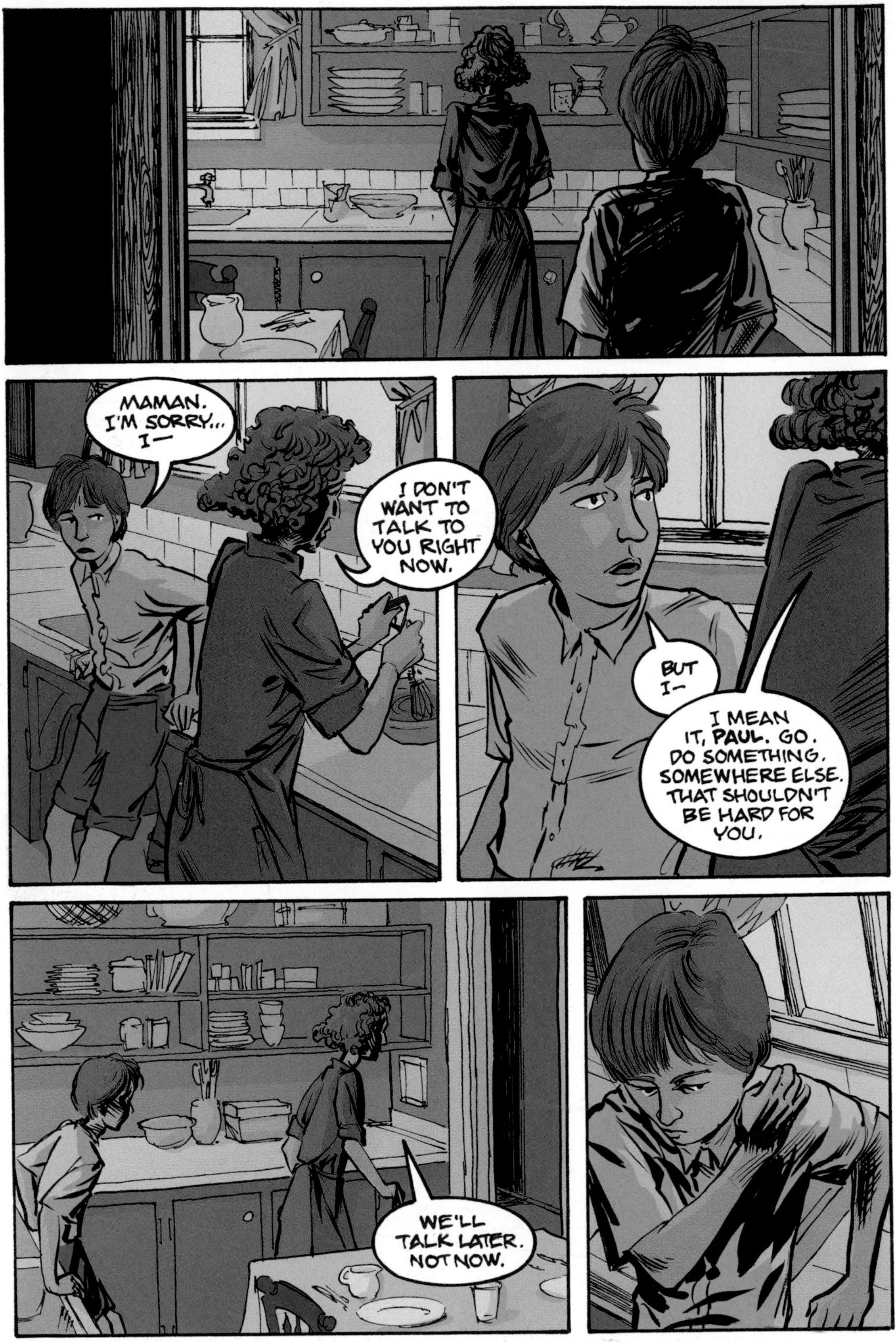
MAMAN. I'M SORRY... I—
I DON'T WANT TO TALK TO YOU RIGHT NOW.
BUT I—
I MEAN IT, **PAUL**. GO. DO SOMETHING. SOMEWHERE ELSE. THAT SHOULDN'T BE HARD FOR YOU.
WE'LL TALK LATER. NOT NOW.

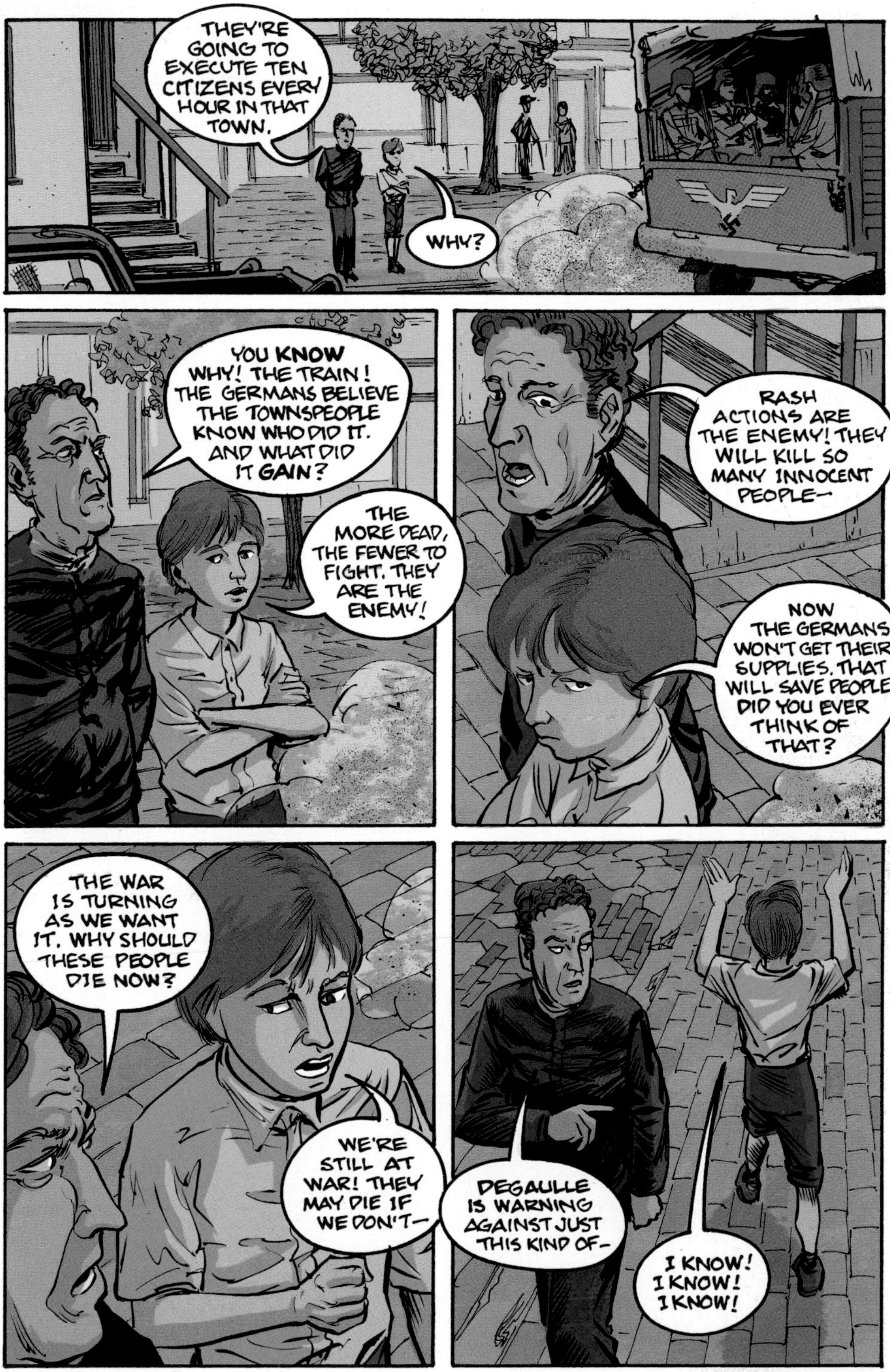
THEY'RE GOING TO EXECUTE TEN CITIZENS EVERY HOUR IN THAT TOWN.
WHY?
YOU KNOW WHY! THE TRAIN! THE GERMANS BELIEVE THE TOWNSPEOPLE KNOW WHO DID IT. AND WHAT DID IT GAIN?
THE MORE DEAD, THE FEWER TO FIGHT. THEY ARE THE ENEMY!
RASH ACTIONS ARE THE ENEMY! THEY WILL KILL SO MANY INNOCENT PEOPLE–
NOW THE GERMANS WON'T GET THEIR SUPPLIES. THAT WILL SAVE PEOPLE, DID YOU EVER THINK OF THAT?
THE WAR IS TURNING AS WE WANT IT. WHY SHOULD THESE PEOPLE DIE NOW?
WE'RE STILL AT WAR! THEY MAY DIE IF WE DON'T–
DEGAULLE IS WARNING AGAINST JUST THIS KIND OF–
I KNOW! I KNOW! I KNOW!

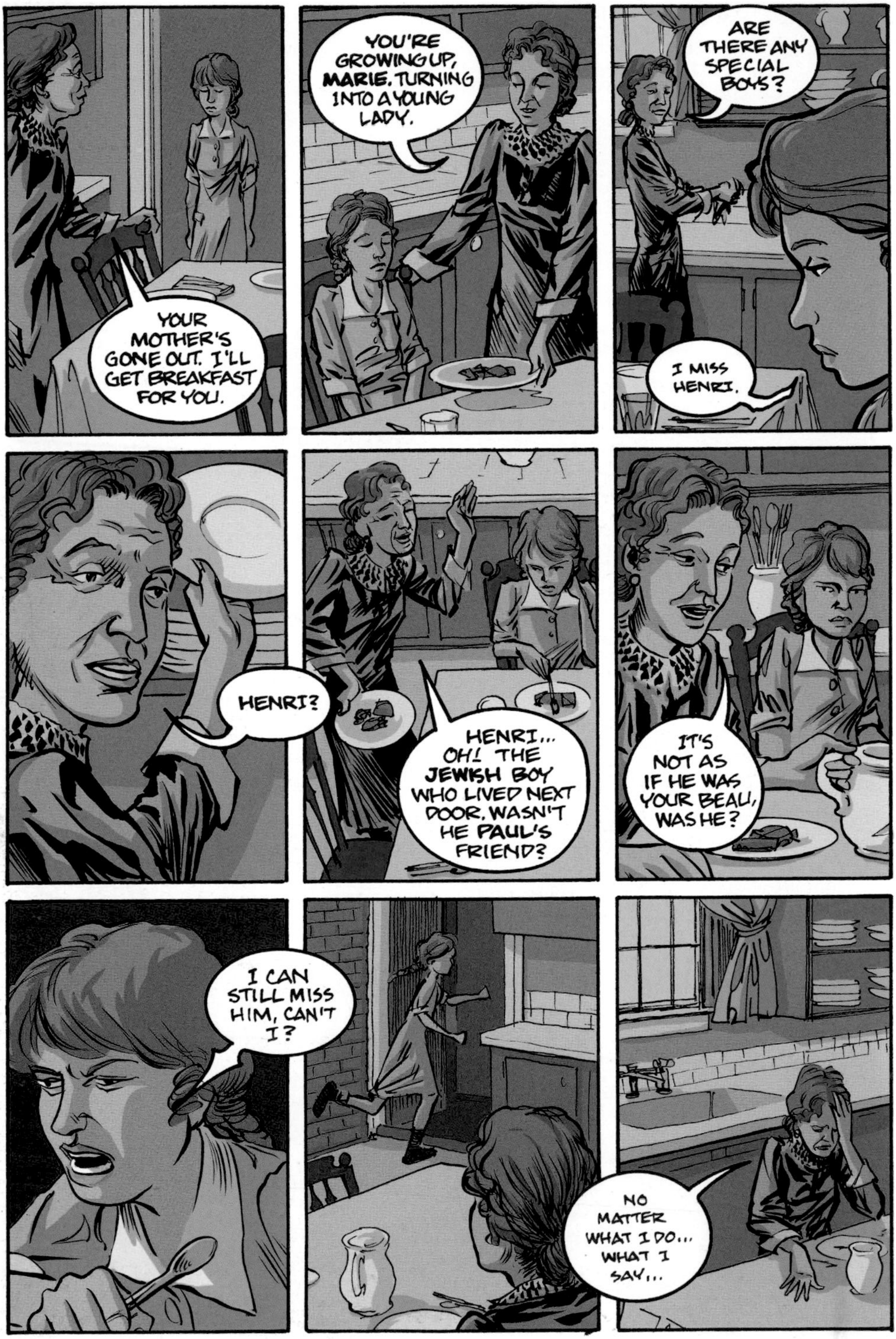
YOUR MOTHER'S GONE OUT. I'LL GET BREAKFAST FOR YOU.
YOU'RE GROWING UP, MARIE. TURNING INTO A YOUNG LADY.
ARE THERE ANY SPECIAL BOYS?
I MISS HENRI.
HENRI?
HENRI... OH! THE JEWISH BOY WHO LIVED NEXT DOOR, WASN'T HE PAUL'S FRIEND?
IT'S NOT AS IF HE WAS YOUR BEAU, WAS HE?
I CAN STILL MISS HIM, CAN'T I?
NO MATTER WHAT I DO... WHAT I SAY...

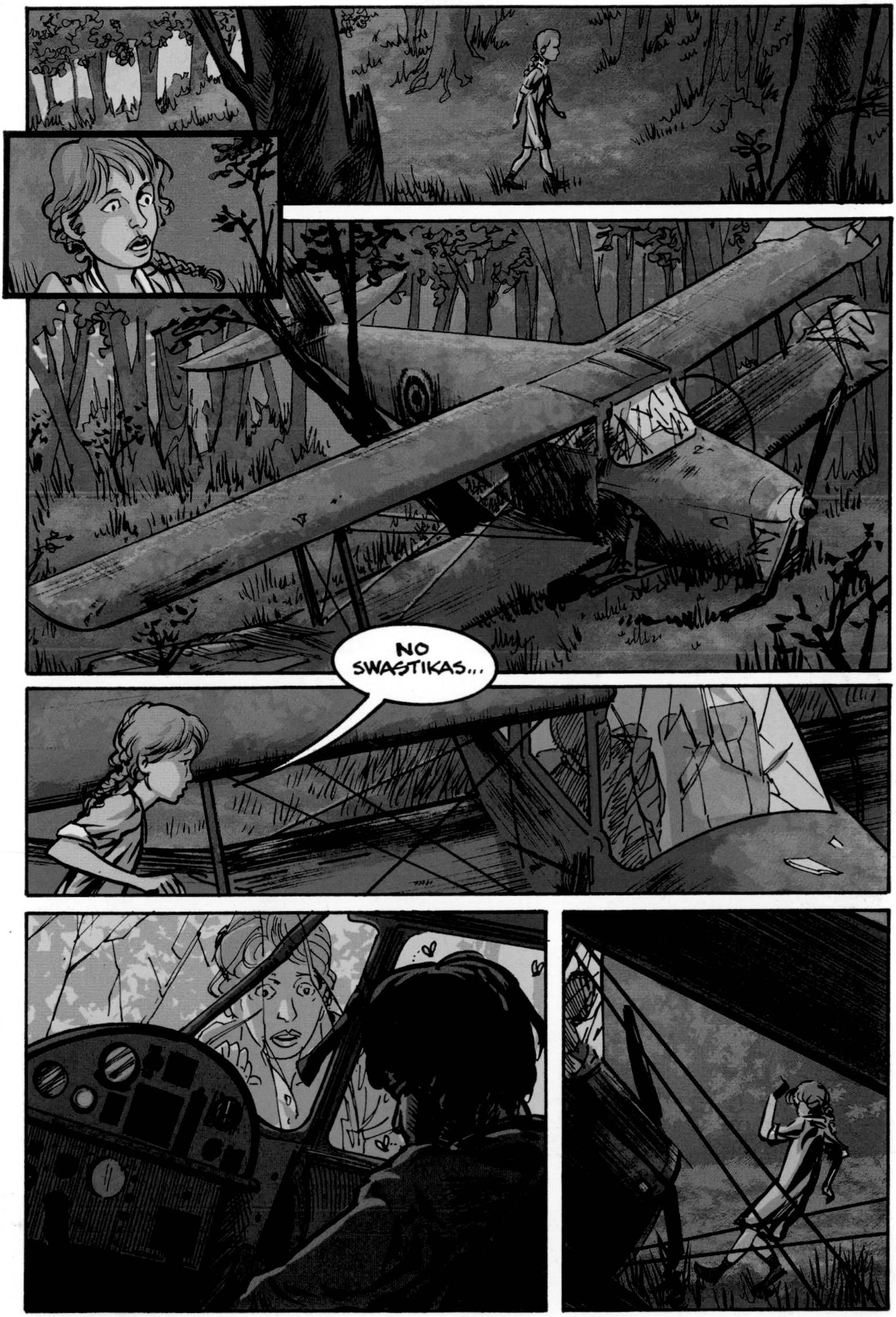
NO SWASTIKAS...

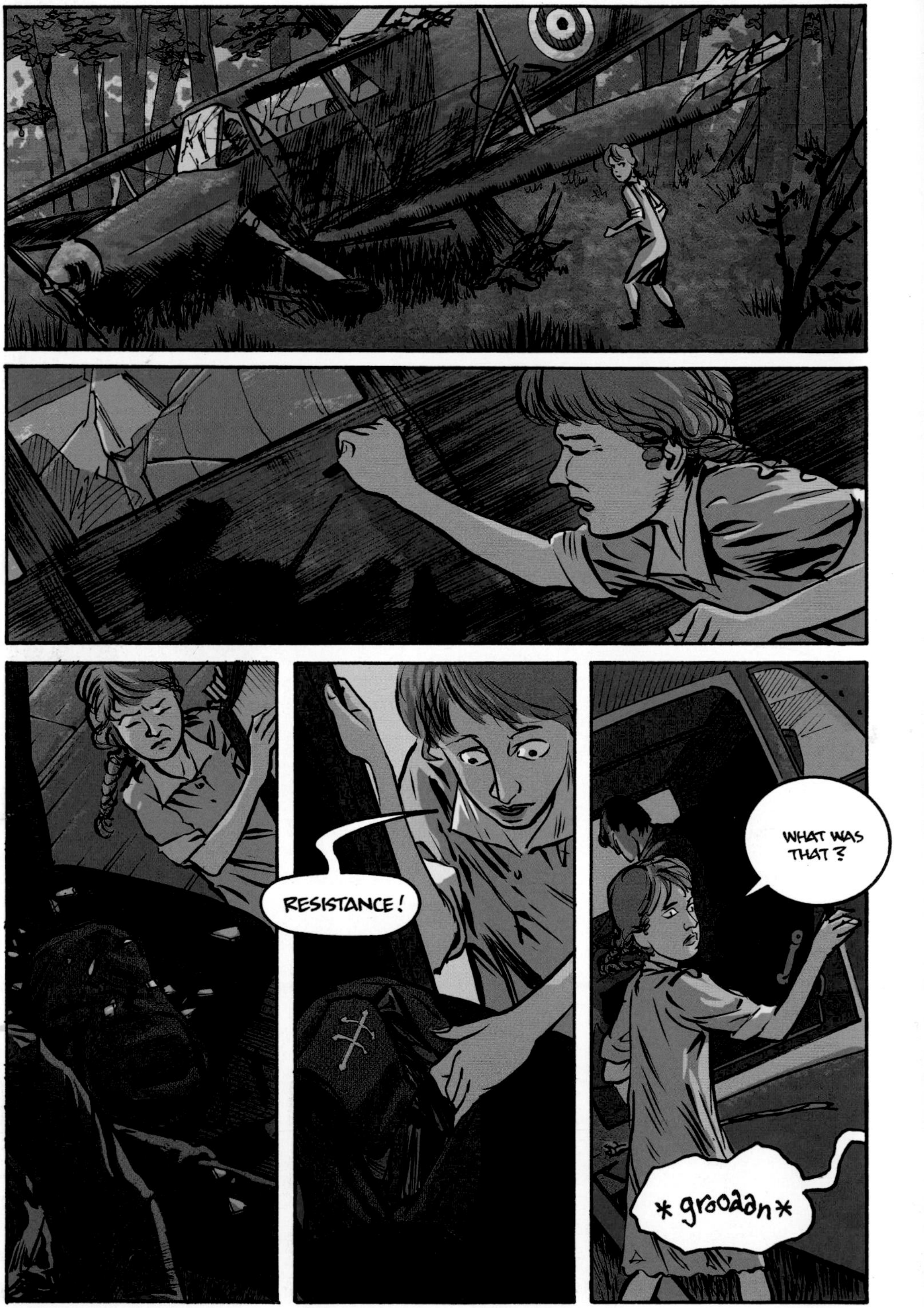
RESISTANCE!
WHAT WAS THAT?
* groaan *

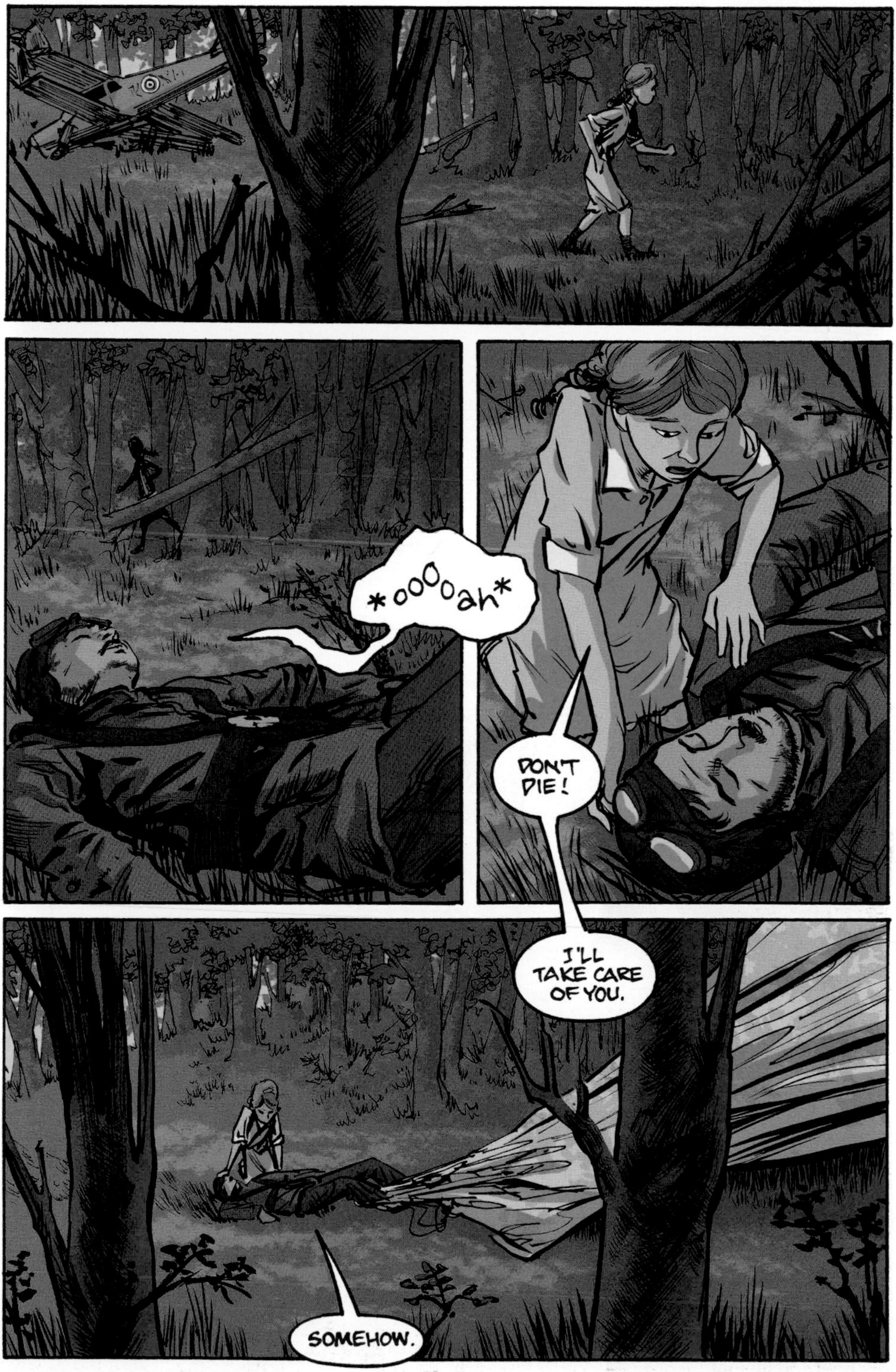
oooOah
DON'T DIE!
I'LL TAKE CARE OF YOU.
SOMEHOW.

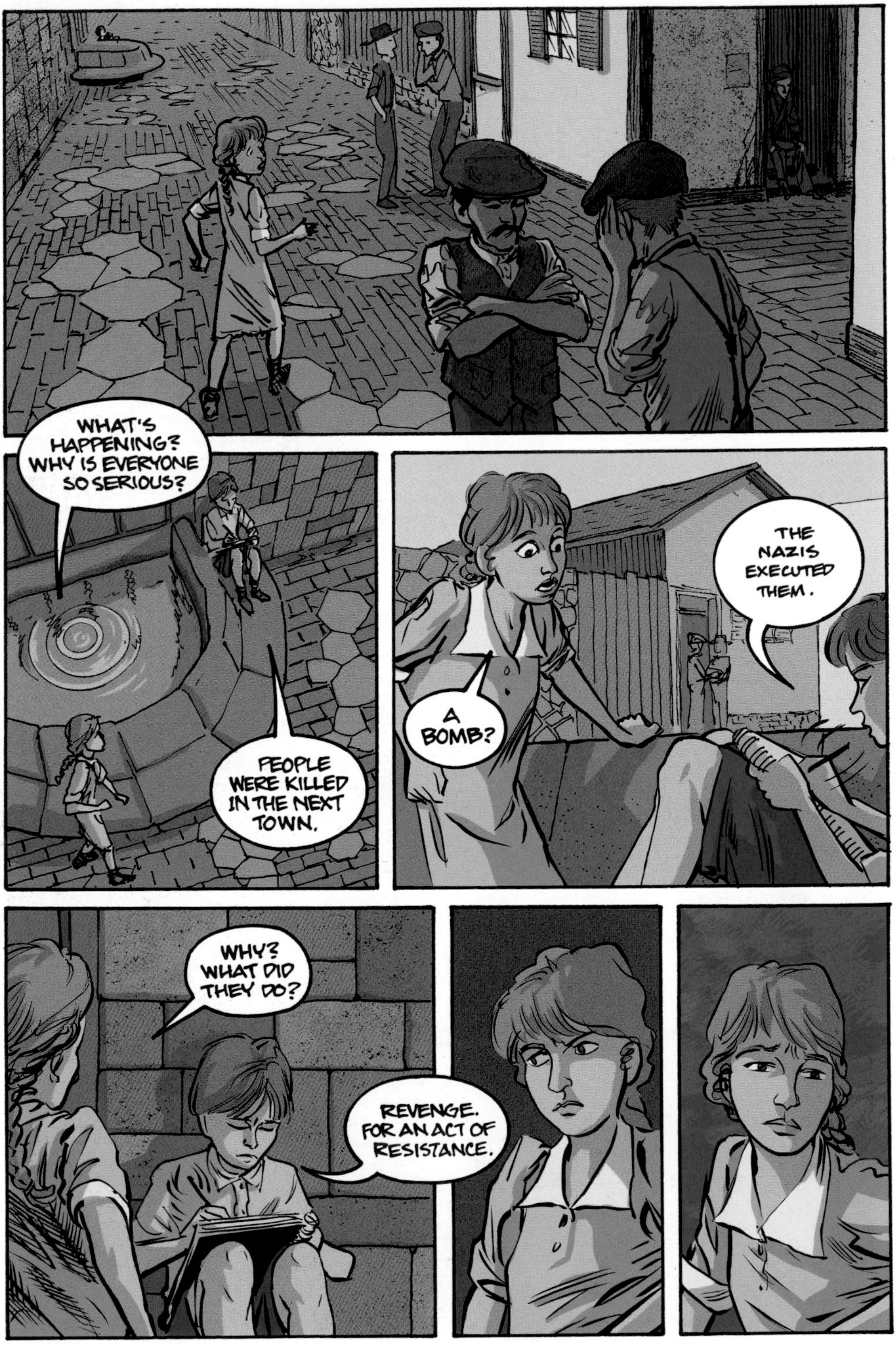
WHAT'S HAPPENING? WHY IS EVERYONE SO SERIOUS?
PEOPLE WERE KILLED IN THE NEXT TOWN.
A BOMB?
THE NAZIS EXECUTED THEM.
WHY? WHAT DID THEY DO?
REVENGE. FOR AN ACT OF RESISTANCE.

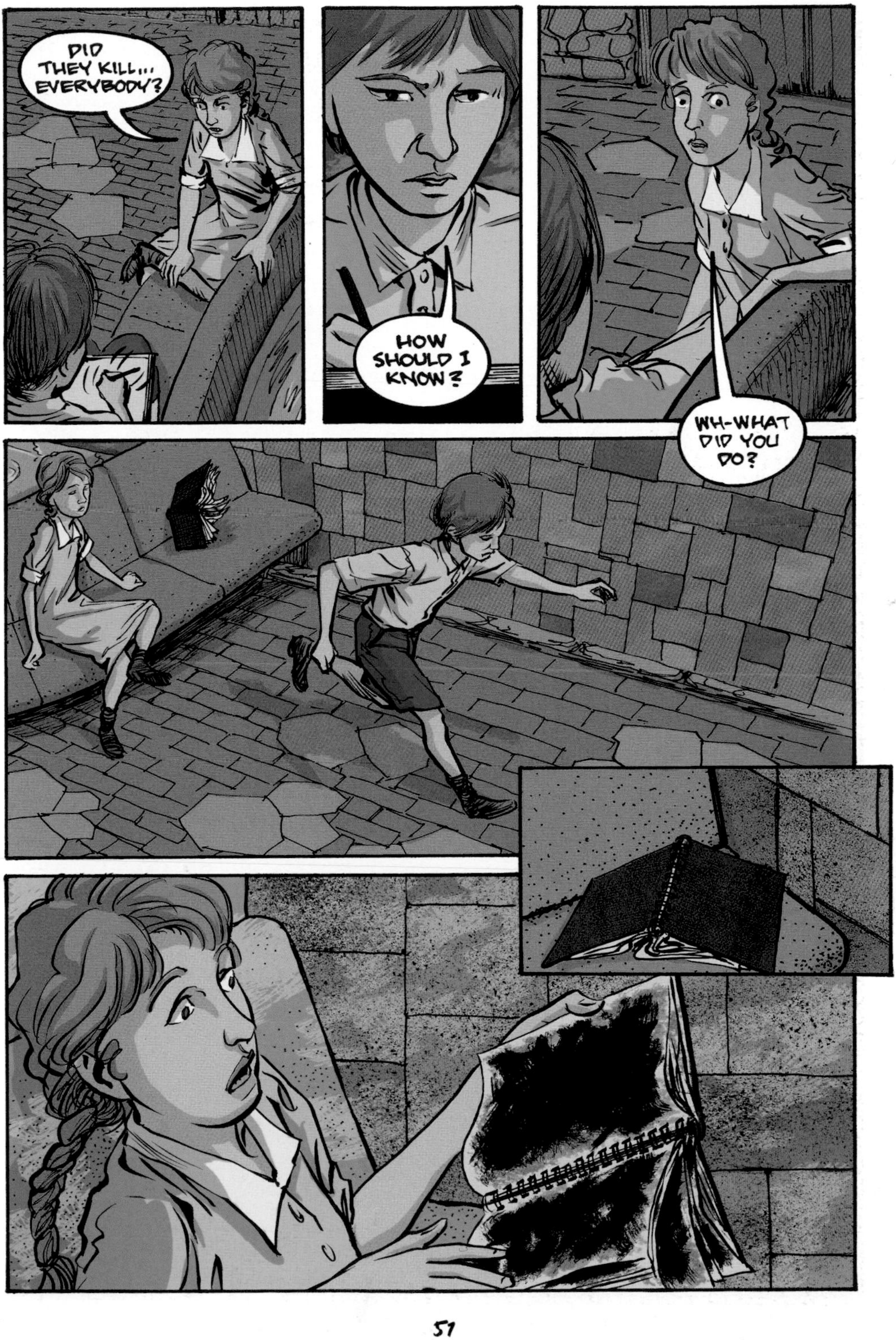
DID THEY KILL... EVERYBODY?
HOW SHOULD I KNOW?
WH-WHAT DID YOU DO?

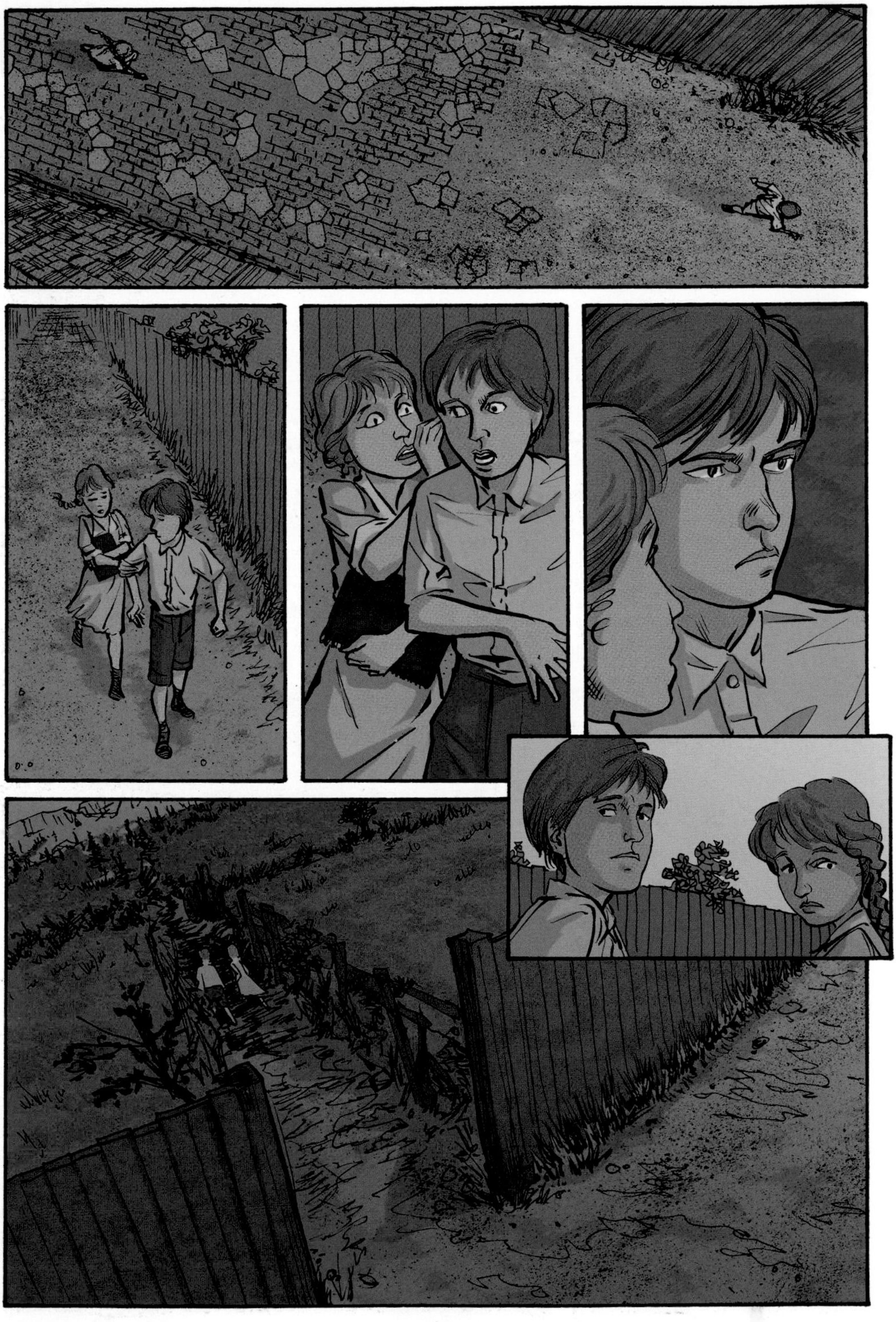

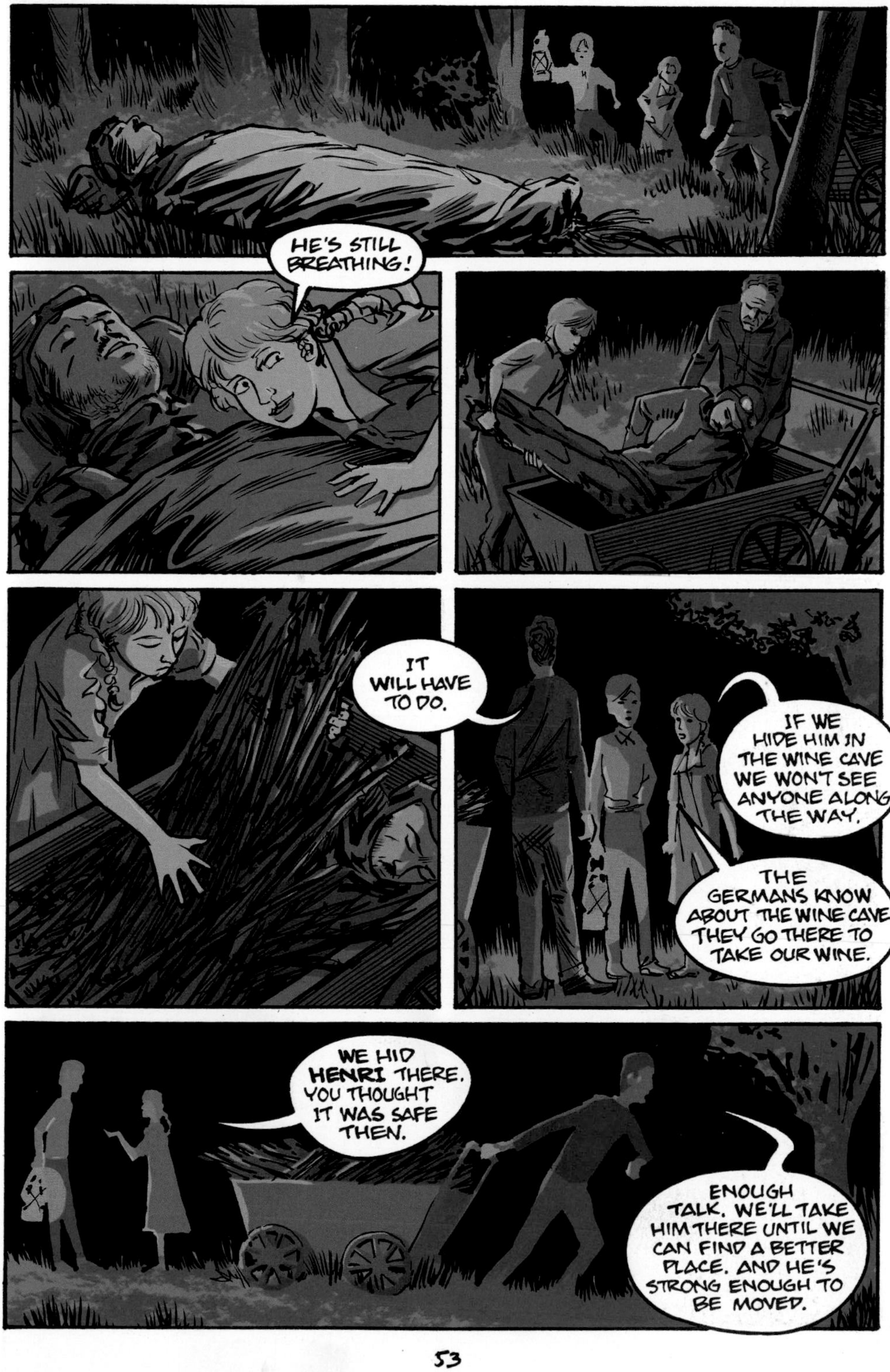
HE'S STILL BREATHING!
IT WILL HAVE TO DO.
IF WE HIDE HIM IN THE WINE CAVE WE WON'T SEE ANYONE ALONG THE WAY.
THE GERMANS KNOW ABOUT THE WINE CAVE. THEY GO THERE TO TAKE OUR WINE.
WE HID **HENRI** THERE. YOU THOUGHT IT WAS SAFE THEN.
ENOUGH TALK. WE'LL TAKE HIM THERE UNTIL WE CAN FIND A BETTER PLACE. AND HE'S STRONG ENOUGH TO BE MOVED.

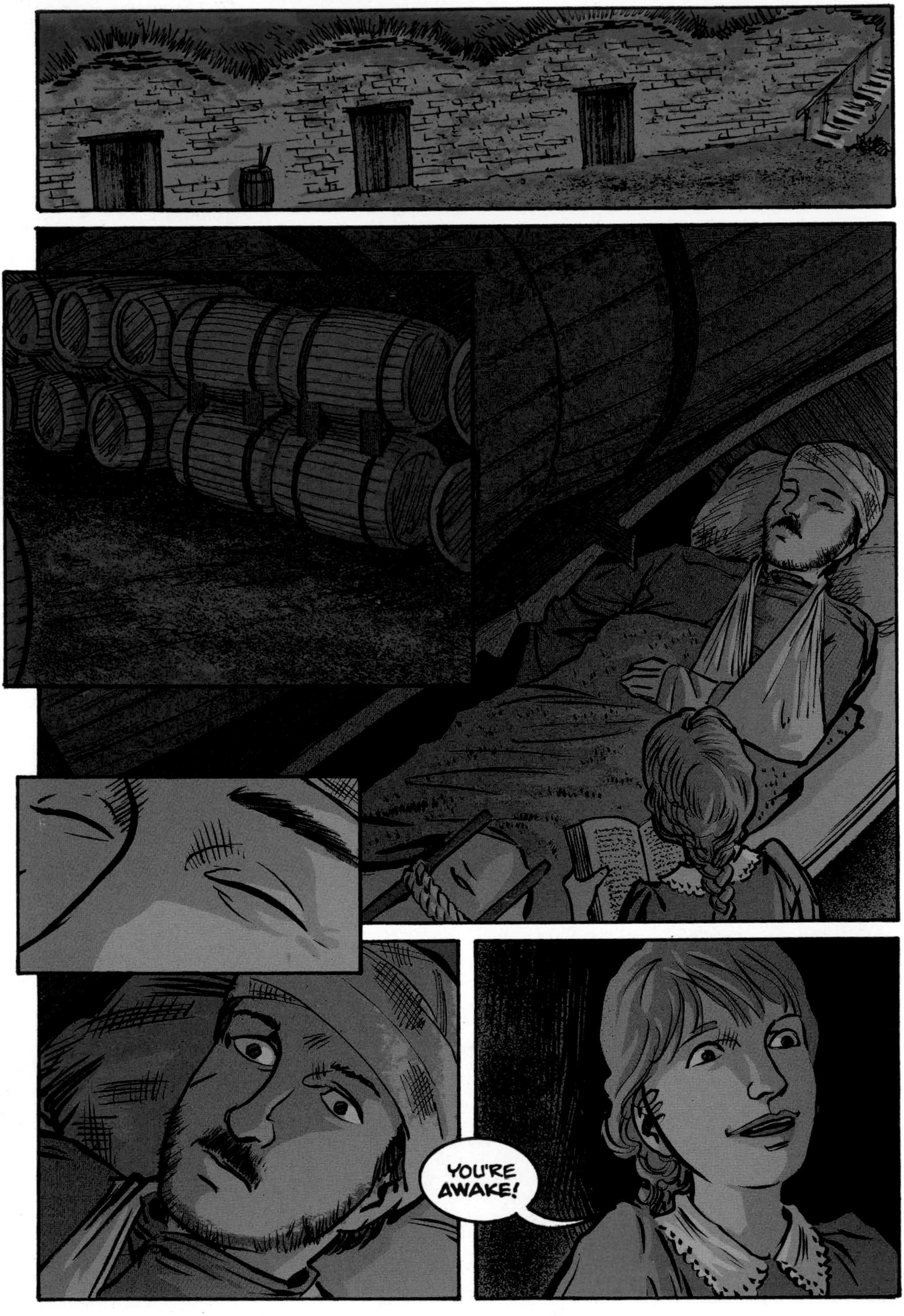
YOU'RE AWAKE!

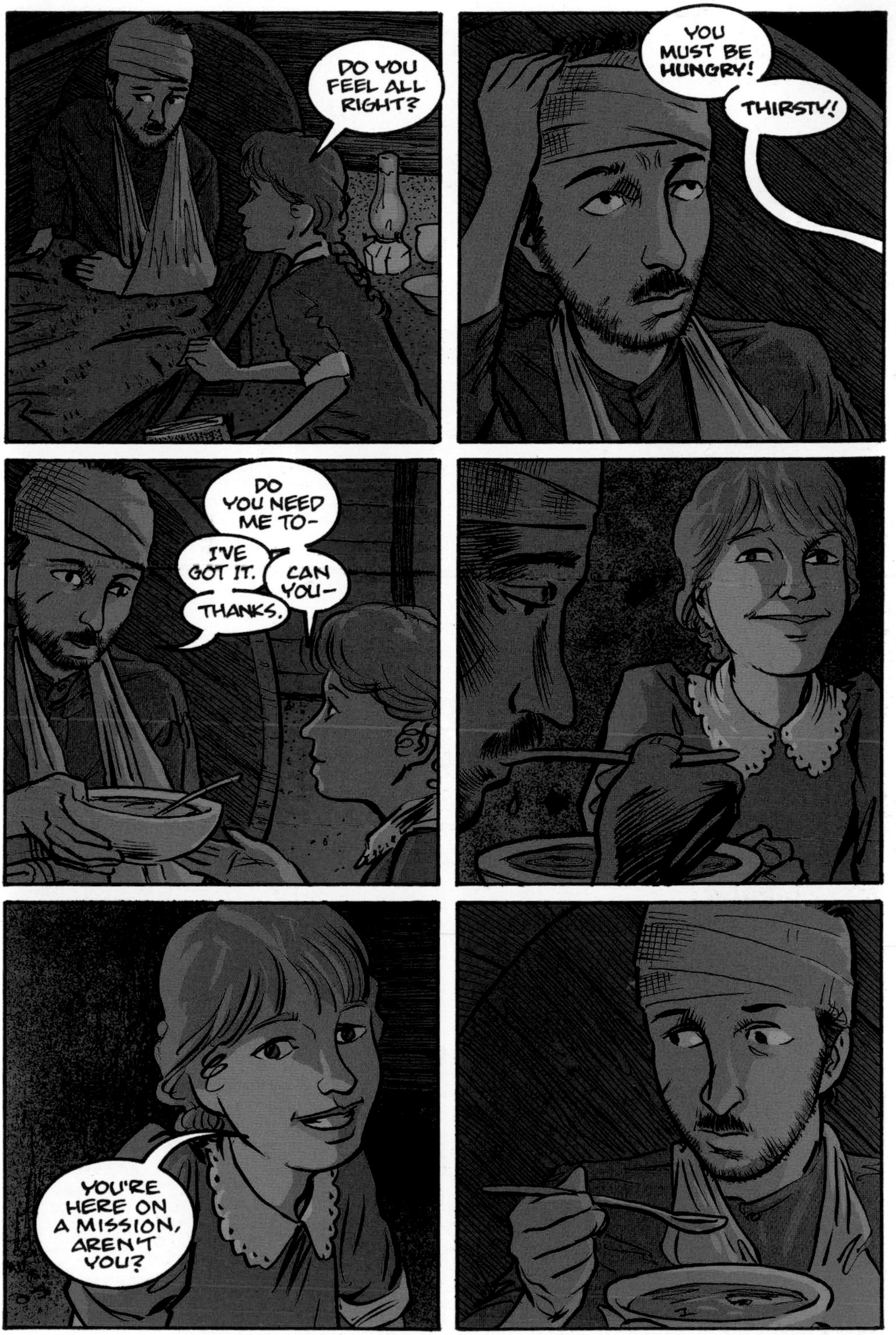
DO YOU FEEL ALL RIGHT?
YOU MUST BE HUNGRY!
THIRSTY!
DO YOU NEED ME TO-
I'VE GOT IT.
CAN YOU-
THANKS.
YOU'RE HERE ON A MISSION, AREN'T YOU?

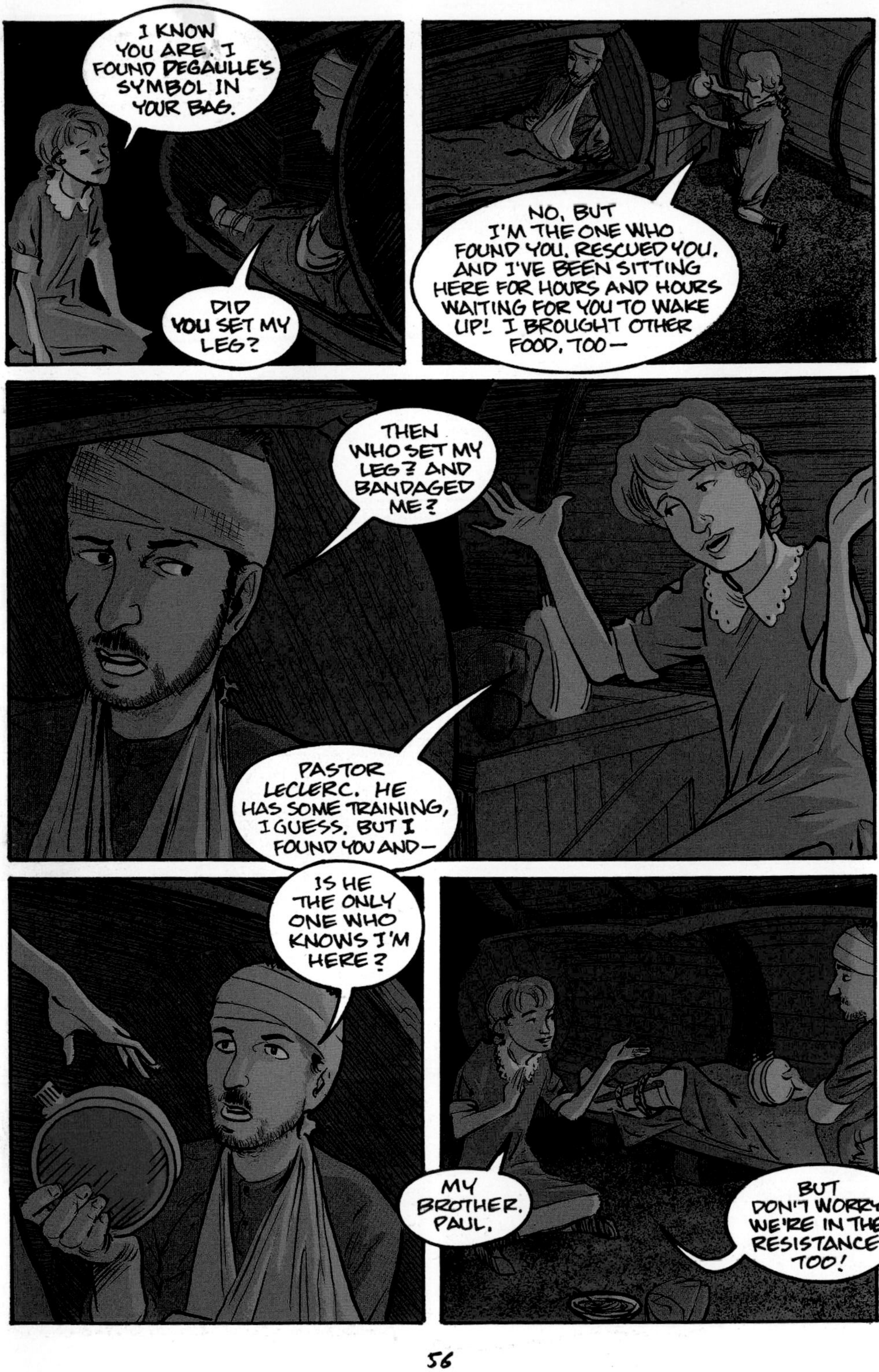
I KNOW YOU ARE. I FOUND DEGAULLE'S SYMBOL IN YOUR BAG.
DID YOU SET MY LEG?
NO, BUT I'M THE ONE WHO FOUND YOU, RESCUED YOU, AND I'VE BEEN SITTING HERE FOR HOURS AND HOURS WAITING FOR YOU TO WAKE UP! I BROUGHT OTHER FOOD, TOO—
THEN WHO SET MY LEG? AND BANDAGED ME?
PASTOR LECLERC. HE HAS SOME TRAINING, I GUESS. BUT I FOUND YOU AND—
IS HE THE ONLY ONE WHO KNOWS I'M HERE?
MY BROTHER. PAUL.
BUT DON'T WORRY! WE'RE IN THE RESISTANCE TOO!

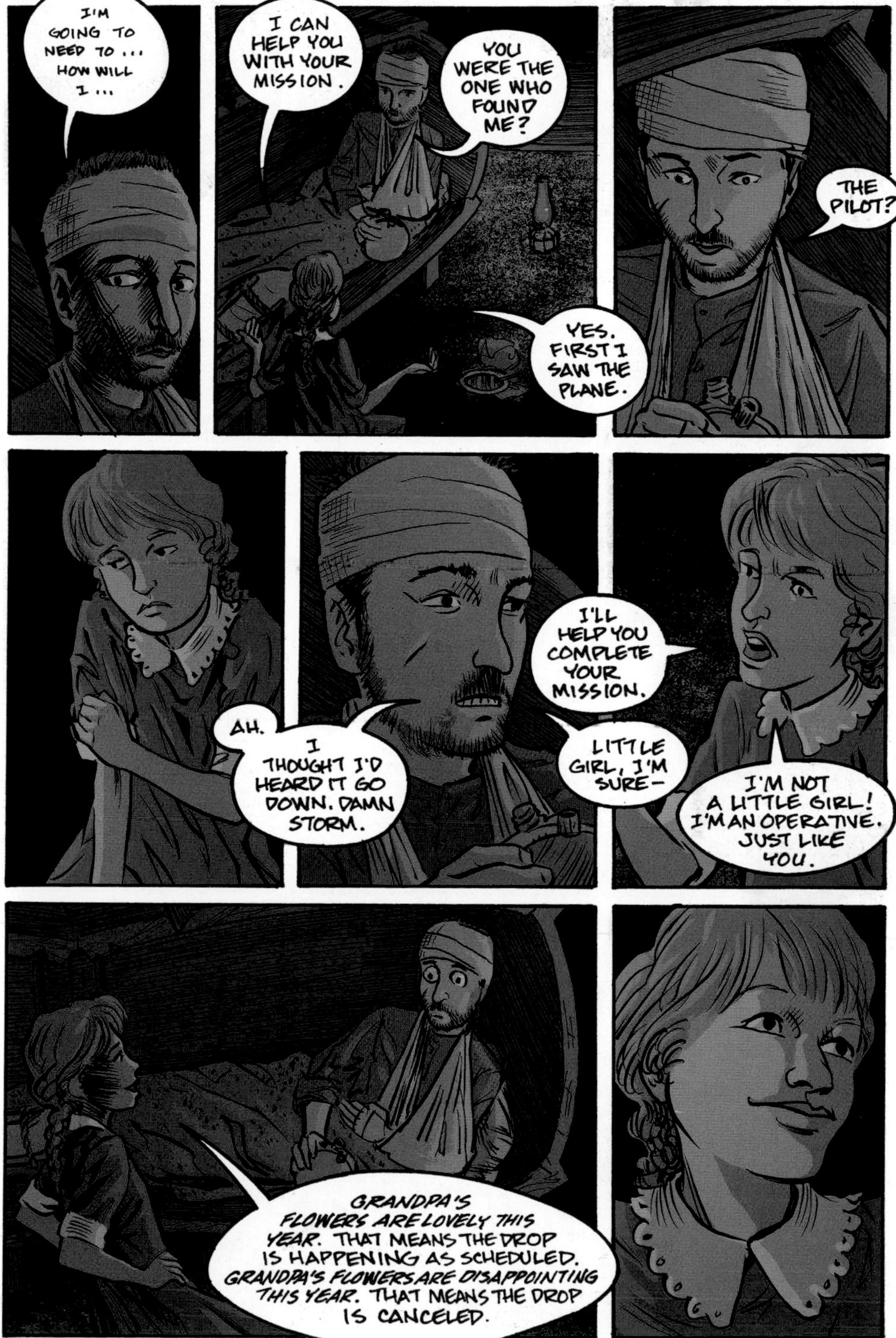
I'M GOING TO NEED TO ... HOW WILL I ...
I CAN HELP YOU WITH YOUR MISSION.
YOU WERE THE ONE WHO FOUND ME?
YES. FIRST I SAW THE PLANE.
THE PILOT?
AH.
I THOUGHT I'D HEARD IT GO DOWN. DAMN STORM.
I'LL HELP YOU COMPLETE YOUR MISSION.
LITTLE GIRL, I'M SURE–
I'M NOT A LITTLE GIRL! I'M AN OPERATIVE. JUST LIKE YOU.
GRANDPA'S FLOWERS ARE LOVELY THIS YEAR. THAT MEANS THE DROP IS HAPPENING AS SCHEDULED. GRANDPA'S FLOWERS ARE DISAPPOINTING THIS YEAR. THAT MEANS THE DROP IS CANCELED.

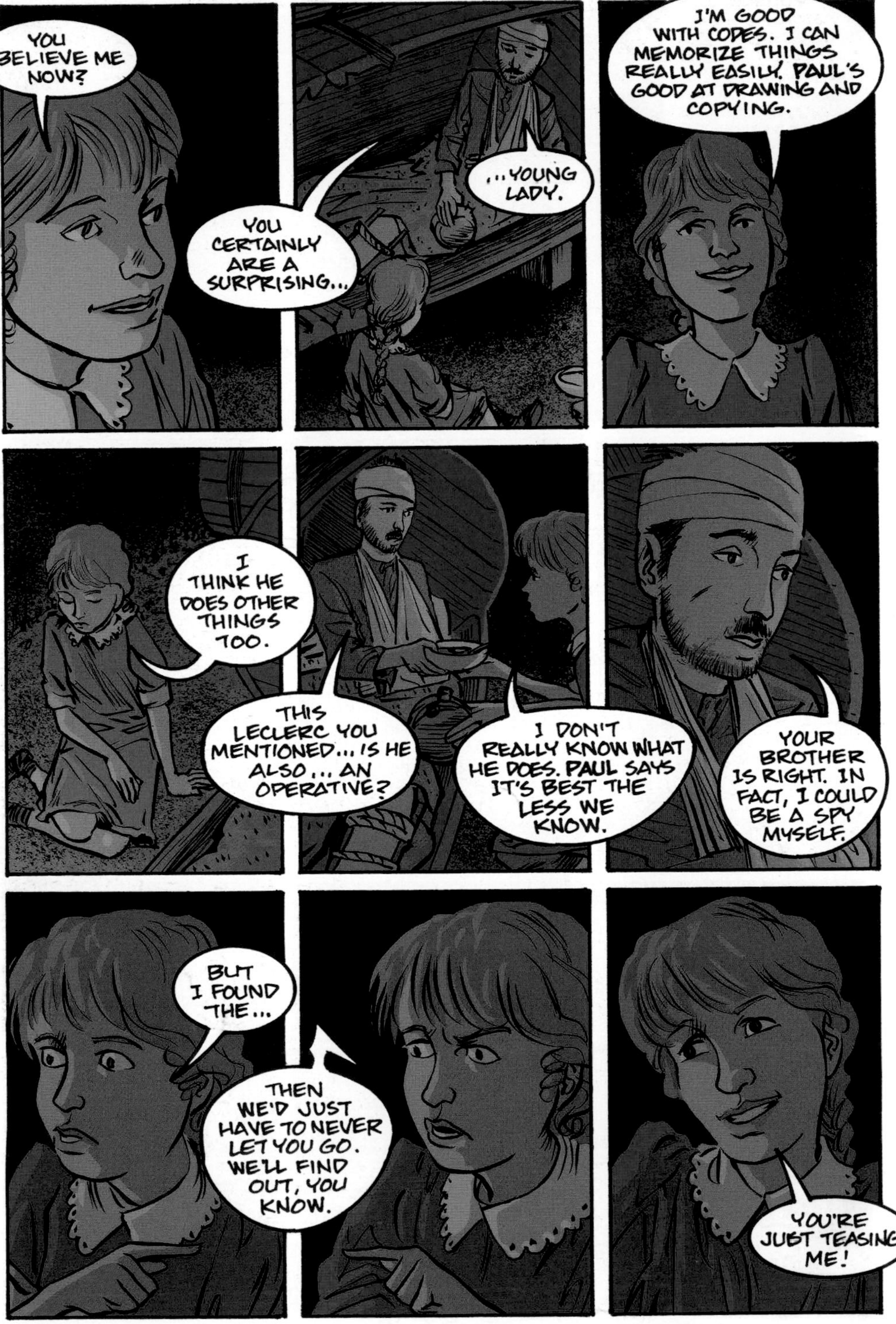
YOU BELIEVE ME NOW?
YOU CERTAINLY ARE A SURPRISING...
...YOUNG LADY.
I'M GOOD WITH CODES. I CAN MEMORIZE THINGS REALLY EASILY. PAUL'S GOOD AT DRAWING AND COPYING.
I THINK HE DOES OTHER THINGS TOO.
THIS LECLERC YOU MENTIONED... IS HE ALSO... AN OPERATIVE?
I DON'T REALLY KNOW WHAT HE DOES. PAUL SAYS IT'S BEST THE LESS WE KNOW.
YOUR BROTHER IS RIGHT. IN FACT, I COULD BE A SPY MYSELF.
BUT I FOUND THE...
THEN WE'D JUST HAVE TO NEVER LET YOU GO. WE'LL FIND OUT, YOU KNOW.
YOU'RE JUST TEASING ME!

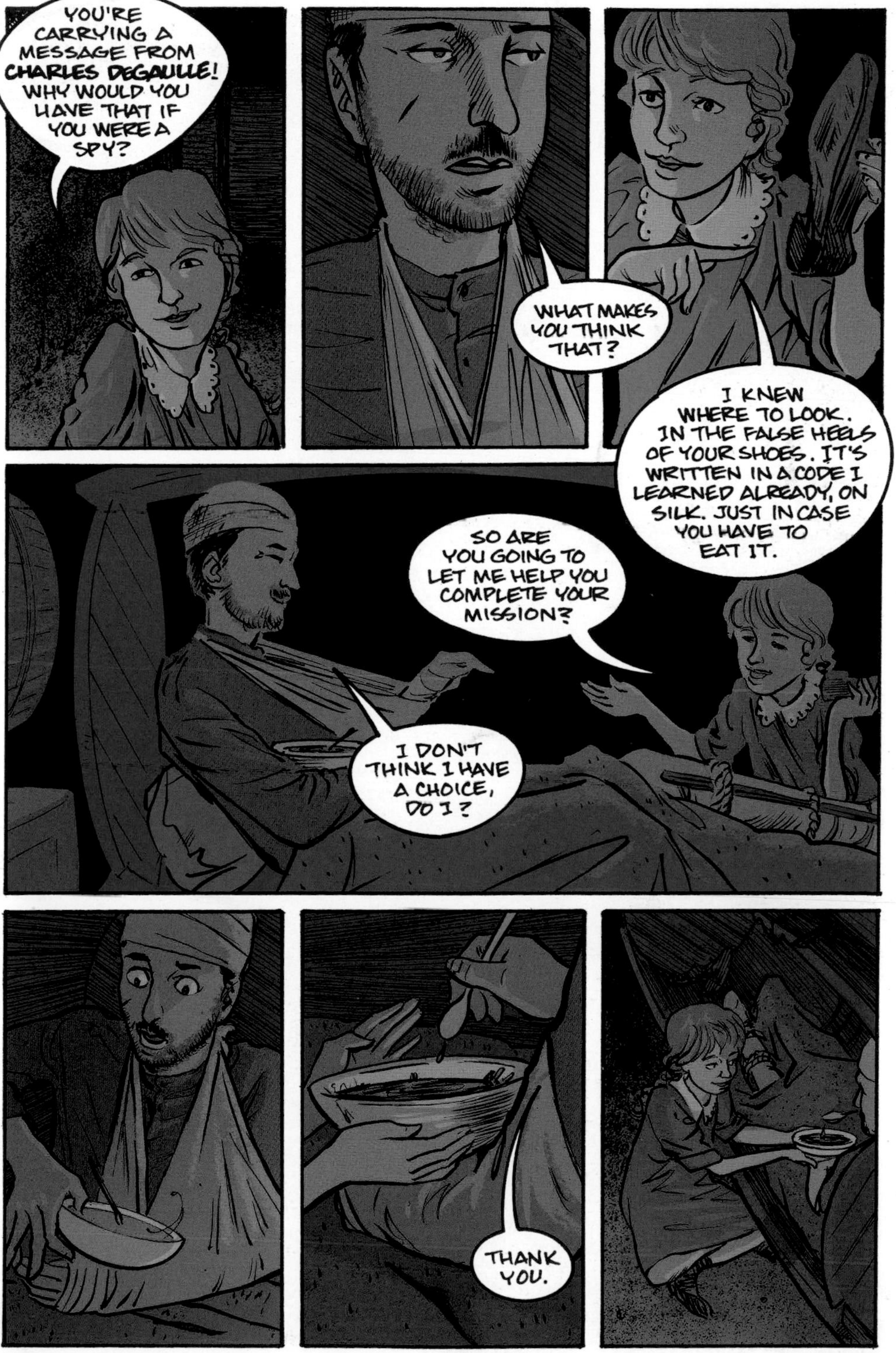
YOU'RE CARRYING A MESSAGE FROM CHARLES DEGAULLE! WHY WOULD YOU HAVE THAT IF YOU WERE A SPY?
WHAT MAKES YOU THINK THAT?
I KNEW WHERE TO LOOK. IN THE FALSE HEELS OF YOUR SHOES. IT'S WRITTEN IN A CODE I LEARNED ALREADY, ON SILK. JUST IN CASE YOU HAVE TO EAT IT.
SO ARE YOU GOING TO LET ME HELP YOU COMPLETE YOUR MISSION?
I DON'T THINK I HAVE A CHOICE, DO I?
THANK YOU.

YOU DID WHAT YOU HAD TO DO.

BUT ALL THOSE PEOPLE!

THE MISSION WAS A SUCCESS.

AT WHAT COST?

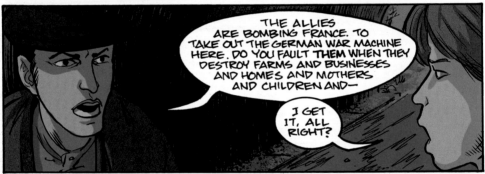

THE ALLIES ARE BOMBING FRANCE. TO TAKE OUT THE GERMAN WAR MACHINE HERE. DO YOU FAULT **THEM** WHEN THEY DESTROY FARMS AND BUSINESSES AND HOMES AND MOTHERS AND CHILDREN AND—

I GET IT, ALL RIGHT?

DO YOU KNOW WHERE THAT TRAIN WAS HEADED? THE P.O.W. CAMPS. TO SLAUGHTER THE PRISONERS. YOU MAY HAVE SAVED YOUR OWN FATHER'S LIFE!

WE'RE IN A WAR, PAUL. THERE ARE CASUALTIES. CIVILIAN AND MILITARY.

AND EVERYONE IN BETWEEN. LIKE US.

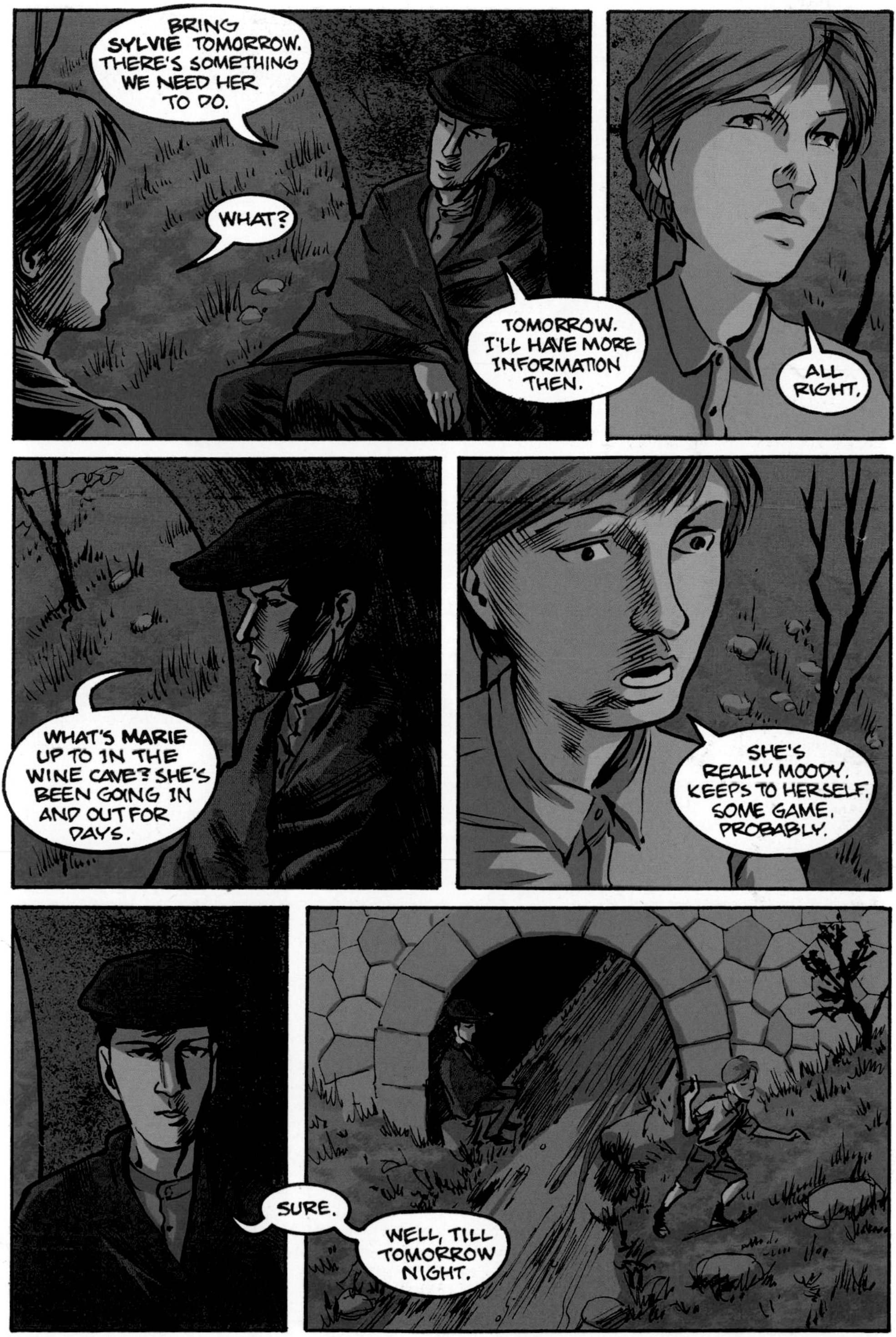
BRING SYLVIE TOMORROW. THERE'S SOMETHING WE NEED HER TO DO.
WHAT?
TOMORROW. I'LL HAVE MORE INFORMATION THEN.
ALL RIGHT.
WHAT'S MARIE UP TO IN THE WINE CAVE? SHE'S BEEN GOING IN AND OUT FOR DAYS.
SHE'S REALLY MOODY. KEEPS TO HERSELF. SOME GAME, PROBABLY.
SURE.
WELL, TILL TOMORROW NIGHT.

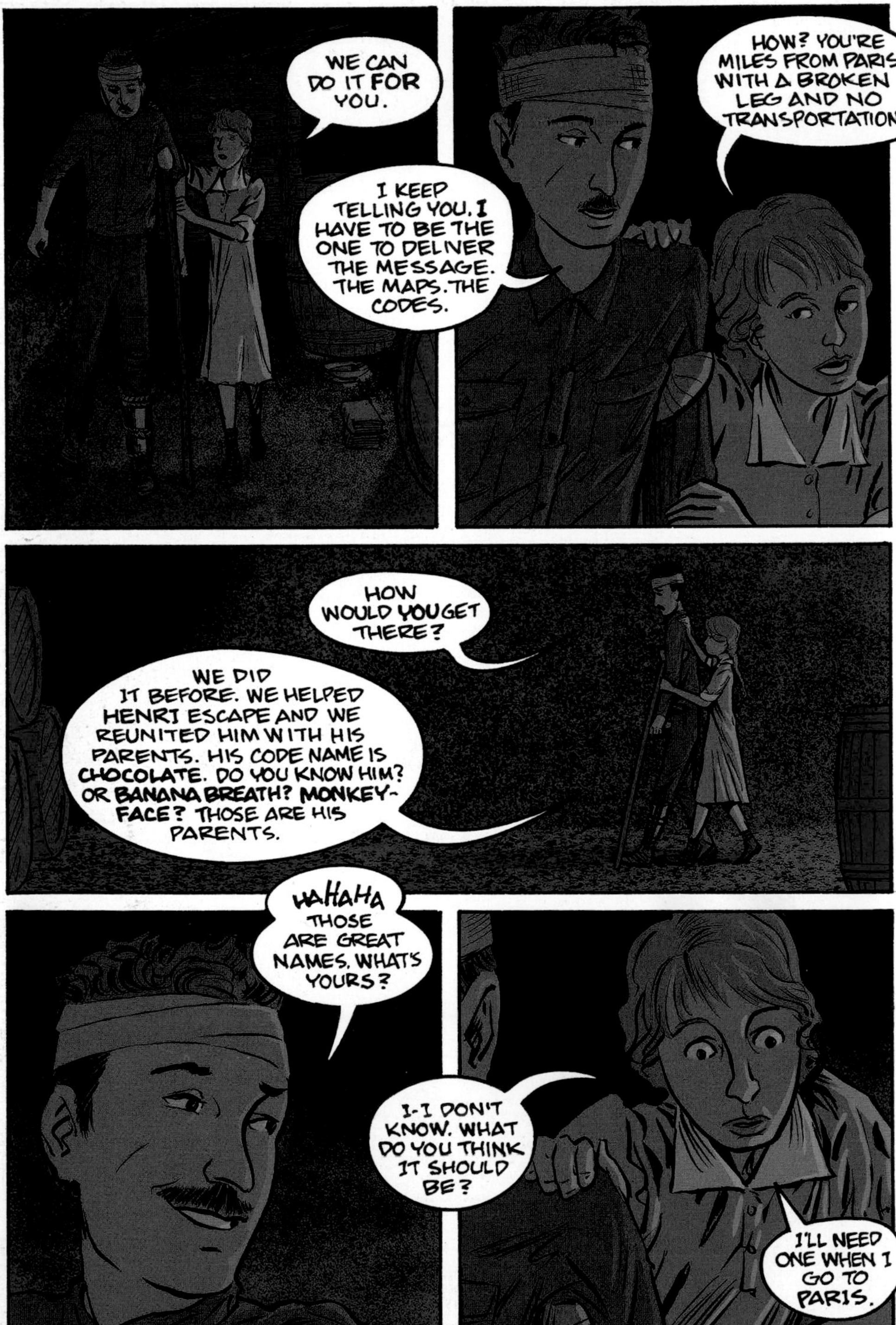
WE CAN DO IT FOR YOU.
HOW? YOU'RE MILES FROM PARIS WITH A BROKEN LEG AND NO TRANSPORTATION.
I KEEP TELLING YOU. I HAVE TO BE THE ONE TO DELIVER THE MESSAGE. THE MAPS. THE CODES.
HOW WOULD YOU GET THERE?
WE DID IT BEFORE. WE HELPED HENRI ESCAPE AND WE REUNITED HIM WITH HIS PARENTS. HIS CODE NAME IS CHOCOLATE. DO YOU KNOW HIM? OR BANANA BREATH? MONKEY-FACE? THOSE ARE HIS PARENTS.
HAHAHA THOSE ARE GREAT NAMES. WHAT'S YOURS?
I-I DON'T KNOW. WHAT DO YOU THINK IT SHOULD BE?
I'LL NEED ONE WHEN I GO TO PARIS.

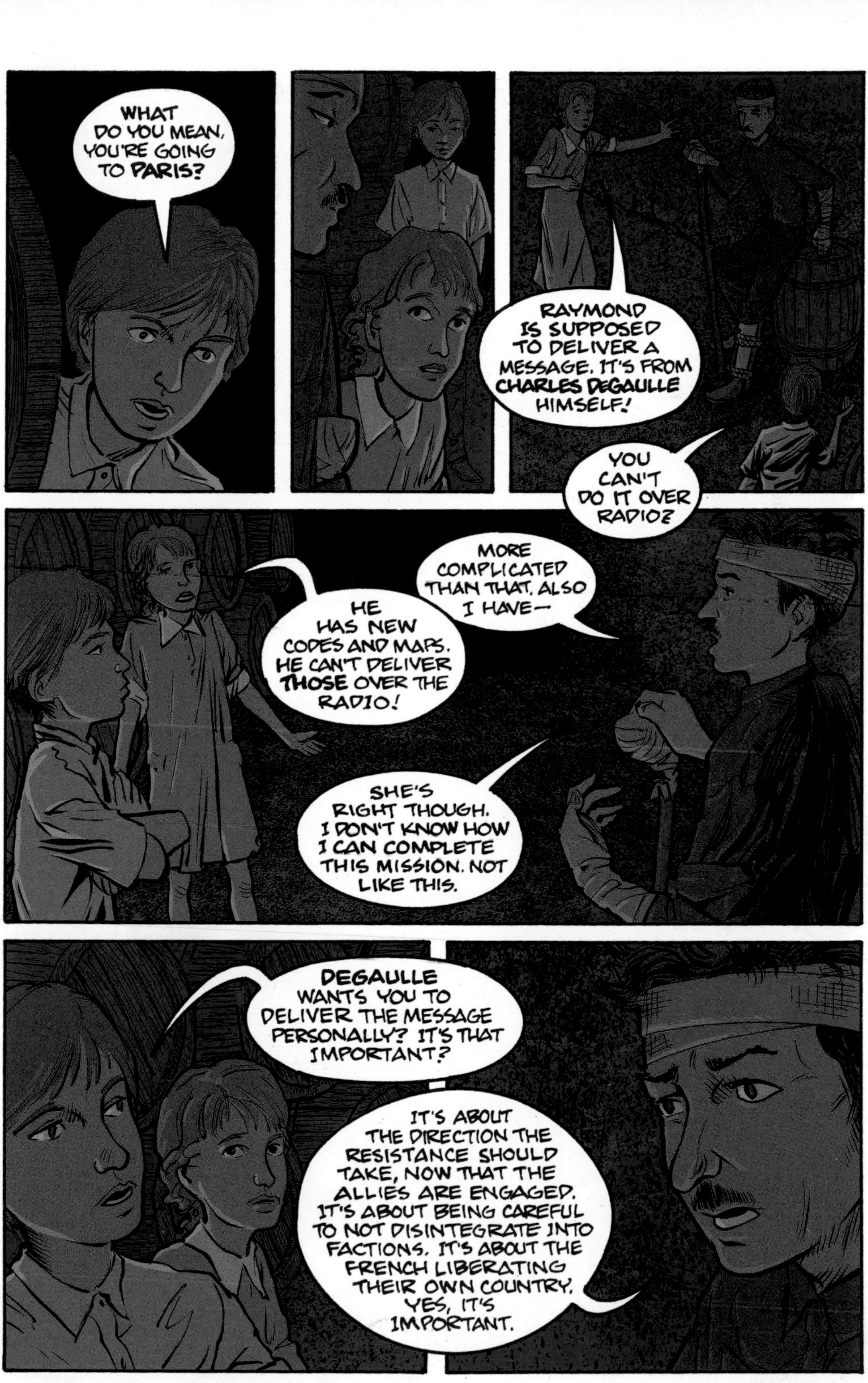
WHAT DO YOU MEAN, YOU'RE GOING TO PARIS?
RAYMOND IS SUPPOSED TO DELIVER A MESSAGE. IT'S FROM CHARLES DEGAULLE HIMSELF!
YOU CAN'T DO IT OVER RADIO?
MORE COMPLICATED THAN THAT. ALSO I HAVE—
HE HAS NEW CODES AND MAPS. HE CAN'T DELIVER THOSE OVER THE RADIO!
SHE'S RIGHT THOUGH. I DON'T KNOW HOW I CAN COMPLETE THIS MISSION. NOT LIKE THIS.
DEGAULLE WANTS YOU TO DELIVER THE MESSAGE PERSONALLY? IT'S THAT IMPORTANT?
IT'S ABOUT THE DIRECTION THE RESISTANCE SHOULD TAKE, NOW THAT THE ALLIES ARE ENGAGED. IT'S ABOUT BEING CAREFUL TO NOT DISINTEGRATE INTO FACTIONS. IT'S ABOUT THE FRENCH LIBERATING THEIR OWN COUNTRY. YES, IT'S IMPORTANT.

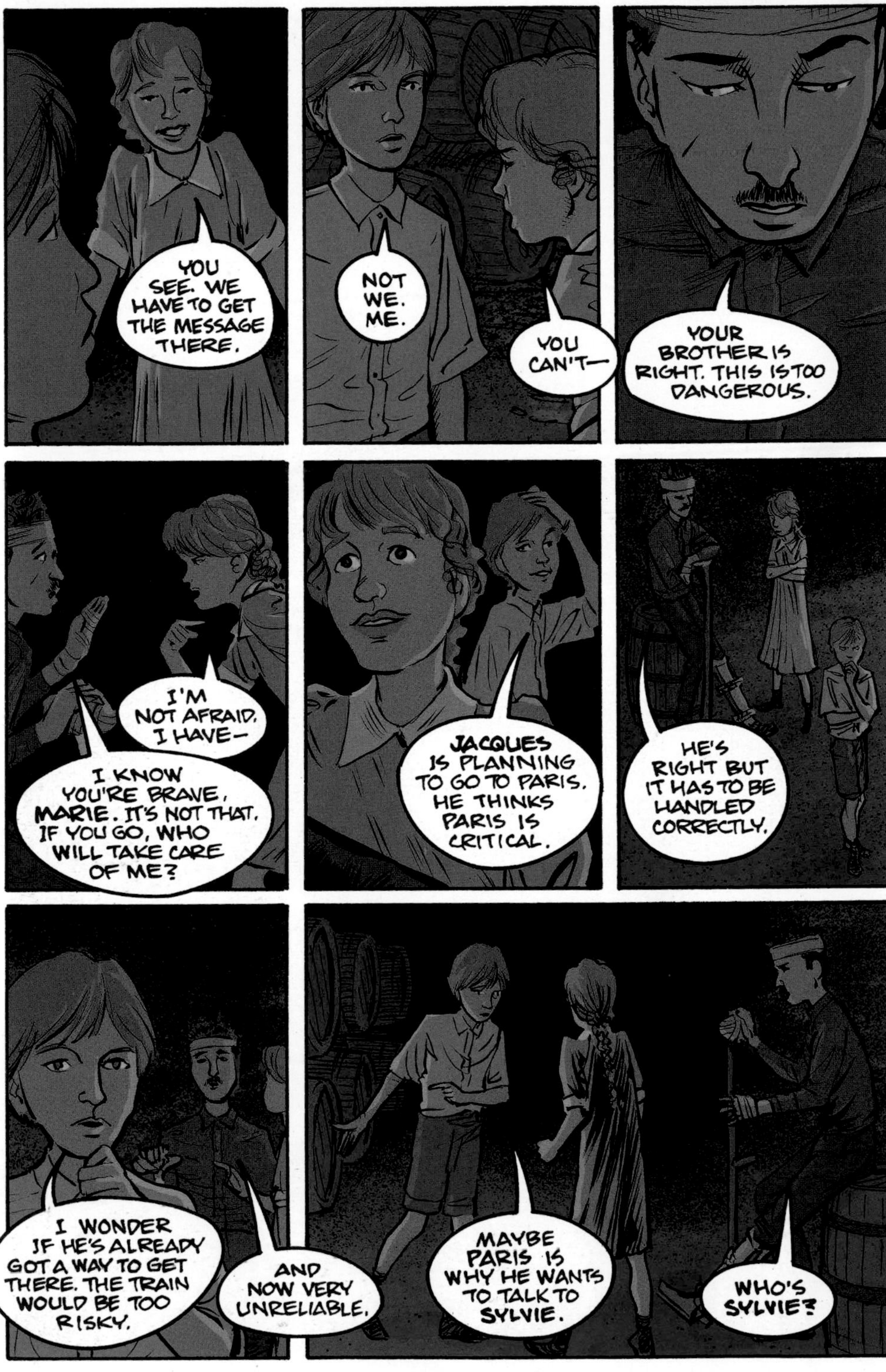
YOU SEE. WE HAVE TO GET THE MESSAGE THERE.
NOT WE. ME.
YOU CAN'T—
YOUR BROTHER IS RIGHT. THIS IS TOO DANGEROUS.
I'M NOT AFRAID. I HAVE—
I KNOW YOU'RE BRAVE, MARIE. IT'S NOT THAT. IF YOU GO, WHO WILL TAKE CARE OF ME?
JACQUES IS PLANNING TO GO TO PARIS. HE THINKS PARIS IS CRITICAL.
HE'S RIGHT BUT IT HAS TO BE HANDLED CORRECTLY.
I WONDER IF HE'S ALREADY GOT A WAY TO GET THERE. THE TRAIN WOULD BE TOO RISKY.
AND NOW VERY UNRELIABLE.
MAYBE PARIS IS WHY HE WANTS TO TALK TO SYLVIE.
WHO'S SYLVIE?

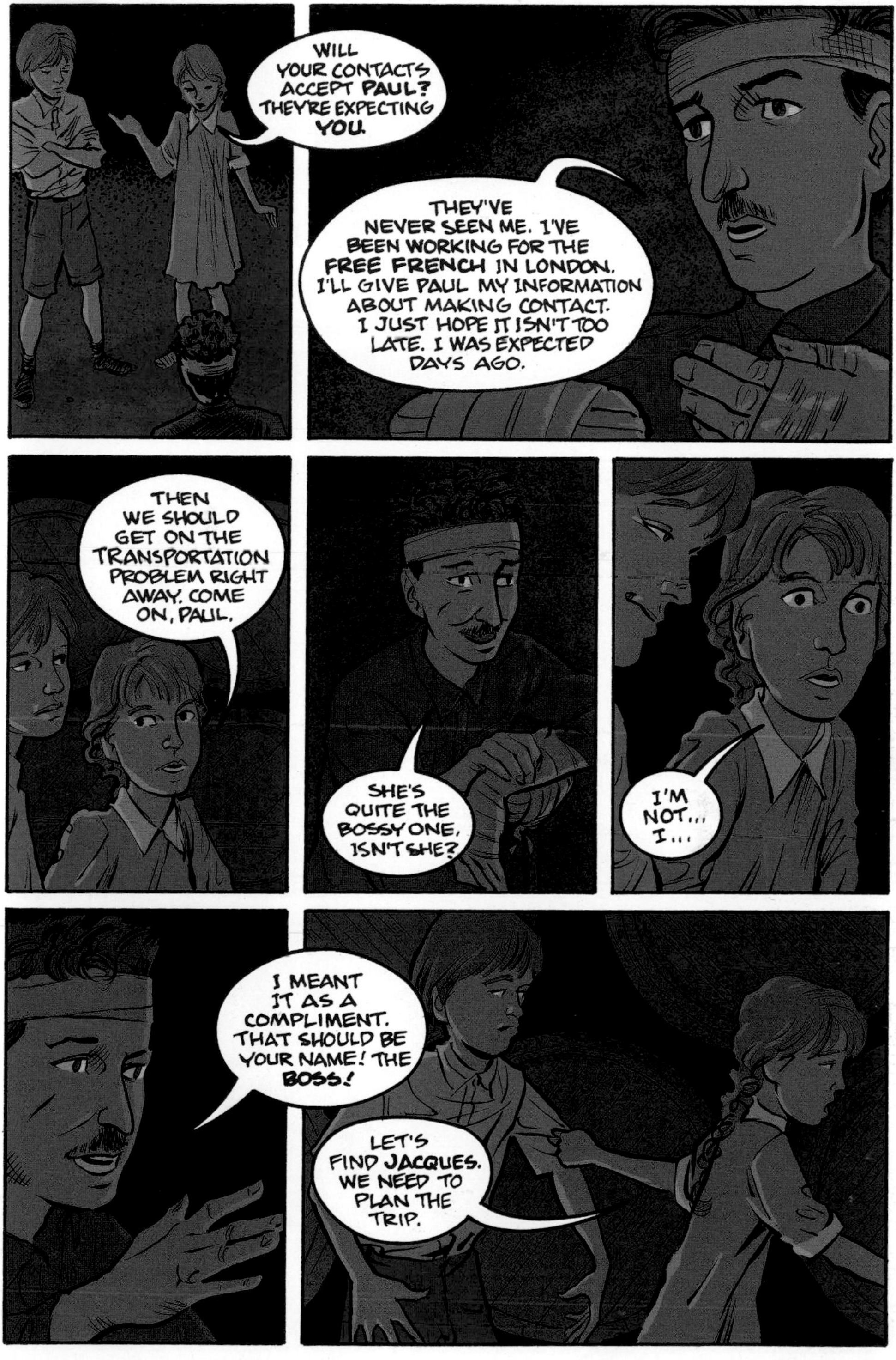
WILL YOUR CONTACTS ACCEPT PAUL? THEY'RE EXPECTING YOU.
THEY'VE NEVER SEEN ME. I'VE BEEN WORKING FOR THE FREE FRENCH IN LONDON. I'LL GIVE PAUL MY INFORMATION ABOUT MAKING CONTACT. I JUST HOPE IT ISN'T TOO LATE. I WAS EXPECTED DAYS AGO.
THEN WE SHOULD GET ON THE TRANSPORTATION PROBLEM RIGHT AWAY. COME ON, PAUL.
SHE'S QUITE THE BOSSY ONE, ISN'T SHE?
I'M NOT... I...
I MEANT IT AS A COMPLIMENT. THAT SHOULD BE YOUR NAME! THE BOSS!
LET'S FIND JACQUES. WE NEED TO PLAN THE TRIP.

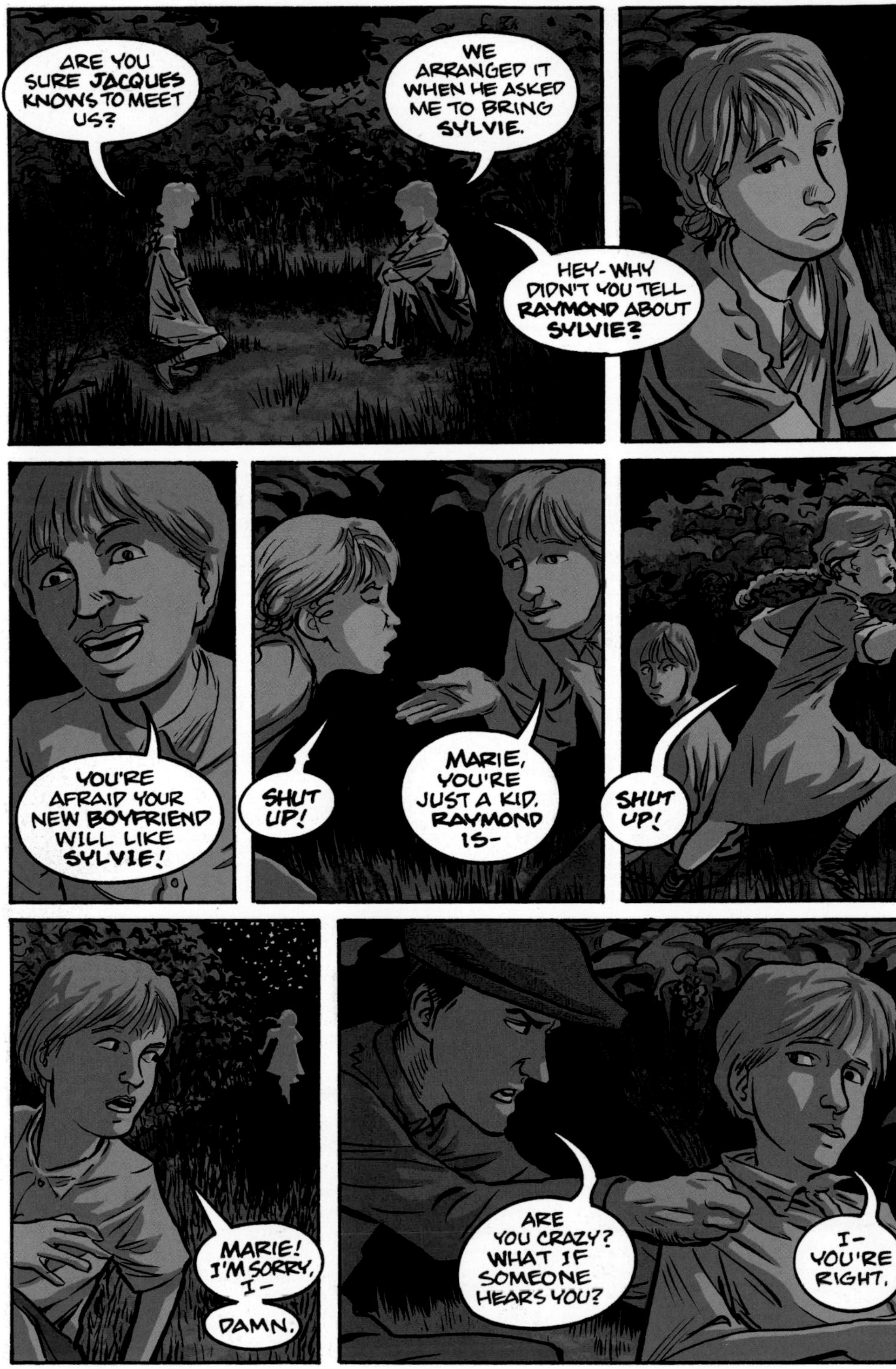
ARE YOU SURE JACQUES KNOWS TO MEET US?
WE ARRANGED IT WHEN HE ASKED ME TO BRING SYLVIE.
HEY- WHY DIDN'T YOU TELL RAYMOND ABOUT SYLVIE?
YOU'RE AFRAID YOUR NEW BOYFRIEND WILL LIKE SYLVIE!
SHUT UP!
MARIE, YOU'RE JUST A KID. RAYMOND IS-
SHUT UP!
MARIE! I'M SORRY, I-
DAMN.
ARE YOU CRAZY? WHAT IF SOMEONE HEARS YOU?
I- YOU'RE RIGHT.

WHERE'S SYLVIE?

SHE PROMISED TO BE HERE.

HOW WILL YOU GET TO PARIS?

STILL WORKING ON IT.

I NEED TO GO WITH YOU.

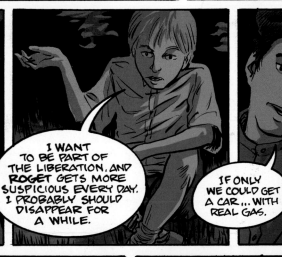

I WANT TO BE PART OF THE LIBERATION, AND ROGET GETS MORE SUSPICIOUS EVERY DAY. I PROBABLY SHOULD DISAPPEAR FOR A WHILE.

IF ONLY WE COULD GET A CAR... WITH REAL GAS.

WE'D HAVE TO BE GERMAN.

HM, YOUR FAMILY MIGHT BE ABLE TO HELP WITH THAT TOO.

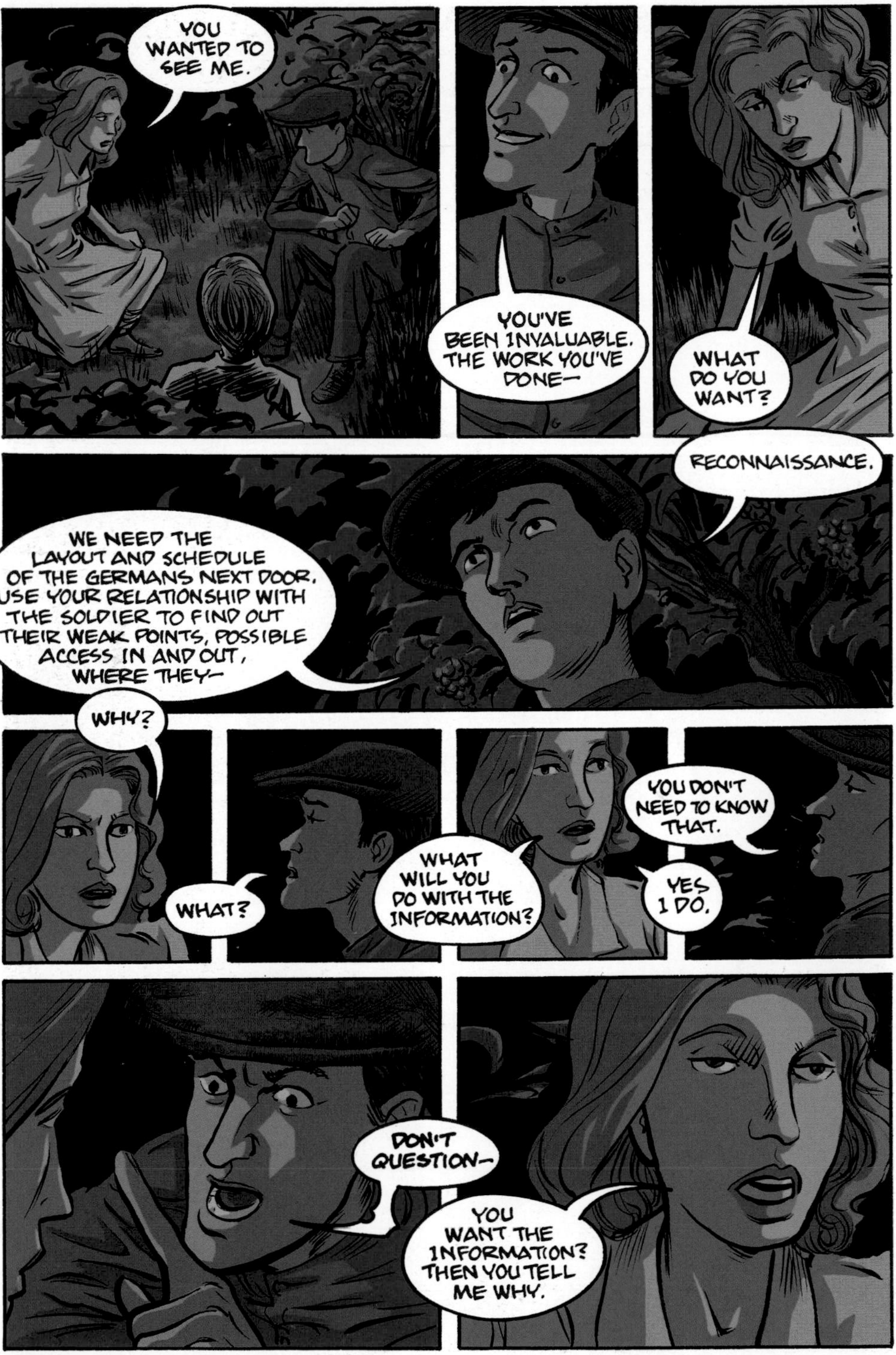
YOU WANTED TO SEE ME.
YOU'VE BEEN INVALUABLE. THE WORK YOU'VE DONE—
WHAT DO YOU WANT?
RECONNAISSANCE.
WE NEED THE LAYOUT AND SCHEDULE OF THE GERMANS NEXT DOOR. USE YOUR RELATIONSHIP WITH THE SOLDIER TO FIND OUT THEIR WEAK POINTS, POSSIBLE ACCESS IN AND OUT, WHERE THEY—
WHY?
WHAT?
WHAT WILL YOU DO WITH THE INFORMATION?
YOU DON'T NEED TO KNOW THAT.
YES I DO.
DON'T QUESTION—
YOU WANT THE INFORMATION? THEN YOU TELL ME WHY.

CAN'T HAVE THE GERMANS INTERFERING WITH THE LIBERATION. SO WE'RE GOING TO GET RID OF THEM, BEFORE THEY GET RID OF US.

WE NEED TO MOVE QUICKLY. WE'VE HEARD—

NO.

WHAT?

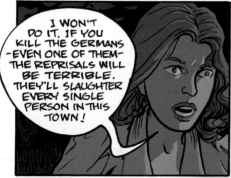

I WON'T DO IT. IF YOU KILL THE GERMANS —EVEN ONE OF THEM— THE REPRISALS WILL BE TERRIBLE. THEY'LL SLAUGHTER EVERY SINGLE PERSON IN THIS TOWN!

YOU KNOW WHAT HAPPENED AFTER THE TRAIN SABOTAGE! ALL THOSE DEAD—

IT IS NOT FOR YOU TO QUESTION!

I CAN'T HAVE IT ON MY CONSCIENCE.

THIS HAS NOTHING TO DO WITH YOUR CONSCIENCE. YOU HAVE FEELINGS FOR THAT GERMAN, YOUR COUNTRY'S ENEMY!

I WON'T HELP YOU.

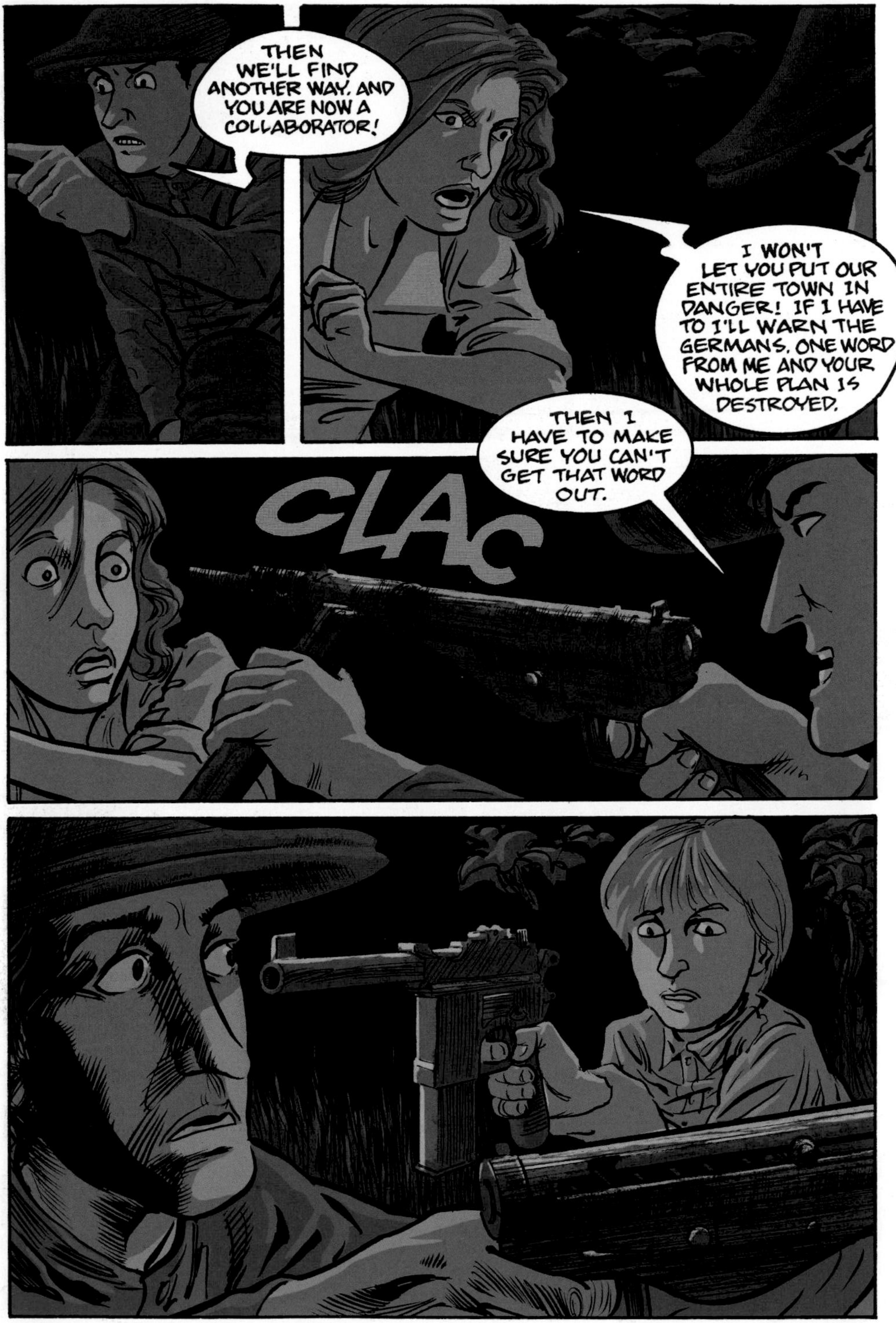
THEN WE'LL FIND ANOTHER WAY. AND YOU ARE NOW A COLLABORATOR!
I WON'T LET YOU PUT OUR ENTIRE TOWN IN DANGER! IF I HAVE TO I'LL WARN THE GERMANS. ONE WORD FROM ME AND YOUR WHOLE PLAN IS DESTROYED.
CLAC
THEN I HAVE TO MAKE SURE YOU CAN'T GET THAT WORD OUT.

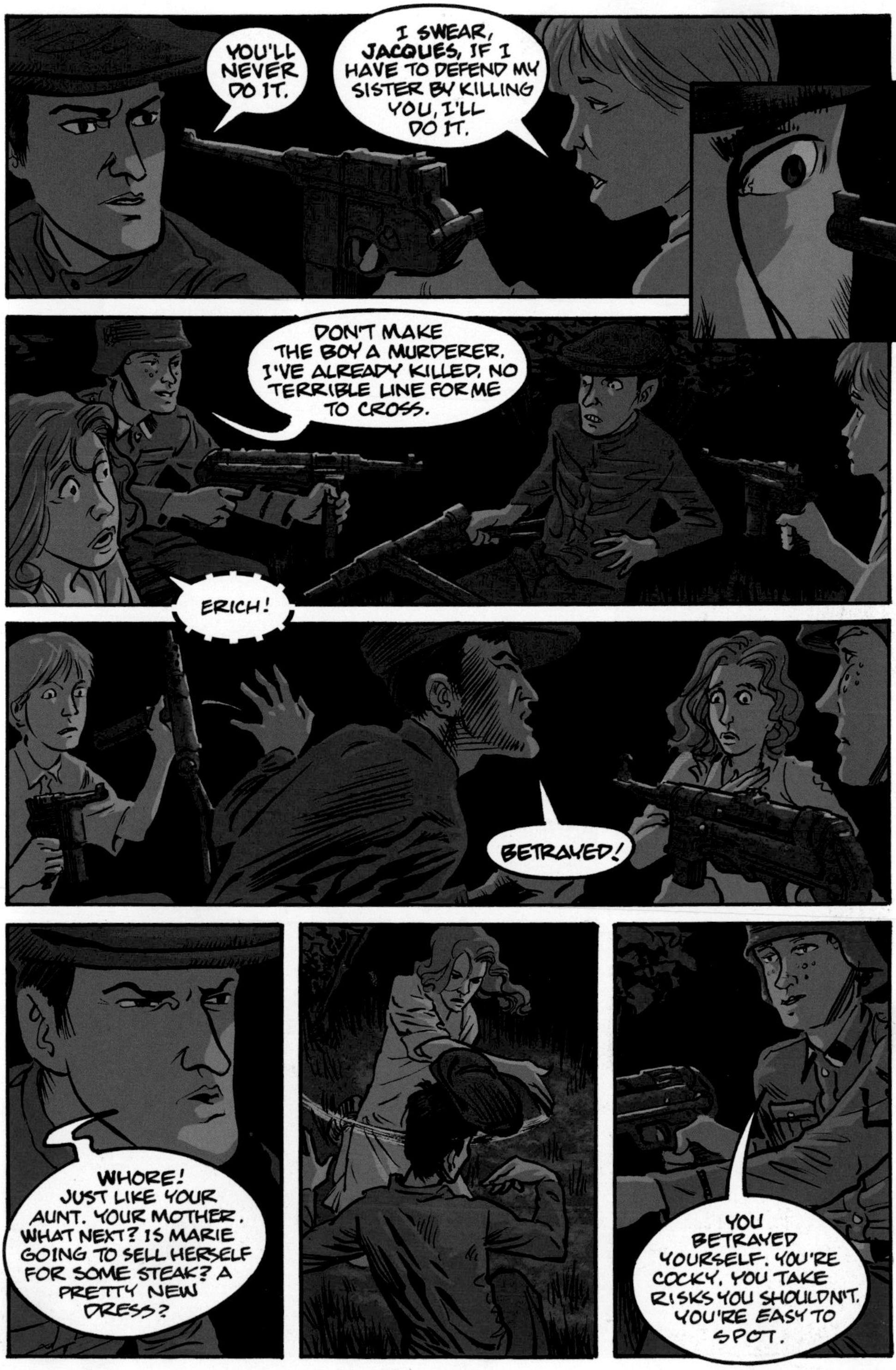
YOU'LL NEVER DO IT.
I SWEAR, JACQUES, IF I HAVE TO DEFEND MY SISTER BY KILLING YOU, I'LL DO IT.
DON'T MAKE THE BOY A MURDERER. I'VE ALREADY KILLED, NO TERRIBLE LINE FOR ME TO CROSS.
ERICH!
BETRAYED!
WHORE! JUST LIKE YOUR AUNT. YOUR MOTHER. WHAT NEXT? IS MARIE GOING TO SELL HERSELF FOR SOME STEAK? A PRETTY NEW DRESS?
YOU BETRAYED YOURSELF. YOU'RE COCKY. YOU TAKE RISKS YOU SHOULDN'T. YOU'RE EASY TO SPOT.

SO NOW WHAT ARE YOU GOING TO DO? TAKE ME PRISONER? TAKE ALL OF US PRISONER?
HITLER IS A MAD MAN. HE WILL DESTROY OUR COUNTRY - HE ALREADY HAS. THESE LATEST ACTIONS...
I HELP YOU, AND YOU HELP ME ESCAPE.
YOU'RE REALLY GOING TO DO IT?
SO YOU'RE A **DESERTER**? A **COWARD**.
HIS MOTHER IS **DYING**!
ARE YOU GOING TO HELP US DESTROY THE COMPOUND? DON'T THINK SO.
NO.
BUT I CAN HELP YOU GET TO **PARIS**.

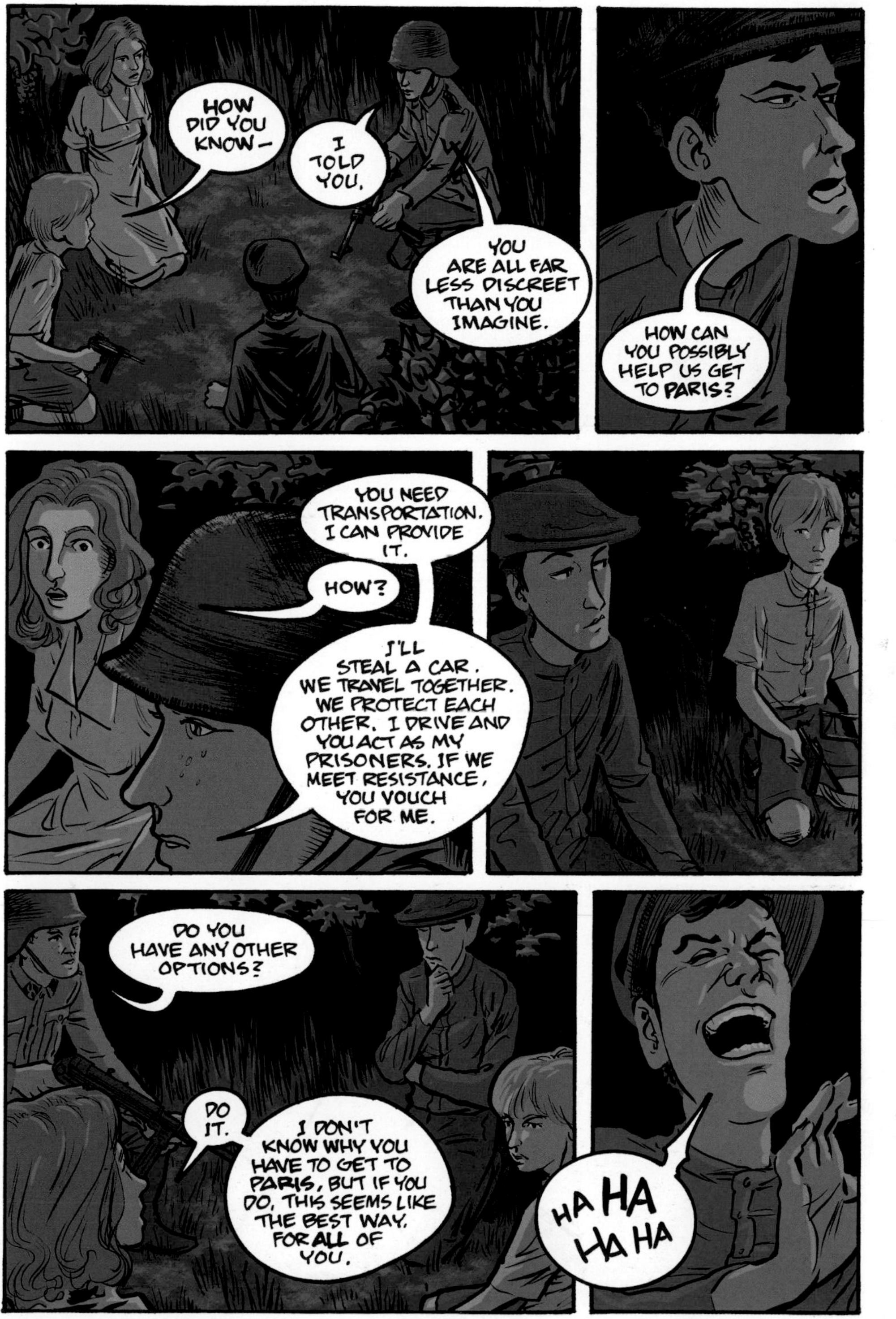
HOW DID YOU KNOW—
I TOLD YOU.
YOU ARE ALL FAR LESS DISCREET THAN YOU IMAGINE.
HOW CAN YOU POSSIBLY HELP US GET TO PARIS?
YOU NEED TRANSPORTATION. I CAN PROVIDE IT.
HOW?
I'LL STEAL A CAR. WE TRAVEL TOGETHER. WE PROTECT EACH OTHER. I DRIVE AND YOU ACT AS MY PRISONERS. IF WE MEET RESISTANCE, YOU VOUCH FOR ME.
DO YOU HAVE ANY OTHER OPTIONS?
DO IT.
I DON'T KNOW WHY YOU HAVE TO GET TO PARIS, BUT IF YOU DO, THIS SEEMS LIKE THE BEST WAY. FOR ALL OF YOU.
HA HA HA HA

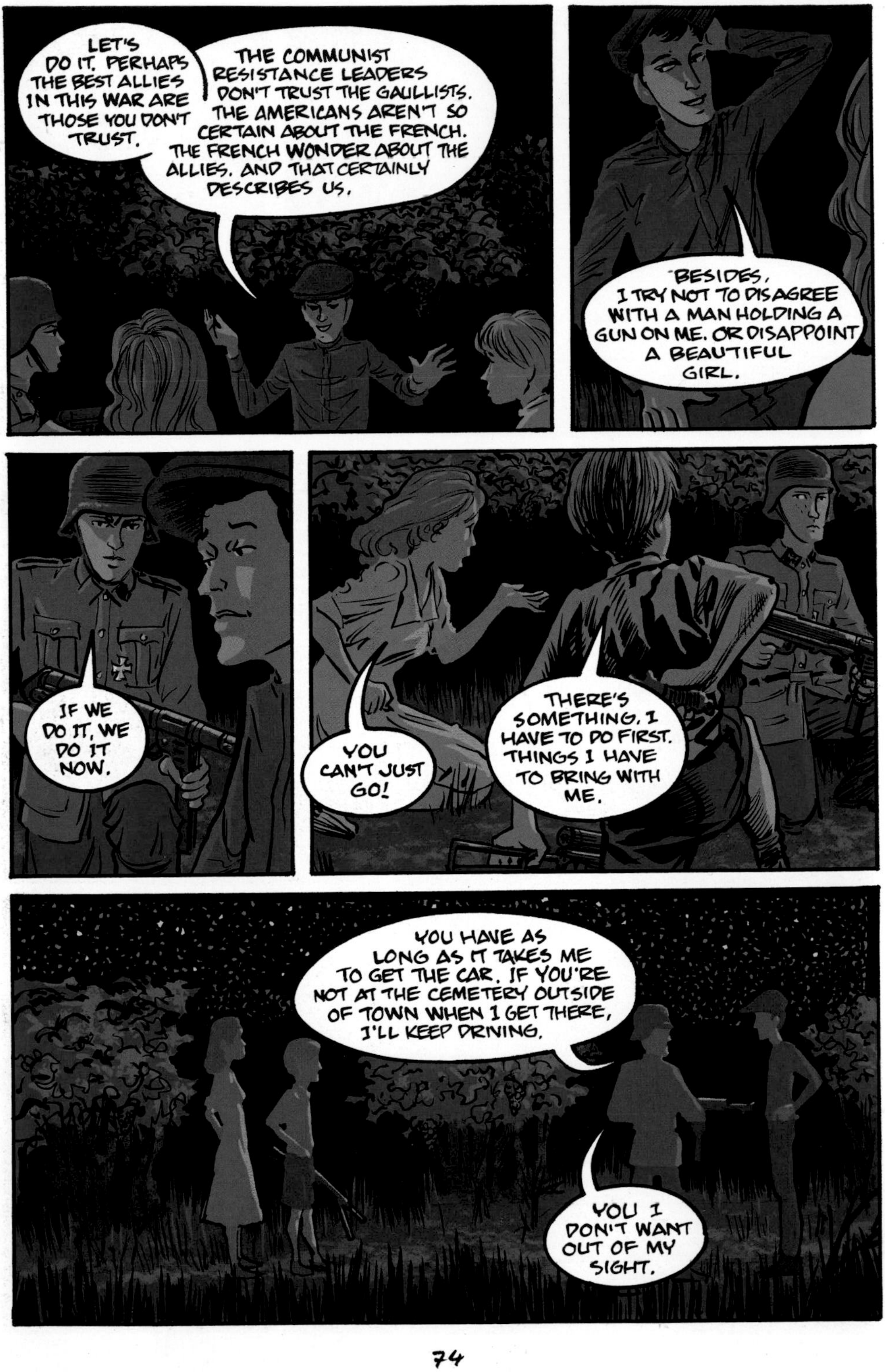
LET'S DO IT. PERHAPS THE BEST ALLIES IN THIS WAR ARE THOSE YOU DON'T TRUST.
THE COMMUNIST RESISTANCE LEADERS DON'T TRUST THE GAULLISTS. THE AMERICANS AREN'T SO CERTAIN ABOUT THE FRENCH. THE FRENCH WONDER ABOUT THE ALLIES. AND THAT CERTAINLY DESCRIBES US.
BESIDES, I TRY NOT TO DISAGREE WITH A MAN HOLDING A GUN ON ME. OR DISAPPOINT A BEAUTIFUL GIRL.
IF WE DO IT, WE DO IT NOW.
YOU CAN'T JUST GO!
THERE'S SOMETHING, I HAVE TO DO FIRST. THINGS I HAVE TO BRING WITH ME.
YOU HAVE AS LONG AS IT TAKES ME TO GET THE CAR. IF YOU'RE NOT AT THE CEMETERY OUTSIDE OF TOWN WHEN I GET THERE, I'LL KEEP DRIVING.
YOU I DON'T WANT OUT OF MY SIGHT.

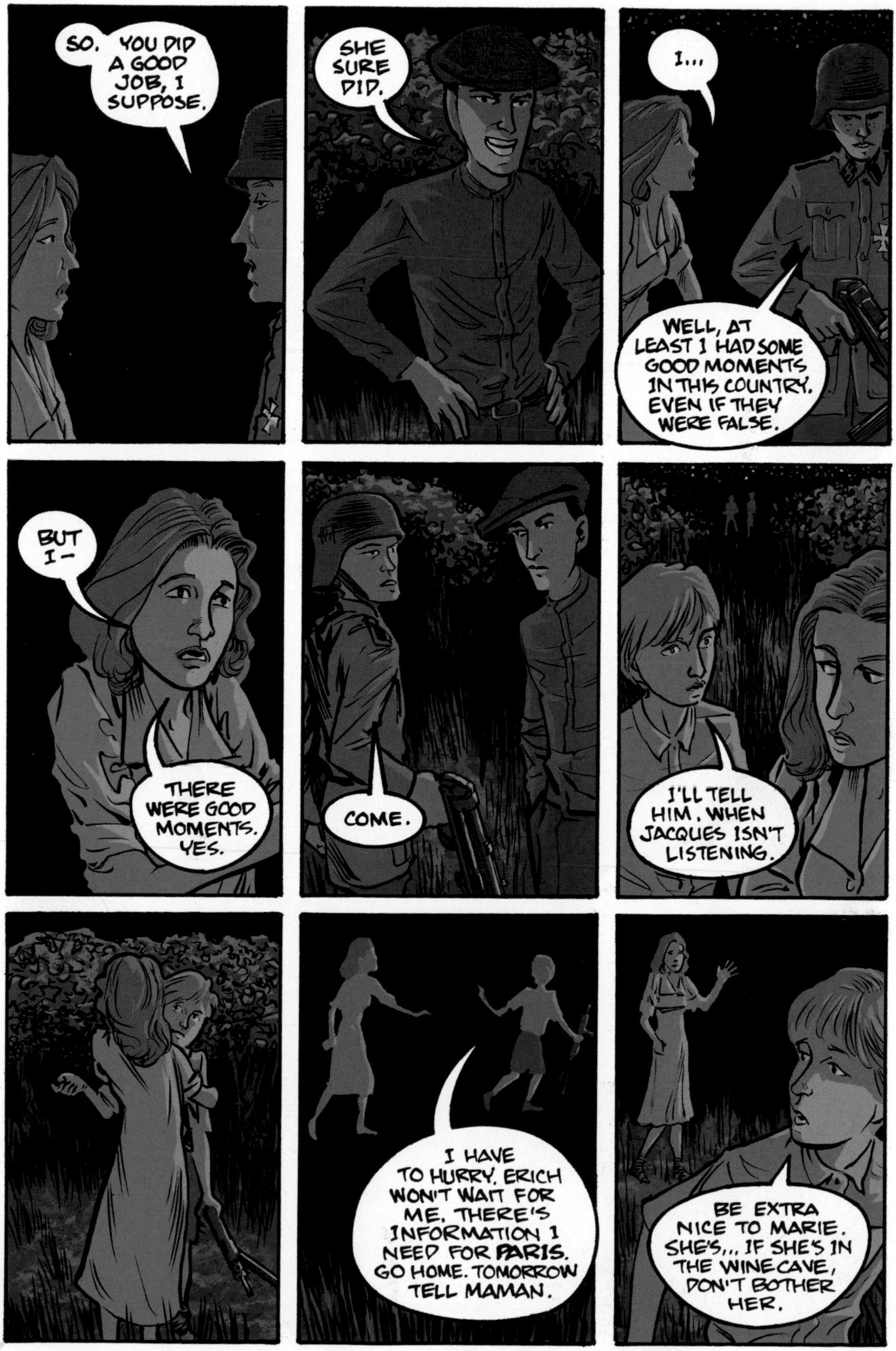

SO. YOU DID A GOOD JOB, I SUPPOSE.
SHE SURE DID.
I...
WELL, AT LEAST I HAD SOME GOOD MOMENTS IN THIS COUNTRY. EVEN IF THEY WERE FALSE.
BUT I-
THERE WERE GOOD MOMENTS. YES.
COME.
I'LL TELL HIM. WHEN JACQUES ISN'T LISTENING.
I HAVE TO HURRY. ERICH WON'T WAIT FOR ME. THERE'S INFORMATION I NEED FOR PARIS. GO HOME. TOMORROW TELL MAMAN.
BE EXTRA NICE TO MARIE. SHE'S... IF SHE'S IN THE WINE CAVE, DON'T BOTHER HER.

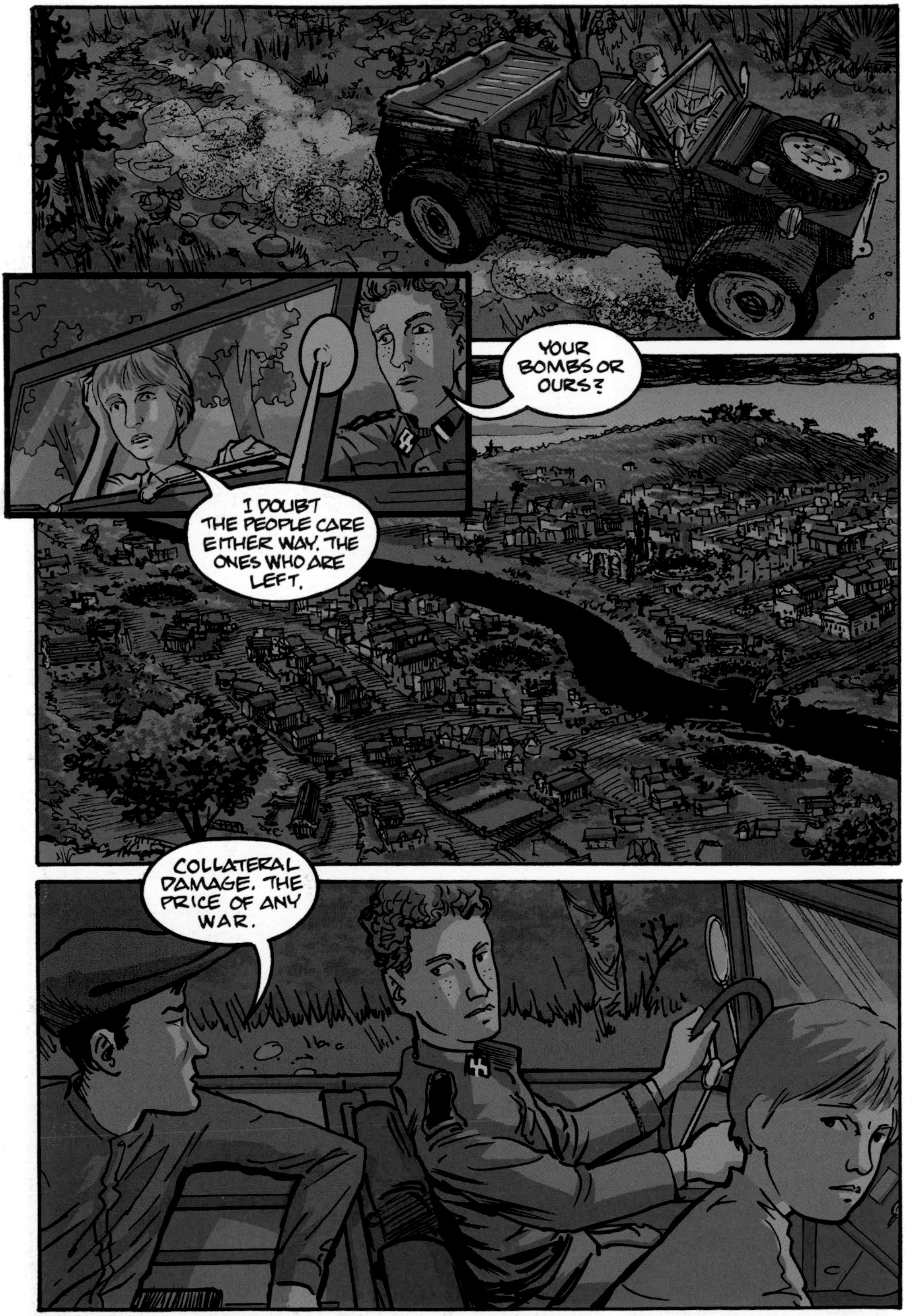
YOUR BOMBS OR OURS?
I DOUBT THE PEOPLE CARE EITHER WAY. THE ONES WHO ARE LEFT.
COLLATERAL DAMAGE. THE PRICE OF ANY WAR.

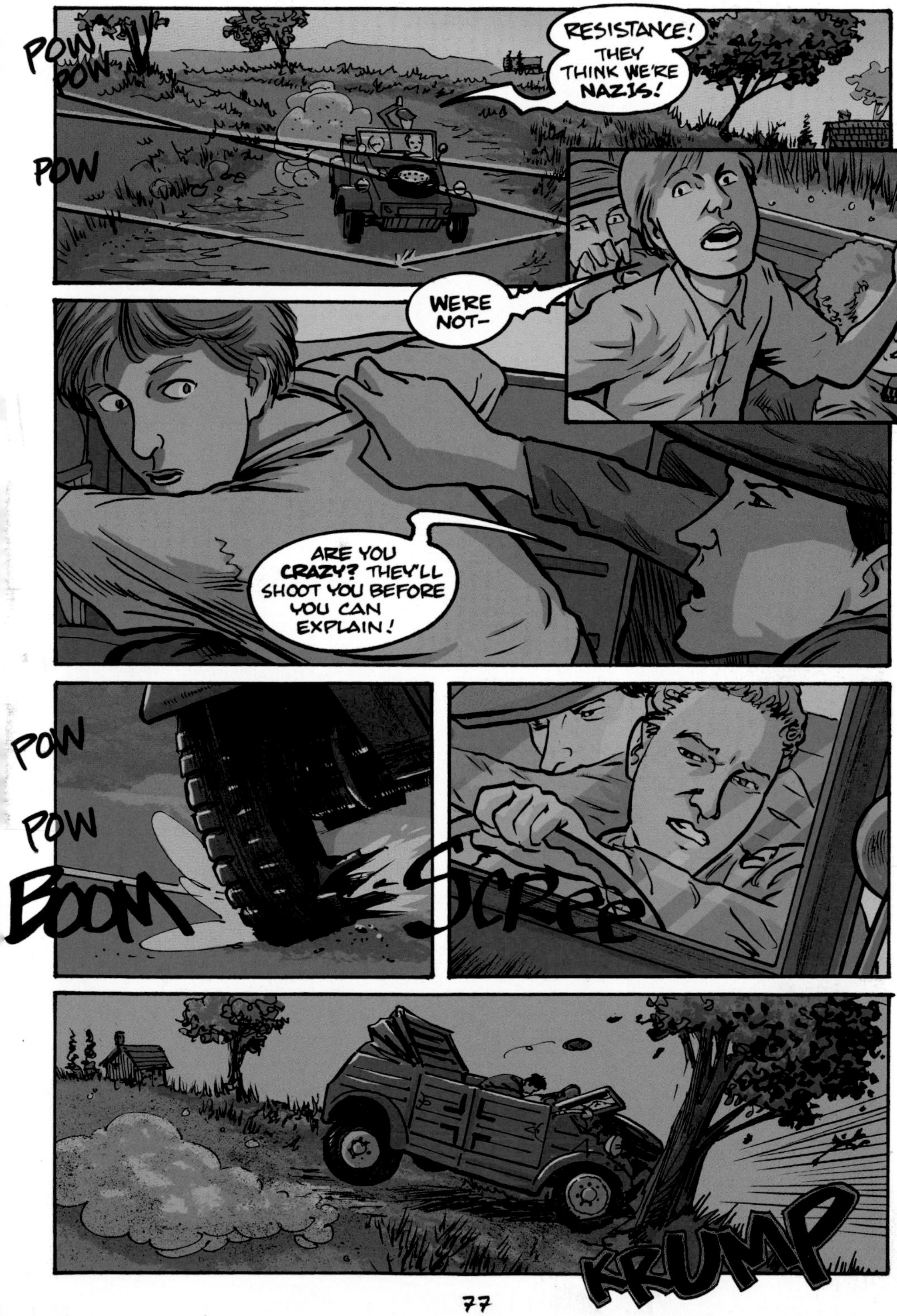
POW
POW
POW
RESISTANCE! THEY THINK WE'RE NAZIS!
WE'RE NOT-
ARE YOU CRAZY? THEY'LL SHOOT YOU BEFORE YOU CAN EXPLAIN!
POW
POW
BOOM
SCREE
KRUMP

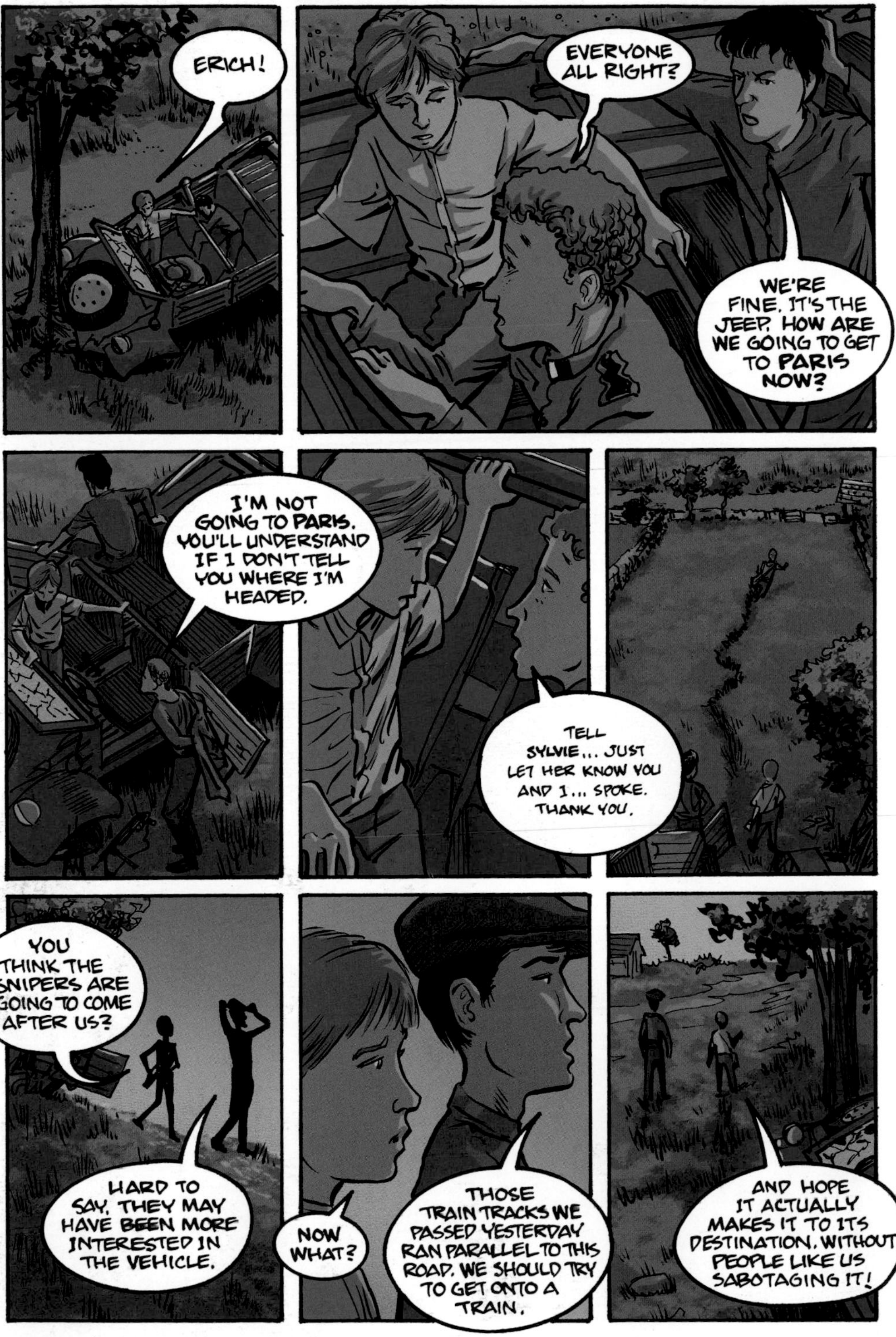
ERICH!
EVERYONE ALL RIGHT?
WE'RE FINE. IT'S THE JEEP. HOW ARE WE GOING TO GET TO PARIS NOW?
I'M NOT GOING TO PARIS. YOU'LL UNDERSTAND IF I DON'T TELL YOU WHERE I'M HEADED.
TELL SYLVIE... JUST LET HER KNOW YOU AND I... SPOKE. THANK YOU.
YOU THINK THE SNIPERS ARE GOING TO COME AFTER US?
HARD TO SAY. THEY MAY HAVE BEEN MORE INTERESTED IN THE VEHICLE.
NOW WHAT?
THOSE TRAIN TRACKS WE PASSED YESTERDAY RAN PARALLEL TO THIS ROAD. WE SHOULD TRY TO GET ONTO A TRAIN.
AND HOPE IT ACTUALLY MAKES IT TO ITS DESTINATION, WITHOUT PEOPLE LIKE US SABOTAGING IT!

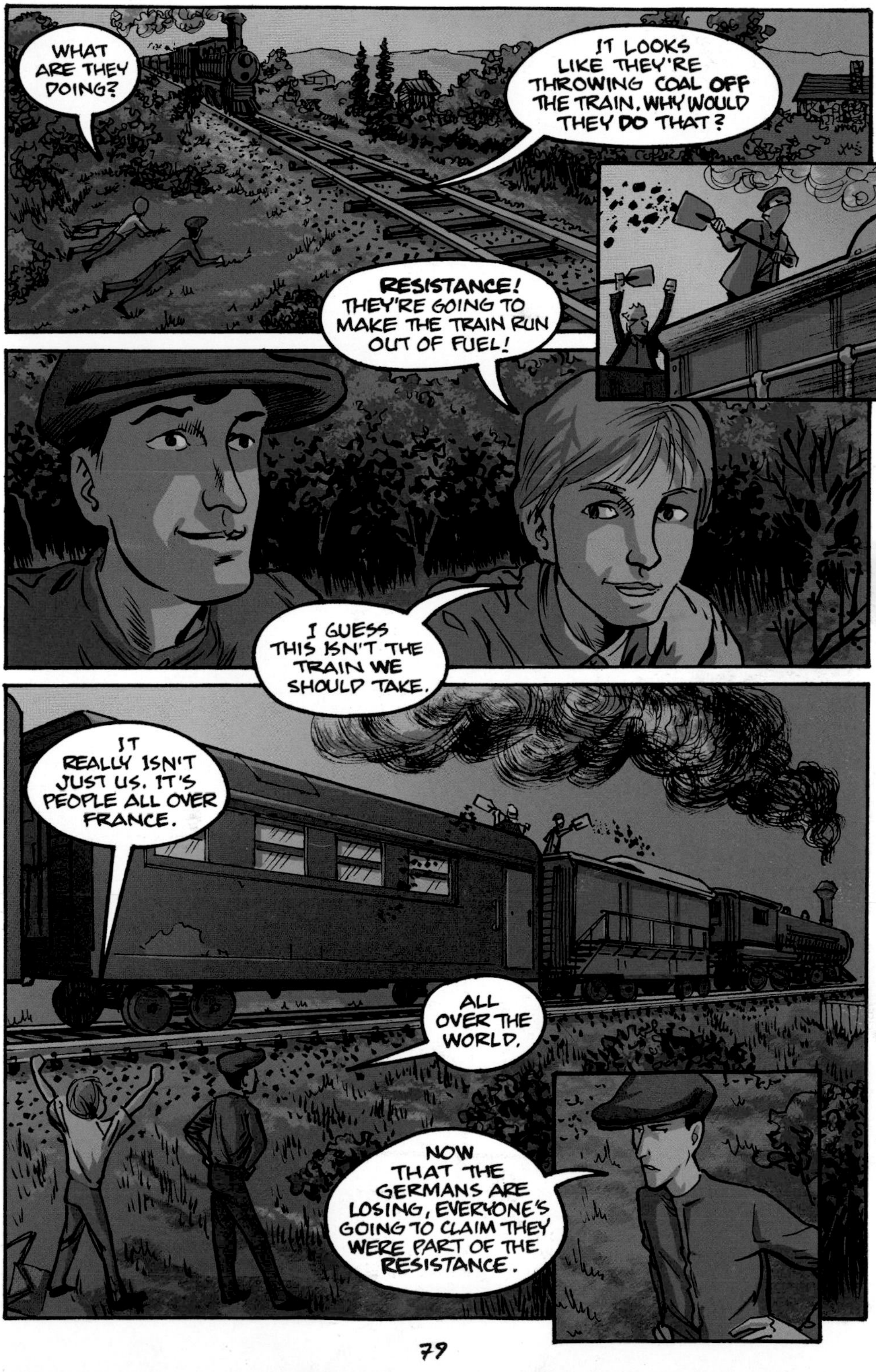
WHAT ARE THEY DOING?
IT LOOKS LIKE THEY'RE THROWING COAL OFF THE TRAIN. WHY WOULD THEY DO THAT?
RESISTANCE! THEY'RE GOING TO MAKE THE TRAIN RUN OUT OF FUEL!
I GUESS THIS ISN'T THE TRAIN WE SHOULD TAKE.
IT REALLY ISN'T JUST US. IT'S PEOPLE ALL OVER FRANCE.
ALL OVER THE WORLD.
NOW THAT THE GERMANS ARE LOSING, EVERYONE'S GOING TO CLAIM THEY WERE PART OF THE RESISTANCE.

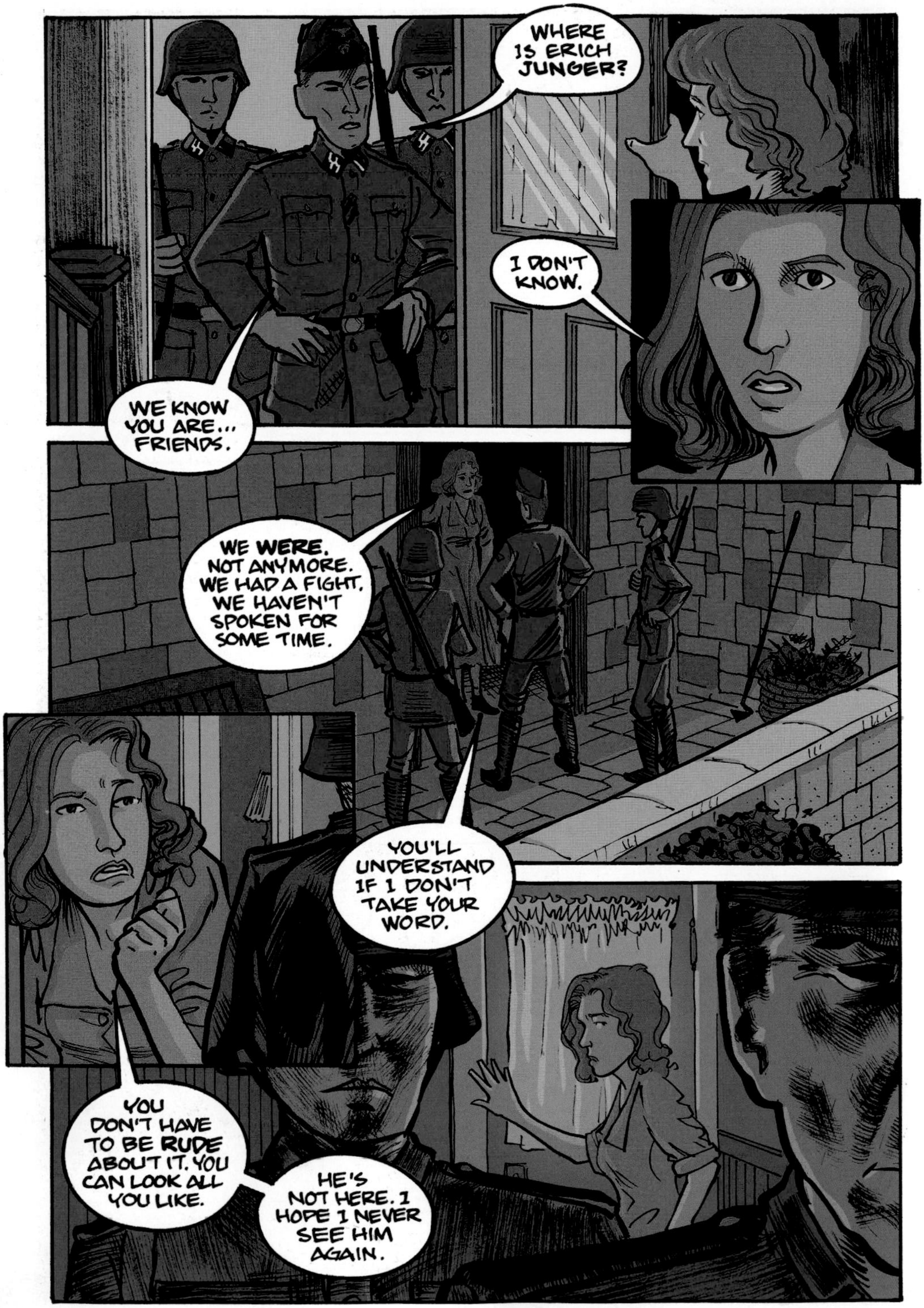
WHERE IS ERICH JUNGER?
I DON'T KNOW.
WE KNOW YOU ARE... FRIENDS.
WE WERE. NOT ANYMORE. WE HAD A FIGHT. WE HAVEN'T SPOKEN FOR SOME TIME.
YOU'LL UNDERSTAND IF I DON'T TAKE YOUR WORD.
YOU DON'T HAVE TO BE RUDE ABOUT IT. YOU CAN LOOK ALL YOU LIKE.
HE'S NOT HERE. I HOPE I NEVER SEE HIM AGAIN.

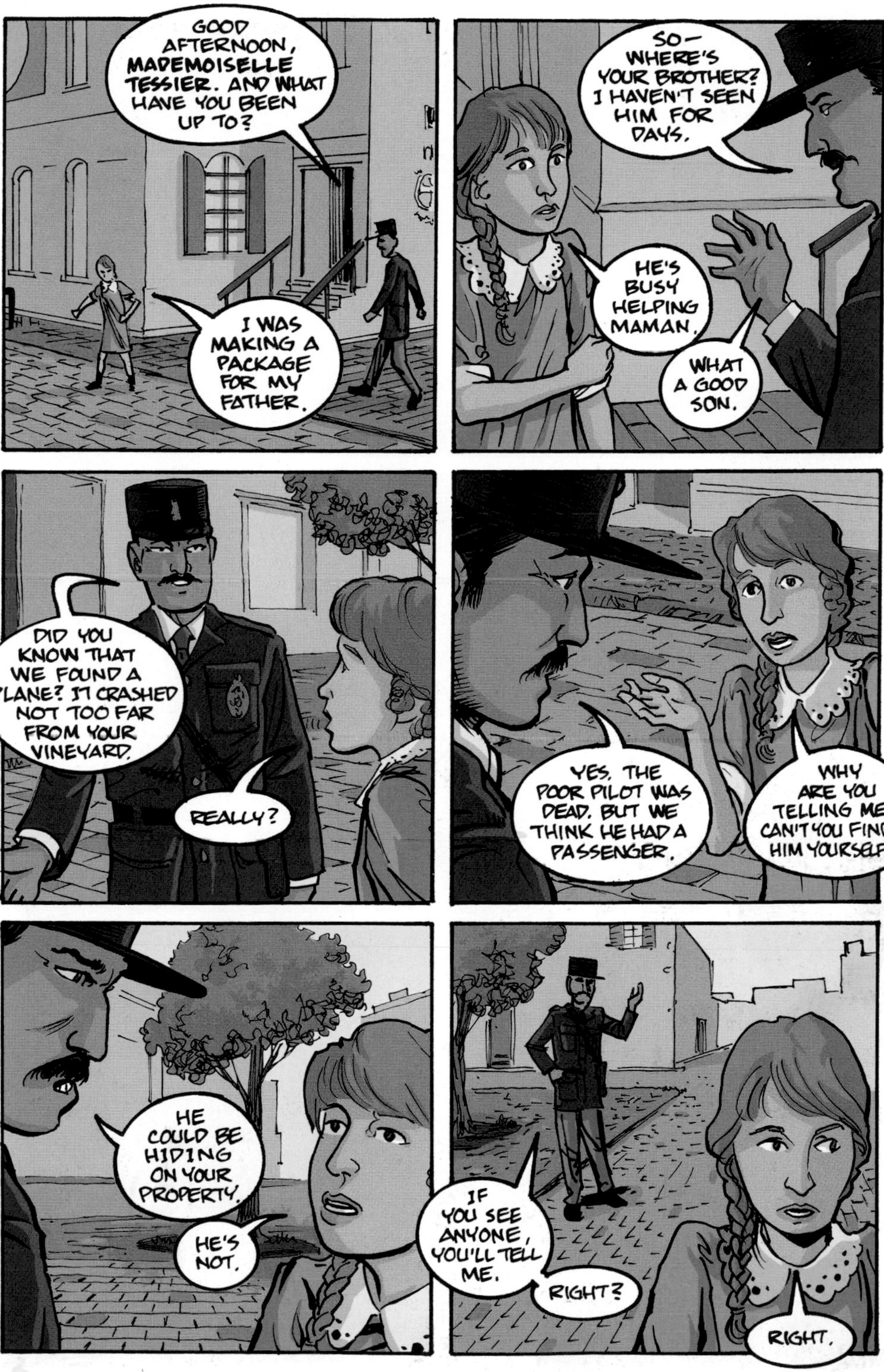
GOOD AFTERNOON, MADEMOISELLE TESSIER. AND WHAT HAVE YOU BEEN UP TO?
I WAS MAKING A PACKAGE FOR MY FATHER.
SO— WHERE'S YOUR BROTHER? I HAVEN'T SEEN HIM FOR DAYS.
HE'S BUSY HELPING MAMAN.
WHAT A GOOD SON.
DID YOU KNOW THAT WE FOUND A PLANE? IT CRASHED NOT TOO FAR FROM YOUR VINEYARD.
REALLY?
YES. THE POOR PILOT WAS DEAD. BUT WE THINK HE HAD A PASSENGER.
WHY ARE YOU TELLING ME? CAN'T YOU FIND HIM YOURSELF?
HE COULD BE HIDING ON YOUR PROPERTY.
HE'S NOT.
IF YOU SEE ANYONE, YOU'LL TELL ME.
RIGHT?
RIGHT.

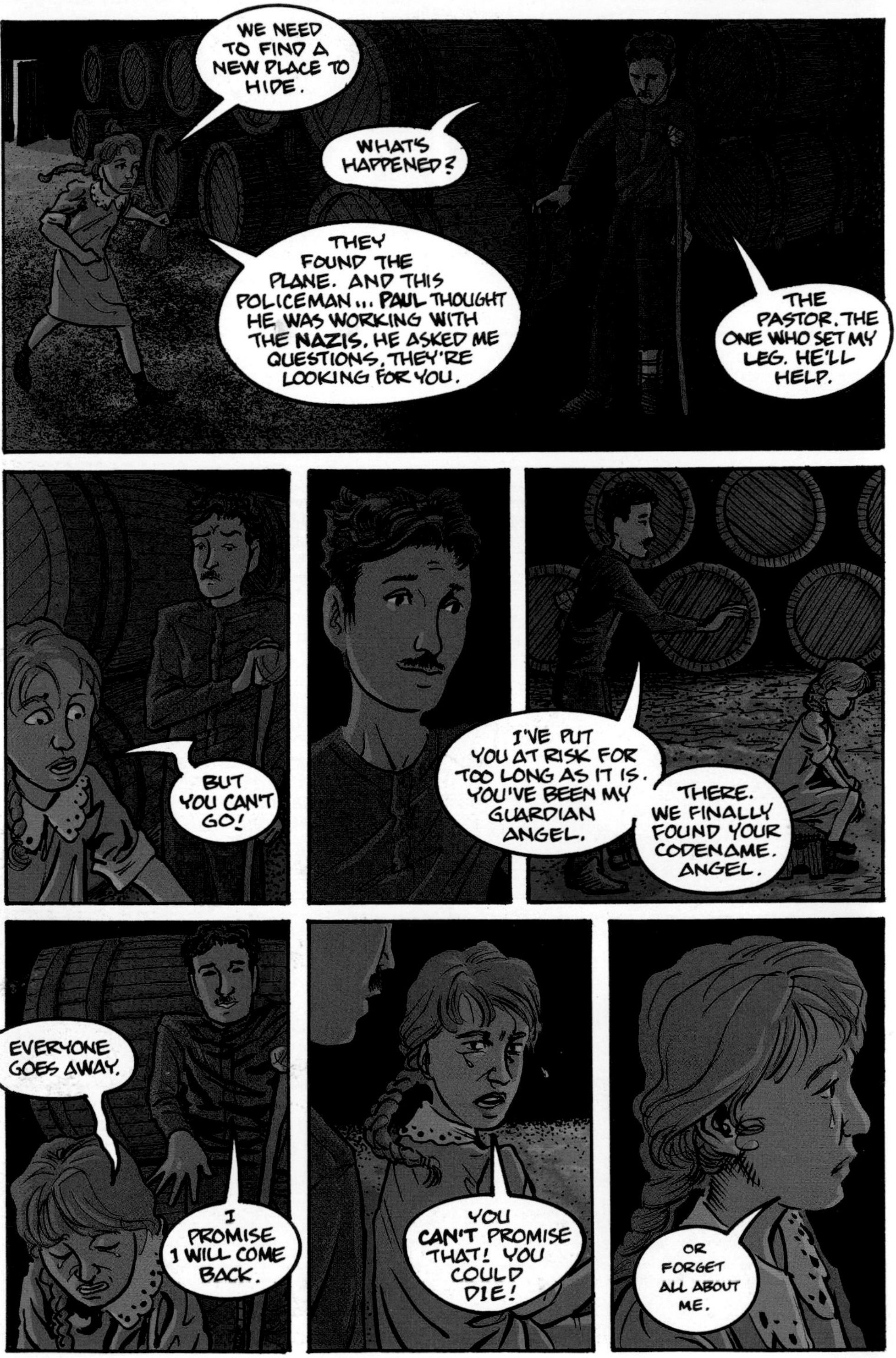
WE NEED TO FIND A NEW PLACE TO HIDE.
WHAT'S HAPPENED?
THEY FOUND THE PLANE. AND THIS POLICEMAN... PAUL THOUGHT HE WAS WORKING WITH THE NAZIS. HE ASKED ME QUESTIONS. THEY'RE LOOKING FOR YOU.
THE PASTOR. THE ONE WHO SET MY LEG. HE'LL HELP.
BUT YOU CAN'T GO!
I'VE PUT YOU AT RISK FOR TOO LONG AS IT IS. YOU'VE BEEN MY GUARDIAN ANGEL.
THERE. WE FINALLY FOUND YOUR CODENAME. ANGEL.
EVERYONE GOES AWAY.
I PROMISE I WILL COME BACK.
YOU CAN'T PROMISE THAT! YOU COULD DIE!
OR FORGET ALL ABOUT ME.

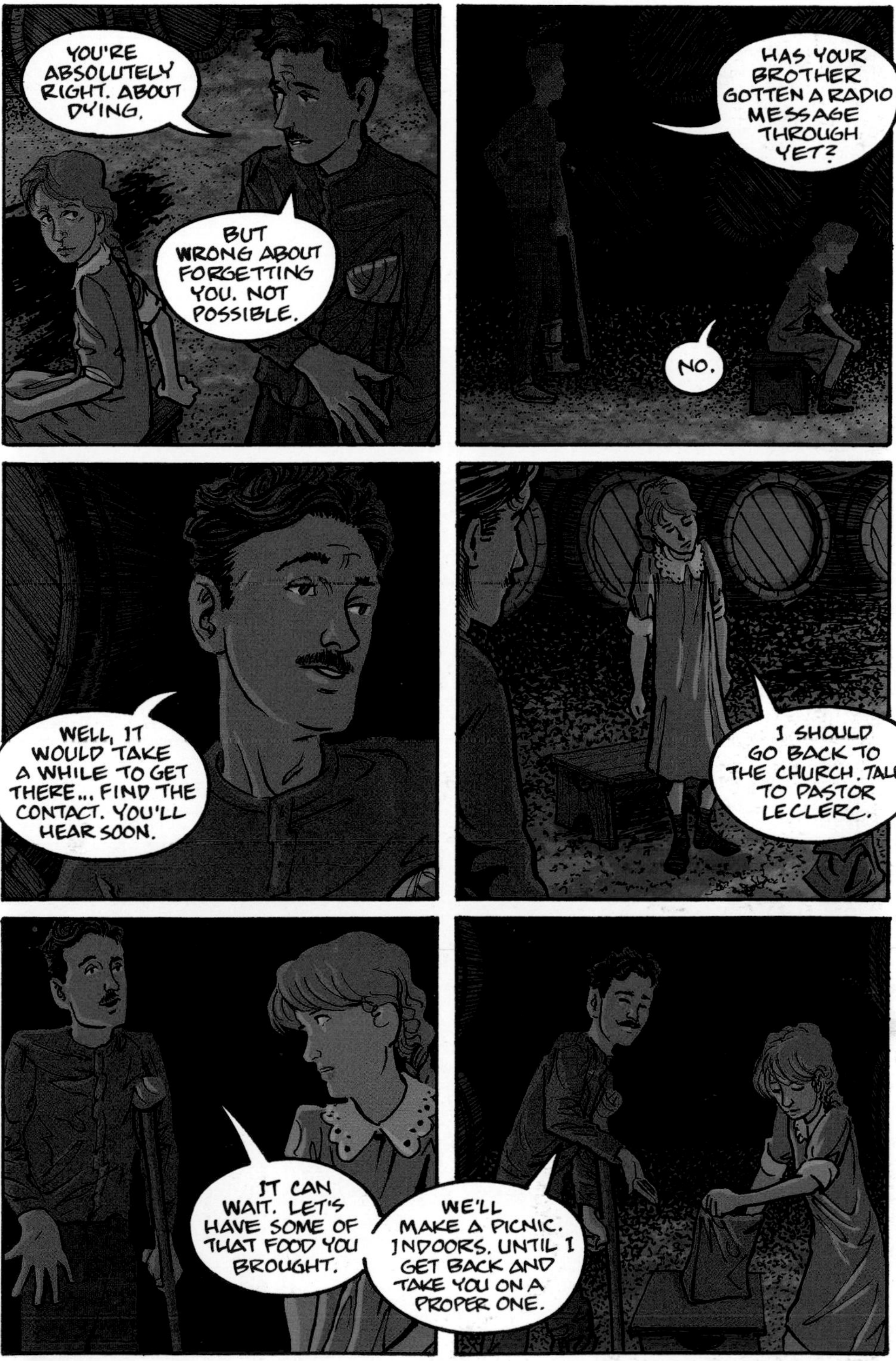
YOU'RE ABSOLUTELY RIGHT. ABOUT DYING.
BUT WRONG ABOUT FORGETTING YOU. NOT POSSIBLE.
HAS YOUR BROTHER GOTTEN A RADIO MESSAGE THROUGH YET?
NO.
WELL, IT WOULD TAKE A WHILE TO GET THERE... FIND THE CONTACT. YOU'LL HEAR SOON.
I SHOULD GO BACK TO THE CHURCH. TALK TO PASTOR LECLERC.
IT CAN WAIT. LET'S HAVE SOME OF THAT FOOD YOU BROUGHT.
WE'LL MAKE A PICNIC. INDOORS. UNTIL I GET BACK AND TAKE YOU ON A PROPER ONE.

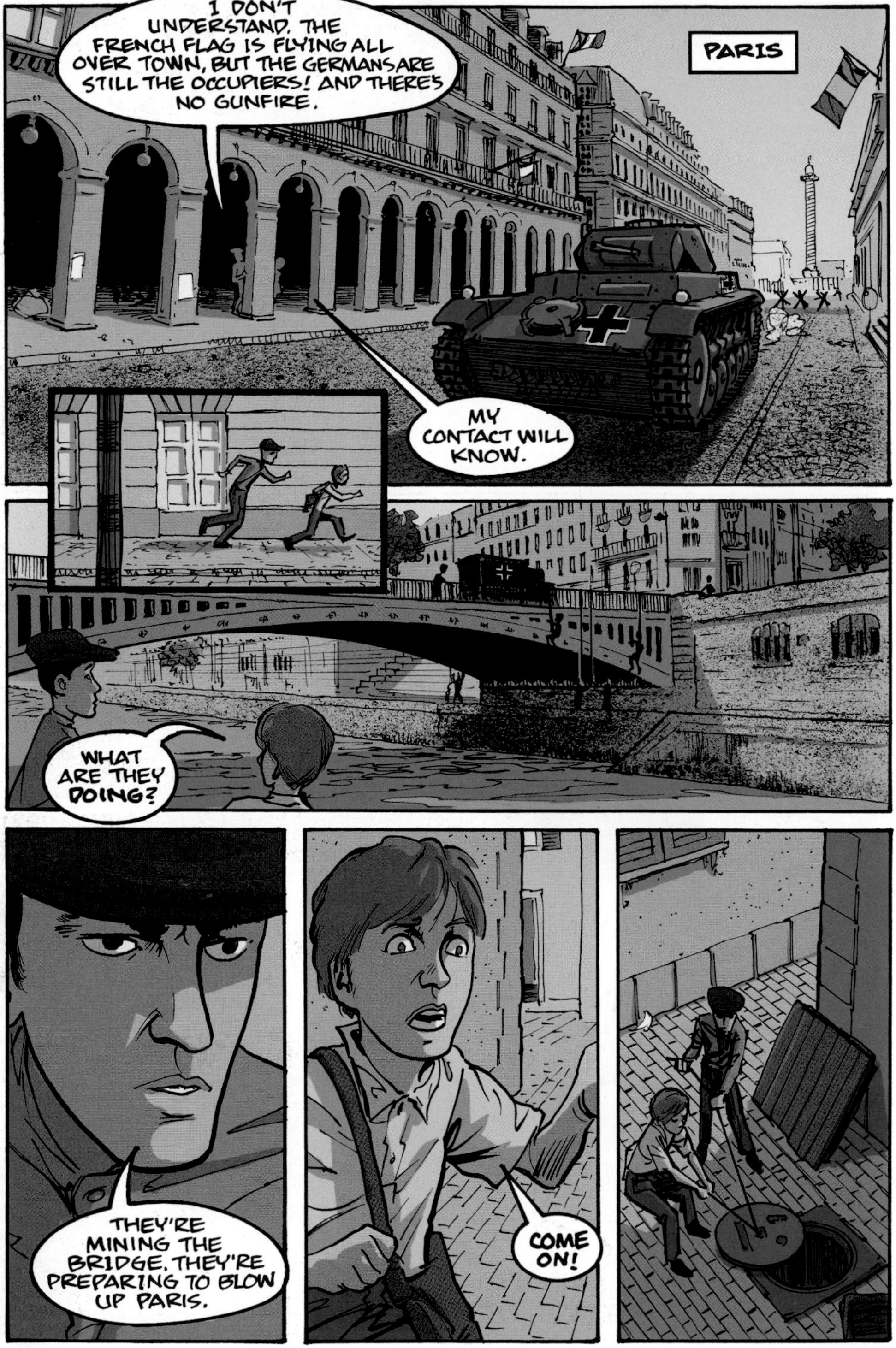
PARIS
I DON'T UNDERSTAND. THE FRENCH FLAG IS FLYING ALL OVER TOWN, BUT THE GERMANS ARE STILL THE OCCUPIERS! AND THERE'S NO GUNFIRE.
MY CONTACT WILL KNOW.
WHAT ARE THEY DOING?
THEY'RE MINING THE BRIDGE. THEY'RE PREPARING TO BLOW UP PARIS.
COME ON!

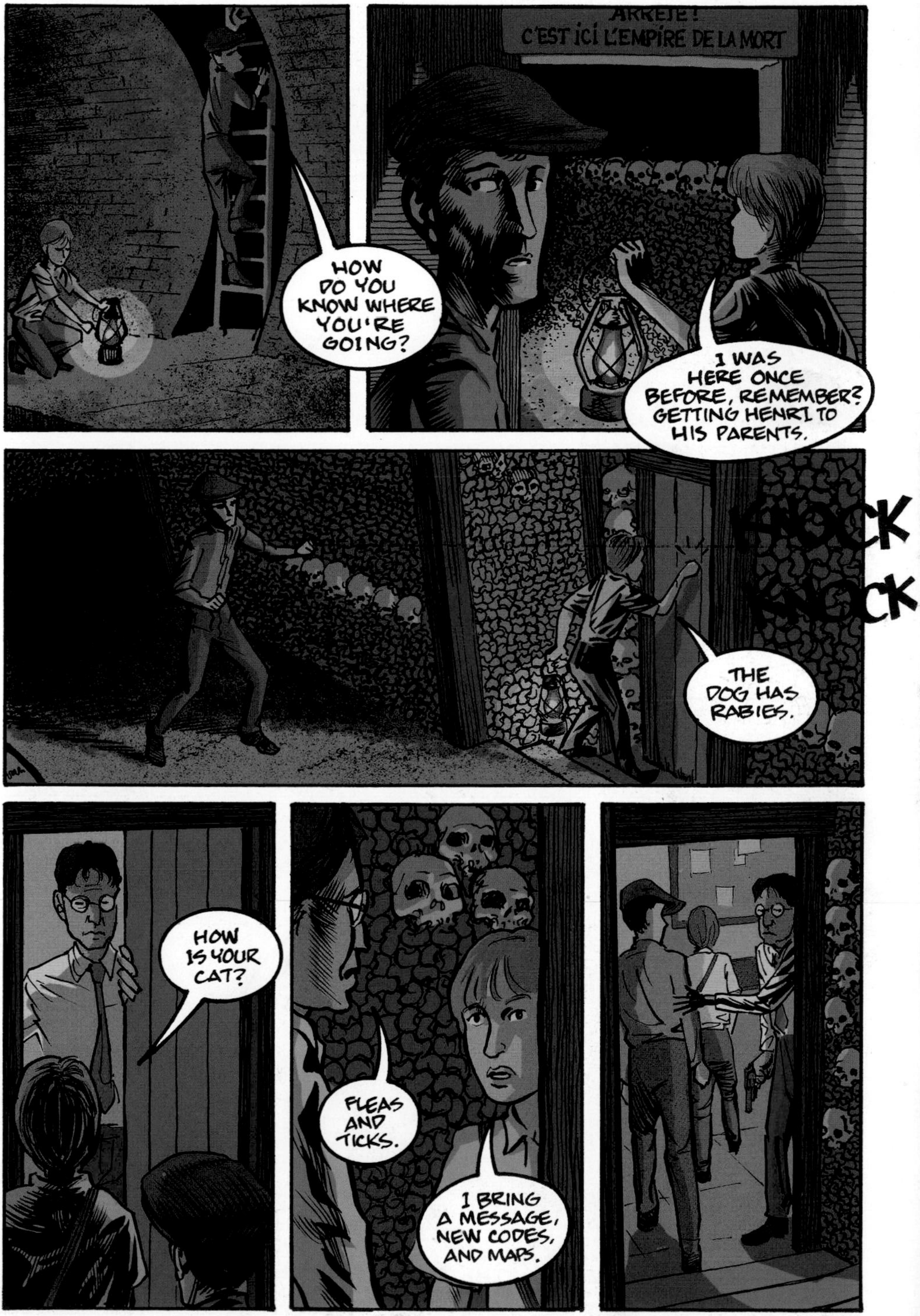
HOW DO YOU KNOW WHERE YOU'RE GOING?
ARRETE! C'EST ICI L'EMPIRE DE LA MORT
I WAS HERE ONCE BEFORE, REMEMBER? GETTING HENRI TO HIS PARENTS.
KNOCK KNOCK
THE DOG HAS RABIES.
HOW IS YOUR CAT?
FLEAS AND TICKS.
I BRING A MESSAGE, NEW CODES, AND MAPS.

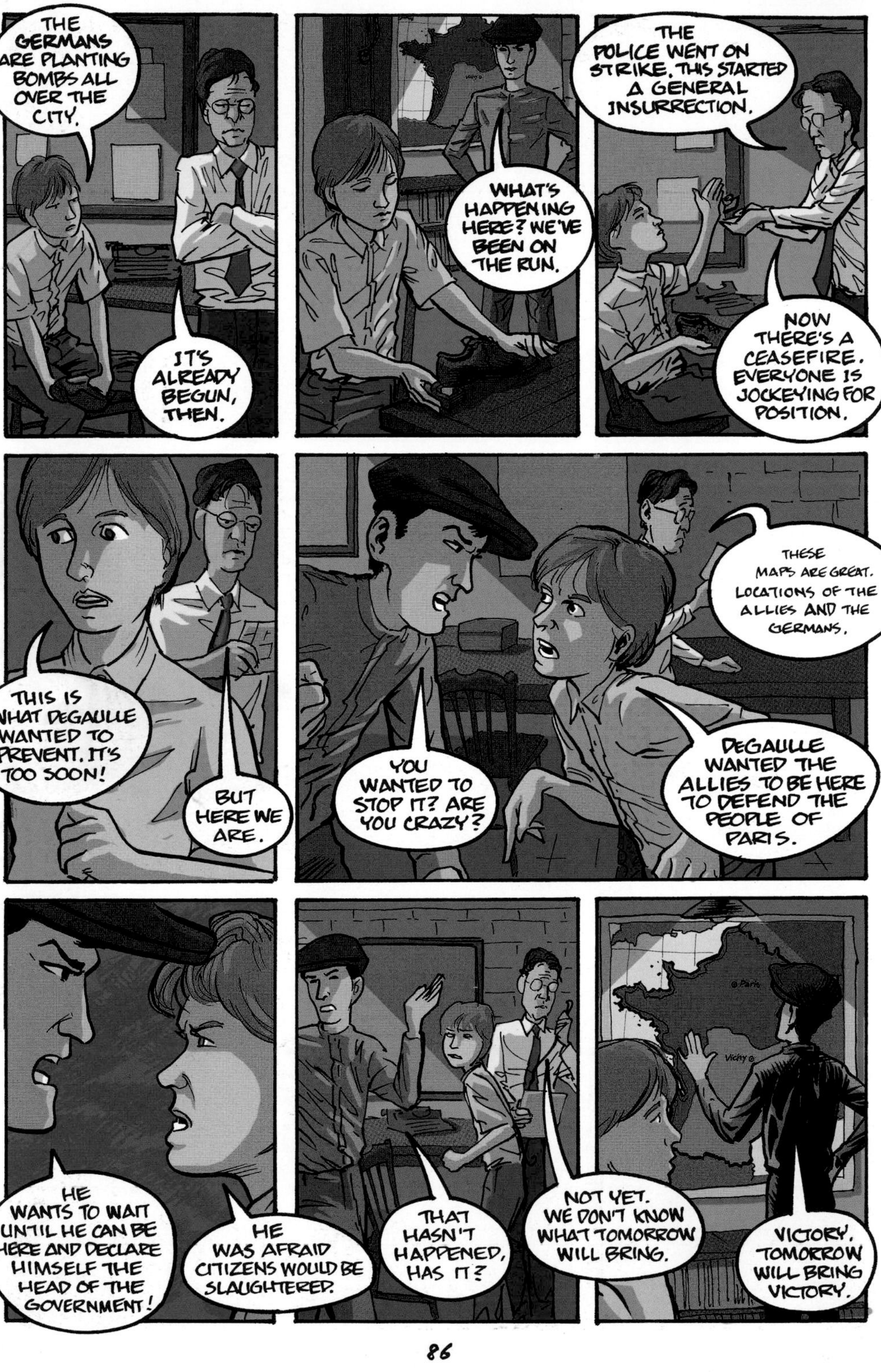
THE GERMANS ARE PLANTING BOMBS ALL OVER THE CITY.
IT'S ALREADY BEGUN, THEN.
WHAT'S HAPPENING HERE? WE'VE BEEN ON THE RUN.
THE POLICE WENT ON STRIKE. THIS STARTED A GENERAL INSURRECTION.
NOW THERE'S A CEASEFIRE. EVERYONE IS JOCKEYING FOR POSITION.
THIS IS WHAT DEGAULLE WANTED TO PREVENT. IT'S TOO SOON!
BUT HERE WE ARE.
THESE MAPS ARE GREAT. LOCATIONS OF THE ALLIES AND THE GERMANS.
YOU WANTED TO STOP IT? ARE YOU CRAZY?
DEGAULLE WANTED THE ALLIES TO BE HERE TO DEFEND THE PEOPLE OF PARIS.
HE WANTS TO WAIT UNTIL HE CAN BE HERE AND DECLARE HIMSELF THE HEAD OF THE GOVERNMENT!
HE WAS AFRAID CITIZENS WOULD BE SLAUGHTERED.
THAT HASN'T HAPPENED, HAS IT?
NOT YET. WE DON'T KNOW WHAT TOMORROW WILL BRING.
Paris
Vichy
VICTORY. TOMORROW WILL BRING VICTORY.

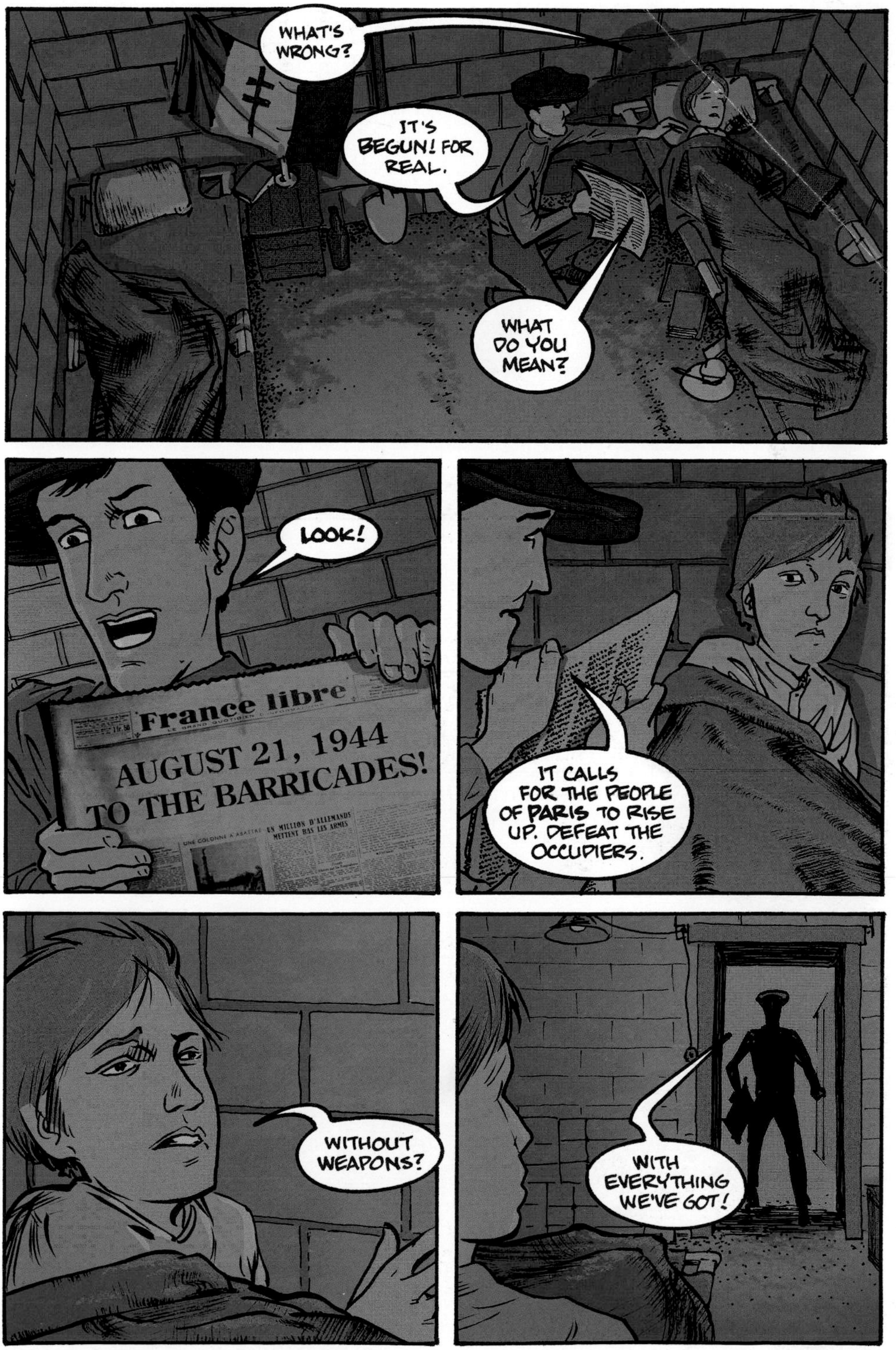
WHAT'S WRONG?
IT'S BEGUN! FOR REAL.
WHAT DO YOU MEAN?
LOOK!
France libre
AUGUST 21, 1944
TO THE BARRICADES!
UN MILLION D'ALLEMANDS METTENT BAS LES ARMES
IT CALLS FOR THE PEOPLE OF PARIS TO RISE UP. DEFEAT THE OCCUPIERS.
WITHOUT WEAPONS?
WITH EVERYTHING WE'VE GOT!

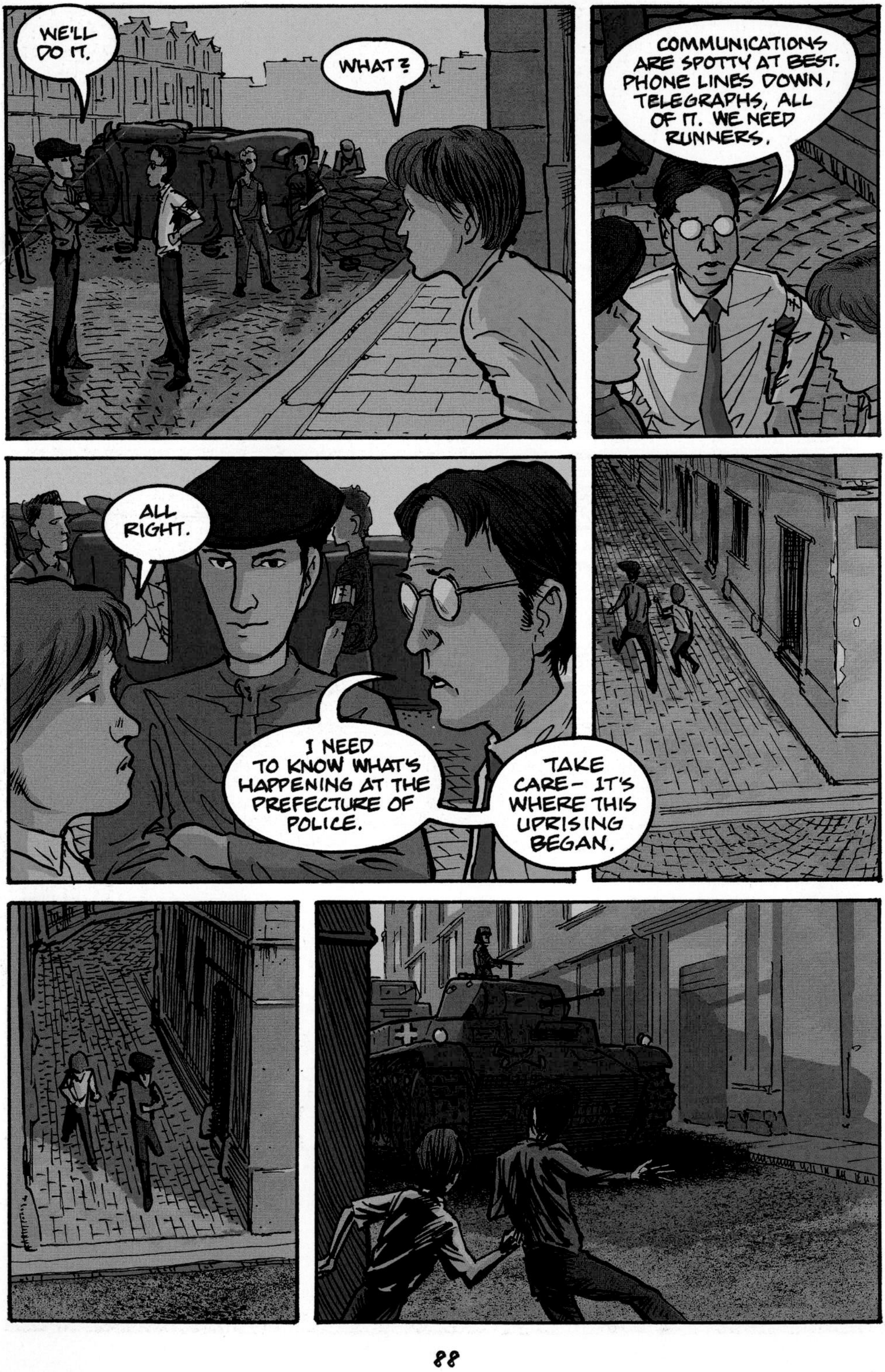
WE'LL DO IT.
WHAT?
COMMUNICATIONS ARE SPOTTY AT BEST. PHONE LINES DOWN, TELEGRAPHS, ALL OF IT. WE NEED RUNNERS.
ALL RIGHT.
I NEED TO KNOW WHAT'S HAPPENING AT THE PREFECTURE OF POLICE.
TAKE CARE– IT'S WHERE THIS UPRISING BEGAN.

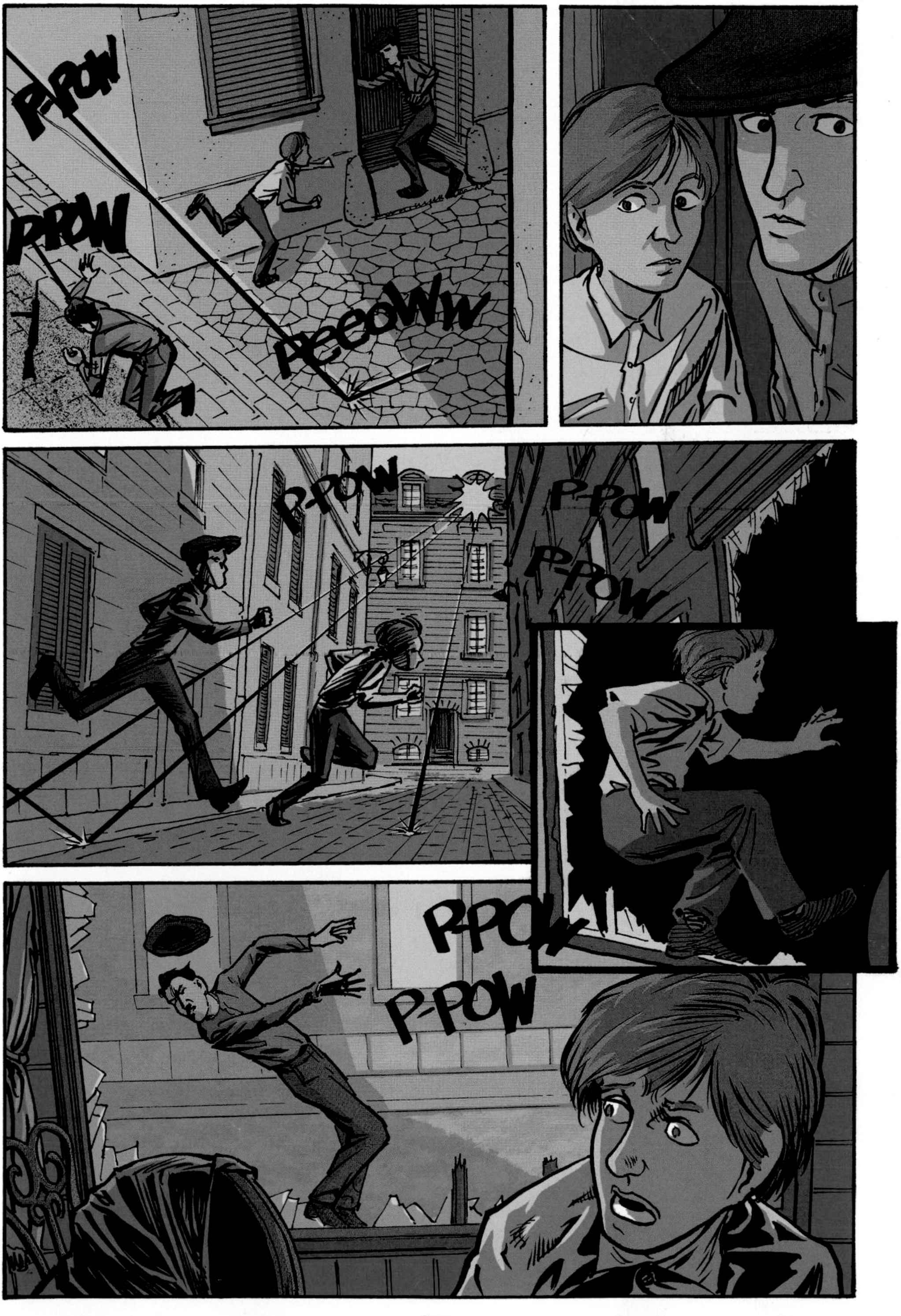
P-POW
P-POW
PEEOWW
P-POW
P-POW
P-POW
P-POW
P-POW

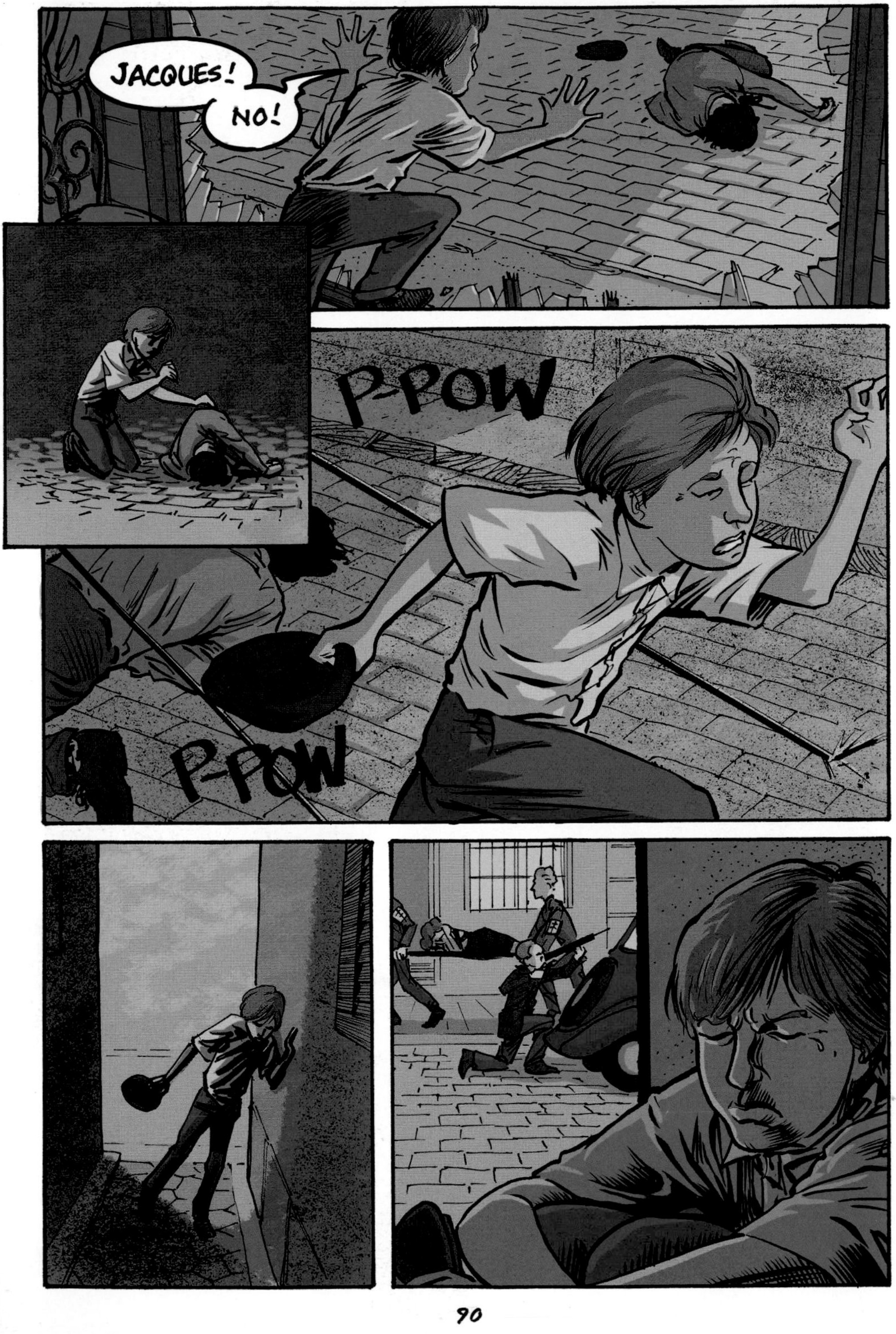
JACQUES!
NO!
P-POW
P-POW

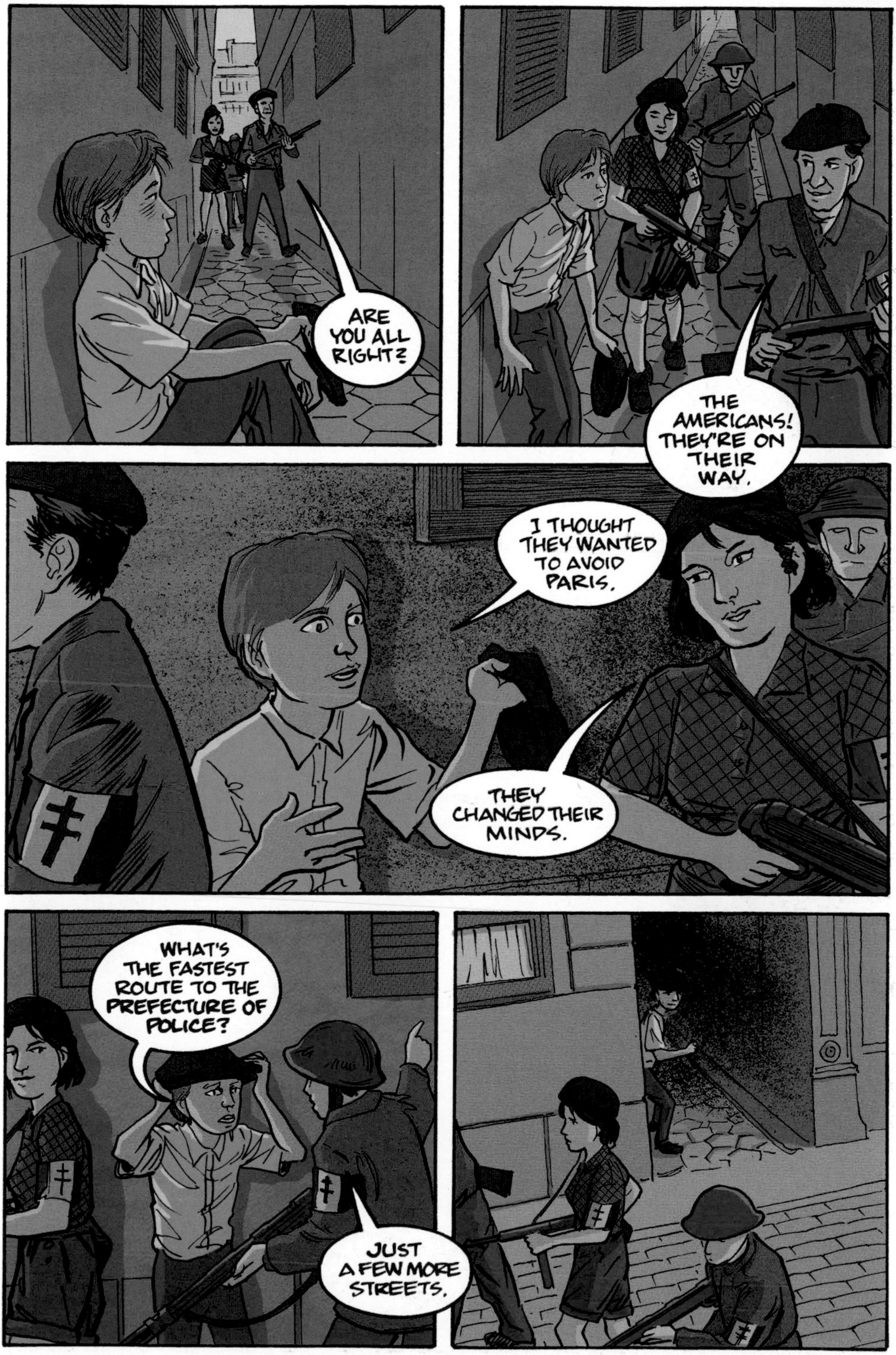
ARE YOU ALL RIGHT?
THE AMERICANS! THEY'RE ON THEIR WAY.
I THOUGHT THEY WANTED TO AVOID PARIS.
THEY CHANGED THEIR MINDS.
WHAT'S THE FASTEST ROUTE TO THE PREFECTURE OF POLICE?
JUST A FEW MORE STREETS.

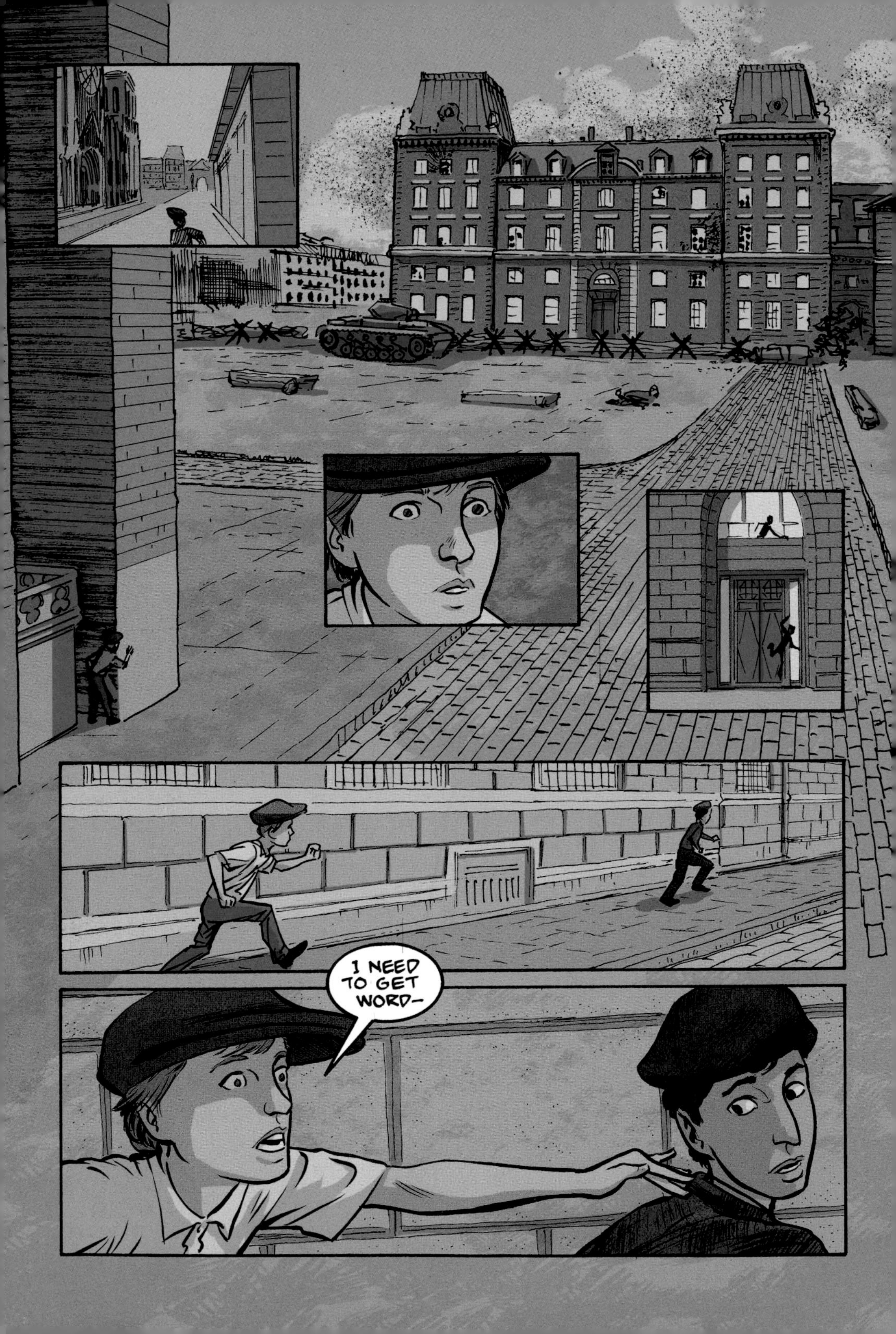
I NEED TO GET WORD-

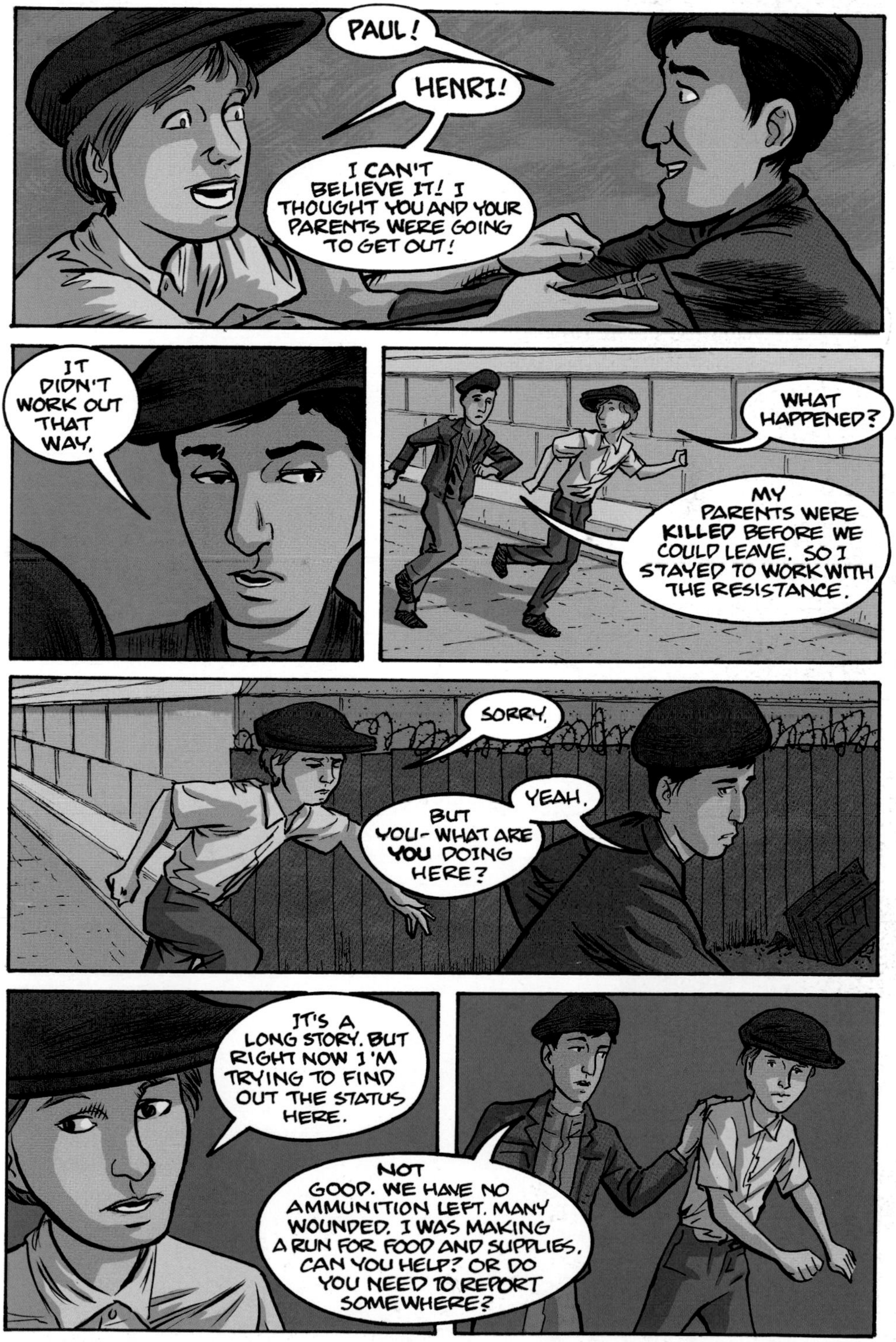
PAUL!
HENRI!
I CAN'T BELIEVE IT! I THOUGHT YOU AND YOUR PARENTS WERE GOING TO GET OUT!
IT DIDN'T WORK OUT THAT WAY.
WHAT HAPPENED?
MY PARENTS WERE KILLED BEFORE WE COULD LEAVE. SO I STAYED TO WORK WITH THE RESISTANCE.
SORRY.
YEAH.
BUT YOU- WHAT ARE YOU DOING HERE?
IT'S A LONG STORY. BUT RIGHT NOW I'M TRYING TO FIND OUT THE STATUS HERE.
NOT GOOD. WE HAVE NO AMMUNITION LEFT. MANY WOUNDED. I WAS MAKING A RUN FOR FOOD AND SUPPLIES. CAN YOU HELP? OR DO YOU NEED TO REPORT SOMEWHERE?

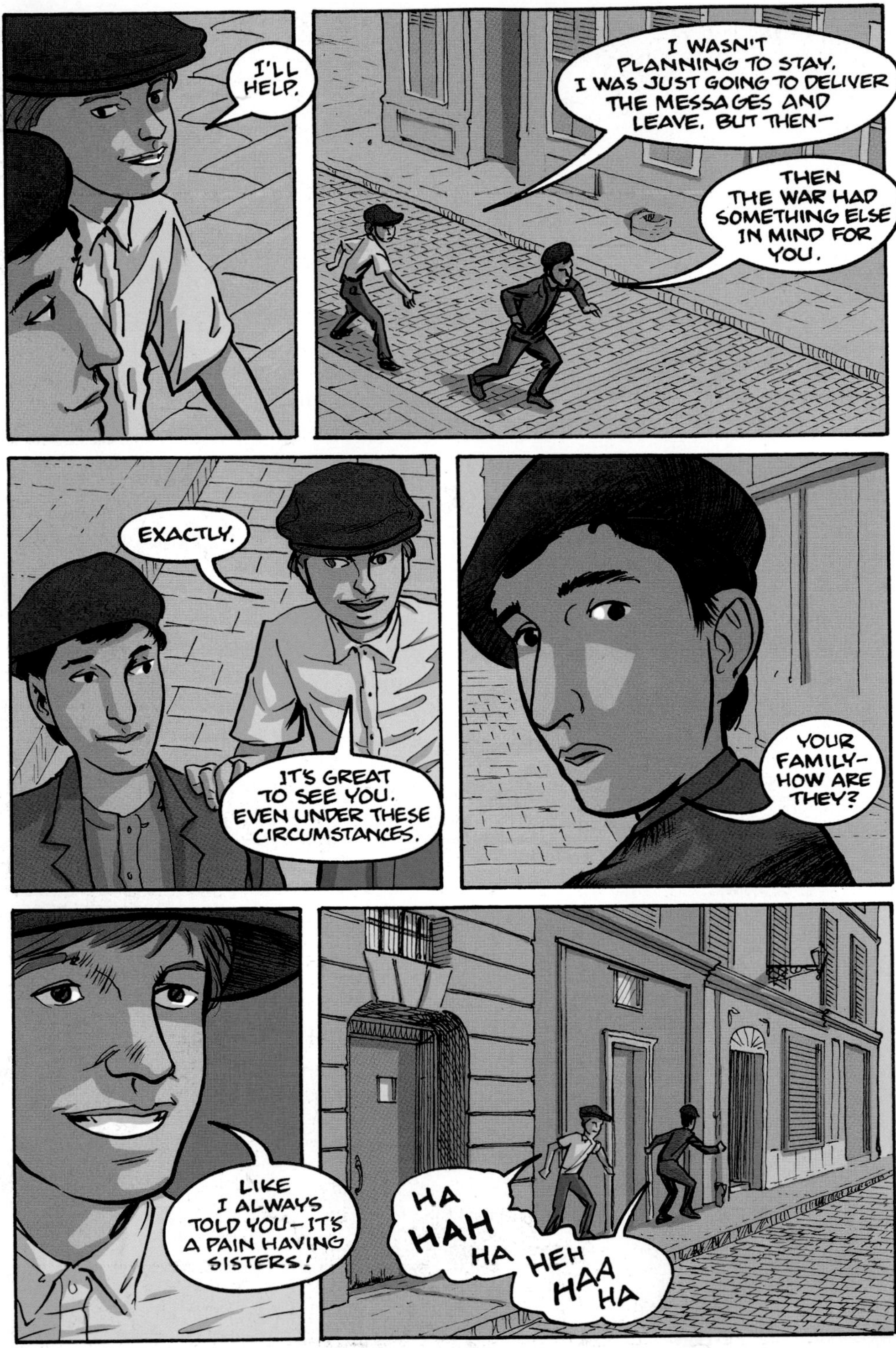

I'LL HELP.
I WASN'T PLANNING TO STAY. I WAS JUST GOING TO DELIVER THE MESSAGES AND LEAVE. BUT THEN—
THEN THE WAR HAD SOMETHING ELSE IN MIND FOR YOU.
EXACTLY.
IT'S GREAT TO SEE YOU. EVEN UNDER THESE CIRCUMSTANCES.
YOUR FAMILY— HOW ARE THEY?
LIKE I ALWAYS TOLD YOU—IT'S A PAIN HAVING SISTERS!
HA HAH HA
HEH HAA HA

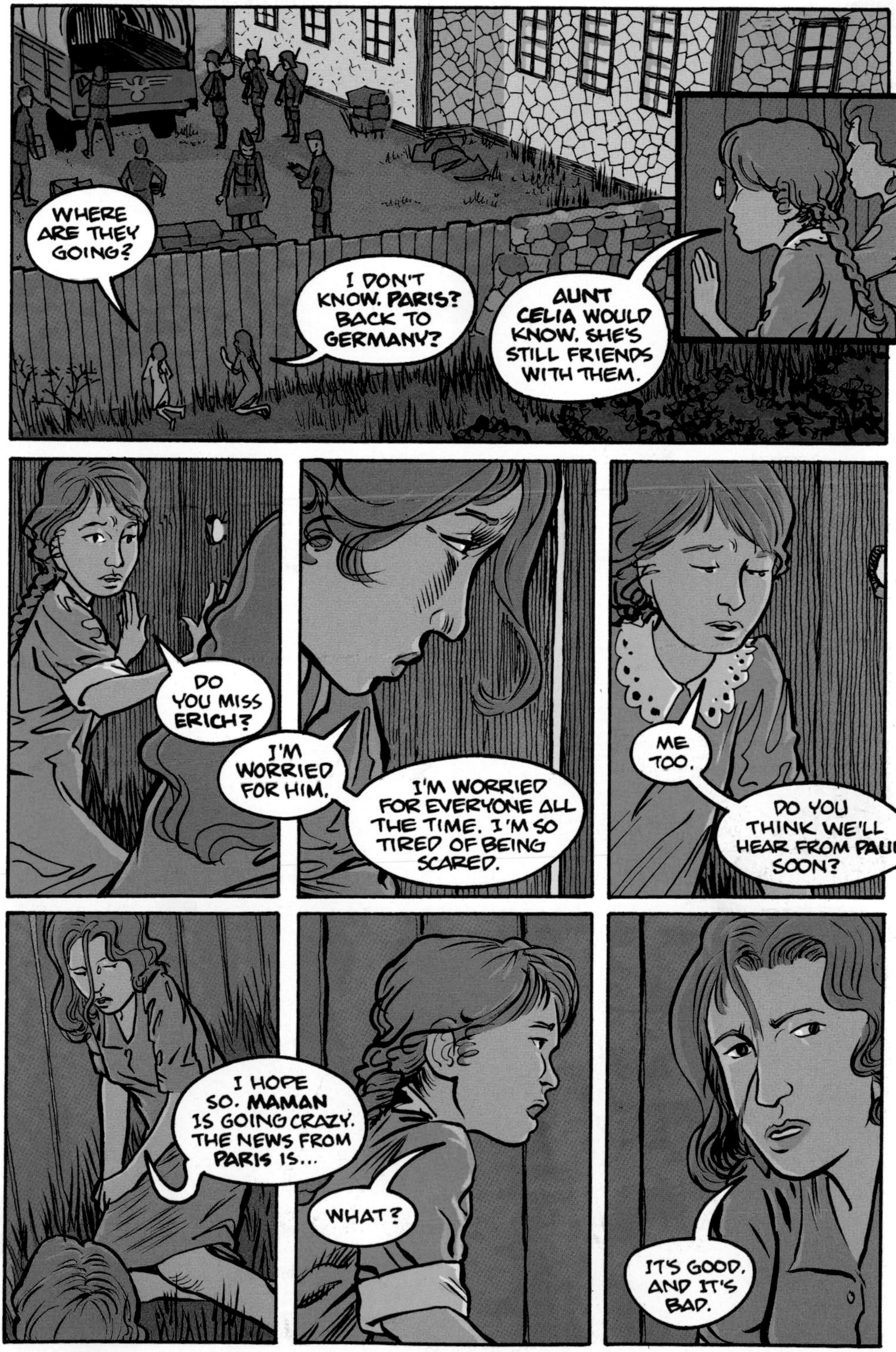
WHERE ARE THEY GOING?
I DON'T KNOW. PARIS? BACK TO GERMANY?
AUNT CELIA WOULD KNOW. SHE'S STILL FRIENDS WITH THEM.
DO YOU MISS ERICH?
I'M WORRIED FOR HIM.
I'M WORRIED FOR EVERYONE ALL THE TIME. I'M SO TIRED OF BEING SCARED.
ME TOO.
DO YOU THINK WE'LL HEAR FROM PAUL SOON?
I HOPE SO. MAMAN IS GOING CRAZY. THE NEWS FROM PARIS IS...
WHAT?
IT'S GOOD. AND IT'S BAD.

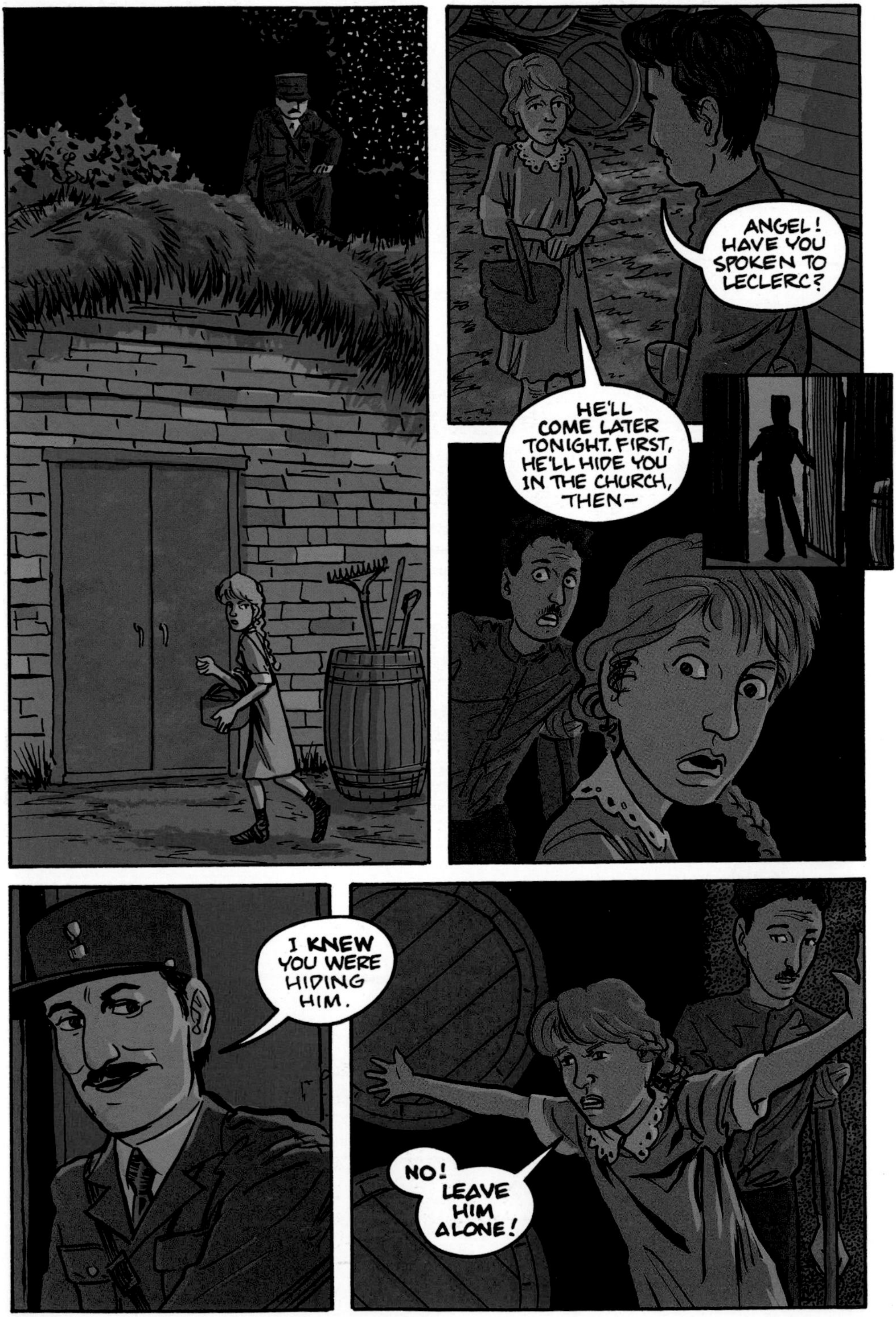
ANGEL! HAVE YOU SPOKEN TO LECLERC?
HE'LL COME LATER TONIGHT. FIRST, HE'LL HIDE YOU IN THE CHURCH, THEN–
I KNEW YOU WERE HIDING HIM.
NO! LEAVE HIM ALONE!

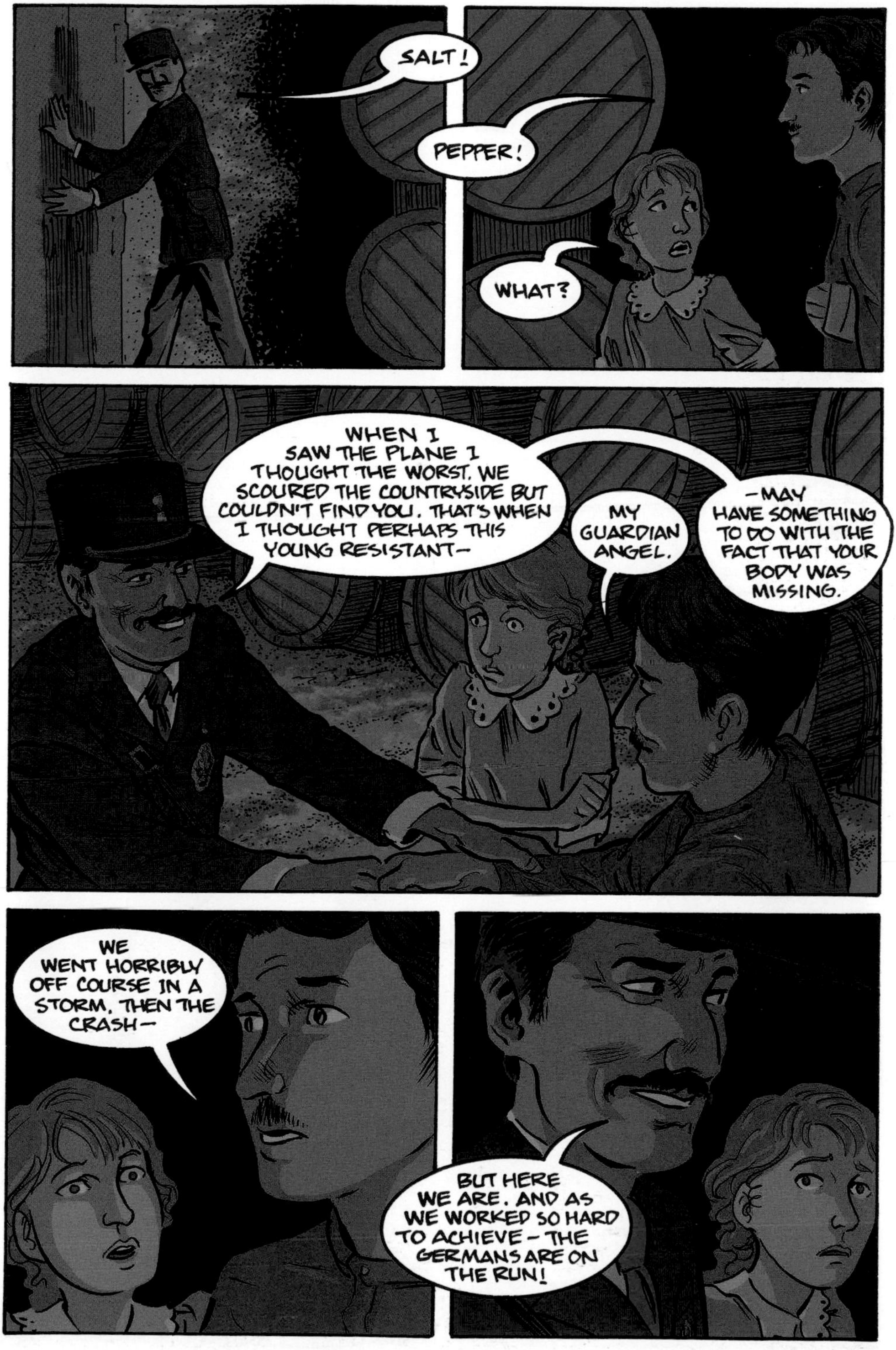
SALT!
PEPPER!
WHAT?
WHEN I SAW THE PLANE I THOUGHT THE WORST. WE SCOURED THE COUNTRYSIDE BUT COULDN'T FIND YOU. THAT'S WHEN I THOUGHT PERHAPS THIS YOUNG RESISTANT—
MY GUARDIAN ANGEL.
—MAY HAVE SOMETHING TO DO WITH THE FACT THAT YOUR BODY WAS MISSING.
WE WENT HORRIBLY OFF COURSE IN A STORM, THEN THE CRASH—
BUT HERE WE ARE. AND AS WE WORKED SO HARD TO ACHIEVE—THE GERMANS ARE ON THE RUN!

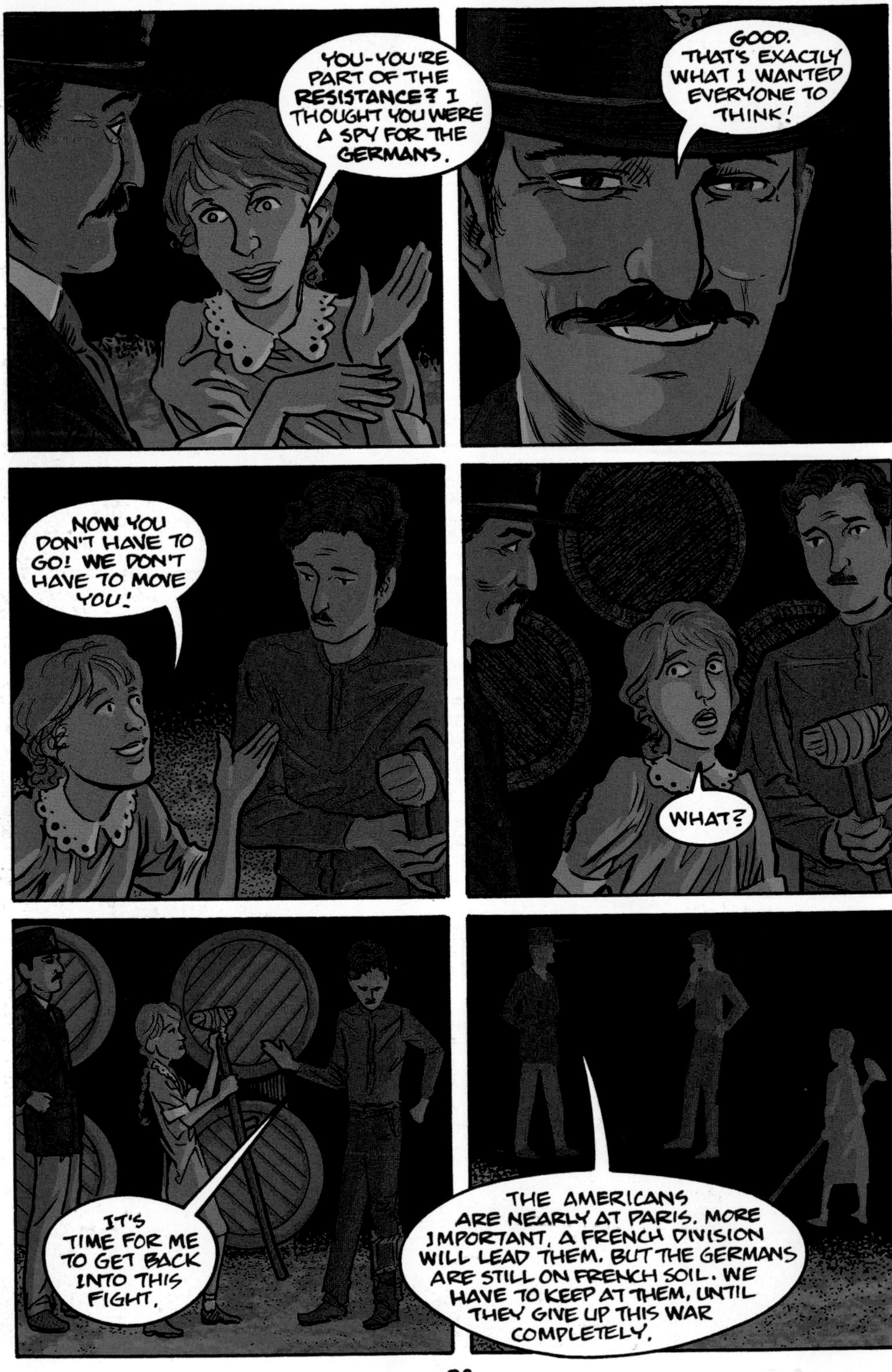
YOU-YOU'RE PART OF THE RESISTANCE? I THOUGHT YOU WERE A SPY FOR THE GERMANS.
GOOD. THAT'S EXACTLY WHAT I WANTED EVERYONE TO THINK!
NOW YOU DON'T HAVE TO GO! WE DON'T HAVE TO MOVE YOU!
WHAT?
IT'S TIME FOR ME TO GET BACK INTO THIS FIGHT.
THE AMERICANS ARE NEARLY AT PARIS. MORE IMPORTANT, A FRENCH DIVISION WILL LEAD THEM. BUT THE GERMANS ARE STILL ON FRENCH SOIL. WE HAVE TO KEEP AT THEM, UNTIL THEY GIVE UP THIS WAR COMPLETELY.

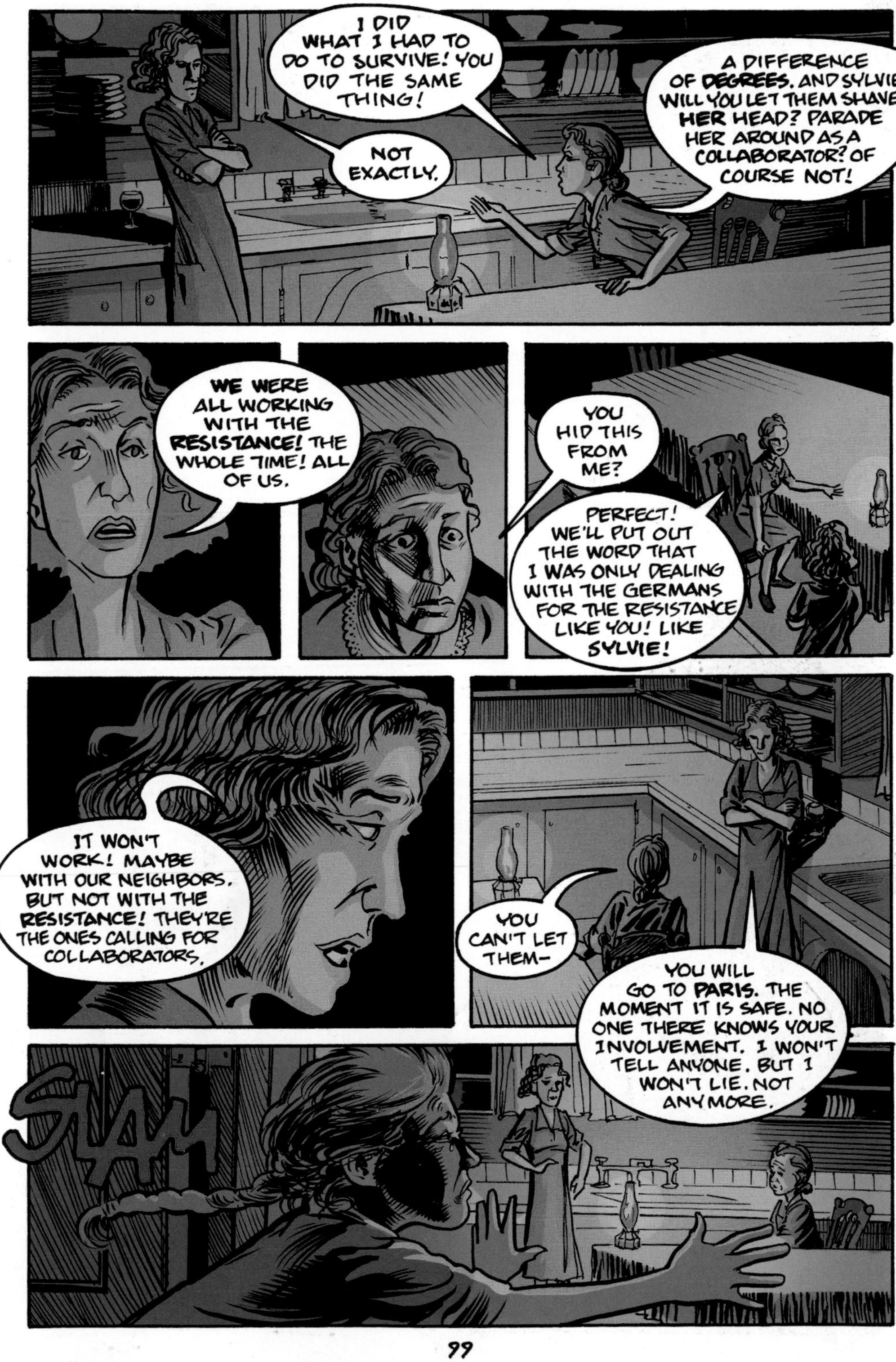
I DID WHAT I HAD TO DO TO SURVIVE! YOU DID THE SAME THING!
NOT EXACTLY.
A DIFFERENCE OF DEGREES. AND SYLVIE! WILL YOU LET THEM SHAVE HER HEAD? PARADE HER AROUND AS A COLLABORATOR? OF COURSE NOT!
WE WERE ALL WORKING WITH THE RESISTANCE! THE WHOLE TIME! ALL OF US.
YOU HID THIS FROM ME?
PERFECT! WE'LL PUT OUT THE WORD THAT I WAS ONLY DEALING WITH THE GERMANS FOR THE RESISTANCE LIKE YOU! LIKE SYLVIE!
IT WON'T WORK! MAYBE WITH OUR NEIGHBORS, BUT NOT WITH THE RESISTANCE! THEY'RE THE ONES CALLING FOR COLLABORATORS.
YOU CAN'T LET THEM-
YOU WILL GO TO PARIS. THE MOMENT IT IS SAFE. NO ONE THERE KNOWS YOUR INVOLVEMENT. I WON'T TELL ANYONE. BUT I WON'T LIE. NOT ANYMORE.
SLAP

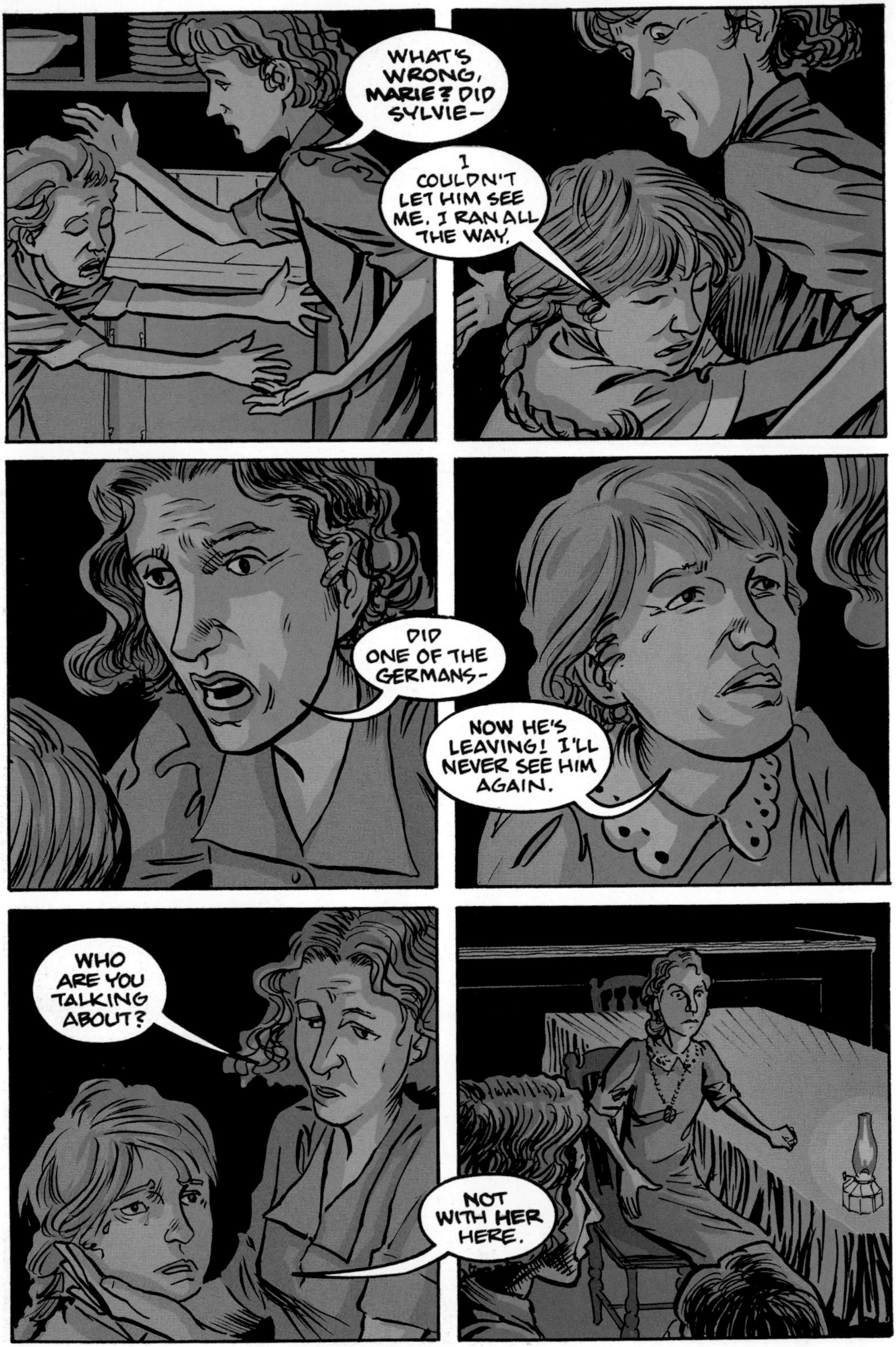
WHAT'S WRONG, MARIE? DID SYLVIE-
I COULDN'T LET HIM SEE ME. I RAN ALL THE WAY.
DID ONE OF THE GERMANS-
NOW HE'S LEAVING! I'LL NEVER SEE HIM AGAIN.
WHO ARE YOU TALKING ABOUT?
NOT WITH HER HERE.

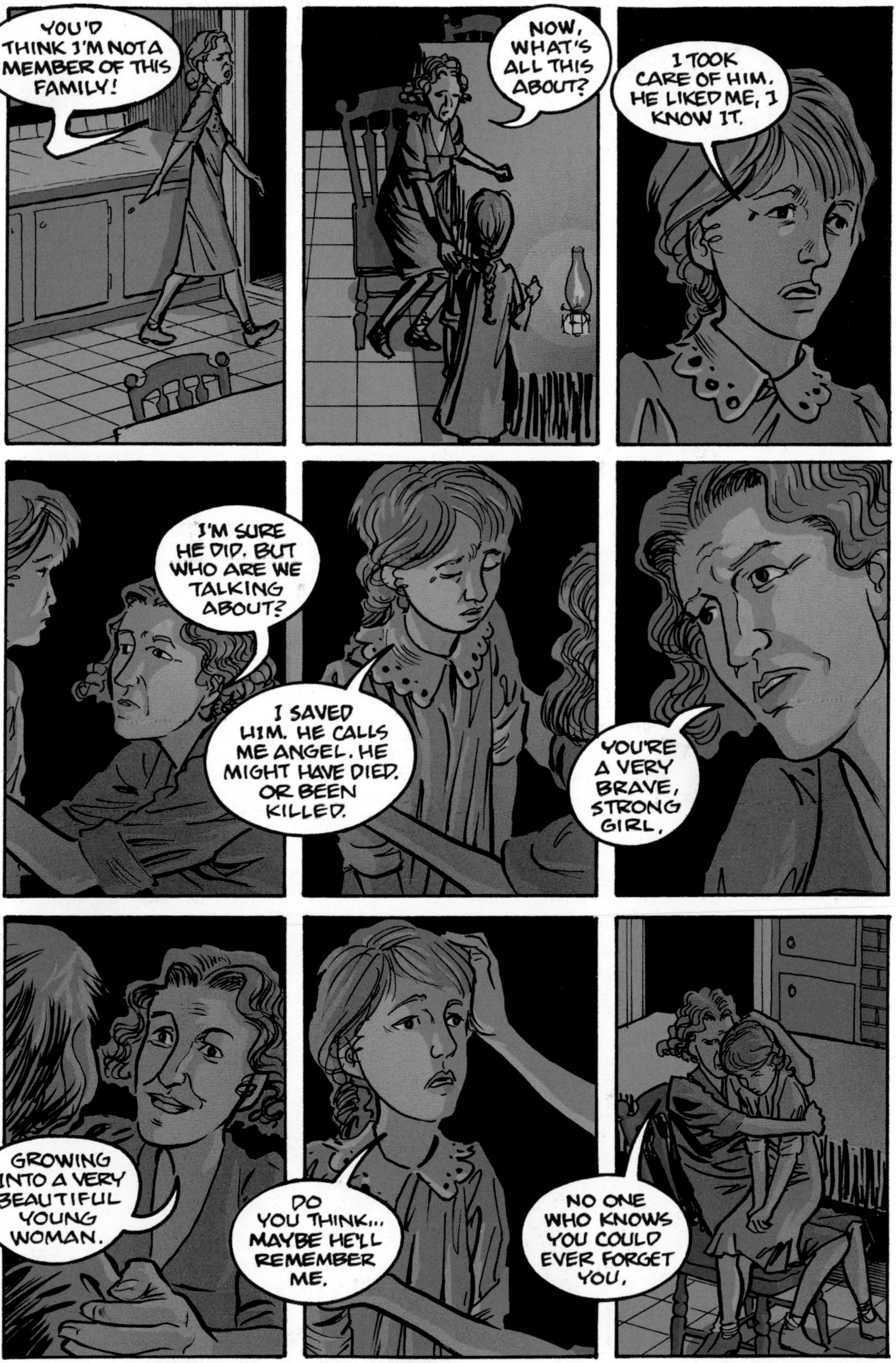
YOU'D THINK I'M NOT A MEMBER OF THIS FAMILY!
NOW, WHAT'S ALL THIS ABOUT?
I TOOK CARE OF HIM. HE LIKED ME, I KNOW IT.
I'M SURE HE DID. BUT WHO ARE WE TALKING ABOUT?
I SAVED HIM. HE CALLS ME ANGEL. HE MIGHT HAVE DIED. OR BEEN KILLED.
YOU'RE A VERY BRAVE, STRONG GIRL,
GROWING INTO A VERY BEAUTIFUL YOUNG WOMAN.
DO YOU THINK... MAYBE HE'LL REMEMBER ME.
NO ONE WHO KNOWS YOU COULD EVER FORGET YOU.

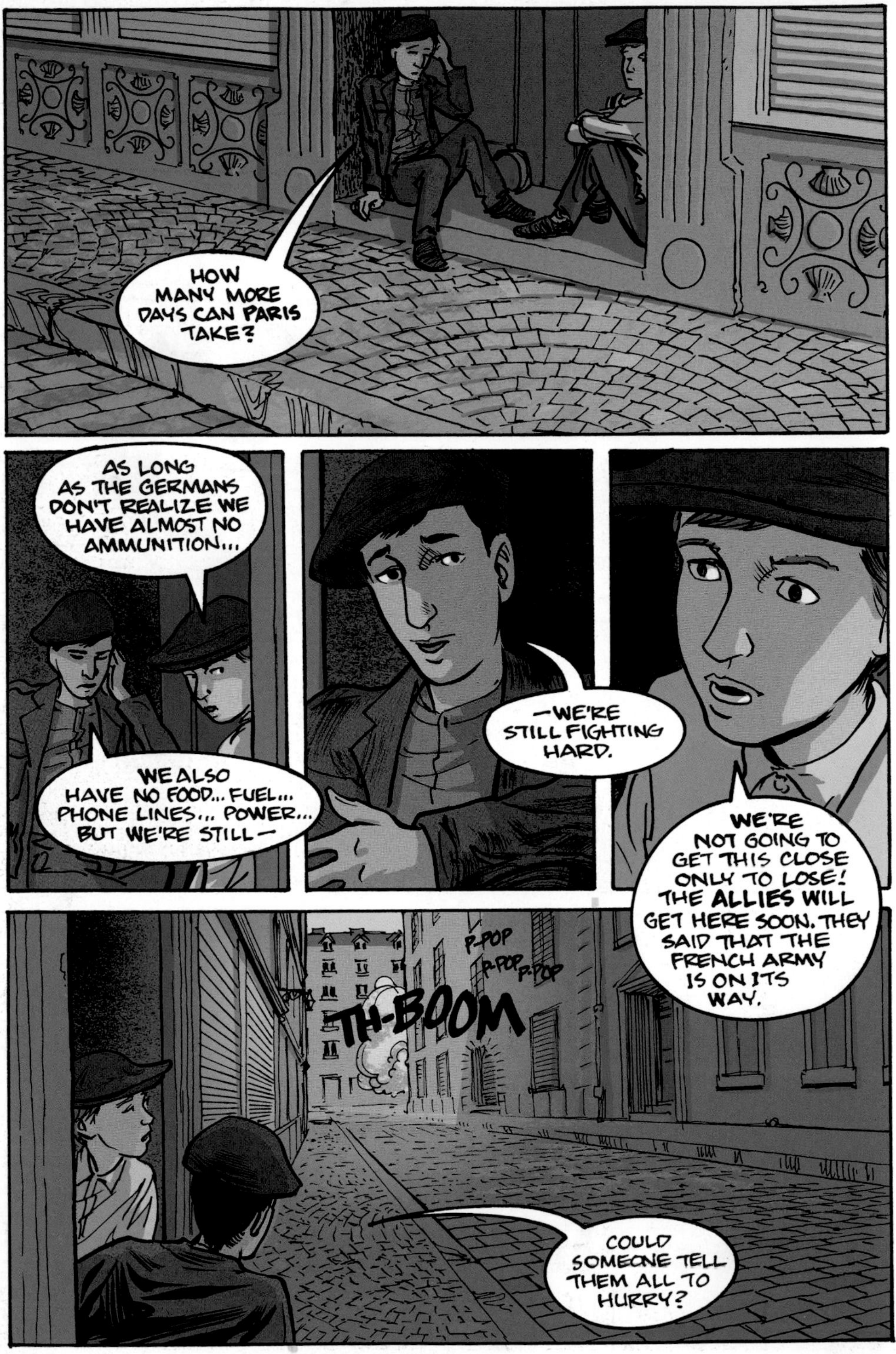
HOW MANY MORE DAYS CAN PARIS TAKE?
AS LONG AS THE GERMANS DON'T REALIZE WE HAVE ALMOST NO AMMUNITION...
WE ALSO HAVE NO FOOD... FUEL... PHONE LINES... POWER... BUT WE'RE STILL—
—WE'RE STILL FIGHTING HARD.
WE'RE NOT GOING TO GET THIS CLOSE ONLY TO LOSE! THE ALLIES WILL GET HERE SOON. THEY SAID THAT THE FRENCH ARMY IS ON ITS WAY.
P-POP
P-POP P-POP
TH-BOOM
COULD SOMEONE TELL THEM ALL TO HURRY?

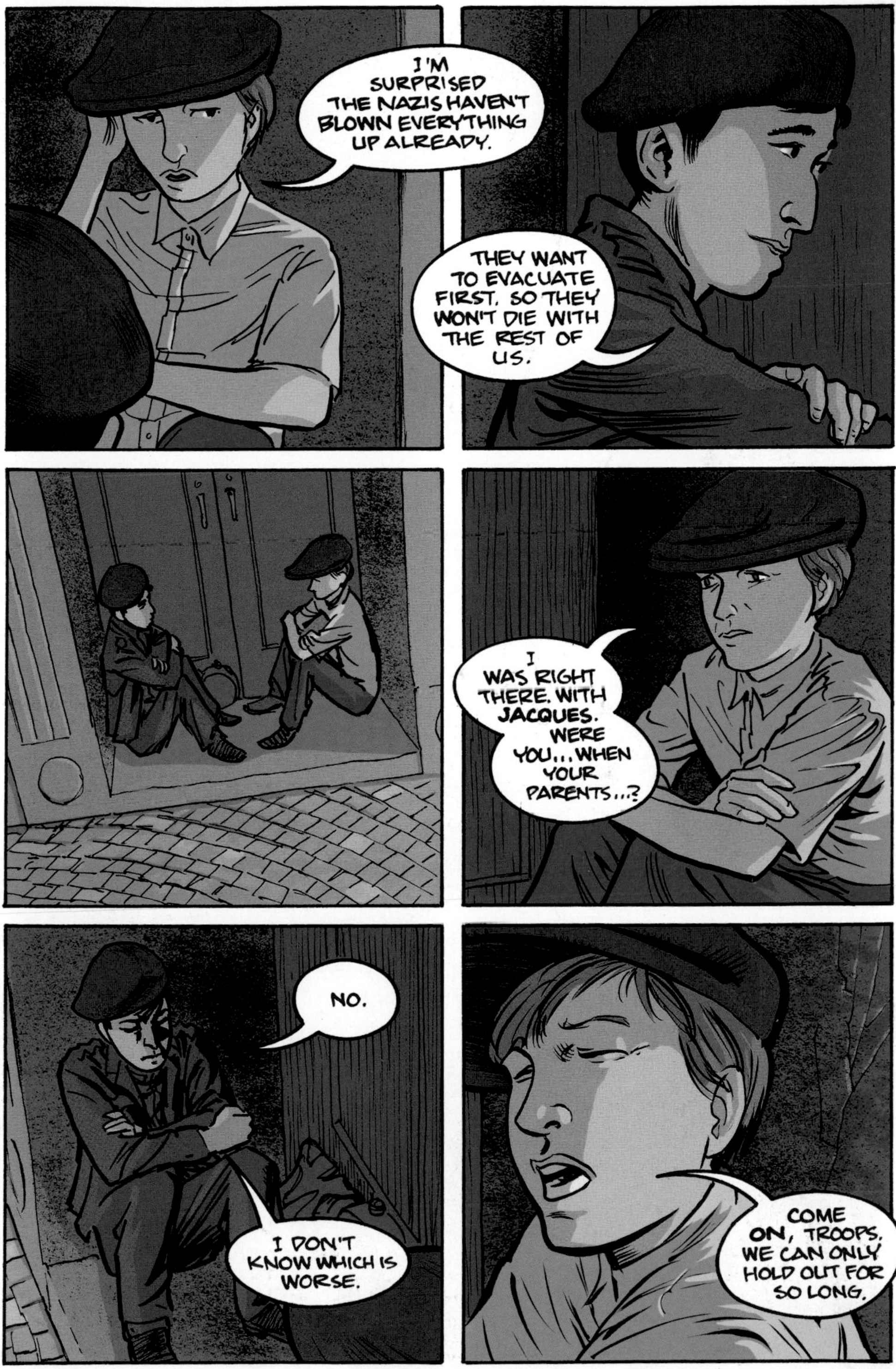
I'M SURPRISED THE NAZIS HAVEN'T BLOWN EVERYTHING UP ALREADY.
THEY WANT TO EVACUATE FIRST. SO THEY WON'T DIE WITH THE REST OF US.
I WAS RIGHT THERE. WITH JACQUES. WERE YOU... WHEN YOUR PARENTS...?
NO.
I DON'T KNOW WHICH IS WORSE.
COME ON, TROOPS. WE CAN ONLY HOLD OUT FOR SO LONG.

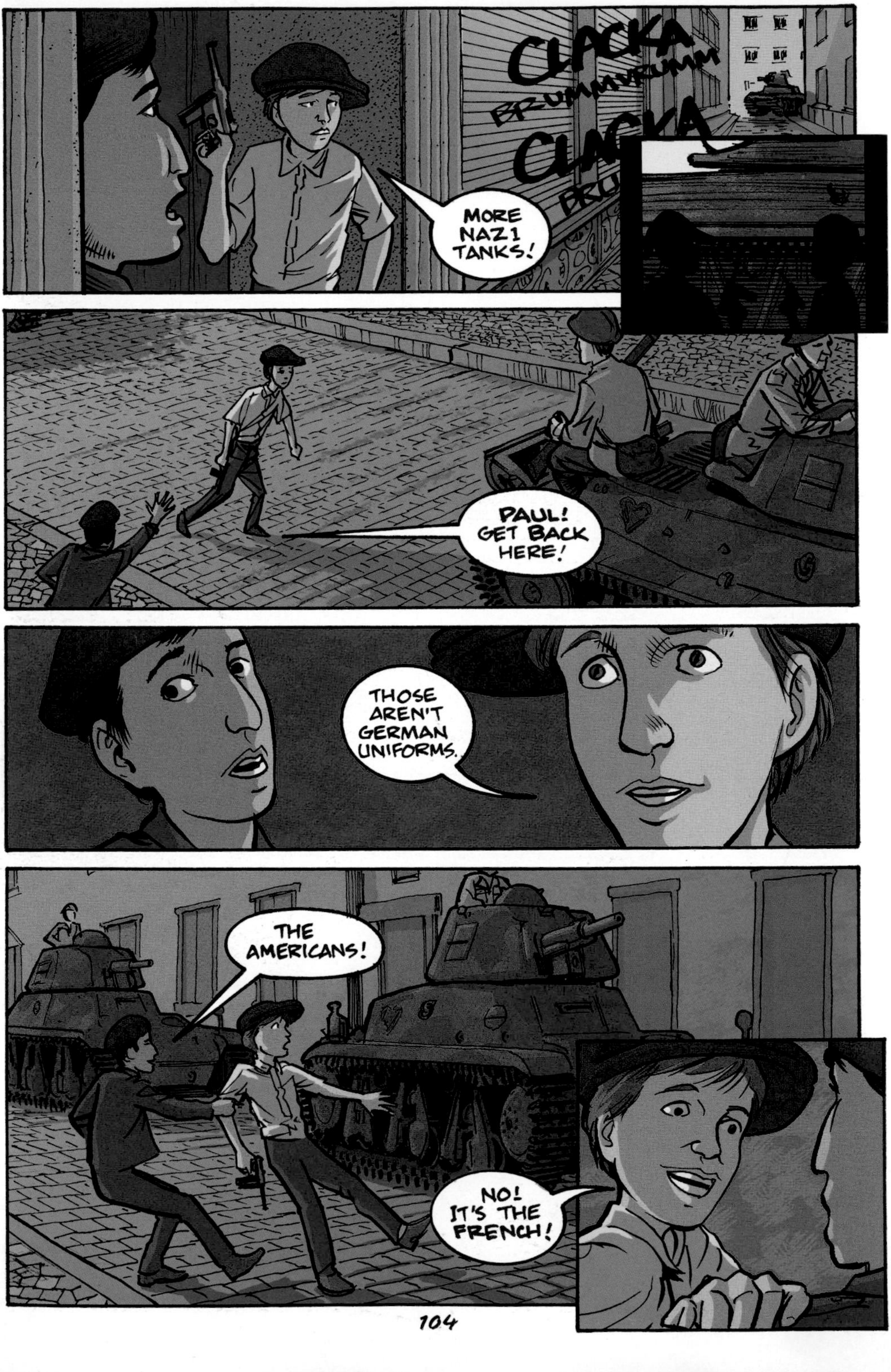
CLACKA
BRUMMVRUMM
CLACKA
MORE NAZI TANKS!
PAUL! GET BACK HERE!
THOSE AREN'T GERMAN UNIFORMS.
THE AMERICANS!
NO! IT'S THE FRENCH!

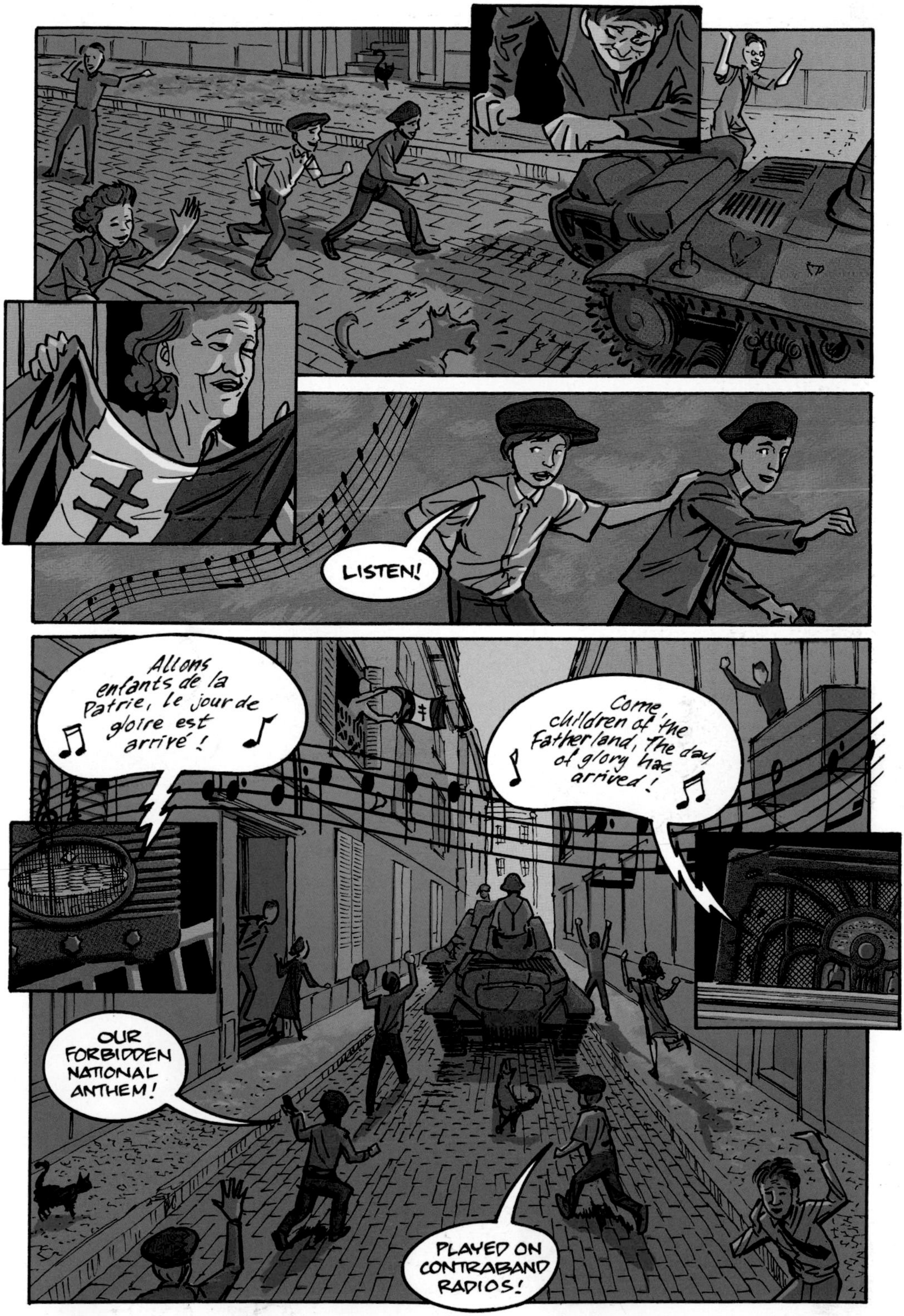
LISTEN!
Allons enfants de la Patrie, le jour de gloire est arrivé!
Come children of the Fatherland, the day of glory has arrived!
OUR FORBIDDEN NATIONAL ANTHEM!
PLAYED ON CONTRABAND RADIOS!

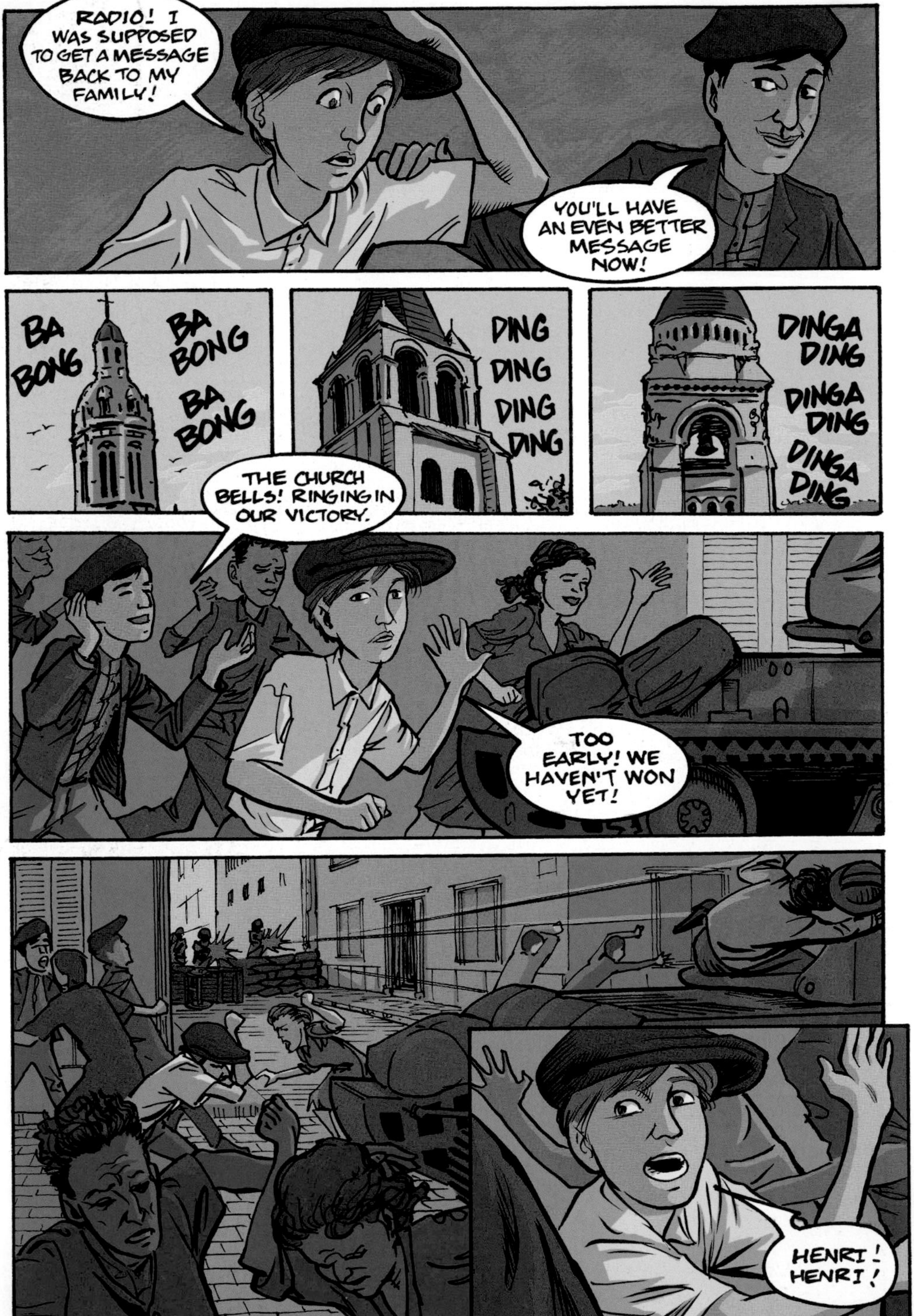
RADIO! I WAS SUPPOSED TO GET A MESSAGE BACK TO MY FAMILY!
YOU'LL HAVE AN EVEN BETTER MESSAGE NOW!
BA BONG
BA BONG
BA BONG
DING DING DING DING
DINGA DING
DINGA DING
DINGA DING
THE CHURCH BELLS! RINGING IN OUR VICTORY.
TOO EARLY! WE HAVEN'T WON YET!
HENRI! HENRI!

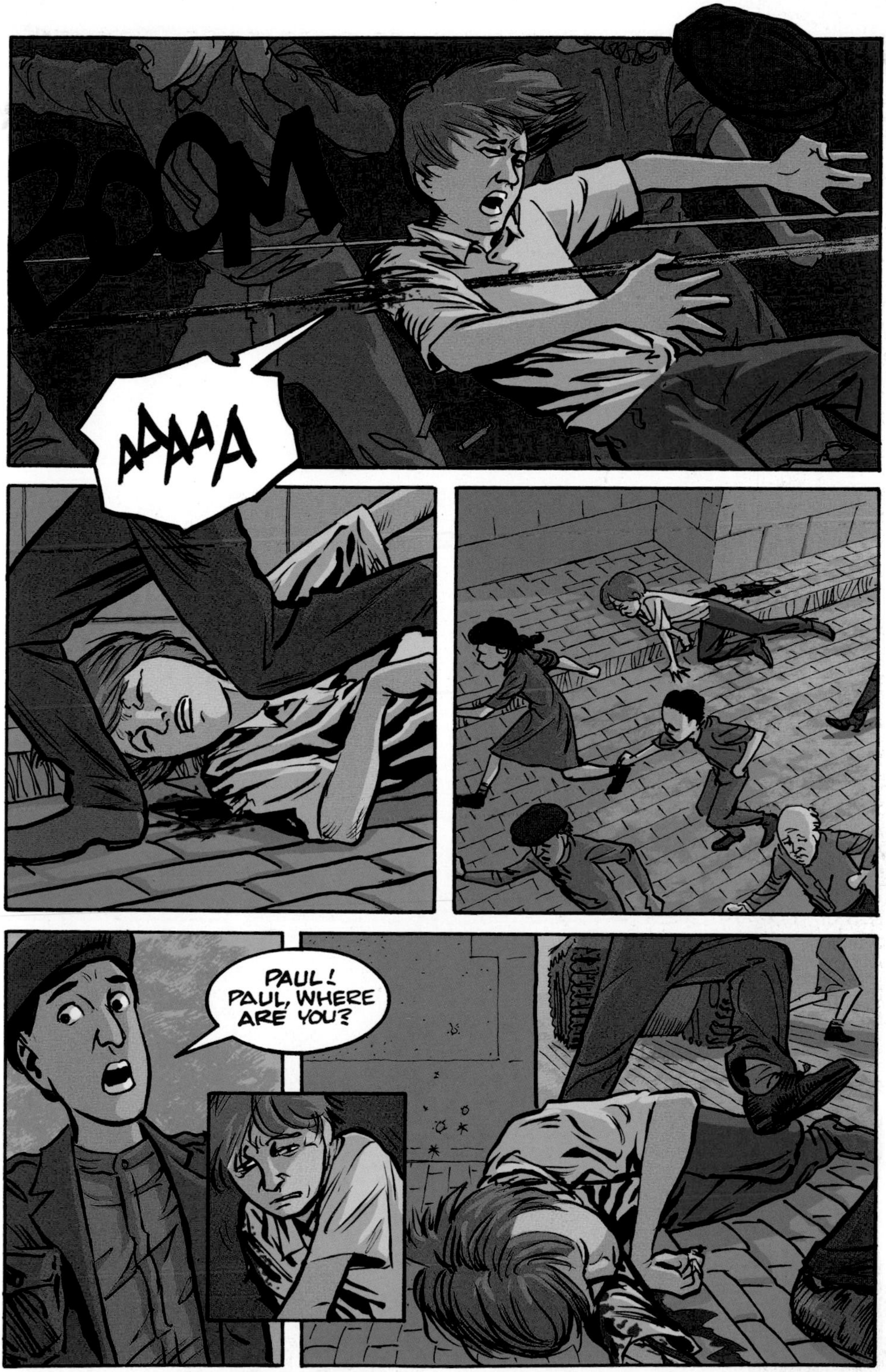
BOOM
AAAAA
PAUL! PAUL, WHERE ARE YOU?

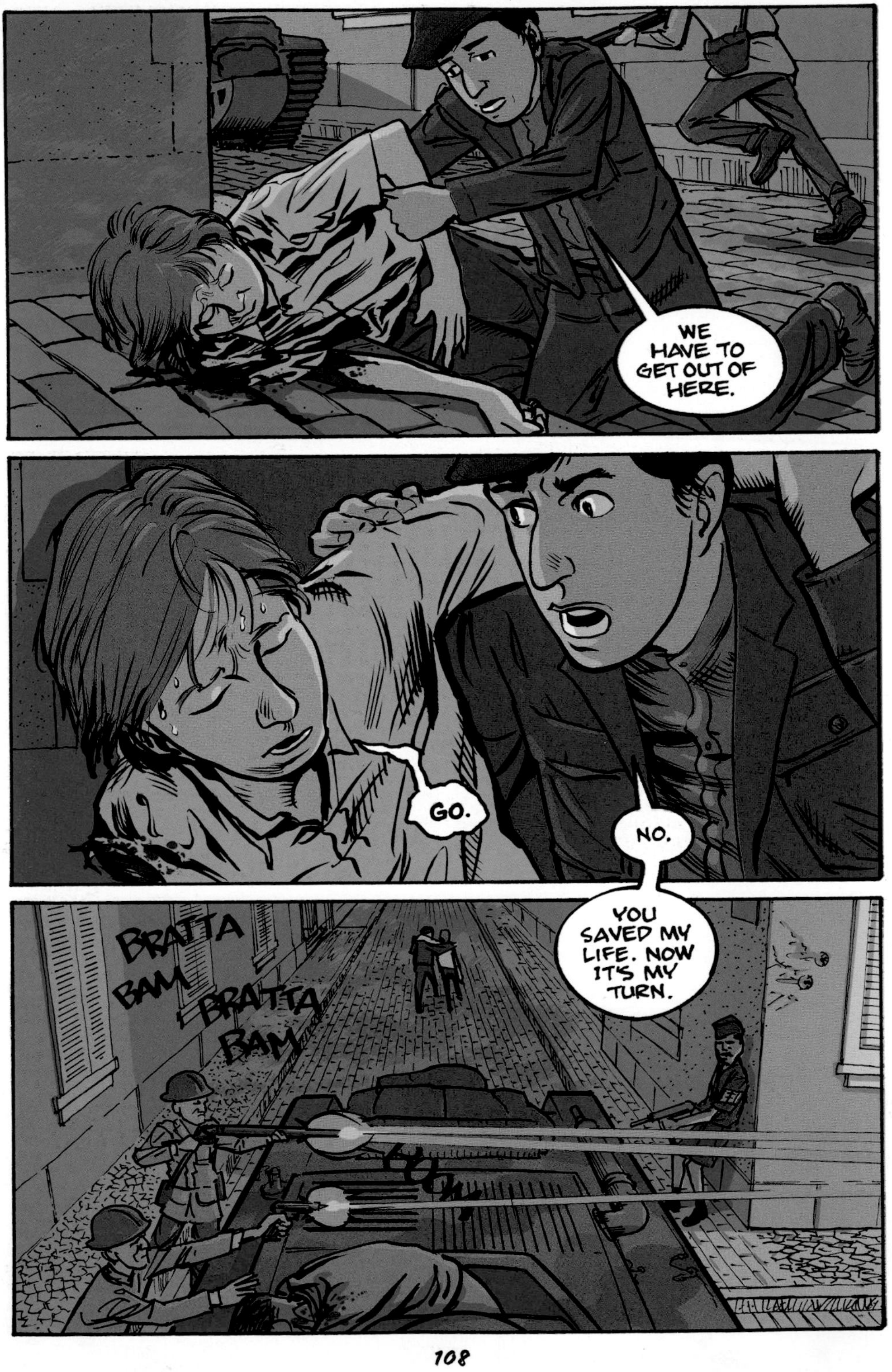
WE HAVE TO GET OUT OF HERE.
GO.
NO.
YOU SAVED MY LIFE. NOW IT'S MY TURN.
BRATTA BAM
BRATTA BAM

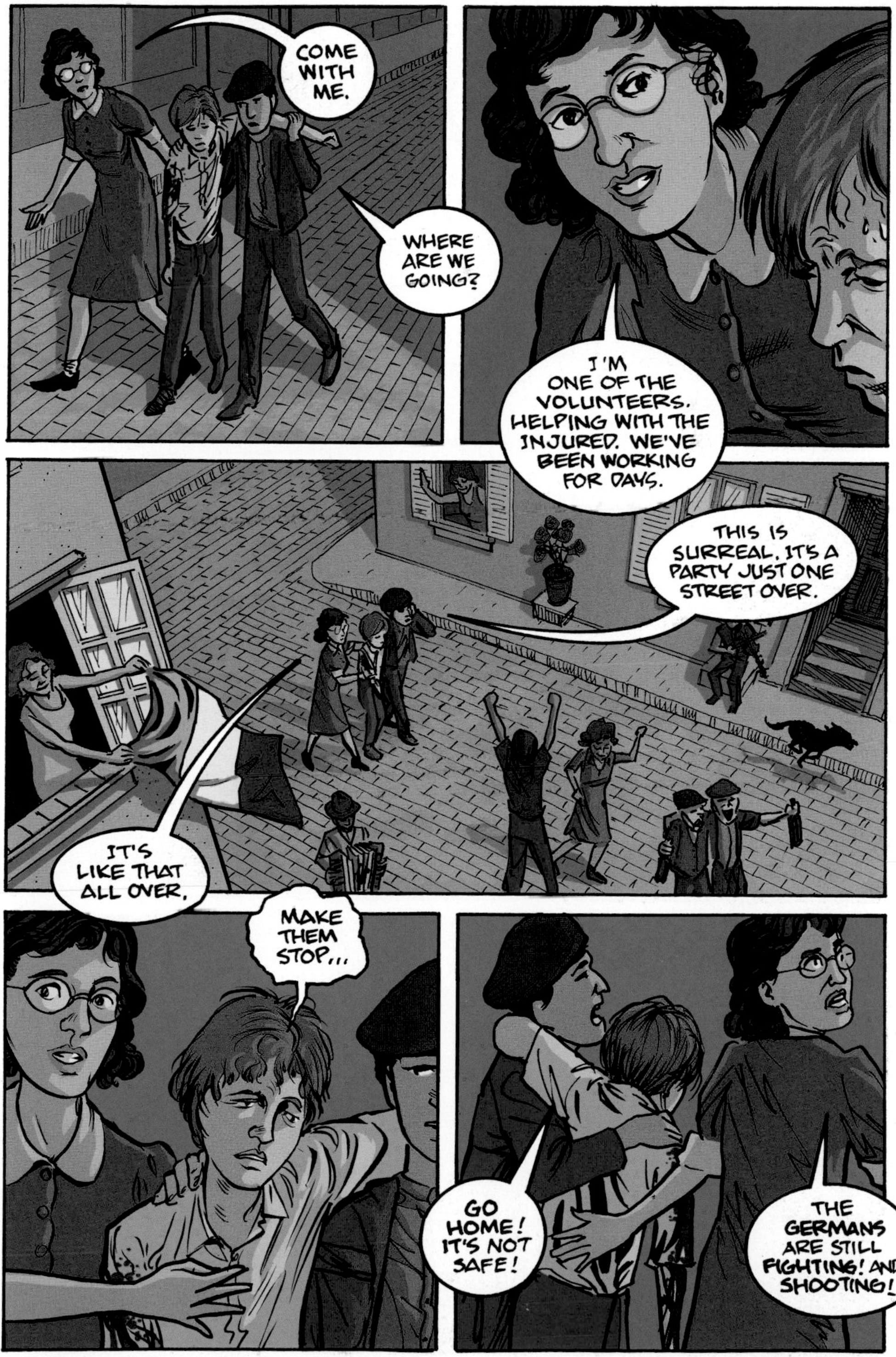
COME WITH ME.
WHERE ARE WE GOING?
I'M ONE OF THE VOLUNTEERS. HELPING WITH THE INJURED. WE'VE BEEN WORKING FOR DAYS.
THIS IS SURREAL. IT'S A PARTY JUST ONE STREET OVER.
IT'S LIKE THAT ALL OVER.
MAKE THEM STOP...
GO HOME! IT'S NOT SAFE!
THE GERMANS ARE STILL FIGHTING! AND SHOOTING!

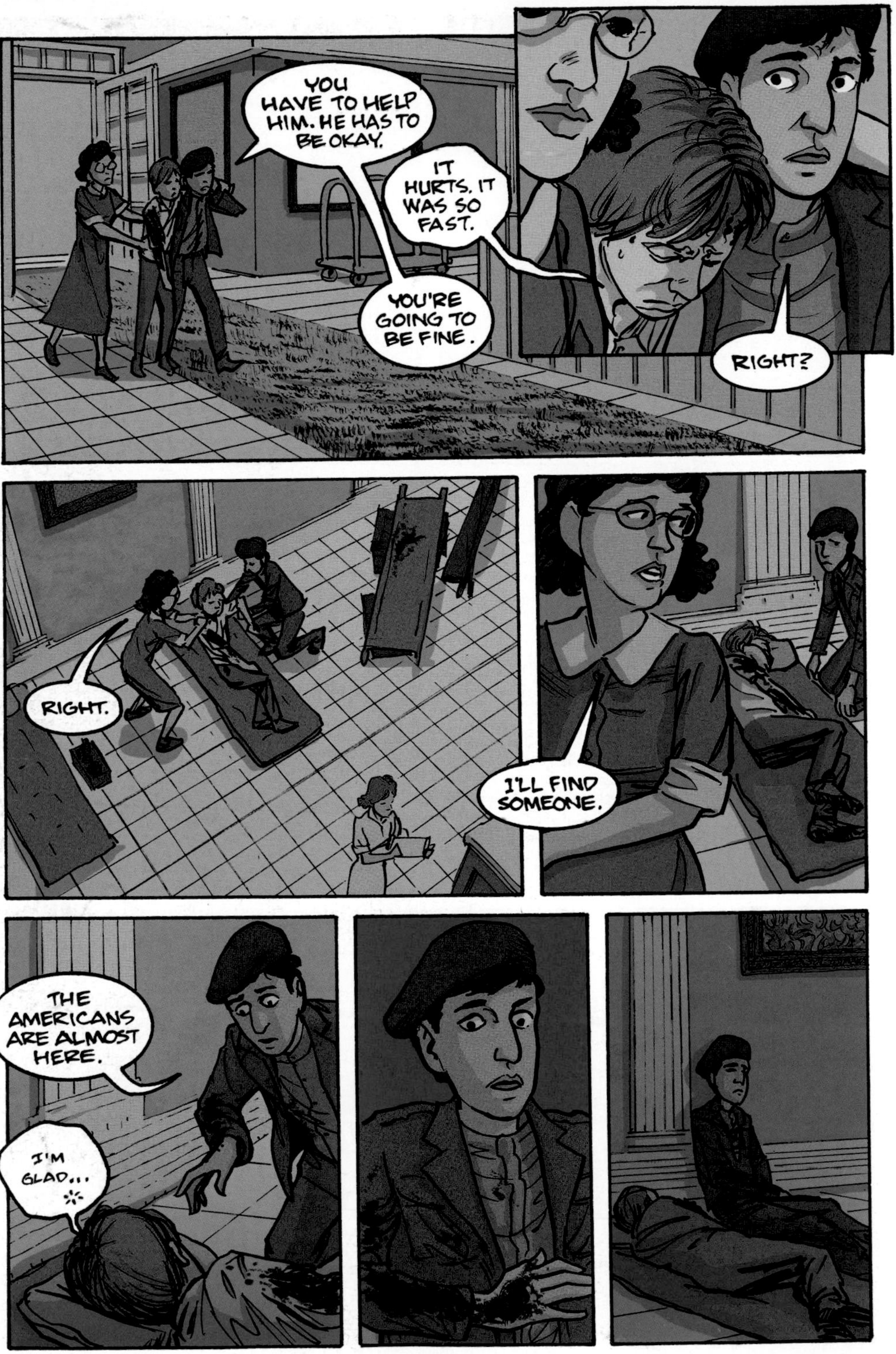
YOU HAVE TO HELP HIM. HE HAS TO BE OKAY.
IT HURTS. IT WAS SO FAST.
YOU'RE GOING TO BE FINE.
RIGHT?
RIGHT.
I'LL FIND SOMEONE.
THE AMERICANS ARE ALMOST HERE.
I'M GLAD...

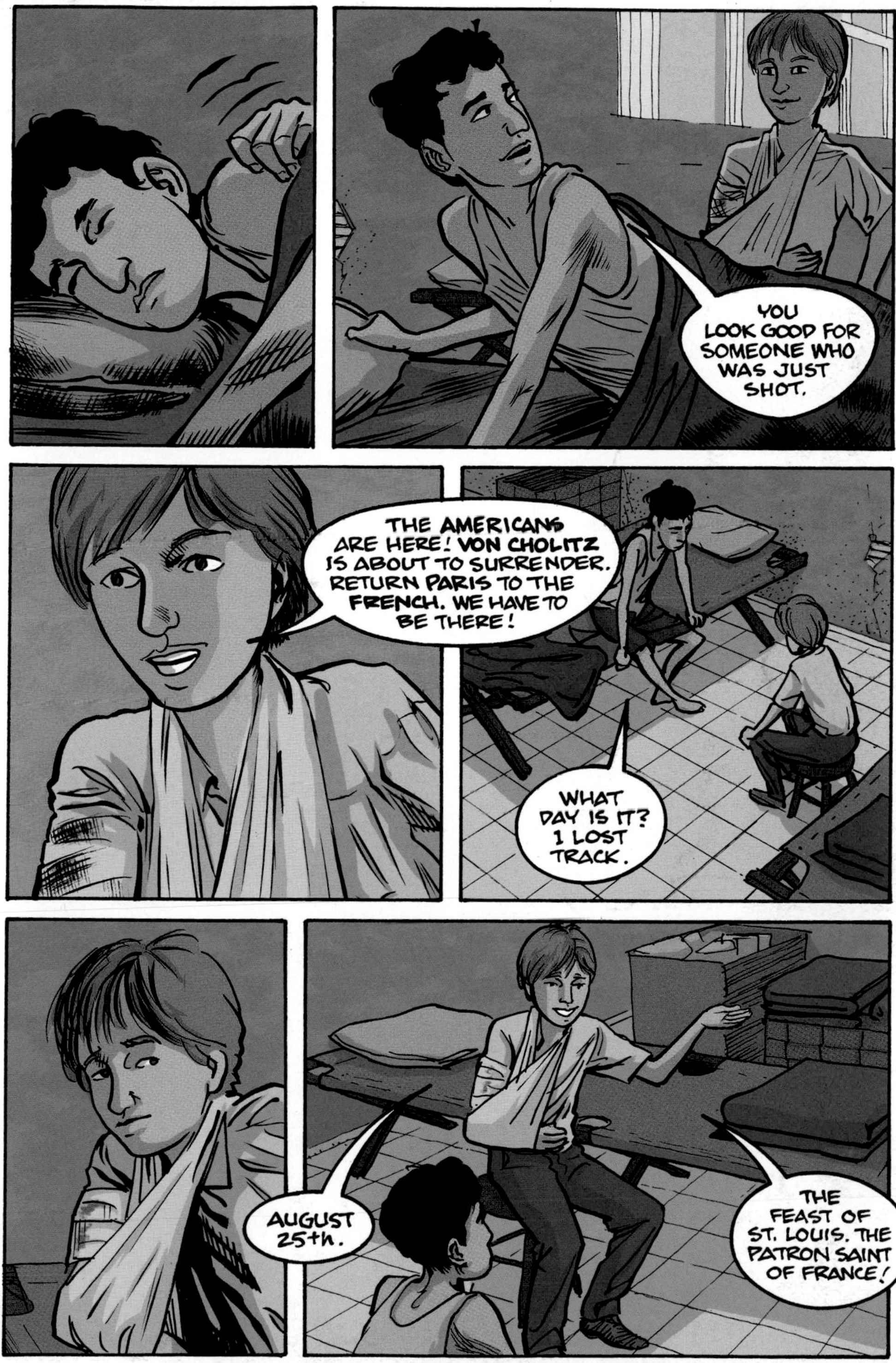
YOU LOOK GOOD FOR SOMEONE WHO WAS JUST SHOT.
THE AMERICANS ARE HERE! VON CHOLITZ IS ABOUT TO SURRENDER. RETURN PARIS TO THE FRENCH. WE HAVE TO BE THERE!
WHAT DAY IS IT? I LOST TRACK.
AUGUST 25th.
THE FEAST OF ST. LOUIS. THE PATRON SAINT OF FRANCE!

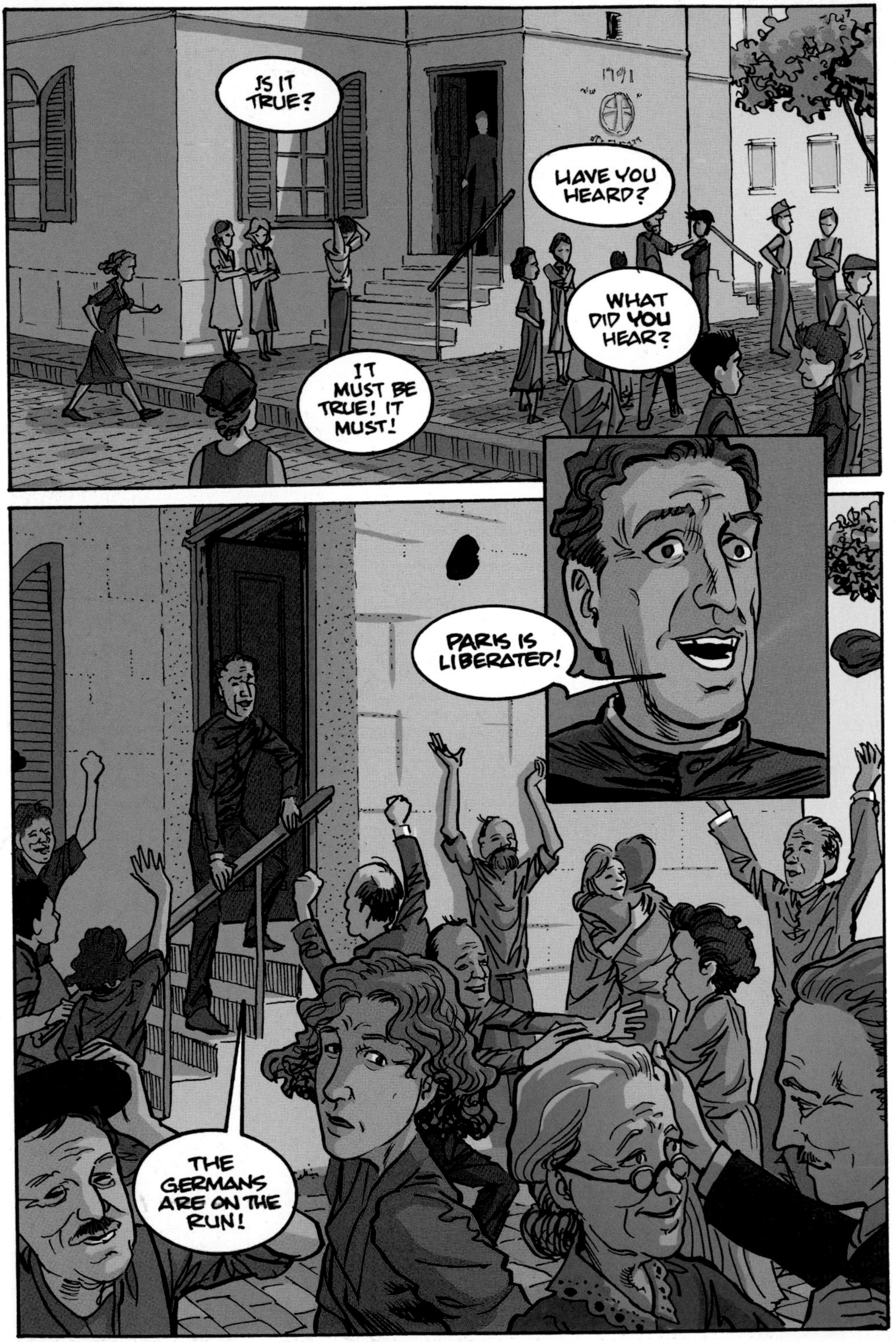
IS IT TRUE?
HAVE YOU HEARD?
WHAT DID YOU HEAR?
IT MUST BE TRUE! IT MUST!
PARIS IS LIBERATED!
THE GERMANS ARE ON THE RUN!

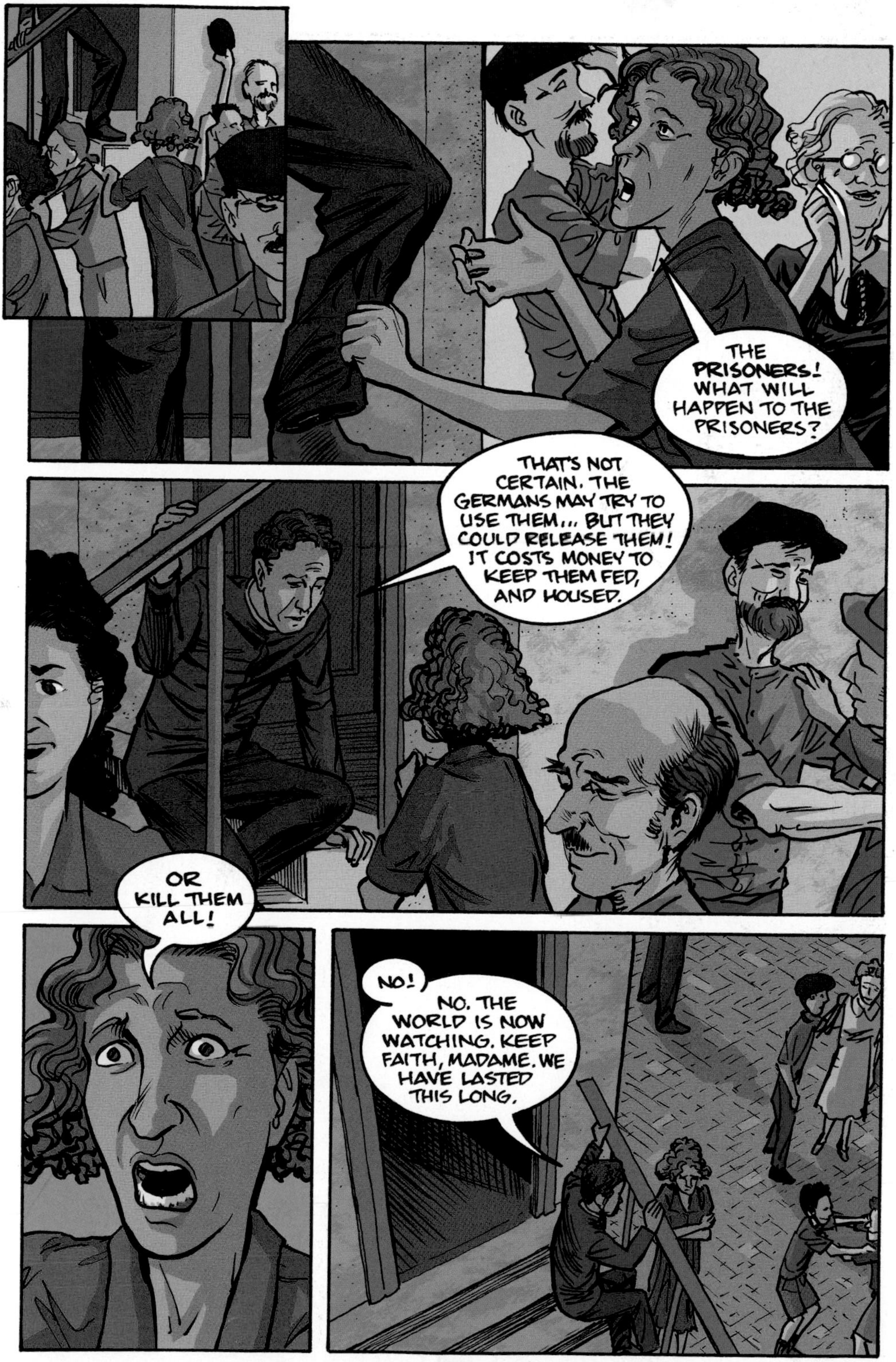
THE PRISONERS! WHAT WILL HAPPEN TO THE PRISONERS?
THAT'S NOT CERTAIN. THE GERMANS MAY TRY TO USE THEM... BUT THEY COULD RELEASE THEM! IT COSTS MONEY TO KEEP THEM FED, AND HOUSED.
OR KILL THEM ALL!
NO!
NO. THE WORLD IS NOW WATCHING. KEEP FAITH, MADAME. WE HAVE LASTED THIS LONG.

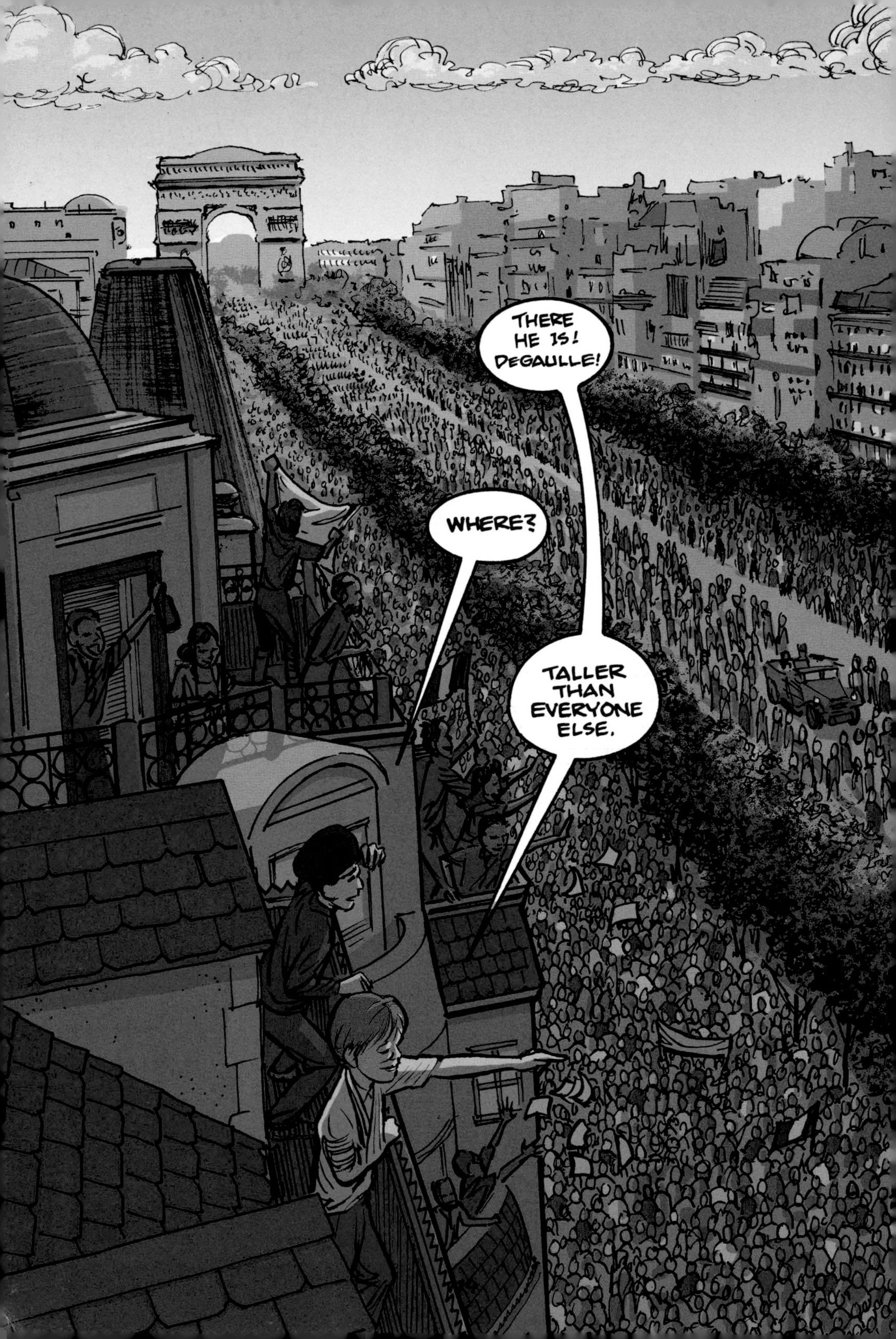
THERE HE IS! DEGAULLE!
WHERE?
TALLER THAN EVERYONE ELSE.

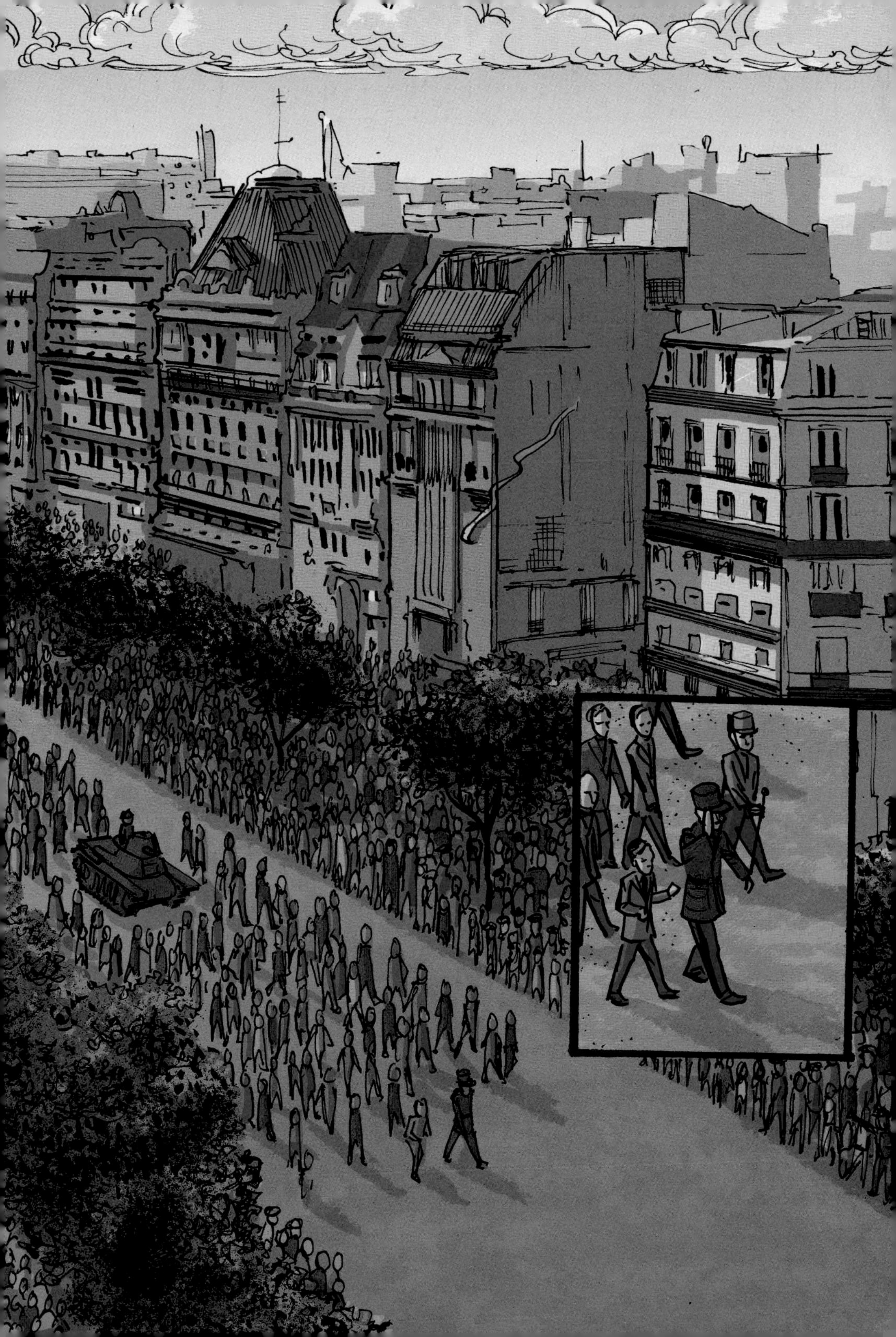

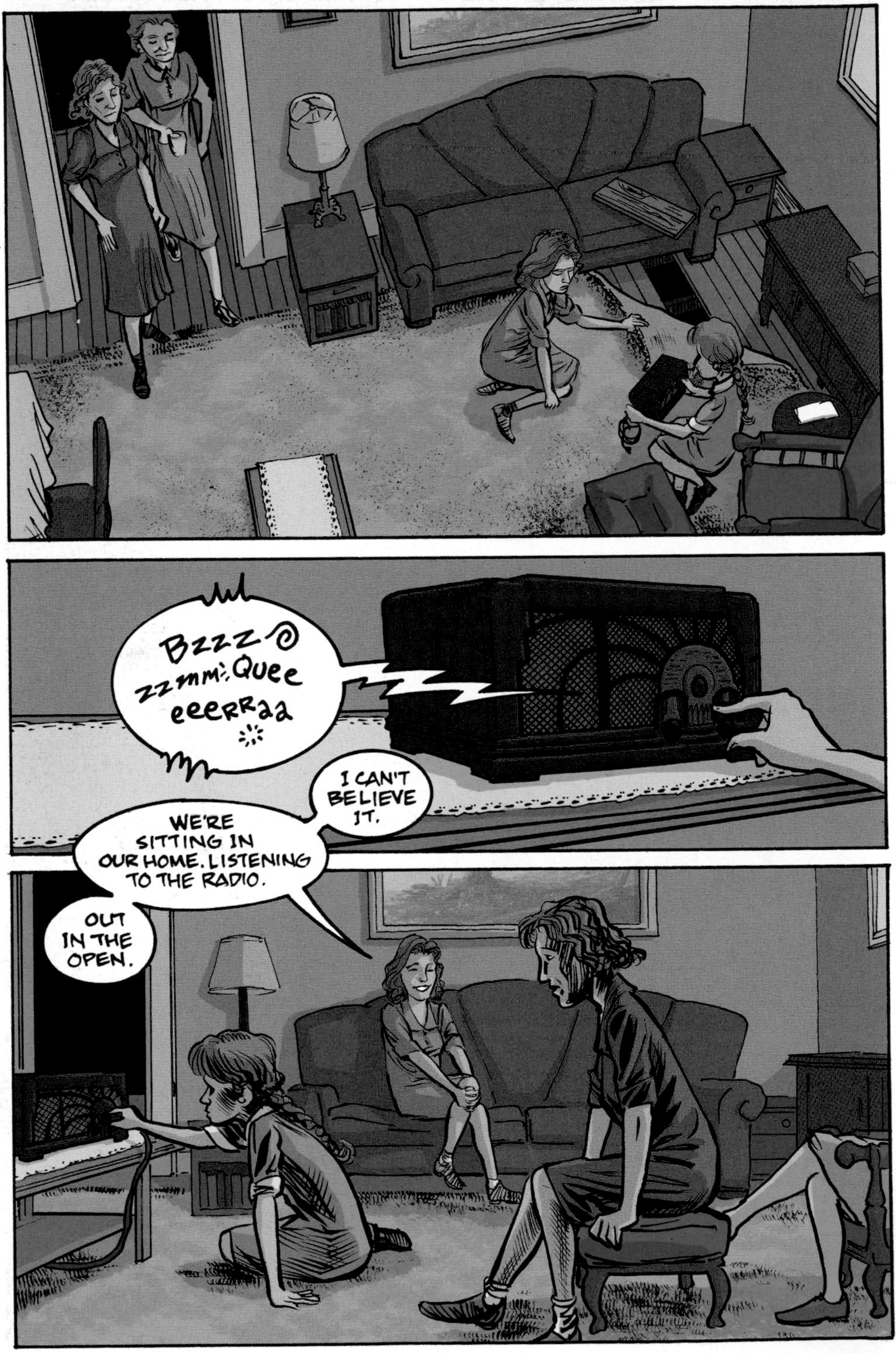
Bzzz zzmm Quee eeerRaa
I CAN'T BELIEVE IT.
WE'RE SITTING IN OUR HOME. LISTENING TO THE RADIO.
OUT IN THE OPEN.

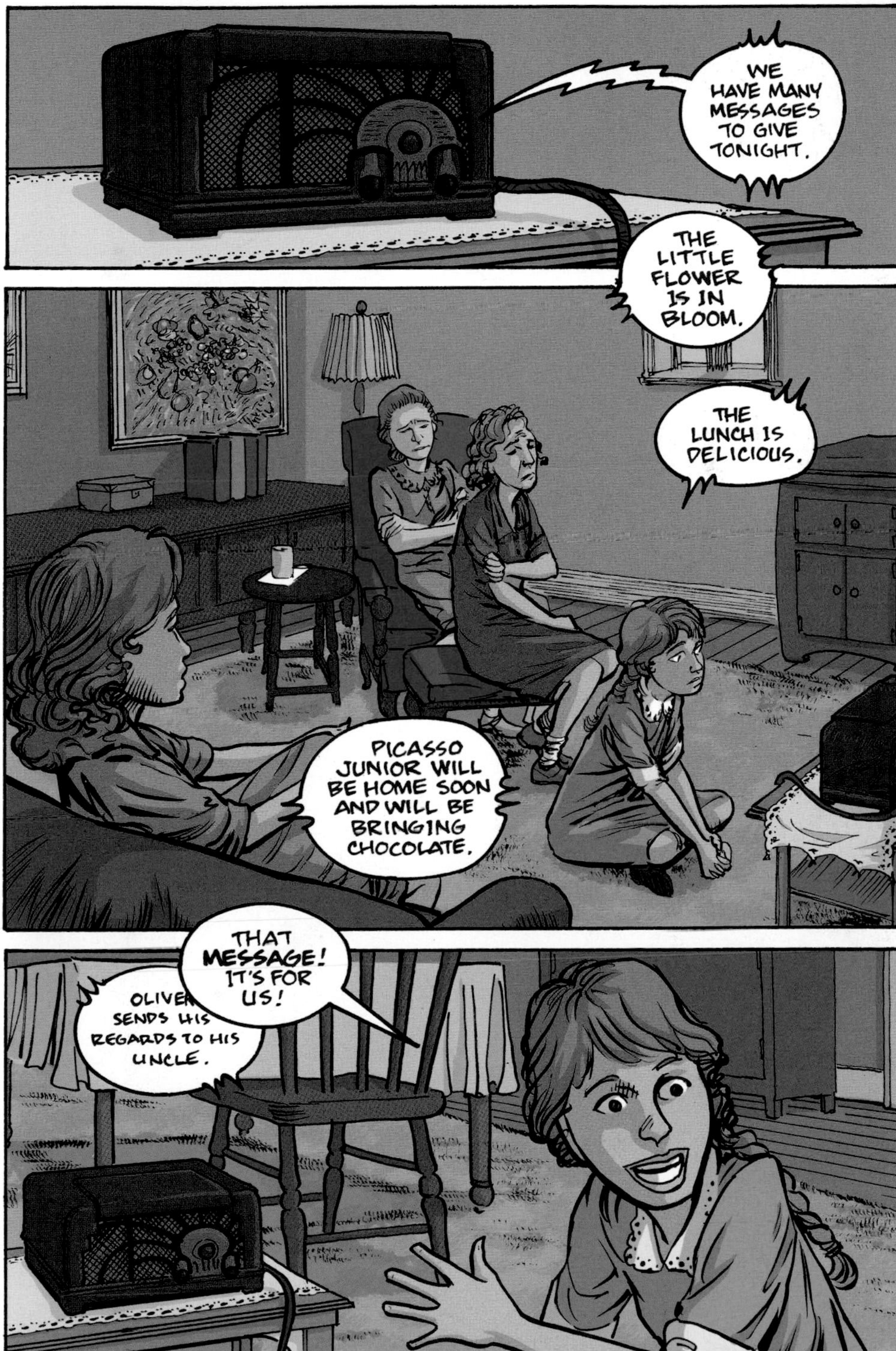
WE HAVE MANY MESSAGES TO GIVE TONIGHT.
THE LITTLE FLOWER IS IN BLOOM.
THE LUNCH IS DELICIOUS.
PICASSO JUNIOR WILL BE HOME SOON AND WILL BE BRINGING CHOCOLATE.
OLIVER SENDS HIS REGARDS TO HIS UNCLE.
THAT MESSAGE! IT'S FOR US!

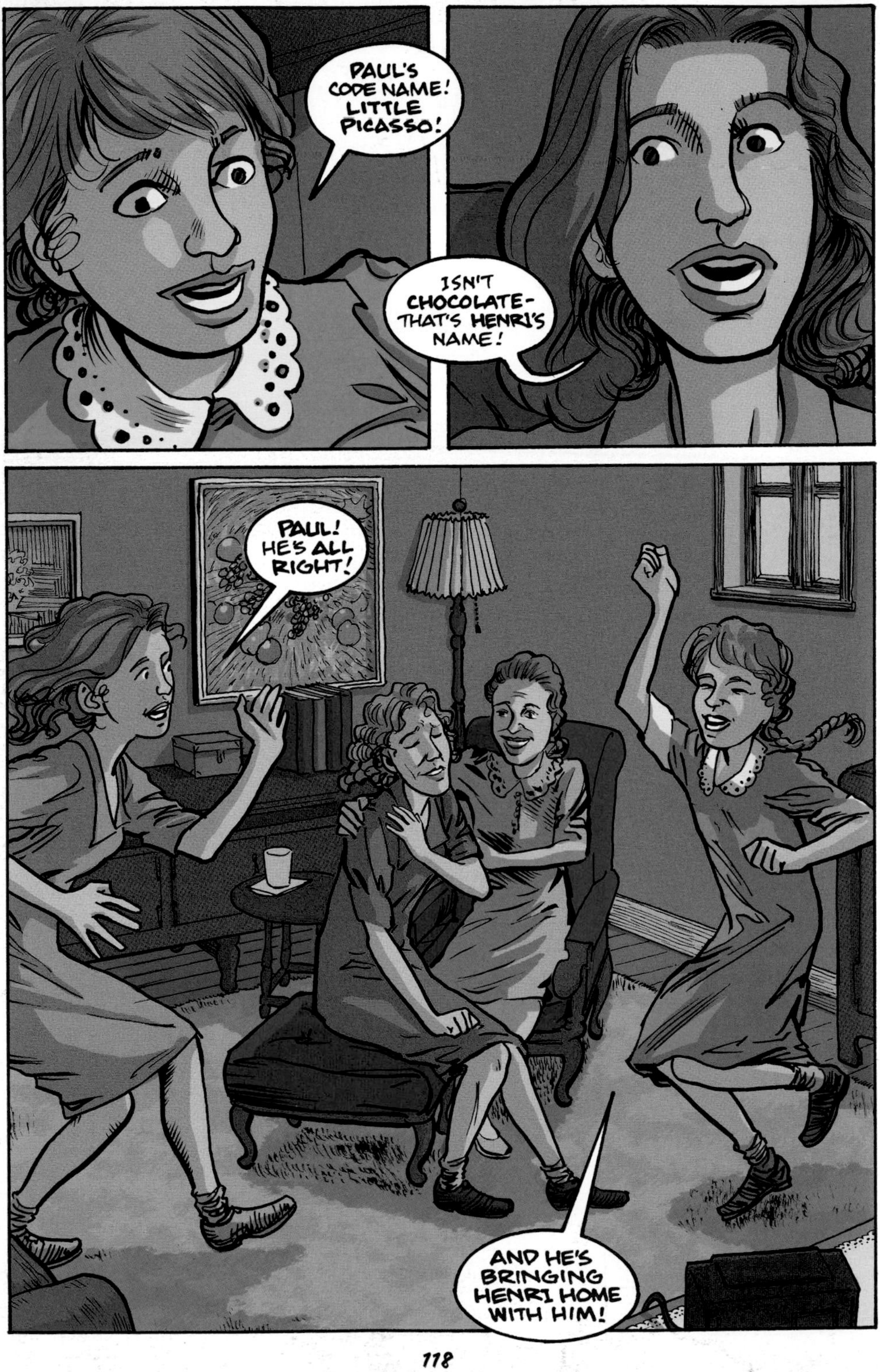
PAUL'S CODE NAME! LITTLE PICASSO!
ISN'T CHOCOLATE- THAT'S HENRI'S NAME!
PAUL! HE'S ALL RIGHT!
AND HE'S BRINGING HENRI HOME WITH HIM!

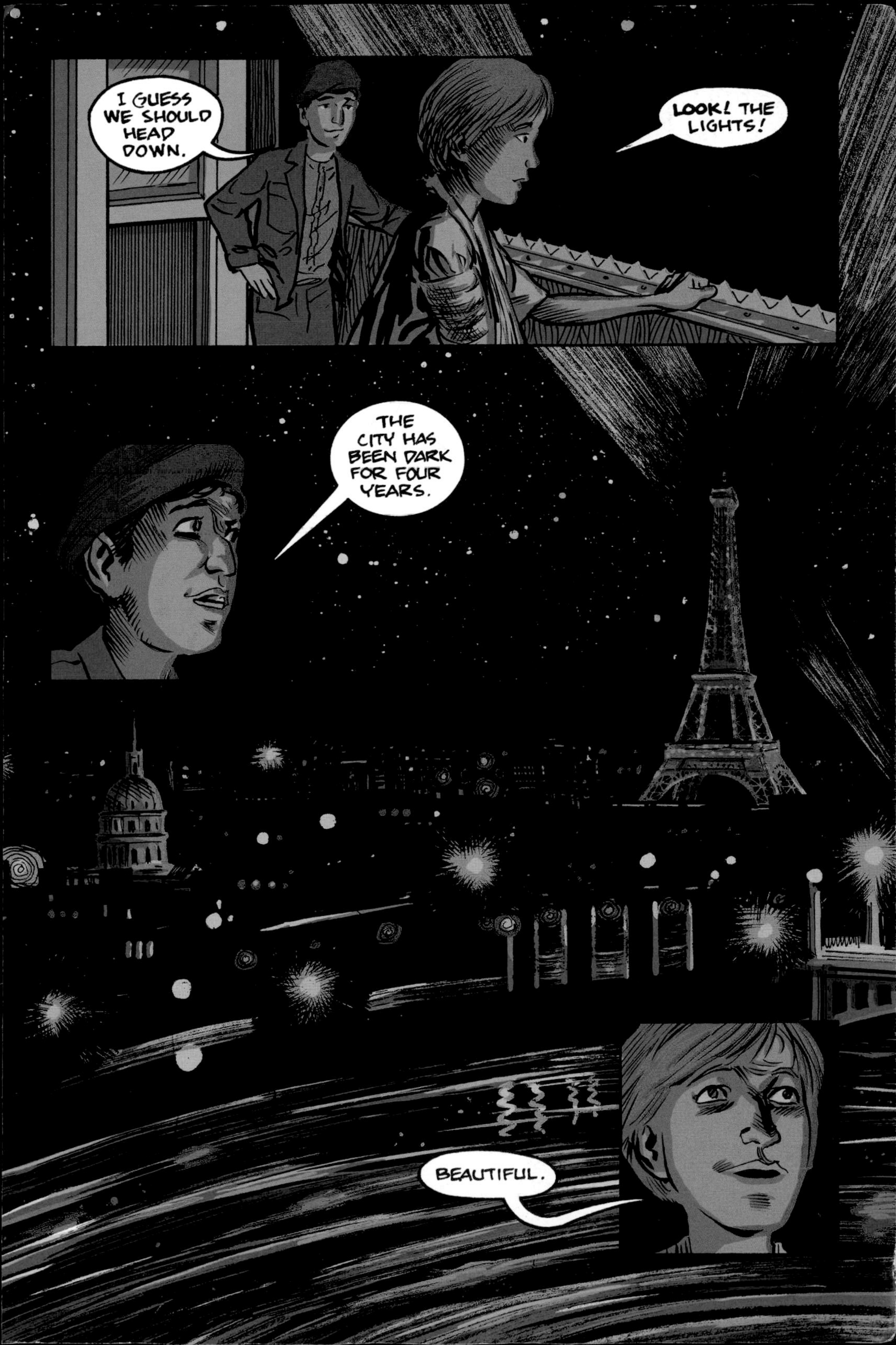
I GUESS WE SHOULD HEAD DOWN.
LOOK! THE LIGHTS!
THE CITY HAS BEEN DARK FOR FOUR YEARS.
BEAUTIFUL.

EPILOGUE

PARIS WAS LIBERATED, BUT THE WAR CONTINUED. GERMANS WERE STILL DEFENDING THEIR POSITIONS IN BRITTANY, BORDEAUX, AND ALSACE. THE VARIOUS RESISTANCE GROUPS JOINED TOGETHER AND BECAME PART OF THE OFFICIAL ARMED FORCES.

THE WAR FINALLY CAME TO AN END WHEN THE GERMANS SURRENDERED IN 1945. REBUILDING IN FRANCE TOOK YEARS, AND FOR MANY OF THE RETURNING POWs THE EFFECTS OF THE WAR LASTED FOR THE REST OF THEIR LIVES.

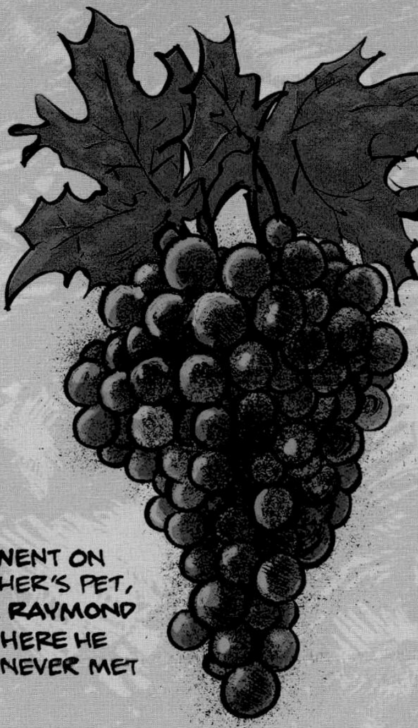

MONSIEUR DIDIER (SYLVIE, PAUL, AND MARIE'S FATHER) DID RETURN HOME. HE WAS IN FRAIL HEALTH, BUT HE SURVIVED. MARIE REMEMBERED HIM AFTER ALL, AND HE AND MME. TESSIER WERE ABLE TO BRING THE VINEYARD BACK TO LIFE.

HENRI CAME TO LIVE WITH THE **TESSIERS**. **PAUL** WENT ON TO ART SCHOOL, **MARIE** WENT BACK TO BEING TEACHER'S PET, AND **SYLVIE** STUDIED TO BECOME A TRANSLATOR. **RAYMOND** SENT A POSTCARD TO **MARIE** FROM THE HOSPITAL WHERE HE RECOVERED FROM NEW INJURIES. ALTHOUGH THEY NEVER MET AGAIN, SHE SAVED IT ALL OF HER LIFE.

EVEN AFTER SHE GREW UP AND MARRIED **HENRI**.

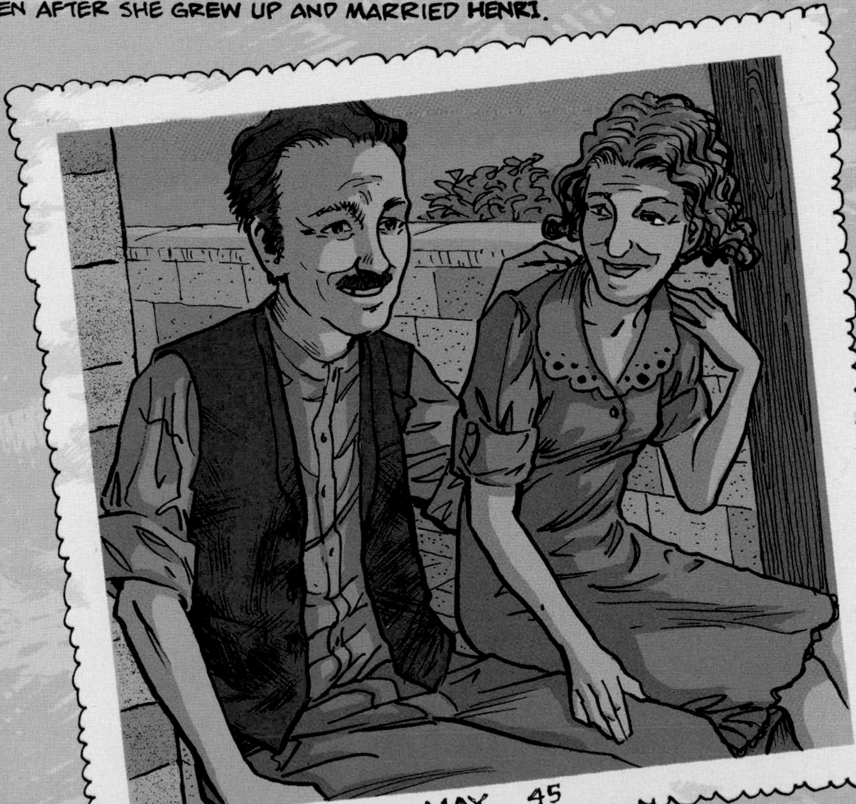
MAY 45

—Author's Note—

France's difficulties didn't end with the liberation of Paris. There were still over two million French people in concentration camps, labor camps, and POW camps. Germans still occupied parts of the country and didn't finally surrender until nearly a year later, in 1945. Shortages, hardships, and fear for loved ones plagued the French after the initial burst of joy and exhilaration on freeing Paris.

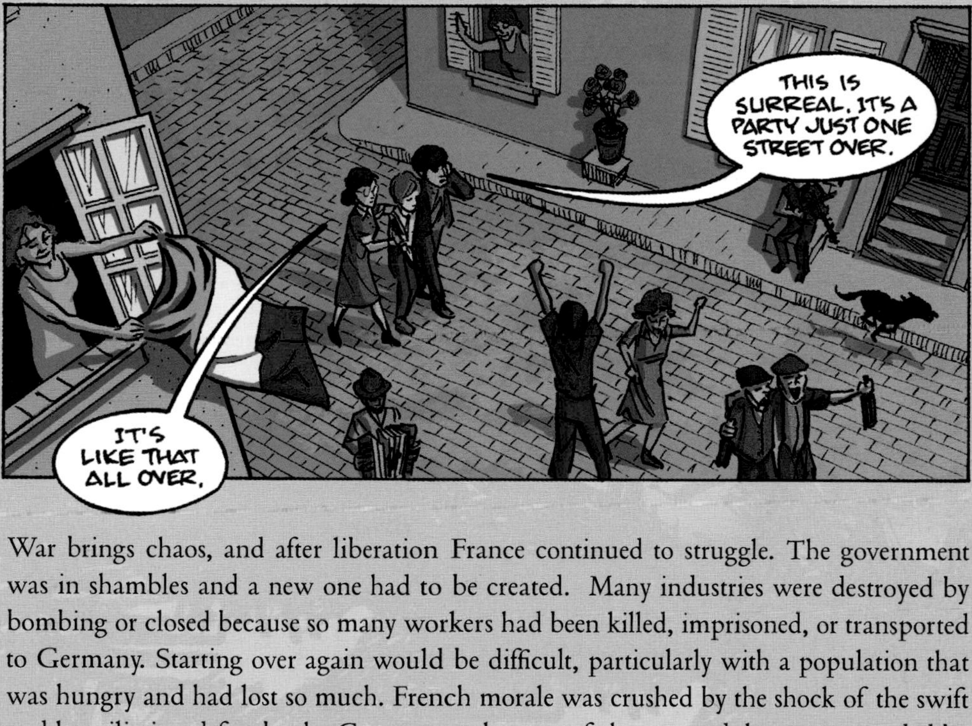
THIS IS SURREAL. IT'S A PARTY JUST ONE STREET OVER.
IT'S LIKE THAT ALL OVER.

War brings chaos, and after liberation France continued to struggle. The government was in shambles and a new one had to be created. Many industries were destroyed by bombing or closed because so many workers had been killed, imprisoned, or transported to Germany. Starting over again would be difficult, particularly with a population that was hungry and had lost so much. French morale was crushed by the shock of the swift and humiliating defeat by the Germans at the start of the war and then compounded by the lengthy occupation.

Complicating things even more was that no one agreed on the best ways to move forward. The same competing interests who jockeyed for position prior to the war fought for power again. De Gaulle had many detractors and enemies and very strong ideas about the new French government. Then there was the question of how to deal with the collaborators. This was an extremely difficult task because collaboration—like resistance—was so hard to define. Toward the end of the war many people suddenly claimed to have been part of the Resistance all along. Some said they were playing a double game, pretending to help the Germans while actually working against them. There were those who insisted that this had been what Petain was doing in running the Vichy government. In some cases, this may have been true—but not all. There were also false accusations (just as there were in the first days of the Nazi occupation); neighbors naming neighbors as collaborators for revenge or personal gain. It took many years (after the first brutal wave of retaliation) for French war criminals to be brought to trial, and many never were. And perhaps there were those who should never have been tried at all.

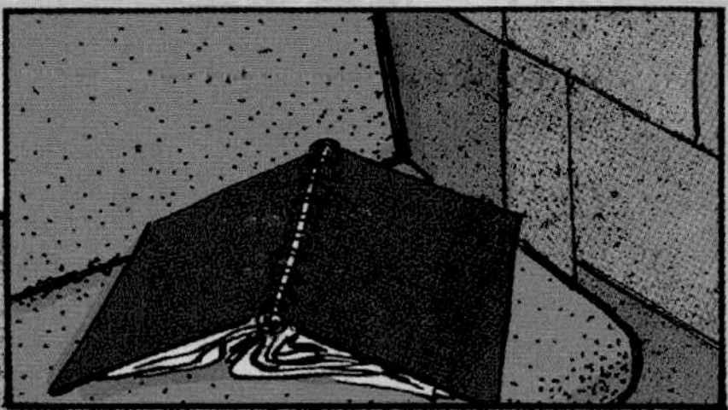

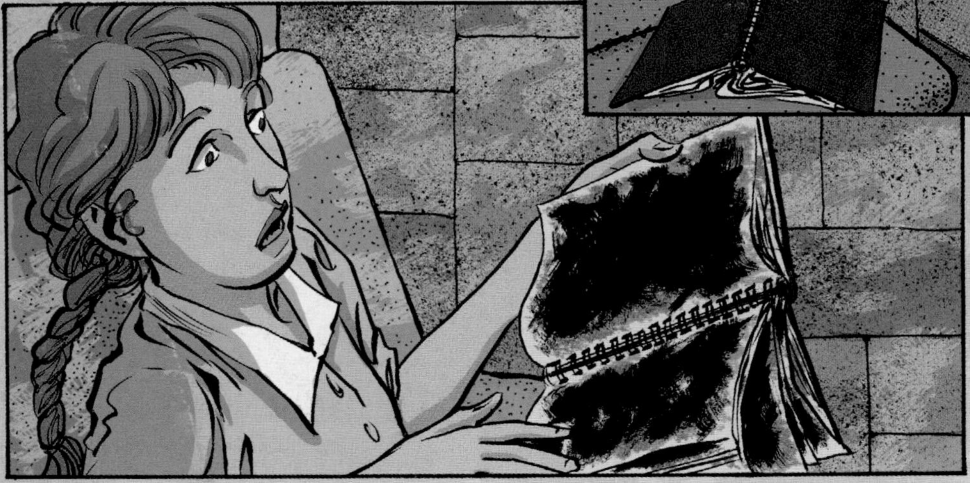

The roles French people played during the occupation and in the Resistance—from the poorest ordinary citizen to the highest commanding military officer, from aristocrats to bureaucrats—continue to be analyzed and argued about even today. Understanding the experience of occupation is hard for anyone who hasn't lived it. Making things even harder is the fact that many files and personal accounts were destroyed or sealed until fairly recently. Shame, confusion, and anger often colored the stories people told after the war was over, as well as a desire to reclaim dignity and honor. It is important to remember that the tales told are different because every person experienced those years differently. Each lived through his or her own war: before, during, and after.

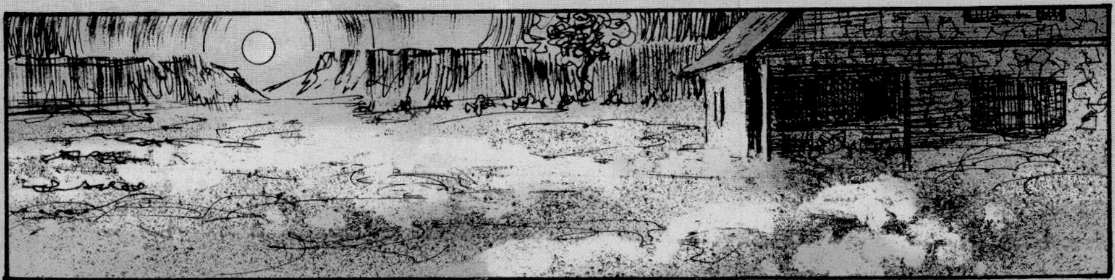